KU-486-421

The Enemy

by the same author

The Enemy

DESMOND BAGLEY

BOOK CLUB ASSOCIATES LONDON

This edition published 1978 by
Book Club Associates
by arrangement with William Collins Sons & Co Ltd

© Literary Publications Limited 1977

Printed in Great Britain by
Richard Clay (The Chaucer Press), Ltd.,
Bungay, Suffolk

We have met the enemy, and he is ours.

OLIVER HAZARD PERRY
Heroic American Commodore

We have met the enemy, and he is us.

WALT KELLY
Subversive Sociological Cartoonist

To all the DASTards

especially

Iwan and Inga
Jan and Anita
Hemming and Annette

ONE

I met Penelope Ashton at a party thrown by Tom Packer. That may be a bit misleading because it wasn't the kind of party that gets thrown very far; no spiked punch or pot, and no wife-swapping or indiscriminate necking in the bedrooms at two in the morning. Just a few people who got together over a civilized dinner with a fair amount of laughter and a hell of a lot of talk. But it did tend to go on and what with Tom's liberal hand with his after-dinner scotches I didn't feel up to driving, so when I left I took a taxi.

Penny Ashton came with Dinah and Mike Huxham; Dinah was Tom's sister. I still haven't worked out whether I was invited as a makeweight for the odd girl or whether she was brought in to counterbalance me. At any rate when we sat at table the sexes were even and I was sitting next to her. She was a tall, dark woman, quiet and composed in manner and not very forthcoming. She was no raving beauty, but few women are; Helen of Troy may have launched a thousand ships but no one was going to push the boat out for Penny Ashton, at least not at first sight. Not that she was ugly or anything like that. She had a reasonably good figure and a reasonably good face, and she dressed well. I think the word to describe her would be average. I put her age at about twenty-seven and I wasn't far out. She was twenty-eight.

As was usual with Tom's friends, the talk ranged far and wide; Tom was a rising star in the upper reaches of the medical establishment and he was eclectic in his choice of dining companions and so the talk was good. Penny joined in but she tended to listen rather than talk and her interjections were infrequent. Gradually I became aware that when she did speak her comments were acute, and there was a sardonic cast to her eye when she was listening to something she didn't agree with. I found her spikiness of mind very agreeable.

9

After dinner the talk went on in the living-room over coffee and brandy. I opted for scotch because brandy doesn't agree with me, a circumstance Tom knew very well because he poured one of his measures big enough to paralyse an elephant and left the jug of iced water convenient to my elbow.

As is common on these occasions, while the dinner-table conversation is general and involves everybody, after dinner the party tended to split into small groups, each pursuing their congenial arguments and riding their hobby-horses hard and on a loose rein. To my mild surprise I found myself opting for a group of two—myself and Penny Ashton. I suppose there were a dozen of us there, but I settled in a corner and monopolized Penny Ashton. Or did she monopolize me? It could have been six of one and half-a-dozen of the other; it usually is in cases like that.

I forget what we talked about at first but gradually our conversation became more personal. I discovered she was a research biologist specializing in genetics and that she worked with Professor Lumsden at University College, London. Genetics is the hottest and most controversial subject in science today and Lumsden was in the forefront of the battle. Anyone working with him would have to be very bright indeed and I was suitably impressed. There was a lot more to Penny Ashton than met the casual eye.

Some time during the evening she asked, 'And what do you do?'

'Oh, I'm someone in the City,' I said lightly.

She got that sardonic look in her eye and said reprovingly, 'Satire doesn't become you.'

'It's true!' I protested. 'Someone's got to make the wheels of commerce turn.' She didn't pursue the subject.

Inevitably someone checked his watch and discovered with horror the lateness of the hour, and the party began to break up. Usually the more congenial the party the later the hour, and it was pretty late. Penny said, 'My God—my train!'

'Which station?'

'Victoria.'

'I'll drop you,' I said and stood up, swaying slightly as I felt Tom's scotch. 'From a taxi.'

I borrowed the telephone and rang for a taxi, and then we

stood around making parting noises until it arrived. As we were driven through the brightly-lit London streets I reflected that it had been a good evening; it had been quite a while since I'd felt so good. And it wasn't because of the quality of Tom's booze, either.

I turned to Penny. 'Known the Packers long?'

'A few years. I was at Cambridge with Dinah Huxham—Dinah Packer she was then.'

'Nice people. It's been a good evening.'

'I enjoyed it.'

I said, 'How about repeating it—just the two of us? Say, the theatre and supper afterwards.'

She was silent for a moment, then said, 'All right.' So we fixed a time for the following Wednesday and I felt even better.

She wouldn't let me come into the station with her so I kept the taxi and redirected it to my flat. It was only then I realized I didn't know if she was married or not, and I tried to remember the fingers of her left hand. Then I thought I was a damned fool; I hardly knew the woman so what did it matter if she was married or not? I wasn't going to marry her myself, was I?

On the Wednesday I picked her up at University College at seven-fifteen in the evening and we had a drink in a pub near the theatre before seeing the show. I don't like theatre crush bars; they're too well named. 'Do you always work as late as this?' I asked.

She shook her head. 'It varies. It's not a nine-to-five job, you know. When we're doing something big we could be there all night, but that doesn't happen often. I laboured tonight because I was staying in town.' She smiled. 'It helped me catch up on some of the paperwork.'

'Ah; the paperwork is always with us.'

'You ought to know; your job is all paperwork, isn't it?'

I grinned. 'Yes; shuffling all those fivers around.'

So we saw the show and I took her to supper in Soho and then to Paddington Station. And made another date for the Saturday.

And, as they say, one thing led to another and soon I was

11

squiring her around regularly. We took in more theatres, an opera, a couple of ballets, a special exhibition at the National Gallery, Regent's Park Zoo, something she wanted to see at the Natural History Museum, and a trip down the river to Greenwich. We could have been a couple of Americans doing the tourist bit.

After six weeks of this I think we both thought that things were becoming pretty serious. I, at least, took it seriously enough to go to Cambridge to see my father. He smiled when I told him about Penny, and said, 'You know, Malcolm, you've been worrying me. It's about time you settled down. Do you know anything about the girl's family?'

'Not much,' I admitted. 'From what I can gather he's some sort of minor industrialist. I haven't met him yet.'

'Not that it matters,' said my father. 'I hope we've gone beyond snobberies like that. Have you bedded the girl yet?'

'No,' I said slowly. 'We've come pretty close, though.'

'Um!' he said obscurely, and began to fill his pipe. 'It's been my experience here at the college that the rising generation isn't as swinging and uninhibited as it likes to think it is. Couples don't jump bare-skinned into a bed at the first opportunity—not if they're taking each other seriously and have respect for each other. Is it like that with you?'

I nodded. 'I've had my moments in the past, but somehow it's different with Penny. Anyway, I've known her only a few weeks.'

'You remember Joe Patterson?'

'Yes.' Patterson was head of one of the departments of psychology.

'He reckons the ordinary man is mixed up about the qualities he wants in a permanent partner. He once told me that the average man's ideal wife-to-be is a virgin in the terminal stages of nymphomania. A witticism, but with truth in it.'

'Joe is a cynic.'

'Most wise men are. Anyway, I'd like to see Penny as soon as you can screw up your courage. Your mother would have been happy to see you married; it's a pity about that.'

'How are you getting on, Dad?'

'Oh, I rub along. The chief danger is of becoming a university eccentric; I'm trying to avoid that.'

We talked of family matters for some time and then I went back to London.

It was at this time that Penny made a constructive move. We were in my flat talking over coffee and liqueurs; she had complimented me on the Chinese dinner and I had modestly replied that I had sent out for it myself. It was then that she invited me to her home for the weekend. To meet the family.

TWO

She lived with her father and sister in a country house near
Marlow in Buckinghamshire, a short hour's spin from London
up the M4. George Ashton was a widower in his mid-fifties who
lived with his daughters in a brick-built Queen Anne house of
the type you see advertised in a full-page spread in *Country
Life*. It had just about everything. There were two tennis-
courts and one swimming-pool; there was a stable block converted into garages filled with expensive bodies on wheels, and
there was a stable block that was still a stable block and filled
with expensive bodies on legs—one at each corner. It was a
Let's-have-tea-on-the-lawn sort of place; The-master-will-see-
you-in-the-library sort of place. The good, rich, upper-middle-
class life.

George Ashton stood six feet tall and was thatched with a
strong growth of iron-grey hair. He was very fit, as I found out
on the tennis-court. He played an aggressive, hard-driving
game and I was hard put to it to cope with him even though he
had a handicap of about twenty-five years. He beat me 5–7,
7–5, 6–3, which shows his stamina was better than mine. I came
off the court out of puff but Ashton trotted down to the
swimming-pool, dived in clothed as he was, and swam a length
before going into the house to change.

I flopped down beside Penny. 'Is he always like that?'

'Always,' she assured me.

I groaned. 'I'll be exhausted just watching him.'

Penny's sister, Gillian, was as different from Penny as could
be. She was the domestic type and ran the house. I don't mean
she acted as lady of the house and merely gave the orders. She
ran it. The Ashton didn't have much staff; there were a
couple of gardeners and a stable girl, a house-man-cum-
chauffeur called Benson, a full-time maid and a daily help who

14

came in for a couple of hours each morning. Not much staff for a house of that size.

Gillian was a couple of years younger than Penny and there was a Martha and Mary relationship between them which struck me as a little odd. Penny didn't do much about the house as far as I could see, apart from keeping her own room tidy, cleaning her own car and grooming her own horse. Gillian was the Martha who did all the drudgery, but she didn't seem to mind and appeared to be quite content. Of course, it was a weekend and it might have been different during the week. All the same, I thought Ashton would get a shock should Gillian marry and leave to make a home of her own.

It was a good weekend although I felt a bit awkward at first, conscious of being on show; but I was soon put at ease in that relaxed household. Dinner that evening, cooked by Gillian, was simple and well served, and afterwards we played bridge. I partnered Penny and Ashton partnered Gillian, and I soon found that Gillian and I were the rabbits. Penny played a strong, exact and carefully calculated game, while Ashton played bridge as he played tennis, aggressively and taking chances at times. I observed that the chances he took came off more often than not, but Penny and I came slightly ahead at the end, although it was nip and tuck.

We talked for a while until the girls decided to go to bed, then Ashton suggested a nightcap. The scotch he poured was not in the same class as Tom Packer's but not far short, and we settled down for a talk. Not unexpectedly he wanted to know something about me and was willing to trade information, so I learned how he earned his pennies among other things. He ran a couple of manufacturing firms in Slough producing something abstruse in the chemical line and another which specialized in high-impact plastics. He employed about a thousand men and was the sole owner, which impressed me. There are not too many organizations like that around which are still in the hands of one man.

Then he enquired, very politely, what I did to earn my bread, and I said, 'I'm an analyst.'

He smiled slightly. 'Psycho?'

I grinned. 'No—economic. I'm a junior partner with McCulloch and Ross; we're economic consultants.'

'Yes, I've heard of your crowd. What exactly is it that you do?'

'Advisory work of all sorts—market surveys, spotting opportunities for new products, or new areas for existing products, and so on. Also general economic and financial advice. We do the general dogsbodying for firms which are not big enough to support their own research group. ICI wouldn't need us but a chap like you might.'

He seemed interested in that. 'I've been thinking of going public,' he said. 'I'm not all that old, but one never knows what may happen. I'd like to leave things tidy for the girls.'

'It might be very profitable for you personally,' I said. 'And, as you say, it would tidy up the estate in the event of your death—make the death duties bit less messy.' I thought about it for a minute. 'But I don't know if this is the time to float a new issue. You'd do better to wait for an upturn in the economy.'

'I've not entirely decided yet,' he said. 'But if I do decide to go public then perhaps you can advise me.'

'Of course. It's exactly our line of work.'

He said no more about it and the conversation drifted to other topics. Soon thereafter we went to bed.

Next morning after breakfast—cooked by Gillian—I declined Penny's invitation to go riding with her, the horse being an animal I despise and distrust. So instead we walked where she would have ridden and went over a forested hill along a broad ride, and descended the other side into a sheltered valley where we lunched in a pub on bread, cheese, pickles and beer, and where Penny demonstrated her skill at playing darts with the locals. Then back to the house where we lazed away the rest of the sunny day on the lawn.

I left the house that evening armed with an invitation to return the following weekend, not from Penny but from Ashton. 'Do you play croquet?' he asked.

'No, I don't.'

He smiled. 'Come next weekend and I'll show you how. I'll have Benson set up the hoops during the week.'

So it was that I drove back to London well contented.

I have given the events of that first weekend in some detail in order to convey the atmosphere of the place and the family. Ashton, the minor industrialist, richer than others of his type because he ran his own show; Gillian, his younger daughter, content to be dutifully domestic and to act as hostess and surrogate wife without the sex bit; and Penny the bright elder daughter, carving out a career in science. And she *was* bright; it was only casually that weekend I learned she was an MD although she didn't practise.

And there was the money. The Rolls, the Jensen and the Aston Martin in the garages, the sleek-bodied horses, the manicured lawns, the furnishings of that beautiful house— all these reeked of money and the good life. Not that I envied Ashton —I have a bit of money myself although not in the same class. I mention it only as a fact because it was there.

The only incongruity in the whole scene was Benson, the general factotum, who did not look like anyone's idea of a servant in a rich household. Rather, he looked like a retired pugilist and an unsuccessful one at that. His nose had been broken more than once in my judgement, and his ears were swollen with battering. Also he had a scar on his right cheek. He would have made a good heavy in a Hammer film. His voice clashed unexpectedly with his appearance, being soft and with an educated accent better than Ashton's own. I didn't know what to make of him at all.

Something big was apparently happening in Penny's line of work that week, and she rang to say she would be in the laboratory all Friday night, and would I pick her up on Saturday morning to take her home. When she got into the car outside University College she looked very tired, with dark smudges under her eyes. 'I'm sorry, Malcolm,' she said. 'This won't be much of a weekend for you. I'm going to bed as soon as I get home.'

I was sorry, too, because this was the weekend I intended to ask her to marry me. However, this wasn't the time, so I grinned and said, 'I'm not coming to see you—I'm coming for the croquet.' Not that I knew much about it—just the bit from Alice and an association with vicars and maiden ladies.

Penny smiled, and said, 'I don't suppose I should tell you

17

this, but Daddy says he can measure a man by the way he plays croquet.'

I said, 'What were you doing all night?'

'Working hard.'

'Doing what? Is it a state secret?'

'No secret. We transferred genetic material from a virus to a bacterium.'

'Sounds finicky,' I remarked. 'With success, I hope.'

'We won't know until we test the resulting strain. We should know something in a couple of weeks; this stuff breeds fast. We hope it will breed true.'

What I knew about genetics could be measured with an eye-dropper. I said curiously, 'What good does all this do?'

'Cancer research,' she said shortly, and laid her head back, closing her eyes. I left her alone after that.

When we got to the house she went to bed immediately. Other than that the weekend was much the same as before. Until the end, that is—then it changed for the worse. I played tennis with Ashton, then swam in the pool, and we had lunch on the lawn in the shade of a chestnut tree, just the three of us, Ashton, Gillian and me. Penny was still asleep.

After lunch I was introduced to the intricacies of match-play croquet and, by God, there *was* a vicar! Croquet, I found, is not a game for the faint-hearted, and the way the Reverend Hawthorne played made Machiavelli look like a Boy Scout. Fortunately he was on my side, but all his tortuous plotting was of no avail against Gillian and Ashton. Gillian played a surprisingly vicious game. Towards the end, when I discovered it's not a game for gentlemen, I quite enjoyed it.

Penny came down for afternoon tea, refreshed and more animated than she had been, and from then on the weekend took its normal course. Put down baldly on paper, as I have done here, such a life may be considered pointless and boring, but it wasn't, really; it was a relief from the stresses of the working week.

Apparently Ashton did not get even that relief because after tea he retired to his study, pleading that he had to attend to paperwork. I commented that Penny had complained of the same problem, and he agreed that putting unnecessary words on paper was the besetting sin of the twentieth century. As he walked away I reflected that Ashton could not have got where he was by idling his time away playing tennis and croquet.

And so the weekend drifted by until it was nearly time for me to leave. It was a pleasant summer Sunday evening. Gillian had gone to church but was expected back at any moment; she was the religious member of the family—neither Ashton nor Penny showed any interest in received religion. Ashton, Penny and I were sitting in lawn chairs arguing a particularly knotty point in scientific ethics which had arisen out of an article in the morning newspaper. Rather, it was Penny and her father doing the arguing; I was contemplating how to get her alone so I could propose to her. Somehow we had never been alone that weekend.

Penny was becoming a little heated when we heard a piercing scream and then another. The three of us froze, Penny in mid-sentence, and Ashton said sharply, 'What the devil was that?'

A third scream came. It was nearer this time and seemed to be coming from the other side of the house. By this time we were on our feet and moving, but then Gillian came into sight, stumbling around the corner of the house, her hands to her face. She screamed again, a bubbling, wordless screech, and collapsed on the lawn.

Ashton got to her first. He bent over her and tried to pull her hands from her face, but Gillian resisted him with all her strength. 'What's the matter?' he yelled, but all he got was a shuddering moan.

Penny said quickly, 'Let me,' and gently pulled him away. She bent over Gillian who was now lying on her side curled in a foetal position, her hands still at her face with the fingers extended like claws. The screams had stopped and were replaced by an extended moaning, and once she said, 'My eyes! Oh, my eyes!'

Penny put her hand to Gillian's face and touched it with her forefinger, rubbing gently. She frowned and put the tip of her finger to her nose, then hastily wiped it on the grass. She turned to her father. 'Take her into the house quickly—into the kitchen.'

She stood up and whirled towards me in one smooth motion. 'Ring for an ambulance. Tell them it's an acid burn.'

19

Ashton had already scooped up Gillian in his arms as I ran to the house, brushing past Benson as I entered the hall. I picked up the telephone and rang 999 and then watched Ashton carry his daughter through a doorway I had never entered, with Penny close behind him.

A voice said in my ear, 'Emergency services.'

'Ambulance.'

There was a click and another voice said immediately, 'Ambulance service.' I gave him the address and the telephone number. 'And your name, sir?'

'Malcolm Jaggard. It's a bad facial acid burn.'

'Right sir; we'll be as quick as we can.'

As I put down the phone I was aware that Benson was staring at me with a startled expression. Abruptly he turned on his heel and walked out of the house. I opened the door to the kitchen and saw Gillian stretched on a table with Penny applying something to her face. Her legs were kicking convulsively and she was still moaning. Ashton was standing by and I have never seen on any man's face such an expression of helpless rage. There wasn't much I could do there and I'd only be in the way so I closed the door gently.

Looking through the big window at the far end of the hall, I saw Benson walking along the drive. He stopped and bent down, looking at something not on the drive but on the wide grass verge. I went out to join him and saw what had attracted his attention; a car had turned there, driving on the grass, and it had done so at speed because the immaculate lawn had been chewed up and the wheels had gouged right down to the soil.

Benson said in his unexpectedly gentle voice, 'As I see it, sir, the car came into the grounds and was parked about there, facing the house. When Miss Gillian walked up someone threw acid into her face here.' He pointed to where a few blades of grass were already turning brown. 'Then the car turned on the grass and drove away.'

'But you didn't see it.'

'No, sir.'

I bent and looked at the wheel marks. 'I think this should be protected until the police get here.'

Benson thought for a moment. 'The gardener made some

hurdles for the new paddock. I'll get those.'

'That should do it,' I agreed.

I helped him bring them and we covered the marks. I straightened as I heard the faint hee-haw of an ambulance, becoming louder as it approached. That was quick—under six minutes. I walked back to the house and rang 999 again.

'Emergency services.'

'The police, please.'

Click. 'Police here.'

'I want to report a criminal assault.'

THREE

They got Gillian into the ambulance very quickly. Penny used her authority as a doctor and went into the ambulance with her, while Ashton followed in a car. I judged he was in no condition to drive and was pleased to see Benson behind the wheel when he left.

Before he went I took him on one side. 'I think you ought to know I've sent for the police.'

He turned a ravaged face towards me and blinked stupidly. 'What's that?' He seemed to have aged ten years in a quarter of an hour.

I repeated what I'd said, and added, 'They'll probably come while you're still at the hospital. I can tell them what they need to know. Don't worry about it. I'll stay here until you get back.'

'Thanks, Malcolm.'

I watched them drive away and then I was alone in the house. The maid lived in, but Sunday was her day off, and now Benson had gone there was no one in the house but me. I went into the living-room, poured myself a drink and lit a cigarette, and sat down to think of just what the hell had happened.

Nothing made sense. Gillian Ashton was a plain, ordinary woman who lived a placid and unadventurous life. She was a homebody who one day might marry an equally unadventurous man who liked his home comforts. Acid-throwing wasn't in that picture; it was something that might happen in Soho or the murkier recesses of the East End of London—it was incongruous in the Buckinghamshire countryside.

I thought about it for a long time and got nowhere. Presently I heard a car drive up and a few minutes later I was talking to a couple of uniformed policemen. I couldn't tell them much; I knew little about Gillian and not much more about Ashton and, although the policemen were polite, I sensed an increasing dissatisfaction. I showed them the tracks and one of them stayed to guard them while the other used his car radio. When I looked from the window a few minutes later I saw he had moved the police car so he could survey the back of the house.

Twenty minutes later a bigger police gun arrived in the person of a plain clothes man. He talked for a while with the constable in the car, then walked towards the house and I opened the door at his knock. 'Detective-Inspector Honnister,' he said briskly. 'Are you Mr Jaggard?'

'That's right. Won't you come in?'

He walked into the hall and stood looking around. As I closed the door he swung on me. 'Are you alone in the house?'

The constable had been punctilious about his 'sirs' but not Honnister. I said, 'Inspector, I'm going to show you something which I shouldn't but which, in all fairness to yourself, I think you ought to see. I'm quite aware my answers didn't satisfy your constable. I'm alone in Ashton's house, admit to knowing hardly anything about the Ashtons, and he thinks I might run away with the spoons.'

Honnister's eyes crinkled. 'From the look of it there's a lot more to run away with here than spoons. What have you to show me?'

'This.' I dug the card out of the pocket which my tailor builds into all my jackets and gave it to him.

Honnister's eyebrows rose as he looked at it. 'We don't get many of these,' he commented. 'This is only the third I've seen.' He flicked at the plastic with his thumbnail as he compared me with the photograph. 'You realize I'll have to test the authenticity of this.'

'Of course. I'm only showing it to you so you don't waste time on me. You can use this telephone or the one in Ashton's study.'

'Will I get an answer this time on Sunday?'

I smiled. 'We're like the police, Inspector; we never close.'

I showed him into the study and it didn't take long. He came out within five minutes and gave me back the card. 'Well, Mr Jaggard; got any notions on this?'

I shook my head. 'It beats me. I'm not here in a professional capacity, if that's what you mean.' From his shrewd glance I could see he didn't believe me, so I told of my relationship with the Ashtons and all I knew of the attack on Gillian which wasn't much.

He said wryly, 'This is one we'll have to do the hard way, then—starting with those tracks. Thank you for your co-operation, Mr Jaggard. I'd better be getting on with it.'

I went with him to the door. 'One thing, Inspector; you never saw that card.'

He nodded abruptly and left.

Ashton and Penny came back more than two hours later. Penny looked as tired as she had the previous morning, but Ashton had recovered some of his colour and springiness. 'Good of you to stay, Malcolm,' he said. 'Stay a little longer—I want to talk to you. Not now, but later.' His voice was brusque and he spoke with authority; what he had issued was not a request but an order. He strode across the hall and went into the study. The door slammed behind him.

I turned to Penny. 'How's Gillian?'

'Not very good,' she said sombrely. 'It was strong acid, un-diluted. Who would do such a barbarous thing?'

'That's what the police want to know.' I told her something of my conversation with Honnister. 'He thinks your father might know something about this. Does he have any enemies?'

'Daddy!' She frowned. 'He's very strong-minded and single-minded, and people like that don't go through life without treading on a few toes. But I can't think he'd make the kind of enemy who would throw acid into his daughter's face.'

Somehow I couldn't, either. God knows some funny things go on in the economic and industrial jungles, but they rarely include acts of gratuitous violence. I turned as Benson came out of the kitchen carrying a tray on which were a jug of water, an unopened bottle of whisky and two glasses. I watched him go into the study then said, 'What about Gillian?'

Penny stared at me. 'Gillian!' She shook her head in dis-belief. 'You're not suggesting Gillian could make that kind of enemy? It's preposterous.'

It was certainly unlikely but not as impossible as Penny

24

thought. Quiet homebodies have been known to lead exotic and secret lives, and I wondered if Gillian had done anything else on her shopping trips into Marlow besides buying the odd pound of tea. But I said tactfully, 'Yes, it is unlikely.'

As I helped Penny get together a scratch meal she said, 'I tried to neutralize the acid with a soda solution, and in the ambulance they had better stuff than that. But she's in the intensive care unit at the hospital.'

We had rather an uncomfortable meal, just the two of us because Ashton wouldn't come out of the study, saying he wasn't hungry. An hour later, when I was wondering if he'd forgotten I was there, Benson came into the room. 'Mr Ashton would like to see you, sir.'

'Thank you.' I made my excuses to Penny and went into the study. Ashton was sitting behind a large desk but rose as I entered. I said, 'I can't tell you how sorry I am that this awful thing should have happened.'

He nodded. 'I know, Malcolm.' His hand grasped the whisky bottle which I noted was now only half full. He glanced at the tray, and said, 'Be a good chap and get yourself a clean glass.'

'I'd rather not drink any more this evening. I still have to drive back to town.'

He put down the bottle gently and came from behind the desk. 'Sit down,' he said, and thus began one of the weirdest interviews of my life. He paused for a moment. 'How are things with you and Penny?'

I looked at him consideringly. 'Are you asking if my intentions are honourable?'

'More or less. Have you slept with her yet?'

That was direct enough. 'No.' I grinned at him. 'You brought her up too well.'

He grunted. 'Well, what are your intentions—if any?'

'I thought it might be a good idea if I asked her to marry me.'

He didn't seem displeased at that. 'And have you?'

'Not yet.'

He rubbed the side of his jaw reflectively. 'This job of yours—what sort of income do you make out of it?'

That was a fair question if I was going to marry his

daughter. 'Last year it was a fraction over £8000; this year will be better.' Aware that a man like Ashton would regard that as chickenfeed I added, 'And I have private investments which being in a further £11,000.'

He raised his eyebrows. 'You still work with a private income?'

'That £11,000 is *before* tax,' I said wryly, and shrugged. 'And a man must do something with his life.'

'How old are you?'

'Thirty-four.'

He leaned back in his chair and said musingly, '£8000 a year isn't bad—so far. Any prospects of advancement in the firm?'

'I'm bucking for it.'

He then asked me a couple of questions which were a damned sight more personal than digging into my finances but, again, in the circumstances they were fair and my answers seemed to satisfy him.

He was silent for a while, then he said, 'You could do better by changing your job. I have an opening which is ideal for a man like yourself. Initially you'd have to spend at least one year in Australia getting things off the ground, but that wouldn't hurt a couple of youngsters like you and Penny. The only trouble is that it must be now—almost immediately.'

He was going too fast for me. 'Hold on a moment,' I protested. 'I don't even know yet if she'll marry me.'

'She will,' he said positively. 'I know my daughter.'

He evidently knew her better than I did because I wasn't nearly so certain. 'Even so,' I said. 'There's Penny to consider. Her work is important to her. I can't see her throwing it up and going to Australia for a year just like that. And that's apart from anything I might think about the advisability of making a change.'

'She could take a sabbatical. Scientists do that all the time.'

'Maybe. Frankly I'd need to know a lot more about it before making a decision.'

For the first time Ashton showed annoyance. He managed to choke it down and disguise it, but it was there. He thought for a moment, then said in conciliatory tones, 'Well, a decision on that might wait a month. I think you'd better pop the question, Malcolm. I can fix a special licence and you can get married towards the end of the week.' He tried to smile genially but the smile got nowhere near his eyes which still had a hurt look in them. 'I'll give you a house for a dowry—somewhere in the South Midlands, north of London.'

It was a time for plain speaking. 'I think you're going a bit too fast. I don't see the necessity for a special licence. In fact, it's my guess that Penny wouldn't hear of it, even if she does agree to marry me. I rather think she'd like to have Gillian at the wedding.'

Ashton's face crumpled and he seemed about to lose what little composure he had. I said evenly, 'It was always in my mind to buy a house when I married. Your offer of a house is very generous, but I think the kind of house it should be—and where it should be—are matters for Penny and me to decide between us.'

He stood up, walked to the desk, and poured himself a drink. With his back to me he said indistinctly, 'You're right, of course. I shouldn't interfere. But will you ask her to marry you—now?'

'Now! Tonight?'

'Yes.'

I stood up. 'Under the circumstances I consider that entirely inappropriate, and I won't do it. Now, if you'll forgive me, I have to go back to town.'

He neither turned nor made an answer. I left him there and closed the study door quietly behind me. I was at a loss to understand his driving insistence that Penny and I should marry quickly. That, and the offer of the job in Australia, had me worried. If this was the way he engaged his staff, not to mention picking a son-in-law, I was surprised how he'd got to where he was.

Penny was telephoning when I entered the hall. She replaced the receiver and said, 'I've been talking to the hospital; they say she's resting easier.'

'Good! I'll be back tomorrow evening and we'll go to see her. It might make her feel better to have someone else around, even a comparative stranger like me.'

'I don't know if that's a good idea,' said Penny doubtfully.

27

'She might be . . . well, self-conscious about her appearance.'

'I'll come anyway and we can decide then. I have to go now—it's late.' She saw me to my car and I kissed her and left, wondering what kind of bee was buzzing in Ashton's bonnet.

FOUR

Next morning, when I walked into the office I shared with Larry Godwin, he looked up from the Czechoslovakian trade magazine he was reading and said, 'Harrison wants to see you.' Harrison was our immediate boss.

'Okay.' I walked straight out again and into Harrison's office, sat in the chair before the desk, and said, 'Morning, Joe. Larry said you wanted to see me.'

Harrison was a bit of a stuffed shirt, very keen on formality, protocol and the line of authority. He didn't like me calling him Joe, so I always did it just to needle him. He said stiffly, 'On checking the weekend telephone log I found you had disclosed yourself to a police officer. Why?'

'I was at a house-party over the weekend. There was a nasty incident—one of the daughters of the house had acid thrown in her face. She was taken to hospital and, when the police pitched up, I was alone in the house and they started to get off on the wrong foot. I didn't want them wasting time on me, so I disclosed myself to the officer in charge.'

He shook his head disapprovingly and tried to hold me in what he supposed to be an eagle-like stare. 'His name?'

'Detective-Inspector Honnister. You'll find him at the cop-shop in Marlow.' Harrison scribbled in his desk book, and I leaned forward. 'What's the matter, Joe? We're *supposed* to co operate with the police.'

He didn't look up. 'You're not supposed to disclose yourself to all and sundry.'

'He wasn't all and sundry. He was a middle-ranking copper doing his job and getting off to a bad start.'

Harrison raised his head. 'You needn't have done it. He would never seriously suspect you of anything.'

I grinned at him. 'The way you tell it co-operation is a one-way street, Joe. The cops co-operate with us when we need them, but we don't co-operate with them when all they need is a little setting straight.'

'It will be noted in your record,' he said coldly.

'Stuff the record,' I said, and stood up. 'Now if you'll excuse me I have work to do.' I didn't wait for his permission to leave and went back to my office.

Larry had switched to something in Polish. 'Have a good weekend?'

'A bit fraught. Who's pinched our *Who's Who*?'

He grinned. 'What's the matter? Wouldn't she play?' He fished out *Who's Who* from among the piles of books which cluttered his desk and tossed it to me. Our job called for a lot of reading; when I retired I'd be entitled to a disability pension due to failing eyesight incurred in the line of duty.

I sat at my desk and ran through the 'A's and found that Ashton was not listed. There are not many men running three or more factories employing over a thousand men who are not listed in *Who's Who*. It seemed rather odd. On impulse I took the telephone directory and checked that, and he was not listed there, either. Why should Ashton have an ex-directory number?

I said, 'Know anything about high-impact plastics, Larry?'

'What do you want to know?'

'A chap called Ashton runs a factory in Slough making the stuff. I could bear to know a little more about him.'

'Haven't heard of him. What's the name of the firm?'

'I don't know.'

'You don't know much. There might be a trade association.'

'Great thinking.' I went to our library and an hour later knew there were more associations of plastics manufacturers than I wotted of—there was even one devoted to high-impact plastics—but none of them had heard of George Ashton. It seemed unnatural.

Gloomily I went back to my office. It's a hard world where a man can't check up on his prospective father-in-law. Ashton, as of that moment, knew a hell of a lot more about me than I knew about him. Larry saw my face and said, 'No luck?'

'The man keeps a bloody low profile.'

He laughed and waved his hand across the room. 'You could ask Nellie.'

30

I looked at Nellie and grinned. 'Why not?' I said lightly, and sat at the console.

You don't have to cuddle up to a computer to ask it question—all you need is a terminal, and we called ours Nellie for no reason I've ever been able to determine. If you crossed an oversized typewriter with a television set you'd get something like Nellie, and if you go to Heathrow you'll see dozens of them in the booking hall.

Where the computer actually was no one had bothered to tell me. Knowing the organization that employed me, and knowing a little of what was in the monster's guts, I'd say it was tended by white-coated acolytes in a limestone cavern in Derbyshire or at the bottom of a Mendip mine-shaft; anywhere reasonably safe from an atomic burst. But, as I say, I didn't really know. My crowd worked strictly on the 'need to know' principle.

I snapped a couple of switches, pushed a button, and was rewarded by a small green question mark on the screen. Another button push made it ask:

IDENTIFICATION?

I identified myself—a bit of a complicated process—and Nellie asked:

CODE?

I answered:

GREEN

Nellie thought about that for about a millionth of a second, then came up with:

INPUT GREEN CODING

That took about two minutes to put in. We were strict about security and not only did I have to identify myself but I had to know the requisite code for the level of information I wanted.

Nellie said:

INFORMATION REQUIRED?

I replied with:

IDENTITY

MALE

ENGLAND

The lines flicked out as Nellie came back with:

NAME?

31

I typed in:

ASHTON, GEORGE

It didn't seem to make much difference to Nellie how you put a name in. I'd experimented a bit and whether you put in Percy Bysshe Shelley—Shelley, Percy Bysshe—or even Percy Shelley, Bysshe—didn't seem to matter. Nellie still came up with the right answer, always assuming that Bysshe Shelley, Percy was under our eagle eye. But I always put the surname first because I thought it would be easier on Nellie's overworked little brain.

This time she came up with:

ASHTON GEORGE—3 KNOWN
PRESENT ADDRESS—IF KNOWN?

There could have been two hundred George Ashtons in the country or maybe two thousand. It's a common name and not surprising that three should be known to the department. As I typed in the address I reflected that I was being a bit silly about this. I tapped the execute key and Nellie hesitated uncharacteristically. Then I had a shock because the cursor scrolled out:

THIS INFORMATION NOT AVAILABLE ON CODE GREEN
TRY CODE YELLOW

I looked pensively at the screen and tapped out:

HOLD QUERY

Dancing electronically in the guts of a computer was a whole lot of information about one George Ashton, my future father-in-law. And it was secret information because it was in Code Yellow. I had picked up Larry Godwin on a joke and it had backfired on me; I hadn't expected Nellie to find him at all—there was no reason to suppose the department was interested in him. But if he had been found I would have expected him to be listed under Code Green, a not particularly secretive batch of information. Practically anything listed under Code Green could have been picked up by an assiduous reading of the world press. Code Yellow was definitely different.

I dug into the recesses of my mind for the coding of yellow, then addressed myself to Nellie. 'Right, you bitch; try again!' I loaded in the coding which took four minutes, then I typed out:

RELEASE HOLD

Nellie's screen flickered a bit and the cursor spelled out:

THIS INFORMATION NOT AVAILABLE ON CODE YELLOW

TRY CODE RED

I took a deep breath, told Nellie to hold the query, then sat back to think about it. I was cleared for Code Red and I knew the information there was pretty much the same as the code colour—redhot! Who the hell was Ashton, and what was I getting into? I stood up and said to Larry, 'I'll be back in a minute. Don't interfere with Nellie.'

I took a lift which went down deep into the guts of the building where there lived a race of troglodytes, the guardians of the vaults. I presented my card at a tungsten-steel grille, and said, 'I'd like to check the computer coding for red. I've forgotten the incantation.'

The hard-faced man behind the grille didn't smile. He merely took the card and dropped it into a slot. A machine chewed on it for a moment, tasted it electronically and liked the flavour but, even so, spat it out. I don't know what would have happened if it hadn't liked the flavour; probably I'd have been struck down by a bolt of lightning. Strange how the real world is catching up with James Bond.

The guard glanced at a small screen. 'Yes, you're cleared for red, Mr Jaggard,' he said, agreeing with the machine. The grille swung open and I passed through, hearing it slam and lock behind me. 'The coding will be brought to you in Room Three.'

Half an hour later I walked into my office, hoping I could remember it all. I found Larry peering at Nellie. 'Do you have red clearance?' I asked.

He shook his head. 'Yellow is my top.'

'Then hop it. Go to the library and study *Playboy* or something elevating like that. I'll give you a ring when I'm finished.'

He didn't argue; he merely nodded and walked out. I sat at the console and loaded Code Red into Nellie and it took nearly ten minutes of doing the right things in the right order. I wasn't entirely joking when I called it an incantation. When faced with Nellie I was always reminded of the medieval sorcerers who sought to conjure up spirits; everything had to be done in the right order and all the right words spoken or the spirit wouldn't appear. We haven't made much progress since then, or not too much. But at least our incantations seem to work and we do get answers from the vasty deep, but whether they're worth anything or not I don't know.

Nellie accepted Code Red or, at least, she didn't hiccough over it.

I keyed in:

RELEASE HOLD

and waited with great interest to see what would come out. The screen flickered again, and Nellie said:

THIS INFORMATION NOT AVAILABLE ON CODE RED

TRY CODE PURPLE

Purple! The colour of royalty and, possibly, of my face at that moment. This was where I was stopped—I was not cleared for Code Purple. I was aware it existed but that's about all. And beyond purple there could have been a whole rainbow of colours visible and invisible, from infra-red to ultra-violet. As I said, we worked on the 'need to know' principle.

I picked up the telephone and rang Larry. 'You can come back now; the secret bit is over.' Then I wiped Nellie's screen clean and sat down to think of what to do next.

FIVE

A couple of hours later I was having a mild ding-dong with Larry. He wasn't a bad chap but his ideals tended to get in the way of his job. His view of the world didn't exactly coincide with things as they are, which can be a bit hampering because a man can make mistakes that way. A spell of field work would have straightened him out but he'd never been given the chance.

My telephone rang and I picked it up. 'Jaggard here.'

It was Harrison. His voice entered my ear like a blast of polar air. 'I want you in my office immediately.'

I put down the phone. 'Joe's in one of his more frigid moods. I wonder how he gets on with his wife.' I went to see what he wanted.

Harrison was a bit more than frigid—he could have been used to liquefy helium. He said chillily, 'What the devil have you been doing with the computer?'

'Nothing much. Has it blown a fuse?'

'What's all this about a man called Ashton?'

I was startled. 'Oh, Christ!' I said. 'Nellie *is* a tattle-tale, isn't she? Too bloody gossipy by half.'

'What's that?'

'Just talking to myself.'

'Well, now you can talk to Ogilvie. He wants to see us both.'

I think I gaped a bit. I'd been with the department for six years and I'd seen Ogilvie precisely that number of times; that's to talk with seriously. I sometimes bumped into him in the lift and he'd exchange pleasantries courteously enough and always asked to be remembered to my father. My monkeying with Nellie must have touched a nerve so sore that the whole firm was going into a spasm.

'Well, don't just stand there,' snapped Harrison. 'He's waiting.'

Waiting with Ogilvie was a short, chubby man who had twinkling eyes, rosy cheeks and a sunny smile. Ogilvie didn't introduce him. He waved Harrison and me into chairs and plunged *in medias res*. 'Now, Malcolm; what's your interest in Ashton?'

I said, 'I'm going to marry his daughter.'

If I'd announced I was going to cohabit with the Prince of Wales I couldn't have had a more rewarding reaction. The clouds came over Mr Nameless; his smile disappeared and his eyes looked like gimlets. Ogilvie goggled for a moment, then barked, *'What's that?'*

'I'm going to marry his daughter,' I repeated. 'What's the matter? Is it illegal?'

'No, it's not illegal,' said Ogilvie in a strangled voice. He glanced at Mr Nameless as though uncertain of what to do next. Mr Nameless said, 'What reason did you have for thinking there'd be a file on Ashton?'

'No reason. It was suggested jokingly that I try asking Nellie, so I did. No one was more surprised than I when Ashton popped up.'

I swear Ogilvie thought I was going round the twist. 'Nellie!' he said faintly.

'Sorry, the computer.'

'Was this enquiry in the course of your work?' he asked.

'No,' I said. 'It was personal and private. I'm sorry about that and I apologize for it. But some odd things have been going on around Ashton over the weekend and I wanted to check him out.'

'What sort of things?'

'Someone threw acid into his daughter's face and...'

Mr Nameless cut in. 'The girl you intend to marry?'

'No—the younger girl, Gillian. Later on Ashton behaved a bit strangely.'

'I'm not surprised,' said Ogilvie. 'When did this happen?'

'Last night.' I paused. 'I had to disclose myself to a copper, so it came through on the weekend telephone log. Joe and I discussed it this morning.'

Ogilvie switched to Harrison. 'You *knew* about this?'

'Only about the acid. Ashton wasn't mentioned.'

'You didn't ask me,' I said. 'And I didn't know Ashton was so bloody important until Nellie told me afterwards.'

Ogilvie said, 'Now let me get this quite right.' He stared at Harrison. 'A member of your staff in this department reported to you that he'd been involved in police enquiries into an acid-throwing attack, and you didn't even ask who was attacked. Is that it?'

Harrison twitched nervously. Mr Nameless paused in the act of lighting a cigarette and said smoothly, 'I think this is irrelevant. Let us get on with it.'

Ogilvie stabbed Harrison with a glance which told him that he'd hear more later. 'Of course. Do you think this is serious?'

'It could be very serious,' said Mr Nameless. 'But I think we're very lucky. We already have an inside man.' He pointed the cigarette at me just as Leonard Bernstein points his baton at the second violins to tell them to get scraping.

I said, 'Now, hold on a minute. I don't know what this is about, but Ashton is going to be my father-in-law. That's bringing things very close to home. You can't be seriously asking me to...'

'You're not being asked,' said Mr Nameless coolly 'You're being told.'

'The hell with that,' I said roundly.

Momentarily he looked startled, and if ever I thought those eyes had twinkled it was then I changed my mind. He glanced at Ogilvie, and said, 'I know this man has a good record, but right now I fail to see how he achieved it.'

'I've said it once this morning, but I'll say it again,' I said. 'Stuff my record.'

'Be quiet, Malcolm,' said Ogilvie irritably. He turned to Harrison. 'I don't think we need you any more, Joe.'

Harrison's expression managed to mirror simultaneously shock, outrage, curiosity and regret at having to leave. As the door closed behind him Ogilvie said, 'I think a valid point has been made. It's not good for an agent to be emotionally involved. Malcolm, what do you think of Ashton?'

'I like him—what I know of him. He's not an easy man to get to know, but then I haven't had much chance yet; just a couple of weekends' acquaintanceship.'

'A point has been made,' conceded Mr Nameless. He twinkled at me as though we were suddenly bosom friends. 'And in rather unparliamentary language. But the fact remains that Mr Jaggard, here, is on the inside. We can't just toss away that advantage.'

Ogilvie said smoothly, 'I think that Malcolm will investigate the circumstances around Ashton as soon as it is properly explained to him why he should.'

'As to that,' said Mr Nameless, 'you mustn't overstep the limits. You know the problem.'

'I think it can be coped with.'

Mr Nameless stood up. 'Then that's what I'll report.'

When he had gone Ogilvie looked at me for a long moment, then shook his head. 'Malcolm, you really can't go about telling high-ranking civil servants to get stuffed.'

'I didn't,' I said reasonably. 'I told him to stuff my record. I didn't even tell him where to stuff it.'

'The trouble about people like you who have private incomes is that it makes you altogether too bloody independent-minded. Now that, while being an asset to the department, as I told his lordship before you came in, can make things difficult for your colleagues.'

His lordship! I didn't know if Ogilvie was being facetious or not.

He said, 'Will you take things a bit easier in future?'

That wasn't asking too much, so I said, 'Of course.'

'Good. How's your father these days?'

'I think he's a bit lonely now that Mother's dead, but he bears up well. He sends you his regards.'

He nodded and checked his watch. 'Now you'll lunch with me and tell me everything you know about Ashton.'

SIX

We lunched in a private room above a restaurant at which
Ogilvie seemed well known. He made me begin right from the
beginning, from the time I met Penny, and I ended my tale
with the abortive checking out of Ashton and my confronta-
tion with Nellie. It took a long time to tell.

When I had finished we were over the coffee cups. Ogilvie lit
a cigar and said, 'All right; you're supposed to be a trained
man. Can you put your finger on anything unusual?'

I thought a bit before answering. 'Ashton has a man called
Benson. I think there's something peculiar there.'

'Sexually, you mean?'

'Not necessarily. Ashton certainly doesn't strike me as being
double-gaited. I mean it's not the normal master-and-servant
relationship. When they came back from the hospital last night
they were closeted in Ashton's study for an hour and a half,
and between them they sank half a bottle of whisky.'

'Um,' said Ogilvie obscurely. 'Anything else?'

'The way he was pressuring me into marrying Penny was
bloody strange. I thought at one time he'd bring out the
traditional shotgun.' I grinned. 'A Purdy, of course—for for-
mal weddings.'

'You know what I think,' said Ogilvie. 'I think Ashton is
scared to death; not on his own behalf but on account of his
girls. He seems to think that if he can get your Penny away
from him she'll be all right. What do you think?'

'It fits all right,' I said. 'And I don't like one damned bit of
it.'

'Poor Ashton. He didn't have the time to polish up a scheme
which showed no cracks, and he sprang it on you too baldly.
I'll bet he pulled that Australian job out of thin air.'

'Who *is* Ashton?' I asked.

'Sorry; I can't tell you that.' Ogilvie blew a plume of smoke.

'I talked very high-handedly to that chap this morning. I told him you'd take on the job as soon as you knew what was involved, but he knew damned well that I can't tell you a thing. That's what he was objecting to in an oblique way.'

'This is bloody silly,' I said.

'Not really. You'll only be doing what you'd be doing anyway, knowing what you know now.'

'Which is?'

'Bodyguarding the girl. Of course, I'll ask you to bodyguard Ashton, too. It's a package deal, you see; one automatically includes the other.'

'And without knowing the reason why?'

'You know the reason why. You'll be guarding Penelope Ashton because you don't want her to get a faceful of sulphuric acid, and that should be reason enough for any tender lover. As for Ashton—well, our friend this morning was right. A commander can't tell his private soldiers his plans when he sends them into battle. He just tells them where to go and they pick up their feet.'

'The analogy is false, and you know it,' I said. 'How can I guard a man if I don't know who or what I'm guarding him against? That's like sending a soldier into battle not only without telling him where the enemy is, but *who* the enemy is.'

'Well, then,' said Ogilvie tranquilly. 'It looks as though you'll have to do it for the sake of my bright blue eyes.'

He had me there and I think he knew it. I had an idea that Mr Nameless, whoever he was, could be quite formidable and Ogilvie had defused what might have been a nasty situation that morning. I owed him something for it. Besides, the cunning old devil's eyes were green.

'All right,' I said. 'But it isn't a one-man job.'

'I'm aware of that. Spend this afternoon thinking out your requirements—I want them on my desk early tomorrow morning. Oh, by the way—you don't disclose yourself.'

I opened my mouth and then closed it again slowly before I swore at him. Then I said, 'You must be joking. I have to guard a man without telling him I'm guarding him?'

'I'm sure you'll do it very well,' he said suavely, and rang for the waiter.

'Then you'll be astonished at what I'll need,' I said acidly.

He nodded, then asked curiously, 'Hasn't it disturbed you that you'll be marrying into a rather mysterious family?'

'It's Penny I'm marrying, not Ashton.' I grinned at him. 'Aren't you disturbed for the same reason?'

'Don't think I'm not,' he said seriously, and left me to make of that what I could.

SEVEN

When I got back to the office Larry Godwin looked me up and down critically. 'I was just about to send out a search party. The griffin is that you've been given a real bollocking. I was just about to go down to the cellar to see if they really do use thumbscrews.'

'Nothing to it,' I said airily. 'I was given the RSPCA medal for being kind to Joe Harrison—that's all.'

'Very funny,' he said acidly, and flapped open a day-old copy of *Pravda*. 'The only time you'll get a medal is when you come with me when I get my knighthood.' He watched me putting a few things into a bag. 'Going somewhere?'

'I won't be around for a couple of days or so.'

'Lucky devil. I never get out of this bloody office.'

'You will one day,' I said consolingly. 'You have to go to Buck House to get a knighthood.' I leaned against the desk. 'You really should be in Slav Section. Why did you opt for General Duties?'

'I thought it would be more exciting,' he said, and added sourly, 'I was wrong.'

'With you around, the phrase "as happy as Larry" takes on an entirely new meaning.' I thought he was going to throw something at me so I ducked out fast.

I drove to Marlow and found the police station. My name presented to the desk sergeant got me Honnister in jig time. He shared an office with another inspector and when I indicated a desire for privacy Honnister shrugged and said, 'Oh, well; we can use an interview room. It's not as comfortable as here, though.'

'That's all right.'

The other copper closed a file and stood up. 'I'm going, anyway. I don't want to pry into your girlish secrets, Charlie.'

He gave me a keen glance as he went out. He'd know me again if he saw me.

Honnister sat at his desk and scowled. 'Secretive crowd, your lot.'

I grinned. 'I don't see you wearing a copper's uniform.'

'I had one of your blokes on the blower this morning—chap by the name of Harrison—threatening me with the Tower of London and unnameable tortures if I talk about you.'

I sat down. 'Joe Harrison is a silly bastard, but he means well.'

'If anyone knows how to keep secrets it's a copper,' said Honnister. 'Especially one in the plain clothes branch. I know enough local secrets to blow Marlow apart. Your chap ought to know that.' He sounded aggrieved.

I cursed Harrison and his ham-fisted approach; if he'd queered my pitch with the local law I'd string him up by the thumbs when I got back. I said, 'Inspector, I told you last night I had no official connection with Ashton. It was true then, but it is no longer true. My people have a definite interest.'

He grunted. 'I know. I've been asked to make an extra copy of all my reports on the Ashton case. As though I don't have enough to do without producing a lot of bloody bumf for people who won't even give me the time of day without consulting the Official Secrets Act.' His resentment was growing.

I said quickly, 'Oh, hell; you can forget that nonsense—just as long as I can see your file copies.'

'You got authority for that?'

I smiled at him. 'A man has all the authority he can take. I'll carry the can if there's a comeback.'

He stared at me and then his lips curved in amusement. 'You and me will get on all right,' he said. 'What do you want to know?'

'First, how's the girl?'

'We haven't been allowed to talk to her so she must be pretty bad. And I need a description. I don't even know the sex of the assailant.'

'So that means no visitors.'

'None except the family. Her sister has been at the hospital most of the day.'

I said, 'I think I might be able to help you there. Suppose I

43

get Penny to ask Gillian for a description. That would do to be going on with until you can ask her yourself.' He nodded. 'I won't be seeing her until later. Where will you be tonight?'

'Theoretically off duty. But I'll be sinking a couple of pints in the Coach and Horses between nine and ten. I'm meeting someone who might give me a lead on another case. You can ring me there. Doyle, the landlord, knows me.'

'Okay. Now, how have you got on with the acid?'

Honnister shrugged. 'About as far as you'd expect. It's battery acid, and the stuff's too common. There are filling stations all around here, and then it might have come from somewhere else.' He leaned back in his chair. 'To me this has the smell of a London job.'

'Have you seen Ashton?'

'Oh, yes, I've seen Ashton. He says he can think of absolutely no reason why his daughter should be attacked in such a manner. No reason whatsoever. It was like talking to a bloody stone wall.'

'I'll be talking to him myself tonight. Maybe I'll get something.'

'Does he know who—and what—you are?'

'No, he doesn't; and he mustn't find out, either.'

'You blokes lead interesting lives,' said Honnister, and grinned crookedly. 'And you wanting to marry his daughter, too.'

I smiled. 'Where did you get that?'

'Just pieced it together from what you told me last night, and from what one of the uniformed boys picked up when talking over a cuppa with the Ashton's maid. I told you I hear secrets—and I'm not a bad jack, even though I say it myself.'

'All right,' I said. 'Tell me a few secrets about Ashton.'

'Not known to the police. Not criminally. The CPO had a few words with him.'

'CPO?'

'Crime Prevention Officer. There are a lot of big houses around here full of expensive loot worth nicking. The CPO calls in to check on the burglar-proofing. You'd be surprised how stupid some of these rich twits can be. A man will fill his house with a quarter of a million quids' worth of paintings and antiques and balk at spending a couple of thousand on keeping the stuff safe.'

44

'How is Ashton's burglar-proofing?'

Honnister grinned. 'It might rank second to the Bank of England,' he conceded.

That interested me. 'Anything more on Ashton?'

'Nothing relevant. But he wasn't the one who was attacked, was he?' He leaned forward. 'Have you thought of the possibility that Gillian Ashton might have been sleeping in the wrong bed? There are two things I think of when I hear of an acid attack on a woman; the first is that it could be a gangland punishment, and the other is that it's one woman taking revenge on another.'

'I've thought of it. Penny discounts it, and I don't go much for it myself. I don't think she's the kind.'

'Maybe, but I've been doing a bit of nosing around. I haven't come up with anything yet, but I can't discount it.'

'Of course you can't.'

I stood up, and Honnister said, 'Don't expect too much too quickly. In fact, don't expect anything at all. I've no great hopes of this case. Anyway, we've not gone twenty-four hours yet.'

That was so, and it surprised me. So much had happened that day that it had seemed longer. 'Okay,' I said. 'I'll be in touch tonight.'

EIGHT

I drove in the direction of Ashton's house and cruised around slowly, making circuits on the country roads and looking for anything out of the ordinary such as cars parked on the verge with people in them doing nothing in particular. There was nothing like that so after an hour of futility I gave up and drove directly to the house.

The gates were locked but there was a bell-push which I pressed. While I waited I studied the gates in the light of what Honnister had said about Ashton's burglar-proofing. They were of ornamental wrought-iron, about ten feet high, very spiky on top, and hung on two massive stone pillars. They barred an opening in an equally high chain-mesh fence, unobtrusive because concealed by trees, which evidently circled the estate. All very good, but the gates hadn't been closed the day before.

Presently a man came down the drive, dressed in rough country clothes. I hadn't seen him before. He looked at me through the gates and said curtly, 'Yes?'

'My name is Malcolm Jaggard. I'd like to see Mr Ashton.'

'He's not in.'

'Miss Ashton?'

'They're not in, either.'

I tugged thoughtfully at my ear. 'What about Benson?'

He looked at me for a moment, then said, 'I'll see.' He stepped to one side behind one of the stone pillars and I heard a click and then the whirr of a telephone dial. There's a phrase for what was happening; it's known as closing the stable door after the horse has gone.

The man came back into sight and wordlessly began to unlock the gate, so I got back into the car and drove up to the house. Benson, in his courtly Boris Karloff manner, ushered me into the living-room, and said, 'I don't expect Miss Penelope will be long, sir. She rang to say she would be back at five.'

'Did she say how Gillian is?'

'No, sir.' He paused, then shook his head slowly. 'This is a bad business, sir. Disgracefully bad.'

'Yes.' I had always been taught that it is bad form to question servants about their masters, but I had no compunction now. Benson had never struck me as being one of your run-of-the-mill house servants, least of all at that very moment because, unless he'd developed a fast-growing tumour under his left armpit, he was wearing a gun. 'I see you have a guard on the gate.'

'Yes; that's Willis. I'll give him your name so he will let you in.'

'How is Mr Ashton taking all this?'

'Remarkably well. He went to his office as usual this morning. Would you care for a drink, sir?'

'Thank you. I'll have a scotch.'

He crossed the room, opened a cabinet, and shortly came back with a tray which he put on a small table next to my elbow. 'If you will excuse me, sir.'

'Thank you, Benson.' He was not staying around to be questioned, but even if he had I doubted if I could have got much out of him. He tended to speak in clichés and bland generalities, but whether he thought that way was quite another matter.

I had not long to wait for Penny and was barely half way through the drink when she came into the room. 'Oh, Malcolm; how good to see you. What a blessed man you are.' She looked tired and drawn.

'I said I'd come. How's Gillian?'

'A little better, I think. She's getting over the shock.'

'I'm very glad to hear it. I had a talk with Honnister, the police inspector in charge of the case. He wants to interview her.'

'Oh, Malcolm; she's not ready for that. Not yet.'

She came to me and I took her into my arms. 'Is it that bad?'

She laid her head on my chest for a moment, and then looked up at me. 'I don't think you know how bad this sort of thing is for a woman. Women seem to care more for their

47

appearance that men—I suppose we have to because we're in the man-catching business, most of us. It's not just the physical shock that's hit Gillian; there's the psychological shock, too.'

'Don't think I'm not aware of it,' I said. 'But put yourself in Honnister's place. He's in a jam—he needs a description. Right now he doesn't even know if he's looking for a man or a woman.'

Penny looked startled. 'I hadn't even thought of that. I assumed it would be a man.'

'Honnister hasn't made that assumption. He hasn't made any assumptions at all because he has damn-all to go on. Is Gillian talking to you?'

'A little, this afternoon.' Penny made a wry face. 'I've kept off the subject of acid-throwing.'

'Could you go to the hospital tonight and see what you can get out of her? Honnister is really at his wits' end about this. Your father couldn't help him and he's stuck.'

'I suppose I could try.'

'Better you than Honnister; he might not have your understanding. I'll come with you; not into the ward, but I'll come along.'

'Will eight o'clock be all right for you? Not too late?'

'All my time is at your disposal.' I didn't tell her that was literally true, by courtesy of one Ogilvie and paid for by the taxpayer. 'You look as though you could do with a drink.'

'I could stand a gin and tonic. Bring it into the kitchen, will you? I have to do something about dinner—Daddy will be home soon.'

She went away and I fixed the drink and took it into the kitchen. I offered to help but she laughed, and said, 'You'd just be in the way. Mary is coming down to help.'

'Mary who?'

'The maid—Mary Cope. You find yourself something to do.'

I went away reflecting that what I really wanted to do was to give Ashton's study a good shake-down. But if it's bad form to question the servants I don't know what the devil it would be called to be found searching through your host's private papers in his *sanctum sanctorum*. Moodily I walked out into the garden.

I was knocking croquet balls about on the lawn when Ashton pitched up. There was a worn and honed look about him as though he was being fined down on some spiritual grindstone. His skin had not lost its tan but he looked paler than usual, and there was still that hurt look in his eyes. It was the look of a little boy who had been punished for something he hadn't done; the anguished look of the injustice of the world. It's hard to explain to a small boy that the world isn't necessarily a just place, but Ashton had been around long enough to know it.

I said, 'Penny's in the kitchen, if you want her.'

'I've seen her,' he said shortly.

'She tells me Gillian is better this evening.'

He looked down, kicking the turf with the toe of his shoe. He didn't speak for some time and I began to think he'd misheard me. But then he looked up and said abruptly, 'She's blind.'

'Christ; I'm sorry to hear that.'

He nodded. 'I had a specialist in this afternoon.'

'Does she know? Does Penny know?'

'Neither of them know. I had it kept from them.'

'I can understand not telling Gillian, but why keep it from Penny?'

'Unlike many sisters they've always been very close even though they are so unalike in temperament—perhaps because of it. I think if Penny knew, Gillian would get it out of her, and she couldn't stand the shock now.' He looked me in the eye. 'Don't tell her.'

Now that was all very logical and carefully thought out, and he had just given me a direct order, there was no doubt about that. 'I won't tell her,' I said. 'But she might find out anyway. She's medically trained and nobody's fool.'

'Just so that it comes later rather than sooner,' he said.

I thought I'd better start to earn my pay. 'I saw Honnister this afternoon. He tells me he didn't get much change out of you this morning. Don't you have any idea why Gillian should be attacked?'

'No,' he said colourlessly.

I studied him carefully. His jacket was much better cut than Benson's but no amount of fine tailoring could hide the slight bulge under his arm. 'You haven't had threatening letters or anything like that?'

'Nothing like that,' he said impatiently. 'I'm at a loss to understand it.'

I felt like asking him, 'Then why carry a gun?' My problem was that I didn't know why he was on our files. Men were listed for many reasons, and to be listed did not make them villains—far from it. The trouble was that no one would tell me which class Ashton came into, and that made this job damned difficult. Difficult to know how to push at him; difficult to identify the cranny into which to push the wedge that would crack him.

But I tried. I said practically, 'Then the reason must lie somewhere in Gillian's own life. Some crowd she's been mixed up with, perhaps.'

He became instantly angry. 'Nonsense!' he said sharply. 'That's a monstrous suggestion. How could she get mixed up with types like that without me knowing? The type who could do such a dreadful thing?'

I was acting the part of the impartial onlooker. 'Oh, I don't know,' I said judiciously. 'It happens all the time judging by what we read in the newspapers. The police arrest a kid and uncover a whole series of offences, from mainlining on heroin to theft to get the cash to feed the habit. The parents are shocked and plead ignorance; they had no idea that little Johnny or little Mary was involved. I believe them, too.'

He took a deep breath. 'For one thing, Gillian isn't a kid; she's a grown woman of twenty-six. And for another, I know my family very well. You paid me a compliment last night; you said I'd brought up Penny too well. That goes for Gillian, too.' He drove his toe viciously into the turf. 'Would you think that of Penny?'

'No, I don't think I would.'

'Then why should you think it of Gillian? It's bloody ridiculous.'

'Because Penny didn't have acid thrown in her face,' I reminded him. 'Gillian did.'

'This is a nightmare,' he muttered.

'I'm sorry; I didn't mean to hurt you. I hope you'll accept my apology.'

He put his hand to his face, rubbing at closed eyelids. 'Oh, that's all right, Malcolm.' His hand dropped to his side. 'It's just that she was always such a good little girl. Not like Penny; Penny could be difficult at times. She still can. She can be very wilful, as you'll find out if you marry her. But Gillian...' He shook his head. 'Gillian was never any trouble at all.'

What Ashton said brought home to me some of the anguish parents must feel when things go wrong with the kids. But I was not so concerned with his agony that I didn't note his reference to *if* I married Penny, not *when* I married her. Evidently the fixation of the previous night had left him.

He disillusioned me immediately. 'Have you given any thought to what we discussed last night?'

'Some.'

'With what conclusion?'

'I'm still pretty much of the same mind,' I said. 'I don't think this is the time to present Penny with new problems, especially if the girls are as close as you say. She's very unhappy, too, you know.'

'I suppose you're right,' he said dispiritedly, and kicked at the grass again. He was doing that shoe no good at all, and it was a pity to treat Lobb's craftsmanship so cavalierly. 'Are you staying to dinner?'

'With your permission,' I said formally. 'I'm taking Penny to the hospital afterwards.'

He nodded. 'Don't tell her about Gillian's eyes. Promise me that.'

'I already have.'

He didn't answer that, but turned on his heel and walked away towards the house. As I watched him go I felt desperately sorry for him. It didn't matter to me then if Nellie had him listed as a hero or a villain; I still felt sorry for him as a simple human being in the deepest of distress.

Penny and I got to the hospital at about half past eight. I didn't go in with her but waited in the car. She was away quite a long time, more than an hour, and I became restive because I had promised to call Honnister. When she came out she said quietly, 'I've got what you wanted.'

I said, 'Will you tell it to Honnister? I have an appointment with him.'

'All right.'

We found Honnister standing at the bar of the Coach and Horses looking broodily into a glass of beer. When we joined him he said, 'My man's been and gone. I've been hanging on waiting for your call.'

'Inspector Honnister—this is Penny Ashton. She has something to tell you.'

He regarded her with gravity. 'Thank you, Miss Ashton. I don't think you need me to tell you that we're doing the best we can on this case, but it's rather difficult, and we appreciate all the help we can get.'

'I understand,' she said.

He turned to me. 'What'll you have?'

'A scotch and ...' I glanced at Penny.

'A gin and tonic.'

Honnister called to the man behind the bar. 'Monte, a large scotch and a gin and tonic.' He turned and surveyed the room. 'We'd better grab that table before the last-minute crowd comes in.'

I took Penny over to the table and presently Honnister joined us with the drinks. He wasted no time and even before he was seated, he said 'Well, Miss Ashton, what can you tell me?'

'Gillian says it was a man.'

'Aah!' said Honnister in satisfaction. He had just eliminated a little more than half the population of Britain. 'What sort of man? Young? Old? Anything you tell me will be of value.'

He led her through the story several times and each time elicited a further nugget of information. What it boiled down to was this: Gillian had walked back from church and, coming up the drive towards the house, had seen a car parked with the bonnet open and a man peering at the engine. She thought he was someone who had broken down so she approached with the intention of offering assistance. As she drew near the man turned and smiled at her. He was no one she knew. She was about to speak when he slammed down the bonnet with one hand and simultaneously threw the acid into her face with the other. The man didn't speak at any time; he was about forty, with a sallow complexion and sunken eyes. She did not know the make of car but it was darkish in colour.

'Let's go back a bit,' said Honnister yet again. 'Your sister saw the man looking at the engine with the bonnet open. Did she mention his hands?'

'No, I don't think so. Is it important?'

'It might be,' said Honnister noncommittally. He *was* a good jack; he didn't put his own ideas into the mouths of his witnesses.

Penny frowned, staring at the bubbles rising in her glass, and her lips moved slightly as she rehearsed her thoughts. Suddenly she said, 'That's it, Inspector. Gillian said she walked up and the man turned and smiled at her, then he took his hands out of his jacket pockets.'

'Good!' said Honnister heartily. 'Very good, indeed!'

'I don't see the importance,' said Penny.

Honnister turned to me. 'Some cars have a rod on a hinge to hold up the bonnet; others have a spring-loaded gadget. Now, if he had his hands in his pockets he couldn't have been holding the bonnet open manually; and if he took them out of his pockets to close the bonnet and throw the acid at the same time then that bonnet was spring-loaded. He wouldn't have time to unhook a rod. It cuts down considerably on the makes of car we have to look for.' He drained his glass. 'Anything more to tell me?'

'I can think of nothing else, Inspector.'

'You and your sister have done very well,' he said as he stood up. 'Now I have to see a man about a dog.' He grinned at me. 'I really mean that—someone pinched a greyhound.'

Penny said, 'You'll let us know if...'

'You'll be first to know when something breaks,' promised Honnister. 'This is one villain I really want to get my hands on.'

As he walked out I said, 'He's a good copper.'

'It seems so,' said Penny. 'I wouldn't have thought of the significance of the way a car bonnet is held open.'

I stared into my glass. I was thinking that if I got hold of that acid-throwing bastard first there wouldn't be much left of him for Honnister to deal with. Presently Penny said, 'I can't say,

"A penny for your thoughts", or you might get the wrong idea; but what are you thinking?'

I said it automatically; I said it without moving my mind. I said, 'I'm thinking it would be a good idea if we got married.'

'Malcolm!'

I'm pretty good at detecting nuances but there were too damn many in that single two-syllable word to cope with. There was something of surprise and something of shock; something, I was afraid, of displeasure and something, I hoped, of delight. All mixed up together.

'Don't *you* think it's a good idea?' I watched her hunt for words. 'But don't say, "This is so sudden!"'

'But it *is* so damned sudden,' she said, and waved her hand at the room. 'Here, of all places.'

'It seems a good pub to me,' I said. 'Does the place matter?'

'I don't suppose it does,' she said quietly. 'But the time—and the timing—does.'

'I suppose I could have picked a better time,' I agreed. 'But it just popped out. I'm not the only one who thinks it's a good idea. Your father does, too; he wanted me to ask you last night.'

'So you two have been discussing me behind my back. I don't know that I like that.'

'Be reasonable. It's traditional—and courteous, too—for a man to inform his prospective father-in-law of his intentions.' I refrained from saying that it had been Ashton who had brought up the subject.

'What would you have done if he had been against it?'

'I'd have asked you just the same,' I said equally. 'I'm marrying you, not your father.'

'You're not marrying anyone—yet.' I was thankful for the saving grace of that final monosyllable. She laid her hand on mine. 'You idiot—I thought you'd never ask.'

'I had it all laid on, but circumstances got in the way.'

'I know.' There was melancholy in her voice. 'Oh, Malcolm; I don't know what to say. I've been so unhappy today, thinking about Gillian, and seeing her in such pain. And then there was that awful task you laid on me tonight of questioning her. I saw it had to be done, so I did it—but I don't like one bit of it. And then there's Daddy—he doesn't say much but I think he's going through hell, and I'm worried about him. And now you come and give me more problems.'

'I'm sorry, Penny; I truly am. Let's put the question back in the deep freeze for a while. Consider yourself unasked.'

'No,' she said. 'You can't unask a question. In a way that's what my work is all about.' She was silent for a while. I didn't know what she meant by that but I had sense enough to keep my mouth shut. At last she said, 'I will marry you, Malcolm—I'd marry you tomorrow. I'm not one for non-essentials, and I don't want a white wedding with all the trimmings or anything like that. I want to marry you but it can't be now, and I can't tell you when it will be. We've got to get this matter of Gillian sorted out first.'

I took her hand. 'That's good enough for me.'

She gave me a crooked smile. 'It won't be the usual kind of engagement, I'm afraid. I'm in no mood for romantic frivolities. Later, perhaps; but not now.' She squeezed my hand. 'Do you remember when I asked you to come here and meet Daddy? It was the night we had the Chinese dinner in your flat.'

'I remember.'

'It was a diversion. I had to stop myself from doing something.'

'Doing what, for God's sake?'

'Marching into your bedroom and getting into your bed.' She disengaged her hand and finished her drink. 'And now you'd better take me home before I change my mind and we start behaving badly.'

As I escorted her to the car my heart was like a singing bird and all the other guff the poets used to write about. They don't any more; they leave it to the writers of pop songs, which is a pity. I drove her home and stopped the car before the gates, and we had five minutes' worth of love before she got out. She had no key and had to press the button for someone to come.

I said, 'We won't announce the engagement, but I think your father ought to know. It seems to be on his mind.'

'I'll tell him now.'

'Are you going to London tomorrow?'

She shook her head. 'Lumsden has given me a few days off. He's very understanding.'

'I'll pop out to see you.'

'But what about your job?'

I grinned. 'I have an understanding boss, too.'

There was a rattle at the gate and it swung open, pushed by Willis, the dour and unfriendly type who had let me in that afternoon. Penny kissed me and then slipped inside and the gate clanged shut. I stepped up to it, and said to Willis, 'Escort Miss Ashton up to the house, see her safe inside, and make sure the house door is locked.'

He looked at me for a moment in silence, then smiled, and it was like an ice floe breaking up. 'I'll do that, sir.'

NINE

I was in the office early next morning and first I had an extended chat with Nellie. I had just moved to the typewriter when Larry came in with a pile of newspapers which he dumped on his desk. 'Thought you were out on a job.'

'I am,' I said. 'I'm not here. I'm a figment of your imagination.'

I finished my list and took it in to Ogilvie, and wasted no time in getting down to the bones of it. I said, 'I don't mind fighting with one hand tied behind my back but I object to having both hands tied. I'll need a list of Ashton's present overt activities and affiliations.'

Ogilvie smiled and pushed a file across the desk. 'I anticipated you.'

In return he got my sheet of paper. 'That's more of what I need.'

He scanned it. 'Six men, six cars, telephone ta...' He broke off. 'Who do you think we are—the CIA?'

I looked studiously at the back of my hands. 'Have you ever been in the field, sir?'

'Of course I've...' I looked up and found him smiling sheepishly. The smile disappeared as he said irritably, 'I know; you people think we desk-bound types have lost touch. You could be right.' He tapped the paper. 'Justify this.'

'I have to do a twenty-four hour secret surveillance of three —perhaps four—people. It'll be...'

He caught me up on that. 'Which three or four?'

'First Ashton and Penny Ashton. Then Gillian Ashton. Just because she's been attacked once doesn't give her a lifelong exemption. I might be able to arrange with Honnister to have one of his chaps at the hospital if I ask him nicely enough. That'll take some of the load off us.'

'And the fourth?'

'Benson. I pushed the lot of them through the computer until I lost them in Code Purple.'

'Benson, too?' Ogilvie thought about it. 'You know, the computer might be going by the address only. Anyone living there might be classed with Ashton.'

'I thought of that and it won't wash. Mary Cope, the maid, lives in and I put her through as a control. Nellie has never heard of her. If Ashton is so damned important then he's six-man-important.'

'I agree—but you can't keep an eye on four people with six men. I'll let you have eight.' He smiled slightly. 'I must be going soft-headed. If Harrison was handling this he'd cut you down to four.'

I was taken aback but rallied enough to discuss who we were going to use on the operation. I said, 'I'd like to take Laurence Godwin.'

'You think he's ready?'

'Yes. If we don't use him soon he'll go sour on us. I've been keeping an eye on him lately; he's been right more times than he's been wrong, which is not bad going in this trade.'

'Very well.' Ogilvie returned to my list. 'I agree that Ashton's telephones should be tapped. If he's being threatened we want to know about it. I'll have to get authorization from upstairs, though; but I'll be as quick as I can. As for the postal surveillance, that's trickier but I'll see what I can do.' He put his finger down. 'This last item worries me. You'll have to have a damned good reason for wanting a pistol.'

'Benson's carrying a gun in his oxter, and Ashton is carrying another. If they are expecting that sort of action I think we should be prepared.'

'You're sure of this?'

'Dead certain. I'd like to know if they have gun permits.'

Ogilvie considered it. 'Under the circumstances Ashton might. I don't know about Benson. I'll check.' I'd have given a lot to know what those circumstances were but I didn't ask because I knew he wouldn't tell me.

We settled a few more minor details, then Ogilvie said, 'Right; that's it. Round up your boys and brief them. I want a recording made of the briefing, the tape to be given to me personally before you leave. Get on with it, Malcolm.' As I was leaving he added, 'I'll authorize two pistols.'

I went back and gave Larry a list of names. 'Get on the blower. I want those men in my office ten minutes ago.' I paused. 'And put yourself on the bottom of the list.'

His expression was a study in pure delight. 'You mean...'

I grinned. 'I mean. Now get busy.' I sat at my desk and opened the file on Ashton. It was very thin. The names and addresses of his firms were given, but his other associations were few, mostly professional men—lawyers, accountants and the like. He was a member of no club, whether social, sporting or intellectual. A millionaire hermit.

The team assembled and I switched on the tape-recorder. The briefing didn't take long. I outlined the problem and then told how we were going to handle it, then allocated jobs and shifts. One pistol would be carried by the man overseeing Ashton, whoever he happened to be at the time; the other I reserved to myself.

I said, 'Now we have radios so we use them. Stay on net and report often so everyone is clued up all the time. Those off-shift to be findable and near a telephone. You might be needed in a hurry.'

Simpson asked, 'Do off-shift men go home?' He'd just got back from his honeymoon.

'No. Everyone books into hotels in or near Marlow.' There was an audible groan. 'As soon as you've done it report which hotel together with its phone number so we can find you. I'm at the Compleat Angler.'

Brent said, 'Living it up on the expense account.'

I grinned, then said soberly, 'I don't think we'll have much time for that on this exercise. I might add that this is an important one. You can judge its importance by the fact that Ogilvie raised the team from six to eight on his own initiative and without me having to needle him. In the light of our staff position that says a lot. So don't lose any of these people—and keep your heads down. Right; that's all.' I switched off the recorder and rewound the tape.

Larry said, 'You haven't given me a job.'

'You stick with me. I'll be back in a minute—I'm going to see Ogilvie.'

As I walked into his outer office his secretary said, 'I was about to ring you, Mr Jaggard. Mr Ogilvie wants to see you.'

'Thanks.' I went on in, and said, 'Here's the tape of the briefing.'

He was frowning and said directly, 'Did you cancel a request given to Inspector Honnister for copies of his reports on the Ashton case?'

I put the cassette on his desk. 'Yes.'

'Why?'

'Because I thought it was a lot of bull,' I said bluntly. 'It was getting in the way of good relations. What Harrison did was bad enough.'

'Harrison! What did Joe do?'

I related Harrison's flat-footed approach and Honnister's reaction to it, and then his views on providing extra copies of his reports. I added, 'If we're going to ask Honnister to provide a guard at the hospital we need to keep in his good books.'

'Very good thinking,' said Ogilvie heavily. 'But for one thing. This department did not request those copies. It came from elsewhere, and someone has just been chewing my ear off by telephone.'

'Oh,' I said, rather inadequately, and then, 'Who?'

'Need you ask?' said Ogilvie acidly. 'The gentleman you met yesterday is sticking his oar in—which, I might add, he is perfectly entitled to do.' He rubbed his jaw and amended the statement. 'As long as he restricts himself to requests for information and does not initiate any action.'

He pondered for a moment, then said, 'All right, Malcolm, you can go. But don't take any precipitate action without referring back to me.'

'Yes. I'm sorry, sir.'

He waved me away.

TEN

There was nearly an hour of bureaucracy to get through before Larry and I could drive to Marlow. On the way I gave him the score up to that point, and his reaction was emphatic. 'This is downright stupid! You mean Ogilvie won't tell you what's behind all this?'

'I think his hands are tied,' I said. 'This is real top-level stuff. He has a character from Whitehall like a monkey on his back.'

'You mean Cregar?'

I glanced sideways at Larry. 'Who?'

'Lord Cregar. Short, chubby little chap.'

'Could be. How did you get on to him? Did you bug Ogilvie's office?'

He grinned. 'I went to the loo yesterday and saw him coming out of Ogilvie's room while you were in there.'

I said musingly, 'Ogilvie did refer to him as "his lordship" but I thought he was joking. How did you know he was Cregar?'

'He got divorced last week,' said Larry. 'His photograph was splashed on the middle inside page of the *Telegraph*.'

I nodded. The *Daily Telegraph* takes a keen interest in the marital ups-and-downs of the upper crust. 'Do you know anything more about him, other than that he's wifeless?'

'Yes,' said Larry. 'He's not womanless—*that* came out very strongly in the court case. But beyond that, nothing.'

We crossed the Thames at Marlow, and I said, 'We'll check the hospital first, then go to the police station and I'll introduce you to a good copper. How good are you at grovelling? I might need a few lessons.'

The hospital car park was full so I put the car illicitly into a doctor's slot. I saw Jack Brent, who was trailing Penny, so that meant she was in the hospital; he was talking to someone over his radio. I was about to go over to him when someone hailed me, and I turned to find Honnister at my elbow.

He seemed quite cheerful as I introduced Larry. I said, 'I got some wires crossed yesterday. My people didn't ask for reports; the request came from elsewhere.'

He smiled. 'I thought the Super was a bit narky this morning. Not to worry, Mr Jaggard. A man can't do more than his best.'

'Any progress?'

'I think we have the make of car. A witness saw a Hillman Sceptre close to Ashton's place on Saturday afternoon. The driver fits the description of the suspect. A dark blue car and spring-loaded bonnet, so it fits.' He rubbed his hands. 'I'm beginning to think we stand a chance on this one. I want to get this man before Miss Ashton for a firm identification.'

I shook my head. 'You won't get it. She's blind.'

Honnister looked stricken. 'Christ!' he said savagely. 'Wait till I lay hands on this whoreson!'

'Stand in line. There's a queue.'

'I'm just going up to see her. The doctor says she's fit to talk.'

'Don't tell her she's blind—she doesn't know yet. And don't tell her sister.' I pondered for a moment. 'We have reason to believe another attack may be made on her. Can you put a man in the hospital?'

'That's asking something,' said Honnister. He paused, then asked, 'Do you know what's wrong with the bloody force? Too many chiefs and not enough Indians. If there's a multiple smash on the M4 we'd be hard put to it to find four uniformed men for crowd control. But go into the nick in Slough and you can't toss a pebble in any direction without it ricocheting off three coppers of the rank of chief inspector or higher.' He seemed bitter. 'But I'll see what I can do.'

I said, 'Failing that, give the hospital staff a good briefing. No stranger to get near Gillian Ashton without authority from you, me or the Ashton family. Pitch it to them strong.'

Brent left his car and joined us and I introduced him to Honnister. 'Everything okay?'

'She's inside now; that's her car over there. But this town is hell on wheels. She went shopping before she came here and led me the devil of a dance. There's nowhere to park—I got two tickets in half an hour.'

'Hell, we can't have that.' I could imagine Penny being abducted while my man argued the toss with a traffic warden. I said to Larry, 'I want CD plates put on all our cars fast.'

'Oh, very tricky!' said Honnister admiringly.

Larry grinned. 'The Foreign Office won't like it.'

'Nothing to do with the Foreign Office,' observed Honnister. 'It's just a convention with no legal significance. A copper once stopped a car with CD plates and found a Cockney driver, so he asked him what CD stood for. The bloke said, "Cake Deliverer". And he was, too.' He strugged. 'There was nothing he could do about it.' He nudged me. 'Coming in?'

'I'll join you inside.'

Jack Brent waited until Honnister was well out of earshot before saying, 'I thought it best not to talk in front of him, but Ashton and Benson haven't been found.'

'Ashton isn't at his office?'

'No, and he isn't at home, either.'

I thought about it. In the course of his business Ashton might be anywhere in the Home Counties; he might even have gone to London. And there was nothing to say that Benson was a prisoner in the house; he had to go out some time. All the same, I didn't like it.

I said, 'I'm going to the house. Come on, Larry.' I turned to Brent. 'And you stick close to Penny Ashton. For Christ's sake, don't lose her.'

I drove a little faster than I should on the way to Ashton's place, and when I got there I leaned on the bell-push until Willis arrived wearing an annoyed expression. 'There's no one in,' he said abruptly.

'I want to make sure of that. Let me in.' He hesitated and then opened the gate reluctantly and I drove up to the house.

Larry said, 'He's a surly devil.'

'But reliable, I'd say.' I stopped before the front door, got out, and rang the bell. It was a fair time before the door opened and I was confronted by the maid who looked surprised to see me. 'Oh, Mr Jaggard, Miss Penny's not here. She's at the hospital.'

'I know. Mr Ashton not in?'

63

'No, he's out, too.'

'What about Benson?'

'I haven't seen him all morning.'

I said, 'Mind if we come in? I'd like to use the telephone.'

In response she opened the door wider. Larry and I walked into the hall, and I said, 'You're Mary Cope, aren't you?'

'Yes, sir.'

'Have you seen either Mr Ashton or Benson at all today?'

'No, sir.'

'When was the last time you saw them?'

'Well, not really to see,' she said. 'But they were in the study last night; I heard them talking. That would be about nine o'clock. Just before, really, because I was going up to my room to catch the nine o'clock news and I switched on five minutes early.' She paused, wondering if she was right in talking of the doings of the family. After all, I hadn't been around all that long. She said nervously, 'Is this anything to do with what happened to Miss Gillian?'

'It could be.'

'Mr Ashton's bed wasn't slept in,' she volunteered.

I glanced at Larry who raised his eyebrows. 'What about Benson's bed?'

'I haven't looked—but he always makes up his own bed.'

'I see. I'll use the telephone if I may.'

I rang the hospital, asking for Penny, and told the operator she'd be in or near the intensive care unit. It was a long time before she came on the line. 'I hope you haven't waited long,' she said. 'I slipped away for a cup of tea. Gillian's much better, Malcolm; she's talking to Honnister now, and she doesn't mind a bit.'

I said, 'Did you tell your father about us last night?'

'No. He'd gone to bed when I got in.'

'Did you tell him this morning?'

'No. I slept late and he'd gone out when I got up. I expect Mary made breakfast for him.'

I didn't comment on that. 'When did you last see Benson?'

Her voice was suddenly wary. 'What's the matter, Malcolm? What's going on?'

I said, 'Look, Penny, I'm at your house. I'd like you to come home because I want to talk to you about something. I expect

Honnister will be at the hospital for quite some time, and there's nothing you can do there.'

'There's something wrong, isn't there?' she said.

'Not really. I'll tell you when I see you.'

'I'm coming now.' She rang off.

I put down the receiver and looked around, to see Mary Cope regarding me curiously from the other end of the hall. I jerked my head at Larry and gave him my keys. 'In the special compartment of my car you'll find a file on Ashton. There's a list of the cars he owns on page five, I think. Nip round to the garage and see what's missing. Then go down to the gate and ask Willis what time Ashton and Benson left here.'

He went quickly and I walked into Ashton's study. On his desk were two envelopes; one addressed to Penny and the other to me. I picked up mine and broke the seal.

The note might have been enigmatic to anyone else, but to me it was as clear as crystal. It read:

My dear Malcolm,

You are far too intelligent a man not to have seen what I was driving at in our more recent conversations. You may be acquainted with the French proverb: *Celui qui a trouvé un bone gendre a gagné un fils; mais celui qui en a rencontré un mauvais a perdu une fille.*

Marry Penny with my blessing and make her happy—but, for her sake, be a bad son-in-law.

Yours,

George Ashton.

I sat down heavily and had a queasy feeling in the pit of my stomach because I knew we'd botched the job. I picked up the telephone to ring Ogilvie.

ELEVEN

I didn't wrap it up for him. 'Our pigeons have flown the coop,' I said baldly.

He was incredulous. 'What! All of them?'

'Just the two cock birds.'

He was silent for a moment, then said slowly, 'My fault, I'm afraid. I ought to have given you your team yesterday. How certain are you?'

'He left me a note.' I read it out.

Ogilvie put the French into English. ' "He who has found a good son-in-law has gained a son, but he who has picked up a bad one has lost a daughter." What the hell is that supposed to mean?'

I said, 'It may be my fault he's cut and run. He tackled me again last evening about marrying Penny, and I gave him another refusal. I think that since he couldn't get her to cut loose from him, he has cut loose from her. If you read the note in that context you'll see what I mean.'

'Um. What was his attitude last evening?'

'He was a walking disaster,' I said flatly.

'How much start have they had?'

I sorted through the details I had picked up, then checked the time. 'I don't know about Benson, but for Ashton say fifteen hours maximum. I might get to know a bit more in the next few minutes.'

'We don't know that he went,' said Ogilvie objectively. 'He might have been taken. That note to you may be a fraud. Either case is serious, of course.'

'I don't think he was taken. The note is too accurately pointed, and this house is well protected.'

'Yes, it would be.' Ogilvie knew enough of the background to make a statement like that. 'How's the girl taking it?'

'She doesn't know yet. Ashton left her a note, too. I haven't opened it—I'll let her do that. I'll let you know anything that's relevant.'

'Think she'll tell you?'

'Yes. It's a funny thing, sir, but I did ask her to marry me last night and she accepted. She was going to tell Ashton when she got home but she said he'd gone to bed. I think he'd already left. If he'd waited another couple of hours he might have decided not to go.'

'Yes,' said Ogilvie meditatively. 'But don't blame yourself for that.' I looked up as Larry came into the study. Ogilvie said, 'Did you disclose yourself to her?'

'No.'

There was a pause. 'You take your duties very seriously, don't you, Malcolm?'

'I try to. Hang on a minute.' I looked up at Larry. 'Well?'

'There's an Aston Martin short, and both Benson and Ashton left last night at about half past nine, and didn't come back.'

The Aston Martin was Penny's car. I said to Ogilvie, 'We've got a pretty firm time. They left together at nine-thirty last night, probably in a hired car.' He seemed to be a long time digesting that, so I said, 'What's the next step?'

'There's going to be a row, of course,' he said, not sounding too perturbed. 'But I'll handle that. What you do is to go through that house like a dose of salts. See if you can find anything to indicate where Ashton has gone. Anything you don't understand bring here for evaluation.'

I said, 'That will blow my cover with Penny. I can't search the house without giving her an explanation.'

'I know.'

'Hold on.' I turned to Larry. 'Get on the radio—I want everyone here as soon as possible.'

'Off-shift boys included?'

'Yes. And go to the gate to make sure they can get in.'

Before speaking to Ogilvie again I glumly contemplated the explanation I'd have to give Penny. It was a hell of a thing to tell a girl you've just proposed to, and I had the feeling that our relationship was about to alter for the worse.

I pushed it out of my mind, and said, 'Do we bring the police in on this?'

I could almost hear Ogilvie's brains creaking as he thought that one out. At last he said, 'Not at this stage. I'll have to push it upstairs for a ruling. Police security is not too good on this sort of thing—they have too many reporters watching them. How long do you think you'll be there?'

'I don't know. It's a big house and I can see at least one safe from here. If we can't find keys we may have to take extreme measures. I'll give you a ring in an hour. I'll have a better idea by then.'

'I can't hold this for an hour. If you look towards London in fifteen minutes you'll see the flames rising from Whitehall. Do your best.' He rang off.

I put down the telephone and looked thoughtfully at the letter addressed to Penny, then crossed to the safe. It had a combination lock and the door didn't open when I turned the handle. I went back to the desk and gave it a quick once-over lightly in the hope of finding something useful immediately. There was nothing. Five minutes later I heard a car draw up outside and, thinking it might be Penny, I went outside.

It was Peter Michaelis, one of the team. He came over with an enquiring look on his face, and I said, 'Stick around.' He had given Larry a lift from the gate, so I called him over. 'Take Ashton's file and start ringing around—his office, factories, every address you find in there. If Ashton is seen he's to ring his home immediately.' I shrugged. 'It won't work but we must cover it.'

'Okay.'

An Aston Martin was coming up the drive so I braced myself. 'Use the telephone in the hall. I want to use the study.'

Larry walked towards the house as Penny's car came to a fast halt, braked hard. She tumbled out, looking uncertainly at Michaelis, then ran towards me. 'I'm being followed,' she said, and whirled around, pointing at the car coming up the drive. 'He followed me into the grounds.'

'It's all right,' I said, as Brent's car stopped. 'I know who he is.'

'What's happening?' she demanded. 'Who are these men?' Her voice caught. 'What's happened to Daddy?'

'As far as I know he's all right.' I took her elbow. 'I want you to come with me.'

I took her into the house and she paused in the hall as she saw Larry at the telephone, then quickened her pace again. We went into the study and I picked up the letter from the desk. 'You'd better read this.'

She looked at me uncertainly before glancing at the superscription. 'It's from Daddy,' she said, and ripped open the envelope. As she read the note she frowned and her face paled. 'But I don't ... I don't understand. I don't ...'

'What does he say?'

Wordlessly she handed the letter to me, then walked over to the window and looked out. I watched her for a moment, then bent my head and read:

My dearest Penny,

For reasons I cannot disclose I must go away for a while. The reasons are not disreputable, nor am I a criminal, although that imputation may be made. My affairs are all in order and my absence should not cause you any trouble financially. I have made all the necessary arrangements: for legal advice consult Mr Veasey of Michelmore, Veasey and Templeton; for financial advice go to Mr Howard of Howard and Page. They have been well briefed for this eventuality.

I do not know for how long I shall have to be away. You will be doing me a great service if you make no attempt at all to find me and, above all, I do not wish the police to be brought into this matter if that can be avoided. I assure you again that my reasons for leaving in this manner are purely private and personal. I will come to no harm because my old friend, Benson, will be looking after me.

It would give me the greatest peace of mind if you would marry your Malcolm as soon as is practically possible. I know that you love him and I know that he wants to marry you very much, and I have a great respect for the intelligence and character of the man you have chosen. Please do not let the matter of poor Gillian impede your plans to marry and, on the occasion, please put a notice in *The Times*.

I have the greatest confidence that the two of you will be very happy together, and I am equally sure that you will both look after Gillian. Forgive me for the abrupt manner of my departure but it is in the best interests of all of us.

Your loving father,
George.

I looked up. 'I'm sorry, Penny.'

'But I don't understand,' she cried desolately. 'Oh, Malcolm, what's *happened* to him?'

She came into my arms and I held her close. 'I don't know—but we'll find out.'

She was still for a while, but pushed herself away as two cars arrived in quick succession. She stared from the window at the gathering knot of men. 'Malcolm, who are all those men? Have you told the police? Daddy said not to.'

'No, I haven't told the police,' I said quietly. 'Sit down, Penny; I have a lot to tell you.' She looked at me wonderingly, and hesitated, but sat in the chair behind the desk. I hesitated, too, not knowing where to begin, then thought it best to give it to her straight and fast.

'I work for the firm of McCulloch and Ross, and I've told no lies about what the firm does. It does everything I've said it does, and does it very well, too. Our clients are most satisfied, and they ought to be because of the amount of public money going into their service.'

'What are you getting at?'

'McCulloch and Ross is a cover for a sort of discreet government department dealing mainly with economic and industrial affairs in so far as they impinge on state security.'

'State security! You mean you're some sort of secret agent. A spy?'

I laughed and held up my hands. 'Not a spy. We're not romantic types with double-o numbers and a licence to kill—no nonsense like that.'

'But you were watching and investigating my father like a common spy.' Anger flamed in her. 'And was I just a means to an end? Did you snuggle up to me just to get to know him better?'

I lost the smile fast—this was where the crunch came. 'Christ, no! I didn't know a damned thing about him until yesterday, and I don't know much more now. Believe me when I say it was something I stumbled into by accident.'

She was disbelieving and contemptuous. 'And just what did you *stumble* into?'

'I can't tell you that because I don't know myself.'

She shook her head as though momentarily dizzy. 'That man in the hall—those men outside: are they in your department, too?'

'Yes.'

'Then I'd like to talk to the man in charge.' She stood up. 'I'd like to tell him just what I think of all this. I knew Daddy was under pressure. Now I know were it was coming from.'

I said deliberately, 'You're talking to the man in charge, and you're dead wrong.'

That stopped her. She sat down with a bump. '*You* are in charge?'

'That's right.'

'And you don't know what you're doing?' She laughed hysterically.

'I know what I'm doing, but I don't know why. There's a hierarchy of levels, Penny—wheels within wheels. Let me tell you how I got into this.'

So I told her. I told her everything, holding nothing back. I told her about Nellie and the colour codes; I told her about Ogilvie and Lord Cregar. I told her a damned sight more than I ought to have done, and to hell with the Official Secrets Act.

She heard me out, then said thoughtfully, 'Your people aren't very trusting, are they?'

'They're not in the trust business.' I lit a cigarette. 'The pressure didn't come from us, Penny. We threw no acid. We came into it after that, and my brief was to watch over your father and protect him—your father, you and Gillian, and Benson, too, if I thought it necessary.' I walked over to the window and looked at the cars. The gang had all arrived. 'I've not done a very good job so far.'

'It's not your fault that Daddy went away.' Her words hung heavily on the air, and she seemed to take another look at her father. 'That he *ran* away.'

I turned to her. 'Don't start blaming him without knowing what you're blaming him for.'

She said pensively, 'I wonder if he'd still want me to marry you, if he knew what I know now?'

'I'll ask him as soon as I catch up with him,' I said grimly.

'You're not going after him?' She picked up her letter. 'He said...'

'I know what he said. I also know he's regarded by my people as a very important man, and he may be going into danger without knowing it. I still have my job to do.'

'But he doesn't want...'

I said impatiently, 'What he wants or doesn't want is immaterial.' I plucked the letter from her fingers and scanned it. 'He says he doesn't want you to go looking for him. Well, you won't—I will. He says not to involve the police. Right; they haven't been told. He says, "I will come to no harm because my old friend, Benson, will be looking after me." Good God, Penny, how old is Benson? He must be pushing sixty-five. He's in no position to protect himself, let alone anyone else.'

She started to weep. She didn't sob or make an outcry, but the tears welled in her eyes and ran down her cheeks. She cried silently and helplessly, and she was shivering as though suddenly very cold. I put my arm around her and she clung to me with a fierce grip. One of the worst things that can happen is when a hitherto cosy and secure world falls apart. An icy wind seemed to be blowing through that pleasant, panelled study from the greater and more vicious world outside.

'Oh, Malcolm, what am I to do?'

I said very quietly, 'You must do what you think is best. If you trust me you will help me to find him, but I wouldn't—I couldn't—blame you if you refuse. I haven't been open with you—I should have told you about this yesterday.'

'But you were under orders.'

'A common plea,' I said. 'All the Nazis made it.'

'Malcolm, don't make it any harder for yourself than you have to.' She put my arm aside, stood up, and went to the window. 'What are your men waiting for?'

I took a deep breath. 'For your decision. I want to search the house, and I can't do that without your permission.'

She came back to the desk and read her father's letter again. I said, 'He wrote to me, too,' and produced the letter. 'You can read it if you like.'

She read it, then gave it back to me. 'Bring in your men,' she said tonelessly.

72

TWELVE

We found a number of surprising things in that house but
nothing that did us much good, at least, not then. In the basement there was a remarkably well-equipped workshop and
chemical laboratory, way beyond amateur standard. There was
also a small computer with a variety of input and output
peripherals including an X–Y plotter. Still on the plotter was a
sketch which had been drawn under computer control; it
seemed to be a schematic of a complicated molecule and it
made no sense to me, but then I'm no expert. For bigger problems with which the little computer couldn't cope there was a
modem and an acoustic coupler so that the little chap could be
used as a terminal to control a big computer by way of the post
office land lines.

In the workshop was a bench on which a thingamajig was
under construction. Whatever it was intended to do it was
going to do under computer control because there were no
fewer than fifteen integrated-circuit microelectronic chips built
into it, and that's a fair amount of computing power. Also
coupled into it was a laser, a cathode ray tube, a lot of laboratory glassware and a couple of gadgets I didn't recognize.

I didn't snap any switches or push any of the unlabelled
buttons because I didn't know what would happen if I did.
Instead I said to Larry, 'Any of Ashton's firms connected with
electronics or computers?'

'No, just chemicals and plastics moulding. Some of the chemical processes might be computer-controlled, though.'

I grunted and had the entire basement sealed. The boffins
from the department would have to check it out, and I wasn't
going to touch anything until they had done so.

Penny had the combination for the safe in the study, and I
knew by that we were unlikely to find anything of consequence
in it. I was right. There was a bit of money, less than £50,

which was not much considering Ashton's resources—I suppose it was emergency pocket money. There were some account books on which I wasted some time until I discovered they related to running the household, the stables and the cars. All very orderly. There was a whole sheaf of balance sheets headed with the name of the firm of accountants, Howard and Page. A quick glance at the bottom lines told me that George Ashton was doing very nicely, thank you, in spite of the economic recession.

And that was all.

Ashton's own quarters were a bit more productive. He had a suite—bedroom, bathroom, dressing-room and sitting-room which were as clean as a whistle. He seemed to live somewhat spartanly; there was less than the usual amount of junk which a man tends to accumulate and it was all very clean and tidy. There was nothing at all in any of the pockets of the clothes hanging in the wardrobes; whoever did his valeting—Benson probably—did a good job.

But a considerable amount of panel-tapping discovered a tambour which, when slid aside after a complicated procedure involving switching on certain lights in all four rooms thus releasing an electrically-controlled lock, revealed a massive metal door of armour-plated steel. The way I've described that might make you think we were lucky to find it, but it wasn't luck. The boys were very good at their jobs.

Not good enough to open that vault door, though. After Simpson had done some architectural measuring with a tape I knew that beyond that door was not merely a safe but a sizeable room, big enough to swing a kitten in, if not a cat. Now, any man who would put a door like that as entrance to a room would be sure to take other precautions. The walls, floor and ceiling would be very thick concrete, well reinforced with toughened steel, and the whole package would weigh a lot even when empty. It was on the second floor which meant that a special underpinning structure must have been built to support it. I made a note to look up Ashton's architect.

When the vault door was shown to Penny she was as surprised as anyone. She had never suspected its existence.

All this doesn't mean that I was prowling about the house personally knocking on walls. I left that to the boys and only inspected the results when they came in. I supervised the search of Ashton's study in Penny's presence, then settled down to talk to her because I assumed she would know more about her father than anyone else.

'Benson,' I said. 'How long have you known Benson?'

She looked surprised. 'He's always been around.'

'That's a long time. How long is always?'

'Always is always, Malcolm. I can't remember a time when there wasn't Benson.'

'As long as that? Twenty-five or twenty-six years?'

Penny smiled. 'Longer than that. He was with Daddy before I was born.

'Always is a long time,' I agreed. 'He does the faithful family retainer bit very well, I must say. But he's more than that, isn't he?'

She crinkled her brow. 'I don't know. That's difficult to assess. When a man had been with a family as long as Benson he tends to become regarded as more of a friend than a servant.'

'To the extent that your father would share a bottle of whisky with him?'

'I don't think he ever did that.'

'He did on Sunday night,' I observed. 'Has Benson always been a personal servant to your father?'

She thought for a moment. 'We moved into the house in 1961—I was twelve then. It was then Benson moved in here as Daddy's valet and dogsbody. Before that we had a house in Slough; just a little one, nothing as grand as this. Benson worked in one of Daddy's factories, but he visited the house quite often—at least once a week.' She smiled. 'He was one of our favourites. He used to bring us sweets—forbidden fruit because Daddy didn't like us to eat too many sweets. Benson used to smuggle them to us.'

'What was Benson doing in the factory?'

'I don't know. I was only a little girl.'

'When did your mother die, Penny?'

'When I was four.'

I thought that was bad luck on Ashton, having to bring up two small daughters. Still, he hadn't made a bad job of it. It seemed he didn't make a bad job of anything. I said, 'Do you

75

know how your father got started? I mean, how did he start in business? Did he have inherited money, for instance?'

She shook her head vigorously. 'Daddy never talked much about his early life but I know he didn't inherit anything because he was an orphan brought up in a foundling home. He was in the army during the war and when he came out he met my grandfather and they set up in business together. They didn't have much money at the time, so my grandfather said before he died. He said Daddy's brains made it a success.'

'What was he in the army?' I asked idly.

'Just a private.'

That rather surprised me. Ashton would have been twenty-six or twenty-seven when he was demobbed and it was strange that a man of his drive and character should still have been a private soldier. Perhaps his army record would bear looking into.

'Did your father ever carry a gun?'

She misunderstood me. 'He did rough shooting at times, but not often.'

'I don't mean a shotgun. I mean a revolver or automatic pistol.'

'Lord, no! He hasn't got such a thing.'

'Would you know?'

'Of course I would.'

'You didn't know about that strong room upstairs.'

She was silent and bit her lip, then said, 'You think he's armed?'

I was saved from answering that because Larry popped his head around the door. 'Can I have a word, Malcolm?' I nodded and joined him in the hall. He said, 'Gillian Ashton's rooms are clean, nothing there of consequence. I read her diaries; she seems to live a quiet, upper-middle-class life— theatre, ballet, opera and so on. She reads a lot, too.'

'Not any more. Any liaisons?'

'Nothing very strong; a string of men who appeared one at a time and then petered out after a while.' He grinned. 'No mysterious assignations with people referred to only by their initials; nothing like that.'

'What about Penny's rooms? Have you checked there?'

Larry looked at me a bit queerly. 'But I thought...'

'I don't care what you thought,' I said evenly. 'Do it.'

'Okay.' He went upstairs again, and I thought that young Larry still had a lot to learn.

I was about to return to the study when Michaelis came through the hall. I said, 'Found anything?'

'Nothing for us. But in an attic there's the damnedest thing — the biggest model railway set-up I've seen in my life.'

'Model railway!' I said incredulously.

'It's a real enthusiast's job,' he said. 'I'm a bit keen, myself, but I've never seen anything like this. There must be over a mile of HO-gauge track up there—it's like a bloody spider web. You'd have to do some smart scheduling to keep that lot running smoothly.'

It was a facet of Ashton I wouldn't have dreamed of, but it didn't have a thing to do with the matter at hand. I dismissed it. 'Where's Jack Brent?'

'Giving the out-buildings a going over—the garages and stables.'

'Tell him I want to see him when he's finished.' I went back into the study and thought it was time to try to find Ogilvie again. I'd been ringing every hour on the hour but each time he'd been out of the office so I'd passed my stuff on to Harrison. I put my hand out to dial again but the telephone shrilled before I got there.

It was Ogilvie. 'What have you got?' he said abruptly.

'I've passed it all to Harrison. Have you spoken to him?'

'No. As you may have gathered the balloon went up on schedule and I've been busy the last few hours. Give me the gist of it.'

'We've got a bloody big vault here,' I said. 'Not a safe, but a professional bank vault. We'll need experts to open it, and it'll probably take *them* a week.'

'It had better not,' said Ogilvie. 'You'll have them within the hour. What else?'

'I'd like some boffins—electronic and chemical. There's a cellar full of scientific stuff to look at. And you'd better send someone competent in computers.' I grinned. 'And maybe a model railway expert.'

'What's that?' he barked.

'Ashton has a model railway lay-out in his attic. I haven't

77

seen it but I'm told it's quite something.'

'This is no time to be funny,' said Ogilvie acidly. 'What else?'

'Damn all. Nothing of use to us.'

'Keep looking,' he said sharply. 'A man can't live fifteen years in a house and not leave something of his personality lying around. There'll be *some* indication of where he's gone.' He thought for a moment. 'But I want you back here. Put someone else in charge.'

'That'll be Gregory,' I said. 'I still have a few things to wrap up—I'll be back in two hours.' I rang off and said to Penny, 'Well, that's it, love. The boss wants me back.'

She said, 'Just before you went out you said something about Daddy having a gun. What did you mean?'

'He's armed,' I said.

She shook her head disbelievingly but, since so many strange things had occurred that day, she could not combat my statement. 'And will you find him?'

'Oh, we'll find him. What's worrying me is that perhaps someone else is looking for him who will find him first. And the hell of it is we aren't sure, one way or another.'

Brent came in. 'You want me?'

I waved him out and joined him in the hall. As I stripped off my jacket I said, 'Find anything?'

'Nothing.'

I unhitched the shoulder-holster from under my left armpit. 'Take this; you might need it.' I waited until he'd put it on, then took him into the study. 'Penny, this is Jack Brent; he's your guardian angel from now on. He sticks with you everywhere you go, excepting the loo and the bedroom—and he inspects those first.'

Penny looked at me as though she suspected me of joking. 'Are you serious?'

'You'll have to find a room for Jack—he'll be living here as long as you do.' I turned to Brent. 'Make yourself acquainted with the burglar precautions here, and make sure the damn things work.'

He nodded, and said, 'Sorry about this, Miss Ashton; I have to do as I'm told.'

'Another man under orders,' she said tightly. There were

pink anger spots in her cheeks. 'Do you really mean that this man goes everywhere I go?'

'As long as you want to keep your schoolgirl complexion.'

Maybe I was a bit brutal about it, but the force of what I said hit her hard. She went very pale. 'My God, Malcolm. What *is* my father?'

'I don't know; but I'm going to wring it out of Ogilvie if it's the last thing I do.'

Jack Brent gave me a look as though he thought it would be the last thing I did. Twisting the boss's arm in any organization is not the way to promotion and that indexed pension.

I said, 'I have things to do. I'll see you before I go, Penny.' I went to brief Gregory on the latest developments and to hand over to him. I found him with Simpson going over Benson's quarters which were a bit more opulent than you'd expect of a house servant—a three-roomed suite. Gregory and Simpson had torn the place apart on my instructions because I was particularly interested in Benson. 'Any luck?'

Gregory grunted. 'Not much. There's this.' He pointed to a small can of oil. 'Recommended for gun actions. And we found a single round of ammunition unfired. It had rolled under the bed and dropped into a crack near the wall.'

It was a 9 mm parabellum round, popular with the military and the police. 'We knew he was armed,' I said. 'Now we know what with—not that it helps. Anything else?'

'Not yet.'

I told Gregory the score and then went to check the activities of the rest of the team. I had to find *something* to take to Ogilvie. In the attic I found two of the boys playing trains. 'Oh, Jesus!' I said. 'Cut it out. We're here on business.'

Michaelis grinned. 'This is business—all in the line of duty. If you want this place searched thoroughly we'll have to look inside every engine, carriage and truck in this lay-out. The only way to do it is to bring them to this central control point a trainload at a time.'

I examined the lay-out and saw he had a point. You might have found a more complicated system in an international model engineering exhibition but I doubted it. There were about ten levels of track and a complexity of points and sidings which was baffling, and the whole lot was controlled from a central console which looked like the flight deck of Concorde. Michaelis seemed to have got the hang of it; maybe he was a budding genius.

'How many trucks and carriages are there?'

'We've looked at about three hundred so far,' he said. 'I reckon that's about a quarter. We're lucky there's an automatic coupling and uncoupling system. See those trucks in the siding over there?' He pointed to a spot about eight yards inside the spider web of rails. 'We'd never be able to get in there without smashing the lot up—so we send an engine in to pull them out. Like this.'

He flicked switches and an engine about five inches long moved into the siding and attached itself to a line of trucks with a slight click. It reversed slowly, drawing out the train of trucks, and Michaelis smiled with pleasure. 'Now the problem is—how do we get it from there to here?'

My God! I thought. What we have to do in the line of duty.

I snorted and left them to it, and went in search of Penny to make my farewells. Somebody said she was in her bedroom. She answered when I tapped on the door, and she was as angry as I'd ever seen her. 'Come in,' she said impatiently, so I did and she slammed the door behind me with a crash. 'Someone has been searching my room.'

'I know. *All* rooms in the house have been searched.'

'On your instructions?'

'Yes.'

'Oh, no! I thought I deserved better of you than that. You were right when you said you people don't deal in trust. Last night you asked me to marry you, and less than twenty-four hours later you show just how much you trust me. What sort of a man are you that you should send someone in here to paw over my things?'

'It's not a question of trusting or not trusting,' I said. 'I do my job in the way I was taught.'

'So you go by the book! It's not the kind of book I'd want to read.'

And so we had a flaming row—our first. I got so boiling mad that in the end I stormed out of the house and jumped into my car. I left a bit of rubber on the drive and got to the office in record time, being lucky not to be picked up by the police for speeding.

I wasn't in the best of moods when I confronted Ogilvie. He said immediately, 'Got anything more?'

I dropped the round of ammunition on his desk. 'Benson has something which shoots those.'

'All right, Malcolm,' he said. 'Let's begin at the beginning.'

So we talked. I told him in detail everything that had happened and we discussed the implications. Or rather, Ogilvie did. I didn't know enough about Ashton to see any implications. At one point in the discussion I said, 'It's obvious that Ashton has been prepared for this a long time. He told Penny that his lawyer and accountant had been well briefed, and he couldn't have done that in a day. I don't know if he expected acid-throwing, but he was certainly ready to jump. Someone has put the frighteners on him.'

Ogilvie made no comment on that. He said, 'You may know—or not know—that there's an inter-departmental committee for organizations like ours which sits to straighten out any demarcational disputes.'

'I didn't know, but it sounds a good idea.'

'There was a special meeting called for this afternoon, and I had to talk very hard and very fast. There was considerable opposition.'

'From Lord Cregar?'

Ogilvie's eyebrows rose. 'How did you identify him?'

'He gets his picture in the papers,' I said sardonically.

'I see. Do you know anything of the early history of this department?'

'Not much.'

He leaned forward and tented his fingers. 'The British way of intelligence and security is rather strange. Over the years we've acquired a reputation for being good at it, good and rather subtle. That is the considered assessment of our American and Russian rivals. They're wrong, of course. What they mistake for subtlety is merely that our right hand hardly ever knows what our left hand is doing.'

He took out a case and offered me a cigarette. 'The politicians are deathly afraid of a centralized intelligence outfit;

they don't want anything monolithic like the CIA or the KGB because they've seen what happens when such a group becomes too big and too powerful. And so, in the classic way of divide and rule, intelligence work in Britain is broken down among relatively small groups.'

He accepted a light. 'That has its drawbacks, too. It leads to amateurism, rivalry between departments, overlapping functions, the building of empires and private armies, lack of co-operation, a breakdown of the lines of communication—a whole litany of petty vices. And it makes my job damned difficult.'

His tone was a mixture of bitterness and resignation. I said, 'I can imagine.'

'In the early 1950s the risks of industrial espionage became noticeable. We weren't really bothered about one firm stealing secrets from another, and we're still not, unless it affects state security. The whole problem was that our friends to the east have no private firms, so any industrial espionage from that direction was *ipso facto* state inspired, and that we couldn't have. In our inimitable British fashion a new department was set up to cope. This department.'

'I know what we're doing, but I didn't know how we got started.'

Ogilvie drew on his cigarette. 'There's an important point. In an attempt to cut down on duplication of effort, several other departments had to hand over large chunks of their interests to us. In fact, a couple of them lost entirely their *raison d'être* and were closed down completely. They were only small fry, though. But it all led to jealousy and bad blood which exists in a dilute form to this day. And that's how we inherited the problem of Ashton.'

I said, 'Who did we pinch Ashton from?'

'Lord Cregar's department.' Ogilvie leaned forward. 'This afternoon the Minister came down on our side. Ashton is still our baby and we have to find him. You are still inside man, and that means *you* find him. Any help you need just ask for.'

'That suits me,' I said. 'I want clearance for Code Purple.'

Ogilvie shook his head. 'Not that.'

I blew up. 'For Christ's sake! How can I look for a man

when I don't know anything about him? Back in Marlow I had an interesting lecture on trust which has soured me to the belly, and this job has already interfered too much with my private life. Now you either trust me or you don't—and the crunch comes here. I get clearance for Code Purple or my resignation will be on your desk at nine tomorrow morning.'

He said sadly, 'I have warned you about being impetuous. To begin with, I couldn't get you clearance in that time, and even if I did you wouldn't find what you're looking for because Ashton is in Code Black.' His voice was grim. 'And you couldn't be cleared for Code Black inside three months—if ever.'

Code Black sounded as though it was the end of the rainbow and Ashton was the pot of gold. There was a silence which I broke by saying diffidently, 'That's it, then. I'd better go along to my office and type my resignation.'

'Don't be a young fool!' snapped Ogilvie. He drummed on the desk, then said, 'I've come to a decision. If it gets out I could be fired. Wait here.'

He got up and went to an unobtrusive door behind his desk and disappeared. I waited a long time and wondered what I'd done. I knew I'd laid my career on the line. Well, I was prepared for that and with my financial backing I could stand it. Maybe I wouldn't have done it if I had only my pay to depend on. I don't know. And I'd pushed Ogilvie into doing something he might be sorry for, and that was bad because I liked him.

Presently he opened the door, and said, 'Come in here.' I followed him into a small room where there was one of the ubiquitous computer terminals. 'I'm cleared for Code Black,' he said. 'The information on Ashton is coming on line. If you sit there you'll find out what you need to know. The computer won't know who is pushing the buttons.' He checked the time. 'I'll be back in two hours.'

I was a bit subdued. 'All right, sir.'

'I want your word,' he said. 'I don't want you roving at random in Code Black. I want to know that you'll stick to Ashton and only to Ashton. There are other matters in Code Black that are better for you not to know—for your own peace of mind.'

I said, 'You can make sure of that just by sitting here with me.'

He smiled. 'You made a point just now about trust. Either I trust you or I don't, and there's an end to it.'

'You have my word.'

He nodded abruptly and left, closing the door behind him.

I glanced at Nellie who was staring at me with an interrogative bright green question mark, and then glanced around the small room which was really more of a cubicle. On one side of the terminal was a small plotter, very much like the one in Ashton's cellar; on the other side was a line printer.

I sat at the console and reflected that if Ashton was so important and had been around and of interest since before the department had started then there was probably reams of stuff about him in Nellie's guts. This idea was reinforced by the two hours Ogilvie had allowed for reviewing the information, so I switched on the printer, and typed:

OUTPUT MODE—PRINTER

Nellie had an attack of verbal diarrhoea. She came back at me with

PRINTER OUTPUT NEGATIVED UNDER CODE BLACK

NOTE WELL: NO WRITTEN RECORD TO BE MADE

UNDER CODE BLACK

NOTE WELL: NO TAPE-RECORDED TRANSCRIPTIONS

TO BE MADE UNDER CODE BLACK

NOTE WELL: NO PHOTOGRAPHS TO BE TAKEN OF

THE CRT UNDER CODE BLACK

I sighed and switched off the printer.

I've described before how one juggles with Nellie so there's no point in going into that again. What I haven't said is that Nellie is accommodating; if she's going too fast you can slow her down, and if she's producing something of no interest you can speed her up. You can also skip about in the record, going back to items forgotten or neglected. She's quite a toy.

I did quite a bit of skipping when swanning around in Ashton's life. He'd lived quite a bit.

THIRTEEN

Aleksandr Dmitrovitch Chelyuskin was born to poorish, but respectable, parents in the small town of Tesevo-Netyl'skiy, just to the north of Novgorod in Russia. The year was 1919. Both parents were schoolteachers; his mother taught in an infants' school and his father taught mathematics and allied subjects to older boys.

These were the years of revolution, and whether the Whites or the Reds were to come on top had not yet been decided in 1919. Armies of foreigners—British, French, American—were on Russian soil, and it was a time of turmoil and conflagration. Little Aleksandr was very nearly snuffed out just after birth as the waves of war swept over the country. In fact, his elder brother and his two sisters did die during this period as the family was buffeted in the storm; the record did not disclose just how they died.

Eventually, in 1923, the family Chelyuskin came to haven in the town of Aprelevka, just outside Moscow. The family had been reduced to three and, since Aleksandr had been a late child and his mother was now apparently barren, there were to be no more children and he was brought up as an only child. His father found a job teaching mathematics and they settled down to a life of relative security

Although Dmitri Ivanovitch Chelyuskin was a teacher of mathematics he was not a good mathematician himself in the sense that he produced original work. His role in life was to teach to small boys the elements of arithmetic, algebra and geometry, which he did largely by rote, a sarcastic tongue and a heavy hand. But he was good enough at his job to notice that he did not have to tell young Aleksandr anything twice, and when the time came that he found he did not have to tell the boy once and that his son was beginning to ask unanswerable questions it was then that he thought he might have an infant prodigy on his hands.

Aleksandr was about ten years old at the time.

He played chess very well and joined the chess club in Aprelevka where he proceeded to lick the pants off his elders and betters. The elder Chelyuskin forgot about the mathematics and thought of the possibility of having a Grand Master in the family, a great honour in Russia.

One Suslov, a member of the chess club, disagreed. He persuaded Chelyuskin *père* to write to a friend of his in Moscow, a member of the Board of Education. Letters and months passed, and eventually, after a series of supposedly gruelling examinations which Aleksandr went through without so much as a qualm, he was admitted to a Lycée in Moscow at the hitherto unheard-of age of twelve years and ten months. Whether the fact that Suslov had been the undisputed chess champion of Aprelevka, until the appearance of Aleksandr had anything to do with that, is not known. At least, Suslov said nothing for the record but went on to win the club championship the following year.

In Britain the left wing decries elitism; in Russia the communists foster it. When a bright youngster is found he is whisked away to a special school where his mind is stretched. He can no longer count on having an easy time walking nonchalantly through the school subjects without effort, coming out on top while his duller brethren work like hell plodding along behind. Aleksandr was subjected to a forced draught of education.

He liked it. He had the cast of mind which loves grappling with the abstruse and difficult, and he found much to his liking in pure mathematics. Now, mathematics at its purest is a game for adults and need have no relationship at all to the real physical world, and the fact that it sometimes does is a bit of luck. The pure mathematician is concerned with the concept of number at its most abstract, and Aleksandr played happily among the abstractions for quite a while. At the age of sixteen he wrote a paper, 'Some Observations on the Relationship between Mathieu Functions and Weierstrass Elliptic Functions'. It consisted of three paragraphs of written text and ten pages of mathematical formulae, and was rather well received. He followed it up with another paper the following year, and that brought him under the eye of Peter Kapitza and led to the second great change in his life.

It was 1936 and Kapitza was the white hope of Russian physics. He was born in Kronstadt and studied in Kronstadt and Petrograd, as it was then. But in 1925 he made a change which was rather odd for a Russian at the time. He went to Cambridge, then the leading university dealing with physics. He became a fellow of Trinity College, and assistant director of research at the Cavendish Laboratory under Rutherford. He was elected a Fellow of the Royal Society in 1929, and managed to pick up about every scientific honour that was not absolutely screwed down except the Nobel Prize which he missed. In 1936 he went back to Russia, supposedly on a sabbatical, and never left again. Stalin is reputed to have lowered the portcullis on him.

This, then, is the man who extended his influence over Aleksandr Chelyuskin. Perhaps he looked at the youth and was reminded of himself at the age of seventeen. At any rate, he diverted Aleksandr from his playground of pure mathematics and showed him that there were real problems to be solved in the world. Kapitza introduced him to theoretical physics.

Physics is an experimental science, and most physicists are good mechanics and have broken fingernails caused by putting bits and pieces of equipment together. But there are a few—a very few—who do nothing but think. They tend to sit around, gazing into space, and their favourite weapons are blackboard and chalk. After a few hours, days or years of thought they diffidently suggest that an experiment should be made.

The realm of the theoretical physicist is the totality of the universe, and there are very few good ones around at any one time. Aleksandr Chelyuskin was one of them.

He studied magnetism and low temperature physics under Peter Kapitza and, applying quantum theory to the earlier work of Kamerlingh Onnes, did important work relating to phase II of liquid helium, and the new field of super-conductivity got under way. But this was just one of the many things he thought about. His work was astonishingly wide-ranging and eclectic, and he published profusely. He did not publish everything he thought because he liked to have things wrapped up tidily, but some of his work, reproduced in the record from his notebooks written at this time, clearly anticipated the cosmological theories of Fred Hoyle in the '50s and '60s. Other work from his notebooks included thoughts on the nature of catalytic action and a brief sketch extending these thoughts into the organic field of enzymes.

In 1941 the war came to Russia, but the brain the state had so carefully nurtured was considered too valuable to risk having a bullet put through it, and Chelyuskin never saw a shot fired in anger. For most of the war he sat behind the Urals and thought his thoughts. One of the many things he thought about was the fine structure of metals. The resultant improvement in Russian tank armour was quite noticeable.

In March 1945 he was visited by a high official and told to give careful consideration to the atomic structure of certain rare metals. Stalin had just come back from the Yalta Conference where he had been informed of the existence of the atomic bomb.

In the period immediately following the war Chelyuskin became increasingly dissatisfied, mainly because, although the war was over, he was still constrained to involve himself in weapons research. He did not like what he was doing and deliberately slowed his pace. But a mind cannot stop thinking and he turned to other things than physics—to sociology, for example. In short, he stopped thinking about things and began to think about people.

He looked at the world immediately about him and did not like what he saw. This was the time when Stalin was conducting an extended post-mortem on the mistakes made during the war. Returning Russians who had been taken prisoner were hardly given time to sneeze before being whisked into Siberian camps, and hundreds of former officers mysteriously dropped out of sight. He reflected that continuous purging is as bad for a society as it is for a body, and he knew that the infamous army purge of 1936 had so weakened the army that it had contributed largely to the startling defeats at the beginning of the war. And yet the process was continuing.

He was determined, on moral grounds, not to continue with atomic research, and beyond that he was sure he did not want to put such weapons into the hands of a man like Stalin. But he was equally determined not to end up in a forced labour camp as some of his colleagues had done, so he was presented with quite a problem which he solved with characteristic neatness and economy.

He killed himself.

It took him three months to plan his death and he was ruthless in the way he went about it. He needed the body of a man about his own age and with the same physical characteristics. More complicatedly, he needed the body before it had died so that certain surgical and dental work could be done and given time to age. This could not be done on a corpse.

He found what he wanted on a visit to Aprelevka. A boyhood friend of his own age was afflicted with leukaemia and there was much doubt about his survival. Chelyuskin visited the hospital and chatted to his friend, at first in generalities and then, more directly and dangerously, about politics. He was fortunate in that he found his friend to have much the same convictions as himself, and so he was encouraged to ask the crucial question. Would his friend, in the terminal stages of a killing illness, donate his body for Chelyuskin's survival?

The record does not disclose the name of Chelyuskin's friend but, in my opinion, he was a very brave man. Chelyuskin pulled strings and had him transferred to another hospital where he had the co-operation of a doctor. File entries were fudged, papers were lost and bureaucracy was baffled; it was all very efficiently inefficient and ended up with the fact that Chelyuskin's friend was effectively dead as far as anyone knew.

Then the poor man had his leg broken under surgical and aseptic conditions and suffered a considerable amount of dental work. The fracture in the leg corresponded exactly with a similar fracture in Chelyuskin's leg and the dental structure duplicated Chelyuskin's mouth exactly. The bone knitted together, and all he had to do was to wait for his friend to die.

Meanwhile, going through underground channels, he had contacted British Intelligence and requested political asylum. We were only too glad to oblige, even on his terms. To wave a defecting Russian scientist like a flag is not necessarily a good ploy, and we were quite happy to respect his terms of secrecy as long as we got him. The necessary arrangements were made.

It took a long time for Chelyuskin's friend to die. In fact, for a period there was a marked improvement in his condition which must have infuriated my masters. I doubt if it worried Chelyuskin very much. He went about his work as usual, attending the committees which were an increasing and aggravating part of his life, and soldiered on. But his friends did comment that he appeared to be doing his best to drown himself in the vodka bottle.

Seven months later the Russian scientific community was saddened to learn that Academician A. D. Chelyuskin had been burnt to death when his *dacha*, to which he had retired for a short period of relaxation, had caught fire. There was a post-mortem examination and an enquiry. The rumour got around that Chelyuskin had been smoking in bed when in his cups and that vodka added to the flames had not helped him much. That was a story everybody could believe.

A month later Chelyuskin slipped over the Iranian border. Three days later he was in Teheran and the following day was put down at RAF Northolt by courtesy of Transport Command. He was given an enthusiastic welcome by a select group who turned out to welcome this genius who was then at the ripe age of twenty-eight. There would be a lot of mileage left in him.

The powers-that-be were somewhat baffled by Chelyuskin's comparative youth. They tended to forget that creative abstract thought, especially in mathematics, is a young man's game, and that Einstein had published his Special Theory of Relativity when only nineteen. Even the politicians among them forgot that Pitt was Prime Minister at twenty-four.

They were even more baffled and irritated by Chelyuskin's attitude. He soon made it clear that he was a Russian patriot and no traitor, and that he had no intention of disclosing secrets, atomic or otherwise. He said he had left Russia because he did not want to work on atomics, and that to communicate his knowledge would be to negate the action he had taken. Conversations on atomic theory were barred.

The irritation grew and pressure was applied, but authority found that it could neither bend nor break this man. The more pressure was applied the more stubborn he became, until finally he refused to discuss *any* of his work. Even the ultimate threat did not move him. When told that he could be disclosed to the Russians even at that late stage he merely shrugged and indicated that it was the privilege of the British to do so if they wished, but he thought it would be unworthy of them.

Authority changed its tack. Someone asked him what he wanted to do. Did he want a laboratory put at his disposal, for instance? By now Chelyuskin was wary of the British and their motives. I suppose, in a way, he had been naïve to expect any other treatment, but naïvety in a genius is comparatively normal. He found himself surrounded, not by scientists whom he understood, but by calculating men, the power brokers of Whitehall. Mutual incomprehensibility was total.

He rejected the offer of a laboratory curtly. He saw quite clearly that he was in danger of exchanging one intellectual prison for another. When they asked him again what it was he wanted, he said something interesting. 'I want to live as an ordinary citizen,' he said. 'I want to sink and lose myself in the sea of Western capitalism.'

Authority shrugged its shoulders and gave up. Who could understand these funny foreigners, anyway? A dog-in-the manger attitude was adopted; if we couldn't get at the man's brain then the Russians didn't have it, either, and that was good enough. He could always be watched and, who knows, he might even declare a dividend in the future.

So Chelyuskin got exactly what he asked for.

A REME soldier called George Ashton had been killed in a traffic accident in Germany. He was twenty-seven and had been brought up in a foundling home. Unmarried and with neither kith nor kin to mourn him, he was the perfect answer. Chelyuskin was flown to Germany, put in the uniform of a private in the British Army, and brought back to England by train and sea, accompanied discreetly at all times. He went through a demobilization centre where he was given a cheap suit, a small amount of back pay and a handshake from a sombre unrecruiting sergeant.

He was also given an honorarium of £2000.

He asked for, and was given, something else before he was cast adrift. Because of the necessity for scientific study he had learned English in his youth and read it fluently. But he never had occasion to speak it, which might have been an advantage when he was put through a six months' total immersion course in conversational English, because he had no bad habits to unlearn. He came out of it with a cultured generalized Home Counties accent, and set out to sink or swim in the capitalist world.

£2000 may not seem much now, but it was quite a sizeable piece of change back in 1947. Even so, George Ashton knew he must conserve his resources; he put most of it in a bank deposit account and lived very simply while he explored this strange new world. He was no longer an honoured man, an Academician with a car and a *dacha* at his disposal, and he had to find a way of earning a living. Any position requiring written qualifications was barred to him because he did not have the papers. It was a preposterous situation.

He took a job as a book-keeper in the stores department of a small engineering firm in Luton. This was in the days before computers when book-keeping was done by hand as in the days of Dickens, and a good book-keeper could add a triple column of pounds, shillings and pence in one practised sweep of the eye. But there weren't many of those around and Ashton found himself welcome because, unlike the popular myth, he was an egghead who could add and *always* got his change right. He found the job ridiculously easy if monotonous, and it left him time to think.

He struck up an acquaintanceship with the foreman of the toolroom, a man called John Franklin who was about 50 years of age. They got on very well together and formed the habit of having a drink together in the local pub after work. Presently Ashton was invited *chez* Franklin for Sunday dinner where he met Franklin's wife, Jane, and his daughter, Mary. Mary Franklin was 25 then, and as yet unmarried because her fiancé had been shot down over Dortmund in the final days of the war.

All this time Ashton was being watched. If he was aware of it he gave no sign. Other people were watched, too, and the Franklin family came in for a thorough rummaging on the grounds that those interested in Ashton were *per se* interesting in themselves. Nothing was discovered except the truth; that Jack Franklin was a damned good artisan with his brains in his fingertips, Jane Franklyn was a comfortable, maternal woman, and Mary Franklin had suffered a tragedy in her life.

Six months after they met, Ashton and Franklin left the engineering firm to strike out on their own. Ashton put up £1500 and his brains while Franklin contributed £500 and his capable hands. The idea was to set up a small plastics moulding shop; Franklin to make the moulds and the relatively simple machines needed, and Ashton to do the designing and to run the business.

The small firm wobbled along for a while without overmuch success until Ashton, becoming dissatisfied with the moulding powders he was getting from a big chemical company, devised a concoction of his own, patented it, and started another company to make it. After that they never looked back.

Ashton married Mary Franklin and I dare say a member of some department or other was unobtrusively present at the wedding. A year later she gave him a daughter whom they christened Penelope, and two years later another girl whom they called Gillian. Mary Ashton died a couple of years later, in 1953, from childbirth complications. The baby died, too.

All his life Ashton kept a low profile. He joined no clubs or trade associations; he steered clear of politics, national or local, although he voted regularly, and generally divided his life between his work and his home. This gave him time to look after his two small girls with the help of a nanny whom he brought into the small suburban house in Slough, where he then lived. From the record he was devoted to them.

About 1953 he must have opened his old notebooks and started to think again. As Chelyuskin he had never published any of his work on catalysts and I suppose he thought it was safe to enter the field. A catalyst is a substance which speeds up the chemical reactions between other substances, sometimes by many thousands of times. They are used extensively in chemical processing, particularly in the oil industry.

Ashton put his old work to good use. He devised a whole series of new catalysts tailored to specialized uses. Some he manufactured and sold himself, others he allowed to be made under licence. All were patented and the money began to roll in. It seemed as though this odd fish was swimming quite well in the capitalist sea.

In 1960 he bought his present house and, after fifteen months of extensive internal remodelling, he moved in with his family. After that nothing much seemed to happen except that he saw the portent of North Sea oil, opened another factory in 1970, took out a lot more patents and became steadily richer. He also extended his interest to those natural catalysts, the enzymes, and presumably the sketchy theory presented in the early notebook became filled out.

After about 1962 the record became peculiarly flat and perfunctory, and I knew why. Authority had lost interest in him and he would exist only in a tickler file to remind someone to given an annual check. It was only when I set the bells jangling by my inadvertent enquiry that someone had woken up.

And that was the life of George Ashton, once Aleksandr Dmitrovitch Chelyuskin—my future father-in-law.

FOURTEEN

What I have set down about Ashton–Chelyuskin is a mere condensation of what was in the computer together with a couple of added minor assumptions used as links to make a sustained narrative. Had I been able to use the printer it would have churned out enough typescript to make a book the size of a family bible. To set down in print the details of a man's life needs a lot of paper. Yet I think I have presented the relevant facts.

When I finished I had a headache. To stare at a cathode ray screen for two and a half hours is not good for the eyes, and I had been smoking heavily so that the little room was very stuffy. It was with relief that I emerged into Ogilvie's office.

He was sitting at his desk reading a book. He looked up and smiled. 'You look as though you need a drink.'

'It would go down very well,' I agreed.

He got up and opened a cabinet from which he took a bottle of whisky and two glasses; then he produced a jug of iced water from a small built-in refrigerator. The perquisites of office. 'What do you think?'

'I think Ashton is one hell of a man. I'm proud to have known him.'

'Anything else?'

'There's one fact that's so damned obvious it may be overlooked.'

'I doubt it,' said Ogilvie, and handed me a glass. 'A lot of good men have checked that file.'

I diluted the whisky and sat down. 'Do you have all of Ashton in there?'

'All that we know is there.'

'Exactly. Now, I've gone through Ashton's work in some detail and it's all in the field of applied science—technology, if you like. All the things he's been doing with catalysts is derived from his earlier unpublished work; there's nothing fundamentally new there. Correct me if I'm wrong.'

'You're quite right, although it took a man with Ashton's brains to do it. We've given our own top chemists photocopies of those notebooks and their attitude was that the stuff was all right from a theoretical point of view but it didn't seem to lead anywhere. Ashton made it lead somewhere and it's made him rich. But, in general, your point is good; it's all derivative of earlier work—even his later interest in enzymes.'

I nodded. 'But Chelyuskin was a theoretician. The point is this—did he stop theorizing and, if not, what the hell has he been thinking about? I can understand why you want that bloody vault opened.'

'You're not too stupid,' said Ogilvie. 'You've hit the nail smack on the head. You're right; you can't stop a man thinking, but what he's been thinking about is difficult to figure. It won't be atomic theory.'

'Why not?'

'We know what he reads; the magazines he subscribes to, the books he buys. We know he's not been keeping up with the scientific literature in any field except catalytical chemistry, and no one thinks in a vacuum. Atomic theory has made great strides since Ashton came out of Russia. To do any original work a man would have to work hard to keep ahead of the pack—attend seminars and so on. Ashton hasn't been doing it.' He tasted his whisky. 'What would you have done in Ashton's position and with a mind like his?'

'Survival would come first,' I said. 'I'd find a niche in society and look for security. Once I'd got that perhaps I'd start thinking again—theorizing.'

'What about? In your struggle for survival the world of thought has passed you by; you've lost touch. And you daren't try to regain touch, either. So what would you think about?'

'I don't know,' I said slowly. 'Perhaps, with a mind like his, I'd think about things other people haven't been thinking about. A new field.'

'Yes,' said Ogilvie thoughtfully. 'It makes one wonder, doesn't it?'

We sat for a few moments in silence. It was late—the light was ebbing from the summer sky over the City—and I was tired. I sipped the whisky appreciatively and thought about Ashton. Presently Ogilvie asked, 'Did you find anything in the file to give you a clue about where he's gone?'

'Nothing springs to mind. I'd like to sleep on it—let the unconscious have a go.' I finished the whisky. 'Where does Cregar fit into this?'

'It was his crowd Ashton approached when he wanted to leave Russia. Cregar went into Russia himself to get him out. He was a young man then, of course, and not yet Lord Cregar—he was the Honourable James Pallton. Now he heads his department.'

I'd come across the name Pallton in reading the file, but I hadn't connected it with Cregar. I said, 'He mishandled Ashton right from the start. He approached him with all the sensitivity of a fifty-pence whore. First he threatened, then he tried to bribe. He didn't understand the type of man he'd come across, and he put Ashton's back up.'

Ogilvie nodded. 'That's one element in the mixture of his resentment. He always thought he could retrieve Ashton; that's why he was so annoyed when the Ashton case was transferred to us. That's why he's sticking his oar in now.'

'What steps have already been taken to find Ashton?'

'The usual. The Special Branch are on the watch at sea ports and airports, and they're checking passenger lists for the past twenty-four hours. You'd better liaise with Scotland Yard on that tomorrow.'

'I'll do that. And I'll have a go from the other end. There's one thing I'd like to know.'

'What's that?'

'Who threw such a scare into Ashton? Who threw that bloody acid?'

I was overtired that night and couldn't get to sleep. As I tossed restlessly Penny was very much on my mind. It was evident from what she had said that she knew nothing of Ashton in the larval stage, before he changed from Chelyuskin. Her account of his early life fitted that of the REME soldier killed in Germany.

I wondered how it would be with Penny and me. I had been damned insensitive that afternoon. Her room had to be searched, but if anyone had done it then it ought to have been me, preferably in her presence. I didn't blame her for blowing her top and I wondered how I could retrieve the situation. I felt very bad about it.

Most people, when they have had a burglary, are not so much concerned about the articles stolen as about the intrusion into the heart of their lives, the home which is so peculiarly their own. It is the thought that strange hands have been delving among their innermost secrets, rummaging in drawers, opening doors in the private parts of the house—all this is profoundly shocking. I knew all that and ought to have applied it to Penny.

At last I sat up in bed, checked the time, then stretched for the telephone. Although it was late I was going to talk to her. Mary Cope answered my call. 'Malcolm Jaggard here; I'd like to talk to Miss Ashton.'

'Just wait a moment, sir,' she said. She wasn't away long. 'Miss Ashton isn't in, sir.' There was a hint of nervousness in her voice as though she thought I wouldn't believe her. I didn't, but there was nothing I could do about it.

It was early morning when I finally slept.

I spent most of the forenoon at Scotland Yard with a Special Branch officer. I had no great hope of success and neither had he but we went through the motions. His crowd had been busy but even so the reports were slow to come in. A lot of people leave from Heathrow in twenty-four hours and that is only one exit from the country.

'Ashton and Benson,' he said morosely, as he ticked off a name. 'Bloody near as bad as Smith and Robinson. Why the hell do people we're interested in never have names like Moneypenny or Gotobed?'

Six Bensons and four Ashtons had left from Heathrow. Half could be eliminated because of sex, and the Ashtons were a family of four. But two of the Bensons would have to be followed up; one had gone to Paris and the other to New York. I got busy on the telephone.

Heathrow may be large but it is still only one place and there are other airports, more than the average person realizes. And there were the sea ports of which islanded Britain has a plenitude. It was going to be a long job with nothing but uncertainty guaranteed.

The Special Branch man said philosophically, 'And, of course, they may have left under other names. Getting a spare passport is dead easy.'

'They may not have left at all,' I said. 'Tell your chaps to keep their eyes open.'

I lunched in a commissary at the Yard and then went back prepared for a slogging afternoon. At three o'clock Ogilvie rang me. 'They'll be opening that vault later today. I want you there.'

A drive to Marlow would be a lot more refreshing than checking passenger lists. 'All right.'

'Now, these are my exact instructions. When that door is opened you will be present, and the head of the safe-cracking team. No one else. Is that clear?'

'Perfectly clear.'

'Then you send him out of the room and check the contents. If they are removable you bring them here under guard. If not, you close and lock the door again, first making sure we can open it again more easily.'

'How long are you staying at the office?'

'All night, if necessary.' He hung up.

So I drove to Marlow and to Ashton's place. I was wearing grooves in that road. Simpson was the gate man and he let me in and I drove up to the house. I met Gregory in the hall. 'Found anything useful?'

He shrugged. 'Not a thing.'

'Where's Miss Ashton?'

'At the hospital. Jack Brent is with her.'

'Good enough.' I went up to Ashton's quarters and found the safe-cracking team at work. I don't know where the department kept its experts when not in use, but they were always available when needed. The chief safe-cracker was a man I'd met before by the name of Frank Lillywhite. 'Afternoon, Frank,' I said. 'How much longer?'

He grunted. 'An hour.' He paused. 'Or two.' There was a longer pause as he did something intricate with a tool he held. 'Or three.'

I grinned. 'Or four. Is this a tricky one?'

99

'They're all tricky. This is a twenty-four hour safe, that's all.'

I was curious. 'What do you mean?'

Lillywhite stepped away from the vault door and an underling moved in. 'Safe manufacturers don't sell security—they sell time. Any safe made can be cracked; all the manufacturer guarantees is the length of time needed to crack it. They reckon this is a twenty-four hour job; I'm going to do it in twenty—with a bit of luck. The tricky part comes in circumventing the booby traps.'

'What booby traps?'

'If I do the wrong thing here, twelve bloody big tungsten steel bars will shoot out all round the door. Then only the maker will be able to open it.'

'Then why didn't we get the maker on the job in the first place?'

Lillywhite sighed, and said patiently, 'The whole vault would have to be ripped out and taken to the factory. They've got a bloody big tin opener there that weighs a thousand tons. Of course the vault wouldn't be good for much after that.'

I contemplated the awful possibility of taking the whole vault out. 'Neither would this house. I'll stop asking silly questions. Don't open the door unless I'm here.'

'Message received and understood.'

I went down to the cellar where I found a couple of studious-looking types being baffled by Ashton's contraption. Their conversation, if you could call it that, was in English, but that's to use the word loosely; it was technical, jargon-ridden and way over my head, so I left them to it. Another man was packing tape cassettes into a box ready to take away. I said, 'What are those?'

He indicated the little computer. 'Program and data tapes for this thing. We're taking them to the lab for analysis.'

'You're listing everything, I hope. You'll have to give a receipt to Miss Ashton.' He frowned at that, and I said acidly, 'We're not thieves or burglars, you know. It's only by courtesy of Miss Ashton that we're here at all.' As I left the cellar he was taking cassettes out of the box and stacking them on a table.

An hour and a half later Gregory found me in Ashton's study. 'They'll be opening the vault in about fifteen minutes.'

'Let's go up.'

We left the study and encountered Lord Cregar in the hall; with him was a big man with the build of a heavyweight boxer. Cregar looked brisk and cheerful but his cheerfulness, if not his briskness, evaporated when he saw me. 'Ah, Mr Jaggard,' he said. 'A fine mess has been made of things, I must say.'

I shrugged. 'Events moved faster than we anticipated.'

'No doubt. I understand there's a vault here which is being opened this afternoon. Has it been opened yet?'

I wondered where he'd got his information. 'No.'

'Good. Then I'm in time.'

I said, 'Am I to understand that you wish to be present when the vault is opened?'

'That's correct.'

'I'm sorry,' I said. 'But I'll have to take that under advisement.'

He looked at me thoughtfully. 'Do you know who I am?'

'Yes, my lord.'

'Very well,' he said. 'Make your telephone call.'

I jerked my head at Gregory and we went back into the study. 'There's no need for a call,' I said. 'Ogilvie's instructions were very precise, and they didn't include Cregar.'

'I know that big chap,' said Gregory. 'His name is Martins. A bad chap to tangle with.' He paused. 'Maybe you'd better check with Ogilvie.'

'No. He's told me what to do and I'm going to do it.'

'So what if Cregar won't take it? A bout of fisticuffs with a member of the House of Lords could have its repercussions.'

I smiled. 'I doubt if it will come to that. Let's tell his lordship the bad news.'

We went back into the hall to find that Cregar and Martins had vanished. 'They'll be upstairs,' said Gregory.

'Come on.' We ran upstairs and found them in Ashton's room. Cregar was tapping his foot impatiently as I stepped forward and said formally, 'My lord, I regret to inform you that you will not be permitted to be present when the vault is opened.'

Cregar's eyes bulged. 'Did Ogilvie say that?'

'I have not spoken to Mr Ogilvie recently. I am merely following instructions.'

'You take a lot upon yourself,' he commented.

I turned to Lillywhite. 'How much longer, Frank?'

'Give me ten minutes.'

'No—stop work now. Don't start again until I tell you.' I turned back to Cregar. 'If you would like to speak to Mr Ogilvie yourself you may use the telephone here or in the study.'

Cregar actually smiled. 'You know when to pass the buck. You're quite right; it's better if I speak to Ogilvie. I'll use the study.'

'Show his lordship where it is,' I said to Gregory, and the three of them left the room.

Lillywhite said, 'What was that all about?'

'A bit of inter-departmental nonsense; nothing to do with humble servants like ourselves. You can carry on, Frank. That vault must be opened come what may.'

He went back to his job and I strolled over to the window and looked down at the drive. Presently Cregar and Martins came out of the house, got into a car, and drove away. Gregory came into the room. 'Cregar was a bit sour when he came out of the study,' he remarked. 'Ogilvie wants to talk to you.'

I walked over and picked up the telephone next to Ashton's bed. 'Jaggard here.'

Ogilvie said quickly: 'On no account must Cregar know what's in that vault. Don't let him pull rank on you—it's got nothing to do with him.'

'He won't,' I said. 'He's gone.'

'Good. When will you open it?'

'Another five minutes.'

'Keep me informed.' He rang off.

Gregory held out a packet of cigarettes and we smoked while Lillywhite and his two assistants fiddled with the door. At last there was a sharp click and Lillywhite said, 'That's it.'

I stood up. 'All right. Everybody out except me and Frank.' I waited until they left then went to the vault. 'Let's get at it.'

'Right.' Lillywhite put his hand to a lever and pulled it down. Nothing happened. 'There you are.'

'You mean it's open now?'

'That's right. Look.' He pulled and the door began to open. It was nearly a foot thick.

102

'Hold it,' I said quickly. 'Now can it be locked again and opened easily?'

'Sure. Nothing to it now.'

'That's all I need to know. Sorry, Frank, but I'll have to ask you to leave now.'

He gave me a crooked smile. 'If what's in here can't even be seen by a member of the House of Lords it's certainly not for Frank Lillywhite.'

He went out and closed the door emphatically.

I opened the vault.

FIFTEEN

Ogilvie gasped. 'Empty!'

'As bare as Mother Hubbard's cupboard.' I considered that. 'Except for a layer of fine dust on the floor.'

'You checked all the shelves and cabinets?'

'There were no cabinets. There were no shelves. It was just an empty cube. I didn't even go inside; I just stuck my head in and looked around. Then I closed the door again and had it relocked. I thought I'd better leave it as it was in case you want the forensic chaps to have a look at it. My bet is that it's never been used since it was built fifteen years ago.'

'Well, my God!' Ogilvie stopped then. He seemed at a total loss for words, but he was thinking furiously. I stepped over to the window and looked down into the empty street. It was late and the bowler-hatted tide had receded from the City leaving it deserted except for a few stragglers. There is no other urban area in the world that can look so empty as the City of London.

Ogilvie said thoughtfully, 'So only you, the chief of the safe-opening team, and now me, know about this.'

I turned. 'Even your Chief Burglar doesn't know. I sent Lillywhite out of the room before I opened the vault.'

'So it's only you and me. Damn!'

He swore so explosively that I said, 'What's wrong?'

'It's backfired on me. Cregar will never believe me now when I tell him the truth about that damned vault. I wish now he'd been there.'

Personally I didn't care what Cregar believed or didn't believe. I took a sheet of paper from my wallet, unfolded it, and laid it on the desk. 'This is the new combination for opening the vault. Lillywhite reset it.'

'This is the only copy?'

'Lillywhite must have a record of it.'

Ogilvie wagged his head. 'This will bear a lot of thinking

about. In the meantime you carry on looking for Ashton and Benson, and don't forget they might have split up. Made any progress?'

'Only by elimination, if you call that progress.'

'All right,' said Ogilvie tiredly. 'Carry on.' I had my hand on the doorknob when he said, 'Malcolm.'

'Yes.'

'Watch out for Cregar. He makes a bad enemy.'

'I'm not fighting Cregar,' I said. 'He's nothing to do with me. What's between you and him is way over my head.'

'He didn't like the way you stood up to him this afternoon.'

'He didn't show it—he was pleasant enough.'

'That's his way, but he'll only pat you on the back to find a place to stick a knife. Watch him.'

'He is nothing to do with me,' I repeated.

'Maybe,' said Ogilvie. 'But Cregar may not share your view.'

After that nothing happened for a while. The Special Branch investigation petered out with no result although their men at the exits were still keeping a sharp watch in case our pair made a late dash for it. Honnister had nothing to offer. On my third enquiry he said tartly, 'Don't ring us—we'll ring you.'

I spent two and a half days reading every word of the bushel or so of miscellaneous papers Gregory had brought back from Ashton's house—appointment books, financial records, business diaries, letters and so on. As a result of that many enquiries were made but nothing of interest turned up. Ashton's companies were given a thorough going-over with like result.

A week after Ashton's disappearance my team was cut in half. I kept Brent with Penny and Michaelis looked after Gillian, leaving two to do the legwork. I was doing a lot of legwork myself, going sixteen hours a day, running like hell like the Red Queen to stay in the same place. Larry Godwin was back at his desk reading the East European journals. His fling at freedom had been brutally brief.

The boffins had nothing much to report. The computer tapes showed nothing out of the ordinary except some very clever program designing, but what the programs did was nothing special. The prototype whatsit Ashton had been tinkering with caused a flood of speculation which left a thin sediment of hard fact. The consensus of opinion was that it was a pilot plant of a process designed to synthesize insulin; very ingenious and highly patentable but still in an early stage of design. It told me nothing to my purpose.

The day after we opened the empty vault I had telephoned Penny. 'Is this to tell me you've found Daddy?' she asked.

'No, I've nothing to tell you about that. I'm sorry.'

'Then I don't think we've much to talk about, Malcolm,' she said, and rang off before I could get in another word. Right at that moment I didn't know whether we were still engaged or not.

After that I kept in touch with her movements through Brent. She went back to doing her work at University College, London, but tended to use her car more instead of the train. She didn't seem to resent Brent; he was her passenger in her daily journeys to and from London, and she always kept him informed of her proposed movements. He was enjoying his assignment and thought she was a very nice person. He didn't think she knew he was armed. And, no, she never talked of me.

Gillian was moved to Moorfields Eye Hospital and I went to see her. After checking with Michaelis I had a few words with her doctor, a specialist called Jarvis. 'She's still heavily bandaged,' he said. 'And she'll need cosmetic plastic surgery, but that will be later and in another place. Here we are concerned only with her eyes.'

'What are the odds, Doctor?'

He said carefully, 'There may be a chance of restoring some measure of sight to the left eye. There's no hope for the right eye at all.' He looked straight at me. 'Miss Ashton doesn't know that yet. Please don't tell her.'

'Of course not. Does she know that her father has—er—gone away?'

'She does, and it's not making my job any easier,' said Jarvis waspishly. 'She's very depressed, and between us we have enough problems without having to cope with a psychologically depressed patient. It's most insensitive of the man to go on a business trip at this time.'

So that's what Penny had told Gillian. I suppose it was marginally better than telling her that Daddy had done a bolt.

I said. 'Perhaps I can cheer her up.'

'I wish you would,' Jarvis said warmly. 'It would help her quite a lot.'

So I went to talk to Gillian and found her flat on her back on a bed with no pillow and totally faceless because she was bandaged up like Claude Rains in the film, *The Invisible Man*. The nursing sister gently told her I was there, and went away. I steered clear of the reasons she was there and asked no questions about it. Honnister was probably a better interrogator than I and would have sucked her dry. Instead I stuck to trivialities and told her a couple of funny items I had read in the papers that morning, and brought her up-to-date on the news of the day.

She was very grateful. 'I miss reading the papers. Penny comes in every day and reads to me.'

Brent had told me of that. 'I know.'

'What's gone wrong between you and Penny?'

'Why, nothing,' I said lightly. 'Did she say there was anything wrong?'

'No, but she's stopped talking about you, and when I asked, she said she hadn't seen you.'

'We've both been busy,' I said.

'I suppose that's it,' said Gillian. 'But it's the way she said it.'

I changed the subject and we chatted some more and when I left I think she was a little better in outlook.

Michaelis found his job boring, which indeed it was. As far as the hospital staff were concerned, he was a policeman set to guard a girl who had been violently attacked once. He sat on a chair outside the ward and spent his time reading paperbacks and magazines.

'I read to Miss Ashton for an hour every afternoon,' he said.

'That's good of you.'

He shrugged. 'Nothing much else to do. There's plenty of time to think on this job, too. I've been thinking about that model railway in Ashton's attic. I've never seen anything to beat it. He was a schedules man, of course.'

'What's that?'

'There's a lot of variety in the people who are interested in model railways. There are the scenic men who are bent on getting all the details right in miniature. I'm one of those. There are the engineering types who insist their stuff should be exact from the engineering aspect; that's expensive. I know a chap who has modelled Paddington station; and all he's interested in is getting the trains in and out according to the timetable. He's a schedules man like Ashton. The only difference is that Ashton was doing it on a really big scale.'

Hobbies are something that people really do become fanatical about, but Ashton hadn't struck me as the type. Still, I hadn't known that Michaelis was a model railwayman, either. I said, 'How big a scale?'

'Bloody big. I found a stack of schedules up there which made me blink. He could duplicate damn nearly the whole of the British railway system—not all at once, but in sections. He seemed to be specializing in pre-war stuff; he had schedules for the old LMS system, for instance; and the Great Western and the LNER. Now that takes a hell of a lot of juggling, so you know what he'd done?'

Michaelis looked at me expectantly, so I said, 'What?'

'He's installed a scad of microprocessors in that control board. You know—the things that have been called a computer on a chip. He could program his timetables into them.'

That sounded like Ashton, all right; very efficient. But it wasn't helping me to find him. 'Better keep your mind on the job,' I advised. 'We don't want anything happening to the girl.'

Two weeks after Ashton bolted Honnister rang me. Without preamble he said, 'We've got a line on our man.'

'Good. When are you seeing him?' I wanted to be there.

'I'm not,' said Honnister. 'He's not in my parish. He's a London boy so he's the Met's meat. A chap from the Yard will be seeing him tonight; Inspector Crammond. He's expecting you to ring him.'

'I'll do that. What's this character's name, and how did you get on to him?'

'His name is Peter Mayberry, aged about forty-five to fifty, and he lives in Finsbury. Apart from that I know damn-all. Crammond will pick it up from there. Mayberry hired the car for the weekend—not from one of the big hire-car firms, but from a garage in Slough. The bobbies over there came across it as a matter of routine and asked a few questions. The garage owner was bloody annoyed; he said someone had spilled battery acid on the back seat, so that made us perk up a bit.'

I thought about that. 'But would Mayberry give his real name when he hired the car?'

'The bloody fool did,' said Honnister. 'Anyway, he'd have to show his driving licence. This one strikes me as an amateur; I don't think he's a pro. Anyway Crammond tells me there's a Peter Mayberry living at that address.'

'I'll get on to Crammond immediately. Thanks, Charlie. You've done very well.'

He said earnestly, 'You'll thank me by leaning bloody hard on this bastard.' I was about to ring off, but he chipped in again. 'Seen anything of Ashton lately?'

It was the sort of innocuous question he might be expected to ask, but I thought I knew Honnister better than that by now; he wasn't the man to waste his time on idle chit-chat. 'Not much,' I said. 'Why?'

'I thought he'd like to know. Every time I ring him he's out, and the beat bobby tells me there's been some funny things going on at the house. A lot of coming and going and to-ing and fro-ing.'

'I believe he went away on a business trip. As for the house I wouldn't know—I haven't been there lately.'

'I suppose that's your story and you're sticking to it,' he said. 'Who's going to tell the Ashton sisters—you or me?'

'I will,' I said. 'After I've made sure of Mayberry.'

'All right. Any time you're down this way pop in and see me. We can have another noggin at the Coach and Horses. I'll be very interested in anything you can tell me.' He rang off.

I smiled. I was sure Honnister would be interested. Something funny was going on in his parish which he didn't know about and it irked him.

I dialled Scotland Yard and got hold of Crammond. 'Oh yes, Mr Jaggard; it's about this acid-throwing attack. I'll be seeing Mayberry tonight—he doesn't get home until about six-thirty, so his landlady tells us. I suggest you meet me here at six and we'll drive out.'

'That's fine.'

'There's just one thing,' Crammond said. 'Whose jurisdiction applies here—ours or yours?'

I said slowly, 'That depends on what Mayberry says. The acid-throwing is straightforward criminal assault, so as far as that's concerned he's your man and you can have him and welcome. But there are other matters I'm not at liberty to go into, and we might like to question him further before you charge him. Informally, of course.'

'I understand,' said Crammond. 'It's just that it's best to get these things straight first. See you at six, Mr Jaggard.'

Crammond was properly cautious. The police were not very comfortable when mixing with people like us. They knew that some of the things we did, if strictly interpreted, could be construed as law-breaking, and it went against the grain with them to turn a blind eye. Also they tended to think of themselves as the only professionals in the business and looked down on us as amateurs and, in their view, they were not there to help amateurs break the law of the land.

I phoned Ogilvie and told him. All he said was, 'Ah well, we'll see what comes of it.'

I met Crammond as arranged. He was a middling-sized thickset man of nondescript appearance, very useful in a plain clothes officer. We went out to Finsbury in his car, with a uniformed copper in the back seat, and he told me what he knew.

'When Honnister passed the word to us I had Mayberry checked out. That was this morning so he wasn't at home. He lives on the top floor of a house that's been broken up into flats. At least, that's what they call them; most of them are single rooms. His landlady describes him as a quiet type—a bit bookish.'

'Married?'

'No. She thinks he never has been, either. He has a job as some kind of a clerk working for a City firm. She wasn't too clear about that.'

'He doesn't sound the type,' I complained.

'He does have a police record,' said Crammond.

'That's better.'

'Wait until you hear it. One charge of assaulting a police officer, that's all. I went into it and the charge should never have been brought, even though he was found guilty. He got into a brawl during one of the Aldermaston marches a few years ago and was lugged in with a few others.'

'A protester,' I said thoughtfully. 'Amateur or professional?'

'Amateur, I'd say. He's not on our list of known rabble-rousers and, in any case, he has the wrong job for it. He's not mobile enough. But his appearance fits the description given by Honnister's witness. We'll see. Who does the asking?'

'You do,' I said. 'I'll hang about in the background. He'll think I'm just another copper.'

Mayberry had not yet arrived home when we got there so his landlady accommodated us in her front parlour. She was plainly curious and said archly, 'Has Mr Mayberry been doing anything naughty?'

'We just want him to help us in our enquiries,' said Crammond blandly. 'Is he a good tenant, Mrs Jackson?'

'He pays his rent regularly, and he's quiet. That's good enough for me.'

'Lived here long?'

'Five years—or is it six?' After much thought she decided it was six.

'Has he any hobbies? What does he do with his spare time?'

'He reads a lot; always got his head in a book. And he's religious—he goes to church twice every Sunday.'

I was depressed. This sounded less and less like our man. 'Did he go to church on the Sunday two weekends ago?' asked Crammond.

'Very likely,' she said. 'But I was away that weekend.' She held her head on one side. 'That sounds like him now.'

Someone walked along the passage outside the room and began to ascend the stairs. We gave him time to get settled then went after him. On the first landing Crammond said to the uniformed man, 'Wait outside the door, Shaw. If he makes a break grab him. It's not likely to happen, but if he is an acid-throwing bastard he can be dangerous.'

I stood behind Crammond as he tapped on Mayberry's door and noted that Shaw was flat against the wall so Mayberry couldn't see him. It's nice to see professionals at work. Mayberry was a man in his late forties and had a sallow complexion as though he did not eat well. His eyes were sunk deep into his skull.

'Mr Peter Mayberry?'

'Yes.'

'We're police officers,' said Crammond pleasantly. 'And we think you can help us. Do you mind if we come in?'

I saw Mayberry's knuckles whiten a little as he gripped the edge of the door. 'How can I help you?'

'Just by answering a few questions. Can we come in?'

'I suppose so.' Mayberry held open the door.

It wasn't much of a place; the carpet was threadbare and the furniture was of painted whitewood and very cheap; but it was clean and tidy. Along one wall was a shelf containing perhaps forty or fifty books; anyone with so many would doubtless be a great reader to Mrs Jackson who probably got through one book a year, if that.

I glanced at the titles. Some were religious and of a decidedly fundamentalist slant; there was a collection of environmental stuff including some pamphlets issued by Friends of the Earth. For the rest they were novels, all classics and none modern. Most of the books were paperbacks.

There were no pictures in the room except for one poster which was stuck on the wall by sticky tape at the corners. It depicted the earth from space, a photograph taken by an astronaut. Printed at the bottom were the words: I'M ALL YOU'VE GOT; LOOK AFTER ME.

Crammond started by saying 'Can I see your driving licence, Mr Mayberry?'

'I don't have a car.'

'That wasn't what I asked,' said Crammond. 'Your driving licence, please.'

Mayberry had taken off his jacket which was hanging on the back of a chair. He bent down and took his wallet from the inside breast pocket, took out his licence and gave it to Crammond who examined it gravely and in silence. At last Crammond said approvingly, 'Clean; no endorsements.' He handed it to me.

'I always drive carefully,' said Mayberry.

'I'm sure you do. Do you drive often?'

'I told you—I don't have a car.'

'And I heard you. Do you drive often?'

'Not very. What's all this about?'

'When did you last drive a car?'

Mayberry said, 'Look, if anyone says I've been in an accident they're wrong because I haven't.' He seemed very nervous, but many people are in the presence of authority, even if innocent. It's the villain who brazens it out.

I put the licence on the table and picked up the book Mayberry had been reading. It was on so-called alternative technology and was turned to a chapter telling how to make a digester to produce methane from manure. It seemed an unlikely subject for Finsbury.

Crammond said, 'When did you last drive a car?'

'Oh, I don't know—several months ago.'

'Whose car was it?'

'I forget. It was a long time ago.'

'Whose car do you usually drive?'

There was a pause while Mayberry sorted that one out. 'I don't *usually* drive.' He begun to sweat.

'Do you ever hire a car?'

'I have.' Mayberry swallowed. 'Yes, I have hired cars.'

'Recently?'

'No.'

'Supposing I said that you hired a car in Slough two weekends ago, what would you say?'

'I'd say you were wrong,' said Mayberry sullenly.

'Yes, you might say that,' said Crammond. 'But would I be wrong, Mr Mayberry?'

Mayberry straightened his shoulders. 'Yes,' he said defiantly.

'Where were you that weekend?'

'Here—as usual. You can ask Mrs Jackson, my landlady.'

Crammond regarded him for a moment in silence. 'But Mrs Jackson was away that weekend, wasn't she? So you were here all weekend. In this room? Didn't you go out?'

'No.'

'Not at all? Not even to church as usual?'

Mayberry was beginning to curl up at the edges. 'I didn't feel well,' he muttered.

'When was the last time you missed church on Sunday, Mr Mayberry?'

'I don't remember.'

'Can you produce one person to testify to your presence here in this room on the whole of that Sunday?'

'How can I? I didn't go out.'

'Didn't you eat?'

'I didn't feel well, I tell you. I wasn't hungry.'

'What about the Saturday? Didn't you go out then?'

'No.'

'And didn't you eat on the Saturday, either?'

Mayberry shifted his feet nervously; the unending stream of questions was getting to him. 'I had some apples.'

'You had some apples,' said Crammond flatly. 'Where and when did you buy the apples?'

'On the Friday afternoon at a supermarket.'

Crammond let that go. He said, 'Mr Mayberry, I suggest that all you've told me is a pack of lies. I suggest that on the Saturday morning you went to Slough by train where you hired a Hillman Sceptre from Joliffe's garage. Mr Joliffe was very upset by the acid damage to the back seat of the car. Where did you buy the acid?'

'I bought no acid.'

'But you hired the car?'

'No.'

'Then how do you account for the fact that the name and address taken from a driving licence—this driving licence'—Crammond picked it up and waved it under Mayberry's nose—'is your name and your address?'

'I can't account for it. I don't have to account for it. Perhaps someone impersonated me.'

'Why should anyone want to impersonate you, Mr Mayberry?'

'How would I know?'

'I don't think anyone would know,' observed Crammond. 'However, the matter can be settled very easily. We have the fingerprints from the car and they can be compared with yours quite easily. I'm sure you wouldn't mind coming to the station and giving us your prints, sir.'

It was the first I'd heard of fingerprints and I guessed Crammond was bluffing. Mayberry said, 'I'm ... I'm not coming. Not to the police station.'

114

'I see,' said Crammond softly. 'Do you regard yourself as a public-spirited citizen?'

'As much as anybody.'

'But you object to coming to the police station.'

'I've had a hard day,' said Mayberry. 'I'm not feeling well. I was about to go to bed when you came in.'

'Oh,' said Crammond, as though illuminated with insight. 'Well, if that's your only objection I have a fingerprint kit in the car. We can settle the matter here and now.'

'You're not taking my fingerprints. I don't have to give them to you. And now I want you to leave.'

'Ah, so that's your true objection.'

'I want you to leave or I'll——' Mayberry stopped short.

'Send for the police?' said Crammond ironically. 'When did you first meet Miss Ashton?'

'I've never met her,' said Mayberry quickly. Too quickly.

'But you know of her.'

Mayberry took a step backwards and banged into the table. The book fell to the floor. 'I know nobody of that name.'

'Not personally, perhaps—but you do know of her?'

I stooped to pick up the book. A thin pamphlet had fallen from the pages and I glanced at it before putting the book on the table. Mayberry repeated, 'I know nobody of that name.'

The pamphlet was a Parliamentary Report issued by the Stationery Office. Beneath the Royal coat-of-arms was the title: *Report of the Working Party on the Experimental Manipulation of the Genetic Composition of Micro-organisms.*

A whole lot of apparently unrelated facts suddenly slotted into place: Mayberry's fundamentalist religion, his environmental interests, and the work Penny Ashton was doing. I said, 'Mr Mayberry, what do you think of the state of modern biological science?'

Crammond, his mouth opened to ask another question, gaped at me in astonishment. Mayberry jerked his head around to look at me. 'Bad,' he said. 'Very bad.'

'In what way?'

'The biologists are breaking the laws of God,' he said. 'Defiling life itself.'

'In what way?'

'By mixing like with unlike—by creating monsters.' Mayberry's voice rose. ' "And God said, 'Let the earth bring forth the living creature after his kind.' " That's what he said—*after his kind*. "Cattle, and creeping thing, and beast of the earth after his kind." *After his kind!* That is on the very first page of the Holy Bible.'

Crammond glanced at me with a mystified expression, and then looked again at Mayberry. 'I'm not sure I know what you mean, sir.'

Mayberry was exalted. 'And God said unto Noah, "Of fowls after their kind"—*after their kind*—"and of cattle after their kind"—*after their kind*—"of every creeping thing of the earth after his kind"—*after his kind*—"two of every sort shall come unto thee, to keep them alive." She's godless; she would destroy God's own work as is set down in the Book.'

I doubted if Crammond knew what Mayberry was saying, but I did. I said. 'How?'

'She would break down the seed which God has made, and mingle one kind with another kind, and so create monsters— chimaeras and abominations.'

I had difficulty in keeping my voice even. 'I take it by "she" you mean Dr Penelope Ashton.'

Crammond's head jerked. Mayberry, still caught up in religious fervour, said thoughtlessly, 'Among others.'

'Such as Professor Lumsden,' I suggested.

'Her master in devilry.'

'If you thought she was doing wrong why didn't you talk to her about it? Perhaps you could have led her to see her error.'

'I wouldn't foul my ears with her voice,' he said contemptuously.

I said, 'Doesn't it say in the Bible that God gave Adam dominion over the fish of the sea, the fowls of the air, and every beast or thing that creeps on the earth? Perhaps she's in the right.'

'The Devil can quote scripture,' said Mayberry, and turned away from me. I felt sick.

Crammond woke up to what was happening. 'Mr Mayberry, are you admitting to having thrown acid into the face of a woman called Ashton?'

Mayberry had a hunted look, conscious of having said too much. 'I haven't said that.'

'You've said enough.' Crammond turned to me. 'I think we have enough to take him.'

I nodded, then said to Mayberry, 'You're a religious man. You go to church every Sunday—twice, so I'm told. Do you think it was a Christian act to throw battery acid into the face of a young woman?'

'I am not responsible to you for my actions,' said Mayberry. 'I am responsible to God.'

Crammond nodded gravely. 'Nevertheless, I believe someone said, "Render unto Caesar the things that are Caesar's." I think you'll have to come along with us, Mr Mayberry.'

'And may God help you,' I said. 'Because you got the wrong girl. You threw the acid into the face of Dr Ashton's sister who was coming back from church.'

Mayberry stared at me. As he had spoken of being responsible to God he had worn a lofty expression but now his face crumpled and horror crept into his eyes. He whispered, 'The wrong ... wrong...' Suddenly he jerked convulsively and screamed at the top of his voice.

'Oh, Christ!' said Crammond as Shaw burst into the room.

Mayberry collapsed to the floor, babbling a string of obscenities in a low and monotonous voice. When Crammond turned to speak to me he was sweating. 'This one's not for the slammer. He'll go to Broadmoor for sure. Do you want any more out of him?'

'Not a thing,' I said. 'Not now.'

Crammond turned to Shaw. 'Phone for an ambulance. Tell them it's religious mania and they might need a restraining jacket.'

SIXTEEN

By the time we'd got Mayberry into an ambulance Ogilvie had left the office and gone home. I didn't bother ringing his home, but I did ring Penny because I thought she ought to know about Mayberry. Mary Cope answered again and said that Penny wasn't in, but this time I pushed it harder. She said Penny had gone to Oxford to attend a lecture and wouldn't be back until late. I rang off, satisfied I wasn't being given another brush-off.

Before seeing Ogilvie next morning I rang Crammond. 'What's new on Mayberry?'

'He's at King's College Hospital—under guard in a private ward.'

'Did he recover?'

'Not so you'd notice. It seems like a complete breakdown to me, but I'm no specialist.'

'A pity. I'll have to talk to him again, you know.'

'You'll have to get through a platoon of assorted doctors first,' warned Crammond. 'It seems he's suffering from everything from ingrowing toenails to psychoceramica.'

'What the hell's that?'

'It means he's a crack-pot,' said Crammond sourly. 'The head-shrinkers are keeping him isolated.'

I thanked him for his help and went to see Ogilvie. I told him about Mayberry and his face was a study in perplexity. 'Are you sure Mayberry isn't pulling a fast one?'

I shook my head. 'He's a nutter. But we've got him, and a psychiatrist will sort him out for us.'

'I'll buy that—for the moment.' Ogilvie shook his head. 'But I wouldn't call psychiatry an exact science. Have you noticed in court cases that for every psychiatrist called for the defence there's another called by the prosecution who'll give an opposing opinion? Still, supposing Mayberry is established as a religious maniac without doubt, there are a few questions which need asking.'

'I know. Why did he pick on Penny—or the girl he thought was Penny? Did he act of his own volition or was he pointed in the right direction and pushed? I'll see he gets filleted as soon as he can be talked to. But you're avoiding the big problem.'

Ogilvie grunted, and ticked points off on his fingers. 'Supposing Mayberry *is* crazy; and supposing he *wasn't* pushed—that he did it off his own bat, and that Penelope Ashton was a more or less random choice among the geneticists. That leaves us up a gum tree, doesn't it?'

'Yes.' I put the big question into words. 'In that case why did Ashton do a bunk?'

I was beginning to develop another headache.

I'd had second thoughts about ringing Penny; it wasn't the sort of thing to tell her on the telephone. But before going to University College I rang Honnister and told him the score. He took it rather badly. His voice rose. 'The wrong girl! The inefficient, crazy bastard picked the wrong girl!' He broke into a stream of profanity.

'I thought you ought to know. I'll keep you informed on future developments.'

I went to University College and was about to enquire at the reception desk when I saw Jack Brent standing at the end of a corridor. I went up to him. 'Any problems?'

'Nary a one.'

'Where's Penny Ashton?'

He jerked his thumb at a door. 'With her boss. That's Lumsden's office.'

I nodded and went in. Penny and Professor Lumsden looked very professional in white laboratory coats, like the chaps who sell toothpaste in TV ads. They were sitting at a desk, drinking coffee and examining papers which looked like computer print-outs. Lumsden was much younger than I expected, not as old as I was; pioneering on the frontiers of science is a young man's game.

Penny looked up. A look of astonishment chased across her face and then she became expressionless, but I noted the tightening of muscles at the angle of her jaw and the firmly compressed lips. I said, 'Good morning, Dr Ashton—Professor Lumsden. Could I have a word with you, Penny?'

'Well?' she said coolly.

I glanced at Lumsden. 'It's official, I'm afraid. In your office, perhaps?'

She said shortly, 'If it is official...' and regarded me distrustfully.

'It is,' I said, matching her curtness.

She made her excuses to Lumsden and we left his office. I said to Brent, 'Stick around,' then followed Penny who led me along another corridor and into her office. I looked around. 'Where's the microscope?'

Unsmilingly she said, 'We're working on things you can't see through microscopes. What do you want? Have you found Daddy?'

I shook my head. 'We've found the man who threw the acid.'

'Oh.' She sat at her desk. 'Who is he?'

'A man called Peter Mayberry. Ever heard of him?'

She thought for a moment. 'No, I can't say that I have. What is he?'

'A clerk in a City office—and a religious maniac.'

She frowned, then said questioningly, 'A religious maniac? But what would he have to do with Gillian? She's an Anglican—and you can't get more unmaniacal than that.'

I sat down. 'Brace yourself, Penny. The acid wasn't intended for Gillian. It was intended for you.'

'For me!' Her forehead creased and then she shook her head as though she wasn't hearing aright. 'You did say ... for me?'

'Yes. Are you sure you haven't heard of this man?'

She ignored my question. 'But why would a religious maniac ...?' She choked on the words. 'Why me?'

'He seemed to think you are tampering with the laws of God.'

'Oh.' Then: 'Seemed? He's not dead?'

'No, but he's not doing much thinking right now. He's gone off into some kind of fugue.'

She shook her head. 'There have been objections to what we've been doing, but they've been scientific. Paul Berg, Brenner, Singer and a few others objected very strongly to...' Suddenly it hit her. 'Oh, my God!' she said. 'Poor Gillian!'

She sat rigidly for a moment, her hands clasped together tightly, and then she began to shake, the tremors sweeping across her body. She moaned a sort of keening sound—and then fell forward across her desk, her head pillowed on her arms. Her shoulders shook convulsively and she sobbed stormily. I located a hand basin in the corner of the office and filled a glass with water and returned quickly to the desk, but there wasn't much I could do until the first shock had abated.

Her sobbing lessened in intensity and I put my arm around her. 'Steady on. Drink this.'

She raised her head, still sobbing, and showed a tear-stained face. 'Oh, Gillian! She'd be ... all right ... if I ... if I hadn't ...'

'Hush,' I said. 'And stop that. Drink this.'

She gulped down some water, then said, 'Oh, Malcolm; what am I to do?'

'Do? There's nothing to do. You just carry on as usual.'

'Oh, no. How can I do that?'

I said deliberately, 'You can't possibly blame yourself for what happened to Gillian. You'll tear yourself apart if you try. You can't hold yourself responsible for the act of an unbalanced man.'

'Oh, I wish it had been me,' she cried.

'No, you don't,' I said sharply. 'Don't ever say that again.'

'How can I tell her?'

'You don't tell her. Not until she's well—if then.' She began to cry again, and I said, 'Penny, pull yourself together—I need your help.'

'What can I do?'

'You can tidy yourself up,' I said. 'Then you can get Lumsden in here, because I want to ask you both some questions.'

She sniffled a bit, then said, 'What sort of questions?'

'You'll hear them when Lumsden comes in. I don't want to go through it all twice. We still don't know why your father went away, but it seemed to be triggered by that acid attack, so we want to find out as much about it as we can.'

She went to the hand basin and washed her face. When she was more presentable she rang Lumsden. I said, 'I'd rather you don't say anything about your father before Lumsden.' She said nothing to that, and sat at the desk.

When Lumsden came in he took one glance at Penny's reddened eyes and white face, then looked at me. 'What's happened here? And who are you?'

'I'm Malcolm Jaggard and I'm a sort of police officer, Professor.' To divert him from asking for my warrant card I added, 'I'm also Penny's fiancé.'

Penny made no objection to that flat statement, but Lumsden showed astonishment. 'Oh, I didn't know...'

'A recent development,' I said. 'You know, of course, of the acid attack on Penny's sister.'

'Yes, a most shocking thing.'

I told him about Mayberry and he became very grave. 'This is bad,' he said. 'I'm deeply sorry, Penny.' She nodded without saying anything.

'I want to know if you or anyone in your department has been threatened—anonymous letters, telephone calls, or anything like that.'

He shrugged. 'There are always the cranks. We tend to ignore them.'

'Perhaps that's a mistake,' I said. 'I'd like some specifics. Do you keep any such letters? If so, I want them.'

'No,' he said regretfully. 'They are usually thrown away. You see ... er ... Inspector?'

'Mister.'

'Well, Mr Jaggard, most of the crank letters aren't threatening—they just tend to ramble, that's all.'

'About what?'

'About supposed offences against God. Lots of biblical quotations, usually from *Genesis*. Just what you might expect.'

I said to Penny, 'Have you had any of these letters?'

'A couple,' she said quietly. 'No threats. I threw them away.'

'Any telephone calls? Heavy breathers?'

'One about six months ago. He stopped after a month.'

'What did he say?'

'What Lummy has described. Just what you might expect.'

'Did you get the calls here or at home?'

'Here. The telephone at home is unlisted.'

I turned to Lumsden. 'You've both used the same phrase—"Just what you might expect". What might I expect, Professor Lumsden?'

'Well, in view of our work here . . .' He threw out his hands expressively.

We were still standing. I said, 'Sit down, Professor, and tell me of your work, or about as much as you can without breaking the Official Secrets Act.'

'Breaking the Official Secrets Act! There's no question of that—not here.'

'In that case, you won't object to telling me, will you?'

'I don't suppose so,' he said doubtfully, and sat down.

He was silent for a moment, marshalling his thoughts, and I knew what was happening. He was hunting for unaccustomed simple words to explain complex ideas to an unscientific clod. I said, 'I can understand words of three syllables—even four syllables if they're spoken slowly. Let me help you. The basis of inheritance is the chromosome; inside the chromosome is an acid called DNA. A thing called a gene is the ultimate factor and is very specific; there are distinct genes for producing the different chemicals needed by the organism. The genes can be thought of as being strung along a strand of DNA like beads on a spiral string. At least, that's how I visualize them. That's where I get lost so you'd better go on from there.'

Lumsden smiled. 'Not bad, Mr Jaggard; not bad at all.' He began to talk, at first hesitantly, and then more fluently. He ranged quite widely and sometimes I had to interrupt and bring him back on to the main track. At other times I had him explain what he meant in simpler terms. The basic concepts were rather simple but I gathered that execution in the laboratory was not as easy as all that.

What it boiled down to was this. A strand of DNA contains many thousands of genes, each gene doing its own particular job such as, for instance, controlling the production of cholinesterase, a chemical which mediates electrical action in the nervous system. There are thousands of chemicals like this and each has its own gene.

The molecular biologist had discovered certain enzymes which could cut up a strand of DNA into short lengths, and other enzymes which could weld the short lengths together again. They also found they could weld a short length of DNA on to a bacteriophage, which is a minute organism capable of penetrating the wall of a cell. Once inside, the genes would be uncoupled and incorporated into the DNA of the host cell.

Put like that it sounds rather simple but the implications are fantastic, and Lumsden was very emphatic about this. 'You see, the genes you incorporate into a cell need not come from the same kind of animal. In this laboratory we have bacterial cultures which contain genetic material from mice. Now a bacterium is a bacterium and a mouse is a mammal, but our little chaps are part bacterium and part mammal.'

'Breaking down the seed, mingling one kind with another, creating chimaeras,' I mused.

'I suppose you could put it that way,' said Lumsden.

'I didn't put it that way,' I said. 'Mayberry did.' At that stage I didn't get the point. 'But what's the use of this?'

Lumsden frowned as though I was being thick-witted, as I suppose I was. Penny spoke up. 'Lummy, what about *Rhizobium*?'

His brow cleared. 'Yes, that's a good example.'

He said that although plants need nitrogen for their growth they cannot take it from the air, even though air is 78 per cent nitrogen. They need it in the form of nitrates which, in man-planted cash crops, are usually spread as artificial fertilizer. However, there is a range of plants, notably the legumes—peas, beans and so on—which harbours in its roots the *Rhizobium* bacterium. This organism has the power of transforming atmospheric nitrogen into a form the plant can use.

'Now,' said Lumsden. 'All plants have bacteria in their roots and some are very specific. Supposing we take the *Rhizobium* bacterium, isolate the gene that controls this nitrogen changing property, and transfer it into a bacterium that is specific to wheat. Then, if it bred true, we'd have self-fertilizing wheat. In these days of world food shortages that seems to me to be a good thing to have around.'

I thought so, too, but Penny said, 'It can be pretty dangerous. You have to be damned sure you've selected the right gene. Some of the *Rhizobium* genes are tumour-causing. If you got one of those you might find the world wheat crop dying of cancer.'

'Yes,' said Lumsden. 'We must be very sure before we let loose our laboratory-changed organisms. There was a hell of a row about that not long ago.' He stood up. 'Well, Mr Jaggard, have you got what you wanted?'

'I think so,' I said. 'But I don't know if it's going to do me a damned bit of good. Thanks for your time, Professor.'

He smiled. 'If you need more information I suggest you ask Penny.' He glanced at her. 'I suggest you take the day off, Penny. You've had a nasty shock—you don't look too well.'

She shivered. 'The thought that there are people in the world who'd want to do that to you is unnerving.'

'I'll take you home,' I said quietly. 'Jack Brent can follow in your car.' She made no objection, and I turned to Lumsden. 'I suggest that any crank letters—no matter how apparently innocuous—should be forwarded to the police. And telephone calls should be reported.'

'I agree,' he said. 'I'll see to it.'

So I took Penny home.

SEVENTEEN

My relationship with Penny improved although neither of us referred to marriage. The shock of Mayberry's error had been shattering and I stuck around and helped her pick up the pieces; from then on propinquity did the rest. She was persuaded by Lumsden to stay with her work and her life took a triangular course—her home, her work, and whatever hospital Gillian happened to be in at the time.

Mayberry was thoroughly investigated, by a band of psychiatrists and by Mansell, the department's best interrogator, a soft-spoken man who could charm the birds from the trees. They all came to the same conclusion: Mayberry was exactly what he appeared to be—a nut case. 'And a bit of a coward, too,' said Mansell. 'He was going for Lumsden at first, but thought a woman would be easier to handle.'

'Why did he pick on Lumsden's crowd?' I asked.

'A natural choice. Firstly, Lumsden is very well known—he's not as averse to talking to newspaper reporters as a lot of scientists are. He gets his name in the papers. Secondly, he hasn't been reticent about what he's been doing. If you wanted a handy geneticist Lumsden would be the first to spring to mind.'

Mayberry was the deadest of dead ends.

Which caused the problem Ogilvie and I had anticipated. If the acid attack had been fortuitous why should Ashton have bolted? It made no sense.

Once Mayberry had been shaken down the guards were taken from Penny and Gillian, and my legmen were put to other work. Ogilvie had little enough manpower to waste and the team investigating the Ashton case was cut down to one—me, and I wasted a lot of time investigating mistaken identities. Ashton's bolt-hole was well concealed.

And so the weeks and then the months went by. Gillian

was in and out of hospital and finally was able to live at home, managing on a quarter of her normal eyesight. She and Penny were making plans to go to the United States where she would undergo plastic surgery to repair her ravaged face.

Once, when I persuaded Penny to dine with me, she asked, 'What did you find in that big vault of Daddy's?'

It was the first time she had shown any interest. 'Nothing.'

'You're lying.' There was an edge of anger.

'I've never lied to you, Penny,' I said soberly. 'Never once. My sins have been those of omission, not commission. I may have been guilty of *suppressio veri* but never *suggestio falsi*.'

'Your classical education is showing,' she said tartly, but she smiled as she said it, her anger appeased. 'Strange. Why should Daddy build such a thing and not use it? Perhaps he did and found it too much trouble.'

'As far as we can make out it was never used,' I said. 'All it contained was stale air and a little dust. My boss is baffled and boggled.'

'Oh, Malcolm, I wish I knew why he disappeared. It's been over three months now.'

I made the usual comforting sounds and diverted her attention. Presently she said, 'Do you remember when you told me of what you really do? You mentioned someone called Lord Cregar.'

'That's right.'

'He's been seeing Lumsden.'

That drew my interest. 'Has he? What about?'

She shook her head. 'Lummy didn't say.'

'Was it about Mayberry?'

'Oh, no. The first time he came was before you told us about Mayberry.' She wrinkled her brow. 'It was two or three days after you opened the vault.'

'Not two or three weeks?'

'No—it was a matter of days. Who is Lord Cregar?'

'He's pretty high in government, I believe.' I could have told her that Cregar had smuggled her father out of Russia a quarter of a century earlier, but I didn't. If Ashton had wanted his daughters to know of his Russian past he would have told them, and it wasn't up to me to blow the gaff. Besides, I couldn't blab about anything listed under Code Black; it would be dangerous for me, for Ogilvie and, possibly, Penny herself. I wasn't supposed to know about that.

All the same it was curious that Cregar had been seeing Lumsden before we knew about Mayberry. Was there a connection between Ashton and Lumsden—apart from Penny—that we hadn't spotted?

I caught the eye of a passing waiter and asked for the bill. As I drained my coffee cup I said, 'It's probably not important. Let's go and keep Gillian company.'

Ogilvie sent for me next morning. He took an envelope, extracted a photograph, and tossed it across the desk. 'Who's that?'

He wore a heavy coat and a round fur hat, the type with flaps which can be tied down to cover the ears but which never are. Wherever he was it was snowing; there were white streaks in the picture which was obviously a time exposure.

I said, 'That's George Ashton.'

'No, he isn't,' said Ogilvie. 'His name is Fyodr Koslov, and he lives in Stockholm. He has a servant, an elderly bruiser called Howell Williams.' Another photograph skimmed across the desk.

I took one look at it, and said, 'That be damned for a tale. This is Benson. Where did you get these?'

'I want you to make quite sure,' said Ogilvie. He took a sheaf of photographs and fanned them out. 'As you know, we had a couple of bad pictures of Ashton and none at all of Benson. You are the only person in the department who can identify them.'

Every one of the photographs showed either Ashton or Benson, and in two of them they were together. 'Positive identification,' I said flatly. 'Ashton and Benson.'

Ogilvie was pleased. 'Some of our associated departments are more co-operative than others,' he remarked. 'I had the pictures of Ashton circulated. These came back from a chap called Henty in Stockholm. He seems to be quite good with a camera.'

'He's very good.' The pictures were unposed—candid camera stuff—and very sharp. 'I hope he's been circumspect. We don't want them to bolt again.'

'You'll go to Stockholm and take up where Henty left off. He has instructions to co-operate.'

I looked out at the bleak London sky and shivered. I didn't fancy Stockholm at that time of year. 'Do I contact Ashton? Tell him about Mayberry and persuade him to come back?'

Ogilvie deliberated. 'No. He's too near Russia. It might startle him to know that British Intelligence is still taking an interest in him—startle him into doing something foolish. He had a low opinion of us thirty years ago which may not have improved. No, you just watch him and find out what the hell he's doing.'

I took the sheet of paper with Henty's address in Stockholm and his telephone number, then said, 'Can you think of any connection between Cregar and Professor Lumsden?' I told him Penny's story.

Ogilvie looked at the ceiling. 'I hear backstairs gossip from time to time. There could be a connection, but it's nothing to do with Ashton. It *can't* have anything to do with Ashton.'

'What is it?'

He abandoned his apparent fascination with the electric fittings and looked at me. 'Malcolm, you're getting to know too damned much—more than is good for you. However, I'll humour you because, as I say, this is only servants' hall rumour. When this department was set up we took a sizeable chunk from Cregar which diminished his outfit considerably, so he began to empire-build in a different direction. The story is that he's heavily involved in CBW—that would explain any interest he has in Lumsden.'

By God it would! Chemical and bacteriological warfare and what Lumsden was doing fitted together like hand in glove. 'Is he still in security?'

'No, he's executive. He mediates between the Minister and the scientists. Of course, with his experience he also handles the security side.'

I could just imagine Cregar happily contemplating some previously inoffensive microbe now armed for death and destruction by genetic engineering. 'Is he in with the Porton Down crowd?'

'The Ministry of Defence is closing down Porton Down,' said Ogilvie. 'I don't know where Cregar does his juggling with life and death. Microbiology isn't like atomics; you don't need a particle accelerator costing a hundred million and a power plant capable of supplying energy for a fair-sized city. The physical plant and investment are both relatively small, and Cregar may have a dozen laboratories scattered about for all I know. He doesn't talk about it—not to me.'

I contemplated this, trying to find a link with Ashton, and failed. There was only Penny, and I said so. Ogilvie asked, 'Has Cregar talked to her?'

'No.'

'I told you it can't have anything to do with Ashton,' he said. 'Off you go to Sweden.'

There was something else I wanted to bring up. 'I'd like to know more about Benson. He's probably filed away in Code Black.'

Ogilvie looked at me thoughtfully then, without speaking, got up and went into the room behind his desk. When he came back he was shaking his head. 'You must be mistaken. Benson isn't listed—not even under Code Green.'

'But I took him up as far as Code Purple,' I said. 'Someone is monkeying around with that bloody computer.'

Ogilvie's lips tightened. 'Unlikely,' he said shortly.

'How unlikely?'

'It's not easy to suborn a computer. It would need an expert.'

'Experts are ten a penny—and they can be bought.'

Ogilvie was palpably uneasy. He said slowly, 'We aren't the only department on line with this computer. I've been pressing for our own computer for several years but without success. Some other department . . .' He stopped and sat down.

'Who determines what material is added to the files—or removed?'

'There's an inter-departmental review committee which meets monthly. No one is authorized to add or subtract without its approval.'

'Someone has subtracted Benson,' I said. 'Or, more likely, he's been blocked off. I'll bet someone has added a tiny sub-program which would be difficult to find—if Benson is asked for say there's no one here of that name.'

'Well it's for me to deal with,' said Ogilvie. 'There's a meeting of the review committee on Friday at which I'll raise a little bit of hell.' He stuck his finger out at me. 'But you know nothing about this. Now, go away. Go to Sweden.'

I got up to leave but paused at the door. 'I'll leave you with a thought. I got into the Ashton case by asking Nellie about Ashton. Two hours later I was on the carpet in your office with you and Cregar asking awkward questions. Did Cregar come to you with it?'

'Yes.'

'In two hours? How did he know who was asking questions about Ashton unless the computer tipped him off? I don't think you have far to look for the chap who is monkeying around with it.'

I left leaving Ogilvie distinctly worried.

EIGHTEEN

It was dark and cold in Stockholm at that time of year. All the time I was in Sweden it didn't stop snowing; not heavily most of the time, but there was a continual fall of fine powder from leaden-grey clouds as though God up there was operating a giant flour-sifter. I was booked into the Grand, which was warm enough, and after I had made my call to Henty I looked out over the frozen Strömmen to the Royal Palace. Edward VII didn't like Buckingham Palace, and called it 'that damned factory'. It's not on record if he said anything about the Palace in Stockholm, but that afternoon it looked like a dark satanic mill.

There were swans on the Strömmen, walking uneasily on the ice and cuddling in clusters as though to keep warm. One was on an ice floe and drifting towards Riddarfjärden; I watched it until it went out of sight under the Ström bridge, then turned away feeling suddenly cold in spite of the central heating. Sweden in winter has that effect on me.

Henty arrived and we swapped credentials. 'We don't have much to do with your mob,' he commented as he handed back my card. He had a raw colonial accent.

'We don't move out of the UK much,' I said. 'Most of our work is counter-espionage. This one is a bit different. If you can take me to George Ashton I'll buy you a case of Foster's.'

Henty blinked. 'Good beer, that. How did you know I'm Australian? I've not been back for twenty years. Must have lost the accent by now.'

I grinned. 'Yes, you've learned to speak English very well. Where's Ashton?'

He went to the window and pointed at the Royal Palace. 'On the other side of that. In Gamla Stan.'

Gamla Stan—the Old Town. A warren of narrow streets threading between ancient buildings and the 'in' place to live

in Stockholm. Cabinet ministers live there, and film directors
—if they can afford it. The Royal Palace is No. 1, Gamla Stan.
I said, 'How did you find him?'

'I got a couple of crummy pictures from London, and the
day I got them I walked slam-bang into this character on the
Vasabron.' Henry shrugged. 'So it's a coincidence.'

'By the laws of statistics we've got to get lucky some time,' I
observed.

'He has a flat just off Västerlånggatan. He's passing himself
off as a Russian called Fyodr Koslov—which is a mistake.'

'Why?'

Henty frowned. 'It's a tip-off—enough to make me take the
pictures and send them back. There's something funny about
the way he speaks Russian—doesn't sound natural.'

I thought about that. After thirty years of non-use Ashton's
Russian would be rusty; it's been known for men to forget
completely their native language. 'And Benson is with him in
the flat?'

'Benson? Is that who he is? He calls himself Williams here.
An older man; looks a bit of a thug. He's definitely British.'

'How can I get a look at them?'

Henty shrugged. 'Go to Gamla Stan and hang around outside the flat until they come out—or go in.'

I shook my head. 'Not good enough. They know me and I
don't want to be seen. What's your status here?'

'Low man on the bloody totem,' said Henty wryly. 'I'm
junior partner in an import-export firm. I have a line into the
Embassy, but that's for emergency use only. The diplomats
here don't like boys like us, they reckon we cause trouble.'

'They could be right,' I said drily. 'Who do I see at the
Embassy?'

'A Second Secretary called Cutler. A toffee-nosed bastard.'
The iron seemed to have entered Henty's soul.

'What resources can you draw on apart from the Embassy?'

'Resources!' Henty grinned. 'You're looking at the resources
—me. I just have a watching brief—we're not geared for
action.'

'Then it will have to be the Embassy.'

He coughed, then said, 'Exactly who is Ashton?' I looked at
him in silence until he said, 'If it's going to be like that . . .'

'It always is like that, isn't it?'

'I suppose so,' he said despondently. 'But I wish, just for once, that I knew why I'm doing what I'm doing.'

I looked at my watch. 'There's just time to see Cutler. In the meantime you pin down Ashton and Benson. Report to me here or at the Embassy. And there's one very important thing —don't scare them.'

'Okay—but I don't think you'll get much change out of Cutler.'

I smiled. 'I wouldn't want either you or Cutler to bet on that one.'

The Embassy was on Skarpögatan, and Cutler turned out to be a tall, slim, fair-haired man of about my age, very English and Old School Tie. His manner was courteous but rather distant as though his mind was occupied by other, and more important, considerations which a non-diplomat could not possibly understand. This minor Metternich reminded me strongly of a shop assistant in one of the more snob London establishments.

When I gave him my card—the special one—his lips tightened and he said coolly, 'You seem to be off your beat, Mr Jaggard. What can we do for you?' He sounded as though he believed there was nothing he could possibly do for me.

I said pleasantly, 'We've mislaid a bit of property and we'd like it back—with your help. But tact is the watchword.' I told him the bare and minimum facts about Ashton and Benson.

When I'd finished he was a shade bewildered. 'But I don't see how . . .' He stopped and began again. 'Look, Mr Jaggard, if this man decides to leave England with his man-servant to come to Sweden and live under an assumed name I don't see what we can do about it. I don't think it's a crime in Swedish law to live under another name; it certainly isn't in England. What exactly is it that you want?'

'A bit of manpower,' I said. 'I want Ashton watched. I want to know what he does and why he does it.'

'That's out of the question,' said Cutler. 'We can't spare men for police work of that nature. I really fail to see what your interest is in the man on the basis of what you've told me.'

'You're not entitled to know more,' I said bluntly. 'But take it from me—Ashton is a hot one.'

'I'm afraid I can't do that,' he said coldly. 'Do you really think we jump when any stranger walks in off the street with an improbable story like this?'

I pointed to my card which was still on the blotter in front of him. 'In spite of that?'

'In spite of that,' he said, but I think he really meant because of it. 'You people amaze me. You think you're James Bonds, the lot of you. Well, I don't think I'm living in the middle of a highly coloured film, even if you do.'

I wasn't going to argue with him. 'May I use your telephone?' He frowned, trying to think of a good reason for denial, so I added, 'I'll pay for the call.'

'That won't be necessary,' he said shortly, and pushed his telephone across the desk.

One of our boffins once asked me what was the biggest machine in the world. After several abortive answers I gave up, and he said, 'The international telephone system. There are 450 million telephones in the world, and 250 million of them are connected by direct dialling—untouched by hand in the exchanges.' We may grouse about the faults of local systems, but in under ninety seconds I was talking to Ogilvie.

I said, 'We have Ashton but there's a small problem. There's only one of Henty, and I can't push in too close myself.'

'Good. Get on to the Embassy for support. We want him watched. Don't approach him yourself.'

'I'm at the Embassy now. No support forthcoming.'

'What's the name of the obstruction?'

'Cutler—Second Secretary.'

'Wait a moment.' There was a clatter and I heard the rustle of papers in distant London. Presently Ogilvie said, 'This will take about half an hour. I'll dynamite the obstruction. For God's sake, don't lose Ashton now.'

'I won't,' I said, and hung up. I stood up and picked my card from Cutler's blotter. 'I'm at the Grand. You can get me there.'

'I can't think of any circumstances in which I should do so,' he said distantly.

I smiled. 'You will.' Suddenly I was tired of him. 'Unless you want to spend the next ten years counting paper clips in Samoa.'

Back at the hotel there was a curt note from Henty: 'Meet

me at the Moderna Museet on Skeppsholmen.' I grabbed a taxi and was there in five minutes. Henty was standing outside the main entrance, his hands thrust deep into his pockets and the tip of his nose blue with cold. He jerked his head at the gallery. 'Your man is getting a bit of culture.'

This had to be handled carefully. I didn't want to bump into Ashton face to face. 'Benson there, too?'

'Just Ashton.'

'Right. Nip in and locate him—then come back here.'

Henty went inside, no doubt glad to be in the warm. He was back in five minutes. 'He's studying blue period Picassos.' He gave me a plan of the halls and marked the Picasso Gallery.

I went into the Musuem, moving carefully. There were not many people in the halls on that cold winter's afternoon, which was a pity because there was no crowd to get lost in. On the other hand there were long unobstructed views. I took out my handkerchief, ready to muffle my face in case of emergency, turned a corner and saw Ashton in the distance. He was contemplating a canvas with interest and, as he turned to move on to the next one, I had a good sight of his face.

To my relief this *was* Ashton. There would have been a blazing row if I had goosed Cutler to no purpose.

NINETEEN

Cutler jumped like a startled frog. An hour later, when I was unfreezing my bones in a hot bath and feeling sorry for Henty who was still tagging Ashton, the telephone rang to announce that he was waiting in the hotel foyer. 'Ask him to come up.' I dried myself quickly and put on a dressing-gown.

He brought two men whom he introduced as Askrigg and Debenham. He made no apologies for his previous attitude and neither of us referred to it. All the time I knew him he maintained his icily well-bred air of disapproval; that I could stand so long as he did what he was told and did it fast, and I had no complaints about that. The only trouble was that he and his people were lacking in professionalism.

We got down to business immediately. I outlined the problem, and Askrigg said, 'A full-time surveillance of two men is a six-man job.'

'At least,' I agreed. 'And that's excluding me and Henty. Ashton and Benson know me, so I'm out. As for Henty, he's done enough. He spotted Ashton for us and has been freezing his balls off ever since keeping an eye on him. I'm pulling him out for a rest and then he'll be in reserve.'

'Six men,' said Cutler doubtfully. 'Oh, well, I suppose we can find them. What are we looking for?'

'I want to know everything about them. Where they go, what they eat, who they see, do they have a routine, what happens when they break that routine, who they write to—you name it, I want to know.'

'It seems a lot of fuss over a relatively minor industrialist,' sniffed Cutler.

I grinned at him, and quoted, ' "Yours not to reason why, Yours but to do or die." Which could happen because they're probably armed.'

That brought a moment of silence during which Cutler

twitched a bit. In his book diplomacy and guns didn't go together. I said, 'Another thing: I want to have a look inside Ashton's apartment, but we'll check their routine first so we can pick the right moment.'

'Burglary!' said Cutler hollowly. 'The Embassy mustn't be involved in that.'

'It won't be,' I said shortly. 'Leave that to me. All right; let's get organized.'

And so Ashton and Benson were watched, every movement noted. It was both wearisome and frustrating as most operations of this nature are. The two men led an exemplary life. Ashton's was the life of a gentleman of leisure; he visited museums and art galleries, attended the theatre and cinemas, and spent a lot of time in bookshops where he spent heavily, purchasing fiction and non-fiction, the non-fiction being mostly biographies. The books were over a spread of languages, English, German and Russian predominating. And all the time he did not do a stroke of what could reasonably be called work. It was baffling.

Benson was the perfect manservant. He did the household shopping, attended to the laundry and dry-cleaning, and did a spot of cooking on those occasions when Ashton did not eat out. He had found himself a favourite drinking-hole which he attended three or four times a week, an *ölstuga* more intellectual than most because it had a chess circle. Benson would play a couple of games and leave relatively early.

Neither of them wrote or received any letters.

Neither appeared to have any associates other than the small-change encounters of everyday life.

Neither did a single damned thing out of the ordinary with one large and overriding exception. Their very presence in Stockholm was out of the ordinary.

At the beginning of the third week, when their routine had been established, Henty and I cracked the apartment. Ashton had gone to the cinema and Benson was doing his Bobby Fischer bit over a half-litre of Carlsberg and we would have an hour or longer. We searched that flat from top to bottom and did not find much.

The main prize was Ashton's passport. It was of Israeli issue, three years old, and made out in the name of Fyodr Antono-vitch Koslov who had been born in Odessa in 1914. I photographed every page, including the blank ones, and put it back where I found it. A secondary catch was the counterfoil stub of a used cheque-book. I photographed that thoroughly, too. Ashton was spending money quite freely; his casual expenses were running to nearly £500 a week.

The telephone rang. Henty picked it up and said cautiously, *'Vilket nummer vill ni ha?'* There was a pause. 'Okay.' He put down the receiver. 'Benson's left the pub; he's on his way back.'

I looked around the room. 'Everything in order?'

'I reckon so.'

'Then let's go.' We left the building and sat in Henty's car until Benson arrived. We saw him safely inside, checked his escort, then went away.

Early next morning I gave Cutler the spools of film and re-quested negatives and two sets of prints. I got them within the hour and spent quite a time checking them before my prear-ranged telephone call from Ogilvie. It had to be prearranged because he had to have a scrambler compatible with that at the Embassy.

Briefly I summarized the position up to that point, then said, 'Any breakthrough will come by something unusual—an oddity—and there are not many of those. There's the Israeli passport—I'd like to know if that's kosher. I'll send you the photographs in the diplomatic bag.'

'Issued three years ago, you say?'

'That's right. That would be about the time a bank account was opened here in the name of Koslov. The apartment was rented a year later, also in the name of Koslov; it was sublet until four months ago when Ashton moved in. Our friend had everything prepared. I've gone through cheque stubs covering nearly two months. Ashton isn't stinting himself.'

'How is he behaving? Psychologically, I mean.'

'I've seen him only three times, and then at a distance.' I thought for a moment. 'My impression is that he's more re-laxed than when I saw him last in England; under less of a strain.' There didn't seem much else to say. 'What do I do now?'

'Carry on,' said Ogilvie succinctly.

I sighed. 'This could go on for weeks—months. What if I tackled him myself? There's no need to blow my cover. I can get myself accredited to an international trade conference that's coming up next week.'

'Don't do that,' said Ogilvie. 'He's sharper than anyone realizes. Just keep watching; something will turn up.'

Yes, Mr Micawber, I thought, but didn't say it. What I said was, 'I'll put the negatives and prints into the diplomatic bag immediately.'

Two more weeks went by and nothing happened. Ashton went on his way serenely, doing nothing in particular. I had another, more extended, look at him and he seemed to be enjoying himself in a left-handed fashion. This was possibly the first holiday he'd ever had free from the cares of the businesses he had created. Benson pottered about in the shops and markets of Gamla Stan most mornings, doing his none-too-frugal shopping, and we began to build up quite a picture of the culinary tastes of the *ménage* Ashton. It didn't do us one damned bit of good.

Henty went about his own mysterious business into which I didn't enquire too closely. I do know that he was in some form of military intelligence because he left for a week and went north to Lapland where the Swedish Army was holding winter manoeuvres. When he came back I saw him briefly and he said he'd be busy writing a report.

Four days later he came to see me with disturbing information. 'Do you know there's another crowd in on the act?'

I stared at him. 'What do you mean?'

'I've got a bump of curiosity,' he said. 'Last night, in my copious spare time, I checked to see whether Cutler's boys were up to snuff. Ashton is leading quite a train—our chap follows Ashton and someone else follows him.' I was about to speak but he held up his hand. 'So I checked on Benson and the same is happening there.'

'Cutler's said nothing about this.'

'How would he know?' said Henty scathingly. 'Or any of them. They're amateurs.'

I asked the crucial question. 'Who?'

Henty shrugged. 'My guess is Swedish Intelligence. Those boys are good. They'd be interested in anyone with a Russian name, and even more interested to find out he's under surveillance. They'll have made the connection with the British Embassy by now.'

'Damn!' I said. 'Better not let Cutler know or he'll have diplomatic kittens. I think this is where we join in.'

Next morning, when Ashton took his morning constitutional, we were on the job. Ashton appeared and collected the first segment of his tail who happened to be Askrigg. Henty nudged me and pointed out the stranger who fell in behind. 'That's our joker. I'll cross the road and follow him. You stay on this side and walk parallel, keeping an eye on both of us.'

By God, but Henty was good! I tried to watch both him and the man he was following but Henty was invisible half the time, even though I knew he was there. He bobbed back and forth, letting the distance lengthen and then closing up, disappearing into shop entrances and reappearing in unexpected places and, in general, doing his best not to be there at all. Two or three times he was even in front of the man he was shadowing.

It was one of Ashton's book mornings. He visited two bookshops and spent about three-quarters of an hour in each, then he retired with his plunder to a coffee-house and inspected his purchases over coffee and Danish pastries. It was pretty funny. The coffee-house was on the corner of a block. Askrigg waited outside while, kitty corner across the street, his follower stamped his feet to keep warm while ostensibly looking into a shop window. The third corner held Henty, doing pretty much the same, while I occupied the fourth corner. My own wait was made risible by the nature of the shop in which I was taking an intent interest. Henty was outside a camera shop. Mine sold frilly lingerie of the type known pungently as passion fashion.

Out came Ashton and the train chugged off again, and he led us back to where we had started, but going home by the Vasabron just to make a variation. So far the whole thing was a bust, but better times were coming. Our man went into a tobacconist's shop and I followed. As I bought a packet of cigarettes I heard him speaking in low tones on the telephone.

141

I couldn't hear what he said but the intonation was neither English nor Swedish.

He left the shop and walked up the street while I followed on the other side. A hundred yards up the street he crossed, so I did the same; then he reversed direction. He was doing what he hoped was an unobtrusive patrol outside Ashton's flat.

Fifteen minutes later came the event we'd waited for—his relief arrived. The two men stood and talked for a few moments, their breath steaming and mingling in the cold air, then my man set off at a smart pace and I followed. He turned the corner which led around the back of the Royal Palace, and when I had him in sight again he was dickering with a taxi-driver.

I was figuring out how to say, 'Follow that car!' in Swedish when Henty pulled up alongside in his car. I scrambled in, and Henty said in satisfaction, 'I thought he might do that. We've all had enough walking for the day.' I've said he was good.

So we followed the taxi through Stockholm, which was not particularly difficult, nor did he take us very far. The taxi pulled up outside a building and was paid off, and our man disappeared inside. Henty carried on without slackening speed. 'That does it!' he said expressively.

I twisted in my seat and looked back. 'Why? What is that place?'

'The bloody Russian Embassy.'

TWENTY

I expected my report on that to bring action but I didn't expect it to bring Ogilvie. I telephoned him at three in the afternoon and he was in my room just before midnight, and four other men from the department were scattered about the hotel, Ogilvie drained me dry, and I ended up by saying 'Henty and I did the same this evening with the man following Benson. He went back to a flat on Upplandsgatan. On checking, he proved to be a commercial attaché at the Russian Embassy.'

Ogilvie was uncharacteristically nervous and indecisive. He paced the room as a tiger paces its cage, his hands clasped behind his back; then he sat in a chair with a thump. 'Damn it all to hell!' he said explosively. 'I'm in two minds about this.'

I waited, but Ogilvie did not enlarge on what was on either of his minds, so I said diffidently, 'What's the problem?'

'Look, Ashton hasn't given us what we expected when we sprung him from Russia. Oh, he's done a lot, but in a purely commercial way—not the advanced scientific thought we wanted. So why the hell should we care if he plays silly buggers in Stockholm and attracts the attention of the Russians?'

Looked at in a cold and calculating way that was a good question. Ogilvie said, 'I'd wash my hands of him—let the Russians take him—but for two things. The first is that I don't *know* why he ran, and the hell of it is that the answer might be quite unimportant. It's probably mere intellectual curiosity on my part, and the taxpayer shouldn't be expected to finance that. This operation is costing a packet.'

He stood up and began to pace again. 'The second thing is that I can't get that empty vault out of my mind. Why did he build it if he didn't intend to use it? Have you thought of that, Malcolm?'

'Yes, but I haven't got very far.'

Ogilvie sighed. 'Over the past months I've read and reread

Ashton's file until I've become cross-eyed. I've been trying to get into the mind of the man. Did you know it was he who suggested taking over the persona of a dead English soldier?'

'No. I thought that was Cregar's idea.'

'It was Chelyuskin. As I read the file I began to see that he works by misdirection like a conjuror. Look at how he got out of Russia. I'm more and more convinced that the vault is another bit of misdirection.'

'An expensive bit,' I said.

'That wouldn't worry Ashton—he's rolling in money. If he's got something, he's got it somewhere else.'

I was exasperated. 'So why did he build the safe in the first place?'

'To tell whoever opened it that they'd reached the end of the line. That there are no secrets. As I say—misdirection.'

'It's all a bit fanciful,' I said. I was tired because it was late and I'd been working hard all day. Hammering the ice-slippery streets of Stockholm with my feet wasn't my idea of pleasure, and I was past the point of coping with Ogilvie's fantasies about Ashton. I tried to bring him to the point by saying, 'What do we do about Ashton now?' He was the boss and he had to make up his mind.

'How did the Russians get on to Ashton here?'

'How would I know?' I shrugged. 'My guess is that they got wind of a free-spending fellow-countryman unknown to Moscow, so they decided to take a closer look at him. To their surprise they found he's of great interest to British Intelligence. That would make them perk up immediately.'

'Or, being the suspicious lot they are, they may have been keeping tabs on the British Embassy as a matter of routine and been alerted by the unaccustomed activity of Cutler and his mob, who're not the brightest crowd of chaps.' Ogilvie shrugged. 'I don't suppose it matters how they found out; the fact is that they have. They're on to Koslov but have not, I think, made the transition to Ashton—and certainly not to Chelyuskin.'

'That's about it. They'll never get to Chelyuskin. Who'd think of going back thirty years?'

'Their files go back further, and they'll have Chelyuskin's fingerprints. If they ever do a comparison with Koslov's prints they'll know it wasn't Chelyuskin who died in that fire. They'd be interested in that.'

'But is it likely?'

'I don't know.' He scowled in my direction but I don't think he saw me; he was looking through me. 'That Israeli passport is quite genuine,' he said. 'But stolen three years ago. The real Koslov is a Professor of Languages at the University of Tel Aviv. He's there right now, deciphering some scrolls in Aramaic.'

'Do the Israelis know about our Koslov? That might be tricky.'

'I shouldn't think so,' he said absently. Then he shook his head irritatedly. 'You don't think much of my theories about Ashton, do you?'

'Not much.'

The scowl deepened. 'Neither do I,' he admitted. 'It's just one big area of uncertainty. Right. We can do one of two things. We can pull out and leave Ashton to sink or swim on his own; or we can get him out ourselves.' Ogilvie looked at me expectantly.

I said, 'That's a policy decision I'm not equipped to make. But I do have a couple of comments. First, any interest the Russians have in Ashton has been exacerbated by ourselves, and I consider we have a responsibility towards him because of that. For the rest—what I've seen of Ashton I've liked and, God willing, I'm going to marry his daughter. I have a personal reason for wanting to get him out which has nothing to do with guessing what he's been doing with his peculiar mind.'

Ogilvie nodded soberly. 'Fair enough. That leaves it up to me. If he really has something and we leave him for the Russians then I'll have made a big mistake. If we bring him out, risking an international incident because of the methods we may have to use, and he has nothing, then I'll have made a big mistake. But the first mistake would be bigger than the second, so the answer is that we bring him out. The decision is made.'

TWENTY-ONE

Ogilvie had brought with him Brent, Gregory, Michaelis and, to my surprise, Larry Godwin, who looked very chipper because not only had he got away from his desk but he'd gone foreign. We had an early morning conference to discuss the nuts and bolts of the operation.

Earlier I had again tackled Ogilvie. 'Why don't I approach Ashton and tell him the Russians are on to him? That would move him.'

'In which direction?' asked Ogilvie. 'If he thought for one moment that British Intelligence was trying to manipulate him I wouldn't care to predict his actions. He might even think it better to go back to Russia. Homesickness is a Russian neurosis.'

'Even after thirty years?'

Ogilvie shrugged. 'The Russians are a strange people. And have you thought of his attitude to you? He'd immediately jump to wrong conclusions—I won't risk the explosion. No, it will have to be some other way.'

Ogilvie brought the meeting to order and outlined the problem, then looked about expectantly. There was a lengthy pause while everyone thought about it. Gregory said, 'We have to separate him from the Russians before we can do anything at all.'

'Are we to assume he might defect to Russia?' asked Brent.

'Not if we're careful,' said Ogilvie. 'But it's a possibility. My own view is that he might even be scared of the Russians if he knew they were watching him.'

Brent threw one in my direction. 'How good are the Russians here?'

'Not bad at all,' I said. 'A hell of a lot better than Cutler's crowd.'

'Then it's unlikely they'll make a mistake,' he said glumly. 'I

146

thought if he knew the Russians were on to him he might cut and run. That would give us the opportunity for a spoiling action.'

Ogilvie said, 'Malcolm and I have discussed that and decided against it.'

'Wait a minute,' I said, and turned to Larry. 'How good is your conversational Russian?'

'Not bad,' he said modestly.

'It will have to be better than not bad,' I warned. 'You might have to fool a native Russian.' I didn't tell him Ashton *was* a Russian.

He grinned. 'Which regional accent do you want?'

Ogilvie caught on. 'I see,' he said thoughtfully. 'If the Russians don't make a mistake we make it for them. I'll buy that.'

We discussed it for a while, then Michaelis said, 'We'll need a back-up scheme. If we're going to take him out against his will we'll need transport, a safe house and possibly a doctor.'

That led to another long discussion in which plans were hammered out and roles allocated. Kidnapping a man can be complicated. 'What about Benson?' asked Gregory. 'Is he included in the deal?'

'I rather think so,' said Ogilvie. 'I'm becoming interested in Benson. But the primary target is Ashton. If it ever comes to a choice between taking Ashton or Benson, then drop Benson.' He turned to Michaelis. 'How long do you need?'

'If we use Plan Three we don't need a house, and the closed van I can hire inside an hour. But I'll have to go to Helsingborg or Malmo to arrange for the boat and that will take time. Say three days.'

'How long across the strait to Denmark?'

'Less than an hour; you can nearly spit across it. But someone will have to organize a receiving committee in Denmark.'

'I'll do that.' Ogilvie stood up and said with finality, 'Three days, then; and we don't tell Cutler anything about it.'

Three days later the operation began as planned and started well. The situation in Gamla Stan was becoming positively ridiculous: two of Cutler's men were idling away their time in antique shops ready for the emergence of Ashton and Benson and unaware that they were being watched by a couple of

147

Russians who, in their turn, were not aware of being under the surveillance of the department. It could have been a Peter Sellers comedy.

Each of our men was issued with a miniature walkie-talkie with strict instructions to stay off the air unless it was absolutely necessary to pass on the word. We didn't want to alert the Swedes that an undercover operation was under way; if they joined in there'd be so many secret agents in those narrow streets there'd be no room for tourists.

I sat in my car, strategically placed to cover the bridges leading from Gamla Stan to the central city area, and kept a listening watch. Ogilvie stayed in his room in the hotel next to the telephone.

At ten-thirty someone came on the air. 'Bluebird Two. Redbird walking north along Västerlånggatan.' Ashton was coming my way so I twisted in my seat to look for him. Presently he rounded the corner and walked up the road next to the Royal Palace. He passed within ten feet of me, striding out briskly. I watched him until he turned to go over Helgeandsholmen by way of Norrbro, then switched on the car engine. Ahead I saw Larry slide out of his parking place and roll along to turn on to Norrbro. His job was to get ahead of Ashton.

I followed behind, passing Ashton who was already carrying a tail like a comet, crossed Norrbro and did a couple of turns around Gustav Adolfs Torg, making sure that everything was in order. I saw Gregory leave his parking place to make room for Larry; it was important that Larry should be in the right place at the right time. Michaelis was reserving a place further west should Ashton have decided to go into town via the Vasabron. I switched on my transmitter and said to him, 'Bluebird Four to Bluebird Three; you may quit.'

At that point I quit myself because there was nothing left to do—everything now depended on Larry. I drove the short distance to the Grand Hotel, parked the car, and went to Ogilvie's room. He was nervous under his apparent placidity. After a few minutes' chat he said abruptly, 'Do you think Godwin is up to it? He's not very experienced.'

'And he never will be if he's not given the chance.' I smiled. 'He'll be all right. Any moment from now he'll be giving his celebrated imitation of an inexperienced KGB man. From that point of view his inexperience is an asset.'

Time wore on. At twelve-thirty Ogilvie had smörgåsbord sent up to the room. 'We might as well eat. If anything breaks you'll be eating on the run from now on.'

At five to one the telephone rang. Ogilvie handed me a pair of earphones before he picked up the receiver. It was Brent, who said, 'Redbird is lunching at the Opera—so am I and so is everyone else concerned. He's looking a bit jumpy.'

'How did Godwin handle first contact?'

'Redbird went into that corner bookshop on the Nybroplan. Godwin was standing next to him when he barked his shin on a shelf; Larry swore a blue streak in Russian and Redbird jumped a foot. Then Larry faded out as planned.'

'And then?'

'Redbird wandered around for a bit and then came here. I saw him get settled, then signalled Larry to come in. He took a table right in front of Redbird who looked worried when he saw him. Larry has just had a hell of a row with a waiter in very bad, Russian-accented Swedish—all very noisy. Redbird is definitely becoming uncomfortable.'

'How are the others taking it?'

'The real Russians look bloody surprised. Cutler's chap ... wait a minute.' After a pause Brent chuckled. 'Cutler's chap is heading for the telephones right now. I think he wants to report that the Russians have arrived. I think I'll let him have this telephone.'

'Stay with it,' said Ogilvie. 'Stick to Ashton.' He replaced the receiver and looked up. 'It's starting.'

'Everything is ready,' I said soothingly. I picked up the telephone and asked the hotel operator to transfer my calls to Ogilvie's room.

We had not long to wait. The telephone rang and I answered. Cutler said, 'Jaggard, there may be an important development.'

'Oh,' I said seriously. 'What's that?'

'My man with Ashton seems to think the Russians are interested.'

'In Ashton?'

'That's right.'

'Oh. That's bad! Where is Ashton now?'

149

'Lunching at the Opera. Shall I put someone on to the Russian? There may be time.'

Ogilvie had the earphone to his ear and shook his head violently. I grinned, and said, 'I think not. In fact I think you'd better pull out all your men as soon as you can get word to them. You don't want the Russians to know you're on to Ashton, do you?'

'My God, no!' said Cutler quickly. 'We can't have the Embassy involved. I'll do as you say at once.' He rang off, seeming relieved.

Ogilvie grunted. 'The man's an idiot. He's well out of it.'

'It does clear the field,' I said, and put on my jacket. 'I'm going over to Gamla Stan for the beginning of the second act. If Larry does his stuff we should get a firm reaction from Ashton.' I paused. 'I don't like doing it this way, you know. I'd much prefer we talk to him.'

'I know,' said Ogilvie sombrely. 'But your preferences don't count. Get on with it, Malcolm.'

So I got on with it. I went to Gamla Stan and met Henty in a bar-restaurant on Västerlånggatan, joining him in a snack of herring and aquavit. He had been watching the flat, so I said, 'Where's Benson?'

'Safe at home. His Russian is still with him but Cutler's boy was vanished. Maybe Benson lost him.'

'No. Cutler is no longer with us.' I described what had happened.

Henty grinned. 'Something should break any moment then.' He finished his beer and stood up. 'I'd better get back.'

'I'll come with you.' As we left I said, 'You're our Swedish expert. Supposing Ashton makes a break—how can he do it?'

'By air from Bromma or Arlanda, depending on where he's going. He can also take a train. He doesn't have a car.'

'Not that we know of. He could also leave by sea.'

Henty shook his head. 'At this time of year I doubt it. There's a lot of ice in the Baltic this year—the Saltsjön was frozen over this morning. It plays hell with their schedules. If I were Ashton I wouldn't risk it; he could get stuck on a ship which didn't move for a few hours.'

The bone-conduction contraption behind my ear came to

life. 'Bluebird Two. Redbird by Palace heading for Väster-långgatan and moving fast.' Bluebird Two was Brent.

I said to Henty, 'He's coming now. You go on ahead, spot him and tag that bloody Russian. I don't want Ashton to see me.'

He quickened his pace while I slowed down, strolling from one shop window to the next. Presently there came the news that Ashton was safely back home, and then Henty came back with Larry Godwin. Both were grinning, and Henty remarked, 'Ashton's in a muck sweat.'

I said to Larry, 'What happened?'

'I followed Ashton from the Opera—very obviously. He tried to shake me; in fact, he did shake me twice, but Brent was able to steer me back on course.'

Henty chuckled. 'Ashton came along Västerlånggatan doing heel-and-toe as though he was in a walking race, with Godwin trying hard for second place. He went through his doorway like a rabbit going down a hole.'

'Did you speak to him, Larry?'

'Well, towards the end I called out, "*Grazhdaninu* Ashton—*ostanovites!*" as though I wanted him to stop. It just made him go faster.'

I smiled slightly. I doubt if Ashton relished being called 'citizen' in Russian, especially when coupled with his English name. 'The ball is now in Ashton's court, but I doubt he'll move before nightfall. Larry, go and do an ostentatious patrol before Ashton's flat. Be a bit haphazard—reappear at irregular intervals.'

I had a last word with Henty, and then did the rounds, checking that every man was in his place and the Russians were covered. After that I reported by telephone to Ogilvie.

Larry caught up with me in about an hour. 'One of those bloody Russians tackled me,' he said. 'He asked me what the hell I thought I was doing.'

'In Russian?'

'Yes. I asked him for his authority and he referred me to a Comrade Latiev in the Russian Embassy. So I got a bit shirty and told him that Latiev's authority had been superseded, and if Latiev didn't know that himself he was even more stupid than Moscow thought. Then I said I didn't have time to waste and did a quick disappearing act.'

'Not bad,' I said. 'It ought to hold Comrade Latiev for a while. Any reaction from the flat?'

'A curtain did twitch a bit.'

'Okay. Now, if Ashton makes his break I don't want him to see you—we don't want to panic him more than necessary. Take over Gregory's car, ask him what the score is, and send him to me.'

It was a long wait and a cold wait. The snow came down steadily and, as darkness fell, a raw mist swept over Gamla Stan from the Riddarfjärden, haloing the street lights and cutting down visibility. I spent the time running over and over in my mind the avenues of escape open to Ashton and wondering if my contingency planning was good enough. With Henty there were six of us, surely enough to take out the two Russians and still keep up with Ashton wherever he went. As the mist thickened I thought of the possibility of taking Ashton there and then, but thought better of it. A quiet kidnapping in a major city is hard enough at the best of times and certainly not the subject for improvisation. Better to follow the plan and isolate Ashton.

It happened at ten to nine. Gregory reported Ashton and Benson on Lilla Nygatan moving south, and both had bags. Michaelis chipped in and said that both Russians were also on the move. I summoned up my mental map of Gamla Stan and concluded that our targets were heading for the taxi rank by the Centralbron, so I ordered the cars south ready to follow. More interestingly, on the other side of the Centralbron, in the main city, was Stockholm's Central Railway Station.

Then I ordered Michaelis and Henty, our best strong-arm men, to take the Russians out of the game. They reported that, because of the mist, it was easy and that two Russians would have sore heads the following morning.

After that things became a bit confused. When Ashton and Benson reached the taxi rank they took separate cabs, Benson going over the Centralbron towards the railway station, and Ashton going in the dead opposite direction towards Södermalm. Larry followed Benson, and Brent went after Ashton. I got busy and ordered the rest of the team to assemble at the railway station which seemed the best bet under the circumstances.

At the station I stayed in the car and sent in Henty to find out if Larry was around. He came back with Larry who got into the car, and said, 'Benson bought two tickets for Göteborg.'

They were heading west. From my point of view that was a relief; better west than east. I said, 'When does the train leave?'

Larry checked his watch. 'In a little over half an hour. I bought us four tickets—and I got a timetable.'

I studied the timetable and thought out loud. 'First stop—Söderätlje; next stop—Eskilstuna. Right.' I gave a ticket each to Gregory and Henty. 'You two get on that train; spot Ashton and Benson and report back by radio. Then stick with them.'

They went into the station, and Larry said, 'What do we do?'

'You and I lie as low as Br'er Rabbit.' I turned to Michaelis. 'Scout around in the station and see if you can spot Ashton. Make sure he's on that train when it leaves, then come back here.'

He went away and I wondered how Brent was getting on. Presently Gregory radioed in. 'We're on the train—spotted Redbird Two—but no Redbird One.'

We'd lost Ashton. 'Stay with it.'

The time ticked by. At five minutes to train-time I became uneasy, wondering what had happened to Ashton. At two minutes to train-time Brent pitched up. 'I lost him,' he said hollowly.

'Where did he go?'

'He went bloody island-hopping—Södermalm—Långholmen—Kungsholmen; that's where I lost him. He seemed to be heading in this general direction at the time so I took a chance and came here.'

'We haven't seen him, and he's not on the train so far. Benson is, though; with two tickets to Göteborg.'

'When does it leave?'

I looked over his shoulder and saw Michaelis coming towards the car. He was shaking his head. I said, 'It's just left—and Ashton wasn't on it.'

'Oh, Christ! What do we do now?'

'The only thing we can do—stick with Benson and pray. And this is how we do it. Get yourself a timetable like this one, and check the stops of that train. You and Michaelis take the first stop—that's Södertälje; you check with Gregory and Henty on the train and you team up if Benson gets off. You also report to Ogilvie. In the meanwhile Larry and I will be heading for the next stop at Eskilstuna—same procedure. And so we leapfrog up the line until the train arrives at Göteborg or anything else happens. Got that?'

'Okay.'

'Reporting to Ogilvie is very important because he can keep us all tied in. I'm going to ring him now.'

Ogilvie wasn't at all pleased but he didn't say much—not then. I told him how I was handling it and he just grunted. 'Carry on—and keep me posted.'

I went back to the car, slumped into the passenger seat, and said to Larry, 'Drive to Eskilstuna—and beat that train.'

TWENTY-TWO

From Stockholm to Eskilstuna is about 100 kilometres. The first 40 kilometres are of motorway standard and we were able to make good time, but after that it became more of an ordinary road with opposing traffic and our average speed dropped. It was very dark—a moonless night—but even if there had been a moon it wouldn't have helped because there was a thick layer of cloud from which descended a heavy and continuous fall of snow.

Like all modern Swedish cars ours was well equipped for this kind of weather. The tyres had tungsten-steel studs for traction and the headlights had wipers to clear the encrusting snow, but that didn't mean fast driving and I suppose we didn't average more than 70 KPH and that was a shade fast for the conditions. Neither Larry nor I could be classed as rally drivers, and I was very much afraid the train would be faster. Fortunately, I saw by the map that it had further to go, the track sweeping round in a loop. Also it would stop at Södertälje.

After an hour I told Larry to pull into a filling station where he refuelled while I phoned Ogilvie. When I got back to the car I was smiling, and Larry said, 'Good news?'

'The best. I'll drive.' As we pulled away I said, 'Ashton tried to pull a fast one. When Brent lost him he wasn't on his way to the railway station in Stockholm; he took a taxi ride to the Södertälje station and got on the train there. We've got them both now.'

Thus it was that I was quite happy when we pulled up outside the railway station at Eskilstuna to find the train standing at the platform. I switched on my transmitter, and said, 'Any Bluebirds there? Come in, Bluebirds.'

A voice said in my ear. 'Redbird and friend jumped train.'

'What the hell?'

Henty said, 'What do you want me to do?'

'Get off that bloody train and come here. We're parked outside the station.' Even as I spoke the train clanked and began to move slowly. I was beginning to wonder if Henty had made it when I saw him running towards the car. I wound down the side window. 'Get in and tell me what, for Christ's sake, happened.'

Henty got into the back seat. 'The train pulled up at some bloody whistle-stop called Åkers-styckebruk, and don't ask me why. Nothing happened until it began to move out, then Ashton and Benson jumped for it. Gregory went after them but it was too late for me—and the way he went he was like to break a leg.'

I got out the road map and studied it. 'Åkers-styckebruk! The place isn't even on the map. Have you reported to Ogilvie?'

'No. I was just going to when you called me.'

'Then I suppose I'll have to.'

I went into the station and rang Stockholm, and Ogilvie said testily, 'What the devil's going on? I've just had a call from Gregory in some God-forsaken place. He's either broken or sprained his ankle and he's lost Ashton. He thinks they've gone to somewhere called Strängnäs.'

Strängnäs was back along the road; we'd skirted around the edges. I said, 'We'll be there in an hour.'

'An hour may be too late,' he snapped. 'But get on with it.'

I ran back to the car. 'Get weaving, Larry—back where we came from.' He moved over into the driving seat and I hadn't closed the door before he took off. I twisted around and said to Henty, 'What can you tell me about Strängnäs? Anything there we ought to know about?'

He snapped his fingers. 'Of course! There's a spur-line going into Strängnäs from Åkers-styckebruk—no passenger trains, just the occasional *räslbuss*.'

'What's that?'

'A single coach on the railway—diesel driven.'

'You say it's a spur-line. You mean the rail stops at Strängnäs?'

'It has to, or it would run into Lake Mälaren.'

I contemplated that. 'So it's a dead end.'

'For the railway, but not for cars. There's a road which goes by way of the islands to the north shore of Mälaren. But it's late; I wouldn't bet they'll be able to hire a car at this time of night.'

'True,' I said. 'But step on it, Larry.' I watched the road unwinding out of the darkness against the hypnotic beat of the wipers as they cleared snow from the windscreen. The headlights brightened as Larry operated the light wipers. 'Anything else about Strängnäs?'

'It's not much of a place,' said Henty. 'Population about twelve thousand; a bit of light industry—pharmaceuticals, penicillin, X-ray film—stuff like that. It's also a garrison town for a training regiment, and it's HQ, East Military Command.' His interest sharpened. 'Is Ashton connected with the soldier boys?'

'No,' I said.

Henty persisted. 'You'd tell me if he is? That's my line of country, and I've helped you enough.'

'Definitely not,' I said. 'His interests aren't military, and neither are mine. We're not poaching on your patch.'

'Just so long as I know.' He seemed satisfied.

We didn't bother going back all the way to Åkers-styckebruk; finding Ashton was more important than finding the state of Gregory's ankle. We came to the outskirts of Strängnäs and coasted gently through snow-covered streets towards the lake edge and the centre of town. A few turns around the town centre proved one thing—there was only one hotel—so we pulled up on the other side of the street from the Hotel Rogge and I sent Henty in to find out the form.

He was away about five minutes and when he came back he said, 'They're both there—booked under the names of Ashton and Williams.'

'So he's reverted,' I said. 'Using his own passport. Koslov has suddenly become too hot.'

'I booked in for the three of us.'

'No; you stay, but Larry and I are going to find Gregory. I'll ring Ogilvie now and ask him to retrieve Brent and Michaelis from wherever the hell they are now—they can have the other two beds here. We'll be back at six tomorrow morning and I want a concentration inside and outside the hotel. Where are Ashton and Benson now?'

'Not in any of the public rooms,' said Henty. 'I'd say they're in bed.'

'Yes, they're getting pretty old for this sort of thing,' I said pensively. 'Come to think of it, so am I.'

TWENTY-THREE

Gregory had sensibly waited at the railway station at Åkers-styckebruk for someone to pick him up. He said he was stiff, cold, tired, and that his ankle hurt like hell, so we all booked into a hotel. At five next morning Larry and I were on our way back to Strängnäs, but Gregory was able to sleep in because I decided to send him back to Stockholm. He'd be no good to us because his ankle really was bad, but he had the satisfaction of knowing that, because of him, we'd pinned down Ashton and Benson.

Just before six I parked the car around the corner from the Hotel Rogge, and at six on the button I went on the air. 'Hello,' I said brightly. 'Any Bluebirds awake?'

Henty said disgruntedly into my ear, 'Don't be so bloody cheerful.'

'Did the other two arrive?'

'Yes; at two this morning. They're still asleep.'

'And Redbird and his friend?'

'They're definitely here—I made sure of that—they're asleep, too.' He paused. 'And I wish to Christ I was.'

'Come out here. We're just around the corner on——' I craned my neck to find a street sign—'on Källgatan.'

He said nothing but the transmission hum stopped so I switched off. He did not appear for a quarter of an hour so Larry and I made small talk. There was nothing much to say because we'd talked the subject to death already. When Henty did arrive he was newly shaved and looked in reasonably good shape even though his manner was still a little shaggy. 'Morning,' he said shortly, as he got into the car.

I passed a vacuum flask over my shoulder. 'Be gruntled.'

He unscrewed the top and sniffed appreciatively. 'Ah, scotch coffee!' He poured a cupful and was silent for a moment before he said, 'That's better. What's the drill?'

'What time is breakfast?'

'I don't know. Say, from seven o'clock—maybe seven-thirty. These country hotels all differ.'

'I want the three of you in the breakfast room as soon as it opens; you at one table, Michaelis and Brent at another. They are to talk to each other and one of them has to give a running commentary over the air about Ashton and Benson as soon as they come in to breakfast. I want to know exactly how Ashton is acting—and reacting.'

'We can do that,' said Henty. 'But I don't get the reason.'

I said, 'Half way through breakfast I'm going to send Larry in to do a replay of his Russian act.'

'Jesus! You'll give Ashton a heart attack.'

'We've got to keep the pressure on,' I said. 'I don't want to give them time to hire a car, and I want to herd them out of town pretty early. Where's the closed van Michaelis has been driving?'

Henty pointed across the darkened street. 'In the hotel car park.'

'Good enough. I want him inside it and ready to go as soon as Ashton moves. I want this whole bloody thing cleaned up before eight o'clock if possible. Now you can go in and wake the sleeping beauties.'

When Henty had gone Larry regarded me curiously. 'I know you've been keeping out of sight,' he said. 'But if what you're doing ever comes out you're not going to be popular with the Ashton family.'

'I know,' I said shortly. 'But this is the way Ogilvie wants it done. And I'm making bloody sure I do stay out of sight, not for Ogilvie's reasons but my own.' Christ! I thought. If Penny ever got to know about this she'd never forgive me in a thousand years.

The time passed and we shared the flask of scotch coffee between us. Strängnäs began to wake up and there was movement in the streets, and we occasioned a couple of curious glances from passers-by. I suppose it was strange for a couple of men to be sitting in a parked car so early in the morning so I told Larry to drive into the hotel car park which was more secluded.

The hotel breakfast started at seven-thirty. I knew that because Jack Brent came on the air with a description of the breakfast he was eating. He described the herring and the boiled eggs and the cheese and the coffee and all the trimmings until I began to salivate. He was doing it deliberately, the bastard.

Because I made no response he tired of the game and switched off, but at seven-fifty he said, 'They're here now—Ashton and Benson. Just sitting down—two tables away. Benson looks dour but Ashton seems cheerful enough.'

No one would know Brent was broadcasting; apparently he would be chatting animatedly to Michaelis, but every word was picked up by the throat microphone concealed beneath the knot of his tie. The throat microphone gave a peculiarly dead quality to the broadcast; there was no background noise —no clatter of cutlery or coffee cups to be heard—just Brent's voice and the rasp of his breathing greatly magnified. Even if he spoke in a whisper every word would come across clearly.

I listened to his description and felt increasingly uneasy. Not about Ashton who, according to Brent, seemed fairly relaxed; I was uneasy about myself and my role in this charade. I would have given a lot to be able to walk into the Hotel Rogge, sit at Ashton's table, and have a down-to-earth chat with him. I was convinced I could get him back to England just by talking to him, but Ogilvie wouldn't have that. He didn't want our cover blown.

I was depressed when I turned to Larry and said quietly 'All right. Go in and have your breakfast.' He got out of the car and walked into the hotel.

Brent said, 'Ashton's just poured himself another cup of coffee. He hasn't lost his appetite, that's for certain. Ho, ho! Larry Godwin has just walked in. Ashton hasn't seen him yet, nor has Benson. Larry's talking to the waitress by the door. God, how he's mangling his Swedish—can hear him from here. So can Ashton. He's turned and he's looking at Larry. I can't see his face. He's turned back again and now he's nudging Benson. He's as white as a sheet. The waitress is coming forward with Larry now—showing him to a table. Larry is passing Ashton's table—he turns and speaks to him. Ashton has knocked over his coffee cup. Benson is looking bloody grim; if ever I saw a man capable of murder it's Benson right now.

He's no oil painting at the best of times but you should see him now. Ashton wants to get up and leave, but Benson is holding him back.'

I switched channels on my transmitter and Brent's voice abruptly stopped. I said, 'Henty, finish your breakfast and leave. Cover the front of the hotel. Michaelis, same for you, but get in your van and cover the back.'

I reversed out of the hotel car park and drove a little way up Källgatan and parked where I could see the front entrance of the hotel. When I switched back to Brent he was saying '... looks pretty shattered and Benson is talking to him urgently. I think he's having a hard job keeping control. You'd think it would be the other way round because Benson is only Ashton's servant. Anyway, that's what it looks like from here—Ashton wants to make a break and Benson is stopping him. Larry isn't doing much—just eating his breakfast—but every now and then he looks across at Ashton and smiles. I don't think Ashton can take much more of it. I'll have to stop now because Michaelis is leaving and I'll look bloody funny talking to myself.'

He stopped speaking and the transmission hum ceased. I keyed my transmitter. 'Larry, when Ashton and Benson leave follow them from behind with Brent.' I saw Henty come out of the hotel and walk across the street. Michaelis came next and walked around to the car park where he disappeared from sight.

Ten minutes later Ashton and Benson appeared, each carrying a bag. They stepped out on to the pavement and Ashton looked up and down the street uncertainly. He said something to Benson who shook his head, and it looked as though there was a difference of opinion. Behind them Larry appeared in the hotel entrance.

I said, 'Larry, go and talk to Ashton. Ask him to follow you. If he agrees, take him to the van and put him in the back.'

'And Benson?'

'Him, too—if possible.'

Ashton became aware that Larry was watching him and pulled at Benson's arm. Benson nodded and they began to walk away but stopped at Larry's call. Larry hurried over to them and began talking and, as he did so, Brent came out and stood close to them.

I heard the one-way conversation. Larry talked fast in Russian and twice Ashton nodded, but Benson made interjections, each time accompanied by a headshake, and tried to get Ashton away. At last he succeeded and the pair of them walked off, leaving Larry flat. They were coming straight towards me so I ducked out of sight.

While I was down on the car floor I spoke to Larry. 'What happened?'

'Ashton nearly came, but Benson wouldn't have it. He spoiled it.'

'Did Benson speak Russian?'

'No, English; but he understood my Russian well enough.'

'Where are they now?'

'Going up the street—about thirty yards past your car.'

I emerged from hiding and looked in the mirror. Ashton and Benson were walking away quickly in the direction of the railway station.

After that it all became a little bit sick because we literally herded them out of town. They found the railway station blocked by Brent, and when they tried to duck back to the town centre they were confronted by Larry and Henty. They soon became aware they had a quartet of opponents and, twist and turn as they might, they found themselves being driven to the edge of town. And all the time I orchestrated the bizarre dance, manipulating them like puppets. I didn't like myself at all.

At last we got to the main Stockholm–Eskilstuna road and they plunged across, Benson nearly being hit by a speeding car which went by with a wailing blast of horn. There were no more streets or houses on the other side—just an infinity of pine trees. I had Michaelis go back and pick up the van, and sent the other three into the forest while I parked my car before following. It seemed as though the chase was nearly over—you can't be more private than in a Swedish forest.

They made better time over rough country than I would have expected of two elderly men. Ashton had already proved his fitness to me, but I hadn't expected Benson to have the stamina because he was a few years older than Ashton. Once in the trees you couldn't see far and they kept foxing us by changing direction. Twice we lost them; the first time we picked them up by sheer luck, and the second time, by finding their abandoned bags. And all the time I was leading from the rear, directing the operation by radio.

We had gone perhaps three kilometres into the forest and the going was becoming rougher. Where the ground was not slippery with snow and ice it was even more slippery with pine needles. The ground rose and fell, not much but enough to take your breath away on the uphill slopes. I paused at the top of one such slope just as Brent said in my ear, 'What the hell was that?'

'What?'

'Listen!'

I listened, trying to control my heavy breathing, and heard a rattle of shots in the distance. They seemed to come from somewhere ahead, deeper in the forest.

'Someone hunting,' said Larry.

Brent said incredulously, 'With a machine-gun!'

'Quiet!' I said. 'Is Ashton spotted?'

'I'm standing looking into a little valley,' said Henty. 'Very few trees. I can see both Ashton and Benson—they're about four hundred yards away.'

'That's all very well, but where the hell are you?'

'Just keep coming ahead,' said Henty. 'It's a long valley— you can't miss it.'

'Everybody move,' I said. Again came the sound of firing, this time a sporadic rattling of badly-spaced single shots. Certainly not a machine-gun as Brent had suggested. It could have been the shoot-out at the OK Corral, and I wondered what was happening. Hunters certainly didn't pop off like that.

I pressed on and presently came to a crest where I looked down into the valley. Henty was right; it was relatively treeless and so the snow was thicker. In the distance I saw Ashton and Benson moving very slowly; perhaps they were hampered by the snow, but I thought the chase was telling on them. Henty was at the valley bottom below me, and Brent and Larry were together, bounding down the hillside, closing in on our quarry from an angle.

Again came firing and, by God, this time it was machine-gun

fire, and from more than one machine-gun. Then there came some deeper coughs, followed by thumping explosions. In the distance, not too far ahead, I saw a haze of smoke drifting above the trees on the far side of the valley.

Henty had stopped. He looked back at me and waved, and said over the radio, 'I know what it is. This is an army exercise area. They're having war games.'

'Live ammunition?'

'Sounds like it. Those were mortars.'

I began to run, bouncing and slithering down the slope. When I got to the bottom I saw that Brent and Larry were within fifty yards of Ashton and gaining on him fast. Ashton switched direction, and I yelled, 'Brent—Larry—fall back!'

They hesitated momentarily but then went on, caught in the lust of the chase. I shouted again. 'Fall back! Don't drive him into the guns.'

They checked, but I ran on. I was going to speak to Ashton myself, regardless of what Ogilvie had said. This was a sick game which had to be stopped before somebody was killed. Ashton was climbing the other side of the valley, heading towards the trees on the crest, but going very slowly. Benson was nowhere to be seen. I ran until I thought my chest would burst, and gained on Ashton.

At last I was close enough, and I shouted, 'Ashton— George Ashton—stop!'

He turned his head and looked back at me as a further burst of firing came, and more explosions of mortar bombs. I took off the fur hat I was wearing and threw it away so that he could get a good look at me. His eyes widened in surprise and he hesitated in his upward climb, then stopped and turned around. Brent and Larry were coming in on my left and Henty on the right.

I was about to call out to him again when there was another single shot, this time from quite close, and Ashton stumbled forward as though he had tripped. I was within ten yards of him and heard him gasp. Then there was another shot and he whirled around and fell and came rolling down the slope towards me to stop at my feet.

I was aware that Henty had passed me and momentarily saw a gun in his fist, then I bent over Ashton. He coughed once and blood trickled from the corner of his mouth. His eyes still held surprise at the sight of me, and he said, 'Mal ... colm ... what ...'

I said, 'Take it easy, George,' and put my hand inside his coat. I felt a warm wetness.

He scrabbled in his pocket for something and said, 'The ... the...' His hand came up before my face with the fist clenched. 'The ... the...' Then he fell back, his eyes still open and looking at the sky with deeper surprise. A snowflake fell and settled on his left eyeball, but he didn't blink.

In the distance mortars thumped and machine-guns rattled, and there were more single shots, again from quite close. I looked down at Ashton and cursed quietly. Brent crunched over the snow. 'Dead?'

I withdrew my hand and looked at the blood. Before wiping it clean on the snow I said, 'You try his pulse.'

I stood up as Brent knelt and thought of the unholy mess we—I—had made of the operation. The snow around Ashton's body was changing colour from white to red. Brent looked up at me. 'Yes, he's dead. From the amount of blood here the aorta must have been cut. That's why he went so fast.'

I had never felt so bad in my life. We had driven Ashton towards the guns as beaters drive an animal. It was so stupid a thing to do. I didn't feel very human at that moment.

Henty came crunching down the slope, carrying a pistol negligently in his right hand. 'I got him,' he said matter-of-factly.

I could smell the faint reek of cordite as he came closer. 'Got who, for Christ's sake?'

'Benson.'

I stared at him. *'You shot Benson!'*

He looked at me in surprise. 'Well, he shot Ashton, didn't he?'

I was stupefied. 'Did he?'

'Of course he did. I saw him do it.' Henty turned and looked up the slope. 'Maybe you couldn't see him from this angle—but I did.'

I was unable to take it in. *'Benson* shot Ashton!'

'He bloody nearly shot me,' said Henty. 'He took a crack at

me as soon as I showed myself up there. And if anyone shoots at me I shoot back.'

It had never occurred to me to ask Henty if he was armed. Nobody else was on Ogilvie's instructions, but Henty was from another department. I was still gaping at him when there was a grinding rattle from above and a tank pointed its nose over the crest and began to come down into the valley. Its nose was a 105 mm high-velocity tank gun which looked like a 16-incher as the turret swivelled to cover our small group. They wouldn't have bothered to use that, though; the machine-gun in the turret of that Centurion was capable of taking care of us much more economically.

As the tank stopped I dropped to my knees next to Ashton's body. The turret opened and a head popped out, followed by a torso. The officer raised his anti-flash goggles and surveyed us with slightly popping eyes. Henty moved, and the officer barked, '*Stopp!*' With a sigh Henty tossed his pistol aside in the snow.

I opened Ashton's clenched fist to look at what he had taken from his pocket. It was a crumpled railway timetable of the route from Stockholm to Göteborg.

TWENTY-FOUR

I don't know what sort of heat was generated at a higher level but the Swedes never treated me with anything less than politeness—icy politeness. If I had thought about it all that cold correctitude would have been more frightening than anything else, but I wasn't thinking during that period—I was dead inside and my brains were frozen solid.

The Swedes had found two dead men and four live men on army territory. One of the dead men had two passports, one stolen and the other genuine; the other had three passports, all false. The passports of the four live men were all genuine. It was claimed that one of the dead men had shot the other and, in turn, was shot and killed by one of the live men, an Australian living and working in Sweden. He had no permit for a gun.

It was all very messy.

Ogilvie was out of it, of course, and so were Michaelis and Gregory. Michaelis had waited with the van at the road, but when a squad of infantry in full battle order debouched from the forest and systematically began to take my car to pieces he had tactfully departed. He drove back into Strängnäs and rang Ogilvie who pulled him back to Stockholm. And what Ogilvie heard from the Embassy made him decide that the climate of London was more favourable than the chilliness of Stockholm. The three of them were back in London that night and Cutler was saying, 'I told you so.'

The four of us were taken to the army barracks in Strängnäs, HQ the Royal Södermanland Regiment and HQ East Military Command. Here we were searched and eyebrows were lifted at the sight of our communications equipment. No doubt conclusions were duly drawn. We weren't treated badly; they fed us, and if what we ate was representative of army rations then the Swedish Army does a damned sight better than the British

Army. But we were not allowed to talk; a stricture reinforced by two hefty Swedes armed with sub-machine-guns.

After that I was led into an empty room and, just as I thought the interrogation was about to begin, a civilian arrived and began being nasty to the military. At least, that's the impression I had judging by the rumble of voices from the office next door. Then an army colonel and a civilian came in to see me and, having seen me, went away without saying a word, and I was transferred into a cell in which I spent the next three weeks apart from an hour's exercise each day. During that time I didn't see the others at all, and the Swedes wouldn't give me the time of day, so I ought to have been pretty lonely, but I wasn't. I wasn't anything at all.

I was awakened one morning at three a.m., taken into an ablutions block and told to take a shower. When I came out I found my own clothes—the army fatigues I had been wearing had disappeared. I dressed, checked my wallet and found everything there, and put on my watch. The only things missing were my passport and the radio.

I was marched smartly across the dark and snow-covered parade ground and shown into an office where a man dressed in civilian clothes awaited me. He wasn't a civilian though, because he said, 'I am Captain Morelius.' He had watchful grey eyes and a gun in a holster under his jacket. 'You will come with me.'

We went outside again to a chauffeur-driven Volvo, and Captain Morelius didn't say another word until we were standing on the apron at Arlanda Airport over three hours later. Then he pointed to a British Airways Trident, and said, 'There is your aircraft, Mr Jaggard. You realize you are no longer welcome in Sweden.' And that is all he said.

We walked to the gangway and he handed a ticket to a steward who took me inside and installed me in a first-class seat. Then they let on the common herd and twenty minutes later we were in the air. I had good service from that steward who must have thought I was a VIP, and I appreciated the first drink I had had for nearly a month.

When we landed at Heathrow I wondered how I was going to get by without a passport; I certainly didn't feel like going into tedious explanations. But Ogilvie was waiting for me and we walked around Passport Control and Customs. Once in his car he asked, 'Are you all right, Malcolm?'

'Yes.' I paused. 'I'm sorry.'

'Not to worry,' he said. 'We'll leave the explanations for later.'

Going into town he talked about everything except what had happened in Sweden. He brought me up-to-date on the news, talked about a new show that had opened, and generally indulged in light chit-chat. When he pulled up outside my flat he said, 'Get some sleep. I'll see you in my office tomorrow.'

I got out of the car. 'Wait! How's Penny?'

'Quite well, I believe. She's in Scotland.'

'Does she know?'

He nodded, took out his wallet, and extracted a newspaper cutting. 'You can keep that,' he said, and put the car into gear and drove away.

I went up to the flat and its very familiarity seemed strange. I stood looking around and then realized I was holding the newspaper cutting. It was from *The Times*, and read:

KILLED IN SWEDEN

Two Englishmen, George Ashton (56) and Howard
Greatorex Benson (64) were killed near Strängnäs,
Sweden, yesterday when they wandered on to a
firing range used by the Swedish army. Both
men died instantaneously when they were caught
in a shell explosion.
A Swedish army spokesman said that the area was
adequately cordoned and that all roads leading
into it were signposted. Announcements of the
proposed firing of live ammunition were routinely
made in the local newspaper and on the radio.

The dateline of the story was five days after Ashton and Benson died.

TWENTY-FIVE

When I walked into my office Larry Godwin was sitting at his desk reading *Pravda* and looking as though he had never left it. He looked up. 'Hello, Malcolm.' He didn't smile and neither did I. We both knew there was nothing to smile about.

'When did you get back?'

'Three days ago—the day after Jack Brent.'

'Henty?'

He shook his head. 'Haven't seen him.'

'How did they treat you?'

'Not bad. I felt a bit isolated, though.'

'Has Ogilvie debriefed you?'

Larry grimaced. 'He emptied me as you'd empty a bottle of beer. I still feel gutted. It'll be your turn now.'

I nodded, picked up the telephone, and told Ogilvie's secretary I was available. Then I sat down to contemplate my future and couldn't see a damned thing in the fog. Larry said, 'Someone knew the right strings to pull. I tell you, I wasn't looking forward to a stretch in a Swedish jail. They'd have put us in their version of Siberia—up in the frozen north.'

'Yes,' I said abstractedly. I wondered what *quid pro quo* the Swedes had claimed for our release and their silence.

Ogilvie called me in twenty minutes later. 'Sit down, Malcolm.' He bent to his intercom. 'No more calls for the rest of the morning, please,' he said ominously, then looked at me. 'I think we have a lot to talk about. How are you feeling?'

I felt he really wanted to know, so I said, 'A bit drained.'

'The Swedes treat you all right?'

'No complaints.'

'Right. Let's get to the crux. Who killed Ashton?'

'Of my own knowledge I don't know. At the time I thought he'd caught a couple from the Swedes—there was a lot of shooting going on. Then Henty told me Benson had shot him.'

171

'But you didn't see Benson shoot him.'

'That's correct.'

Ogilvie nodded. 'That fits with what Godwin and Brent told me. Now, who killed Benson?'

'Henty said he did it. He said he saw Benson shooting at Ashton so he drew his own gun and went after him. Apparently Benson was at the top of the slope in the trees. He said that Benson shot at him, too, so he shot back and killed him. I didn't even know Henty was armed.'

'Have you thought why Benson should have killed Ashton? It's not the normal thing for an old family retainer to do to his master.'

A humourless thought crossed my mind: in the less inventive early British detective stories it was always the butler who committed the murder. I said, 'I can think of a reason but it doesn't depend on Benson's status as a servant.'

'Well?'

'Henty was coming up on my right, and Brent and Godwin angling in from the left. Ashton was just above, but there was a big boulder screening me from the top of the slope. I didn't see Benson and I don't think he saw me. But he did see Larry, and Larry was a Russian, remember. When Ashton stopped and turned, and showed signs of coming down, then Benson shot him.'

'To prevent him falling into the hands of the Russians. I see.'

I said, 'And that makes him something more than a family servant.'

'Possibly,' said Ogilvie. 'But I've been going into the history of Howard Greatorex Benson and the man is as pure as the driven snow. Born in Exeter in 1912, son of a solicitor; normal schooling but flunked university entrance to his father's disappointment. Did clerical work for a firm in Plymouth and rose to be the boss of a rather small department. Joined the army in 1940—rose to be a sergeant in the RASC—he was an ideal quarter-master type. Demobilized in 1946, he went to work for Ashton, running the firm's office. There he ran into the Peter Principle; he was all right as long as the firm remained small but, with expansion, it became too much for him. Remember he never rose to be more than sergeant—he was a small-scale man. So Ashton converted him into a general factotum which would seem to be ideal for Benson. There'd be nothing too big for him to handle, and he was glad to be of service. Ashton probably got his money's worth out of him. He never married. What do you think of all that?'

'Did you get that from the computer?'

'No. The brains are still baffled. They're telling me now Benson can't be in the data bank.'

'They're wrong,' I said flatly. 'He popped up when I asked Nellie.'

Ogilvie looked at me doubtfully, then said, 'But what do you think of his history as I've related it?'

'There's nothing there to say why he should kill Ashton. There's nothing there to say why he should be carrying a gun in the first place. Did he have a pistol permit?'

'No.'

'Have you traced the gun?'

Ogilvie shrugged. 'How can we? The Swedes have it.' He pondered for a moment, then opened a quarto-sized, hard-backed notebook and took the cap off his pen. 'I wanted to go for the main point first, but now you'll tell me, in detail, every-thing that happened right from the time Ashton and Benson left their flat in Stockholm.'

That took the rest of the morning. At quarter to one Ogilvie recapped his pen. 'That's it, then. Now you can go home.'

'Am I suspended from duty?'

He looked at me from under lowered eyebrows. 'There are a few people around who would like to see you fired. Others favour a transfer to the Outer Hebrides so you can counter industrial espionage into the production of Harris Tweed; they're talking about a twenty-year tour of duty. Have you any idea of the trouble this enterprise of ours has caused?'

'I have a good imagination.'

He snorted. 'Have you? Well, imagine how the Swedes felt about it, and imagine their reaction when we began to put on the pressure at a high level. It got up to the Cabinet, you know, and the Ministers aren't at all happy. They're talking about bungling amateurs.'

I opened my mouth to speak, but he held up his hand. 'No, you're not suspended from duty. What you did was under my instruction, and I can't see that you could have done differently given the circumstances. Neither of us expected Benson to kill Ashton, so if anyone carries the can it's me, as head of the department. But this department is now under extreme pressure. There's an inter-departmental meeting tomorrow morning at eleven at which the screws will begin to turn. You will be required to attend. So you will go away now and come back here at ten-fifteen tomorrow, rested and refreshed, and prepared to have a hard time. Do you understand?'

'Yes.'

'And I would be obliged if you do not disclose to the committee that you are aware of the Ashton file in Code Black. We're in enough trouble already.'

I stood up. 'All right, but I'd like to know one thing—what happened to the bodies?'

'Ashton and Benson? They were brought back to England two weeks ago. There was a funeral service in Marlow and they are buried in adjoining graves in the cemetery there.'

'How did Penny take it?'

'As you might expect. Both the daughters were hit rather badly. I wasn't there myself, of course, but I was informed of the circumstances. I managed to have word passed to Miss Ashton that you were in America but were expected back in the near future. I thought that advisable.'

Advisable and tactful. 'Thanks,' I said.

'Now go away and prepare your thoughts for tomorrow.' I walked towards the door, and he added, 'And, Malcolm: regardless of how the meeting goes, I want you to know there is much still to be explained about the Ashton case—and it will be explained. I am becoming very angry about this.'

As I left I thought that Ogilvie angry might be formidable indeed.

I was left to my own thoughts for a long time while the committee meeting was in progress; it was twelve-fifteen before an usher entered the ante-room and said, 'Will you come this way, Mr Jaggard.' I followed him and was shown into a large, airy room overlooking an inner courtyard somewhere in Westminster.

There was a long, walnut table around which sat a group of

men, all well-dressed and well-fed, and all in late middle-age. It could have been the annual meeting of the directors of a City bank but for the fact that one of them wore the uniform of a Commander of the Metropolitan Police and another was a red-tabbed colonel from the General Staff. Ogilvie twisted in his chair as I entered and indicated I should take the empty seat next to him.

Chairing the meeting was a Cabinet Minister whose politics I didn't agree with and whose personality I had always thought of as vacillating in the extreme. He showed no trace of vacillation that morning, and ran the meeting like a company sergeant-major. He said, 'Mr Jaggard, we have been discussing the recent Swedish operation in which you were involved, and in view of certain differences of opinion Mr Ogilvie has suggested that you appear to answer our questions yourself.'

I nodded, but the colonel snorted. 'Differences of opinion is putting it mildly.'

'That has nothing to do with Mr Jaggard, Colonel Morton,' said the Minister.

'Hasn't it?' Morton addressed me directly. 'Are you aware, young man, that you've lost me my best man in Scandinavia? His cover is blown completely.'

I concluded that Morton was Henty's boss.

The Minister tapped the table with his pen and Morton subsided. 'The questions we shall ask are very simple and we expect clear-cut, unequivocal answers. Is that understood?'

'Yes.'

'Very well. Who killed Ashton?'

'I didn't see who shot him. Henty told me it was Benson.'

There was a stir from lower down the table. 'But you don't know that he did, other than that you had been told so.'

I turned and looked at Lord Cregar. 'That is correct. But I have, and still have, no reason to disbelieve Henty. He told me immediately after the event.'

'After he had killed Benson?'

'That's right.'

Cregar regarded me and smiled thinly. 'Now, from what you know of Benson, and I'm assuming you had the man investigated, can you give me one reason why Benson should kill the man he had so faithfully served for thirty years?'

175

'I can think of no sound reason,' I said.

His lip curled a little contemptuously. 'Can you think of any unsound reasons?'

Ogilvie said tartly, 'Mr Jaggard is not here to answer stupid questions.'

The Minister said sharply, 'We shall do better if the questions are kept simple, as I suggested.'

'Very well,' said Cregar. 'Here is a simple question. Why did you order Henty to kill Benson?'

'I didn't,' I said. 'I didn't even know he was armed. The rest of us weren't; those were Mr Ogilvie's instructions. Henty was in a different department.'

Colonel Morton said, 'You mean Henty acted on his own initiative?'

'I do. It all happened within a matter of, say, twenty seconds. At the time Benson was killed I was trying to help Ashton.'

Morton leaned forward. 'Now, think carefully, Mr Jaggard. My men are not in the habit of leaving bodies carelessly strewn about the landscape. What reason did Henty give for shooting Benson?'

'Self-defence. He said Benson was shooting at him, so he shot back.'

Colonel Morton leaned back and appeared satisfied, but Cregar said to the company at large, 'This man, Benson, seems to be acting more and more out of character. Here we have an old age pensioner behaving like Billy the Kid. I find it unbelievable.'

Ogilvie dipped his fingers into a waistcoat pocket and put something on to the table with a click. 'This is a round of 9 mm parabellum found in Benson's room in Marlow. It would fit the pistol found with Benson's body. And we know that the bullet recovered from Ashton's body came from that pistol. We got that from the Swedes.'

'Precisely,' said Cregar. 'All you know is what the Swedes told you. How much is that really worth?'

'Are you suggesting that Benson did not kill Ashton?' asked Morton. There was a note of sourness in his voice.

'I consider it highly unlikely,' said Cregar.

'I don't employ men who are stupid enough to lie to me,' said Morton, in a voice that could cut diamonds. 'Henty said he saw Benson kill Ashton, and I believe him. All the evidence we have heard so far does not contradict that.'

Ogilvie said, 'Unless Lord Cregar is suggesting that my department, Colonel Morton's department and Swedish Army Intelligence are in a conspiracy to put the blame for Ashton's death on Benson and so shield the killer.' His voice was filled with incredulity.

The uniformed Commander guffawed and Cregar flushed. 'No,' he snapped. 'I'm just trying to get to the bottom of something damned mysterious. Why, for instance, *should* Benson shoot Ashton?'

'He is not here to be asked,' said the Minister coolly. 'I suggest we stop this chasing of hares and address ourselves to Mr Jaggard.'

The Commander leaned forward and talked to me around Ogilvie. 'I'm Pearson—Special Branch. This Swedish operation isn't in my bailiwick but I'm interested for professional reasons. As I take it, Mr Ogilvie did not want Ashton to become aware that British Intelligence was taking note of him. Do you know why?'

That was a tricky one because I wasn't supposed to know who Ashton really was. I said, 'I suggest you refer that question to Mr Ogilvie.'

'Quite so,' said the Minister. 'It involves information to which Mr Jaggard is not privy.'

'Very well,' said Pearson. 'At the same time he wanted Ashton out of Sweden because the Russians had become attracted, so he put pressure on Ashton by having a man pretend to be Russian and thus "explode Ashton out of Sweden", as he has put it. What I don't understand is why this kidnapping attempt in Strängnäs was necessary. Why did you try it?'

I said, 'They took tickets from Stockholm to Göteborg. That was all right with me. I intended to shepherd them along and, if they took ship from Göteborg to find out where they were going. The important thing was to get them out from under the Russians in Sweden. But when they gave us the slip and went to Strängnäs it became something more complex than a discreet escort operation. Stronger measures were necessary as sanctioned by Mr Ogilvie.'

'I see,' said Pearson. 'That was the point I misunderstood.'

'I misunderstood something, too,' said Cregar. 'Are we to assume that your instructions precluded the disclosure of yourself to Ashton?'

'Yes.'

'Yet according to what I've been told you did so. We have been informed by Mr Ogilvie this morning that you showed yourself to him deliberately. It was only when he saw you that he turned back. Is that not so?'

'That's correct.'

'So you disobeyed orders.'

I said nothing because he hadn't asked a question, and he barked, 'Well, didn't you?'

'Yes.'

'I see. You admit it. Now, with all respect to Colonel Morton's trust in the truthfulness of his staff, I'm not satisfied by the somewhat misty evidence presented here that Benson shot Ashton; but the fact remains that Ashton was shot by someone, and it is highly likely that he was shot *because* he turned back. In other words, he died because you disobeyed an order not to disclose yourself.' His voice was scathing. 'Why did you disobey the order?'

I was seething with rage but managed to keep my voice even. 'The idea was not to kill Ashton but to bring him out alive. At that time he was going into grave danger. There was heavy fire in that part of the forest where he was heading—machine-guns and mortars, together with rifle fire. Just what was going on I didn't know. It seemed imperative to stop him and he did stop and started to come back. That he was shot by Benson came as a complete shock.'

'But *you* don't know he was shot by Benson,' objected Cregar.

The Minister tapped with his pen. 'We have already been over that ground, Lord Cregar.'

'Very well.' Cregar regarded me and said silkily, 'Wouldn't you say that your conduct of this whole operation, right from the beginning, has been characterized by, shall we say, a lack of expertise?'

Ogilvie bristled. 'What Mr Jaggard has done has been on my direct instruction. You have no right or authority to criticize my staff like this. Address your criticisms to me, sir.'

'Very well, I will,' said Cregar. 'Right at the beginning I objected to your putting Jaggard on this case, and all the...'

'That's not my recollection,' snapped Ogilvie.

Cregar overrode him. '... all the events since have proved my point. He let Ashton slip from under his nose at a time when he had free access to Ashton's home. That necessitated the Swedish operation which he has also botched, and botched for good, if I may say so, because Ashton is now dead. As for claiming that all he did was on your direct instruction, you have just heard him admit to disobeying your orders.'

'He used his initiative at a critical time.'

'And with what result? The death of Ashton,' said Cregar devastatingly. 'You have expounded before on the initiative of this man. I wasn't impressed then, and I'm still less impressed now.'

'That will be enough,' said the Minister chillily. 'We will have no more of this. Are there any more questions for Mr Jaggard? Questions that are both simple and relevant, please.' No one spoke, so he said, 'Very well, Mr Jaggard. That will be all.'

Ogilvie said in an undertone, 'Wait for me outside.'

As I walked to the door Cregar was saying, 'Well, that's the end of the Ashton case—after thirty long years. He was a failure, of course; never did come up to expectations. I suggest we drop it and get on to something more productive. I think ...'

What Cregar thought was cut off by the door closing behind me.

They came out of committee twenty minutes later. Ogilvie stuck his head into the ante-room. 'Let's have lunch,' he proposed. He didn't seem too depressed at what had happened, but he never did show much emotion.

As we were walking along Whitehall he said, 'What do you think?'

I summoned a hard-fought-for smile. 'I think Cregar doesn't like me.'

'Did you hear what he said as you were leaving?'

'Something about the Ashton case being over, wasn't it?'

'Yes. Ashton is buried and that buries the Ashton case. He's wrong, you know.'

'Why?'

'Because from now on until everything is accounted for and wrapped up you are going to work full time on the Ashton case.' He paused, then said meditatively, 'I wonder what we'll find.'

TWENTY-SIX

In view of what had been said at the meeting Ogilvie's decision came as a profound surprise. The worst possibility that had come to mind was that I would be fired; drummed out of the department after my special card had been put through the office shredding machine. The best that occurred to me was a downgrading or a sideways promotion. I had the idea that Ogilvie had not been entirely joking when he had spoken of the Hebrides. That he was carrying on with the Ashton case, and putting me in charge, gave me a jolt. I wondered how he was going to make it stick with the Minister.

He told me. 'The Minister won't know a damned thing about it.' He gave me a wintry smile. 'The advantage of organisations like ours is that we really are equipped to work in secret.'

This conversation took place in the privacy of his office. He had refused to speak of the case at all after dropping his bombshell and the luncheon conversation had been innocuous. Back at the office he plunged into the heart of it.

'What I am about to do is unethical and possibly mutinous,' he said. 'But, in this case, I think I'm justified.'

'Why?' I asked directly. If I was going to be involved I wanted to know the true issues.

'Because someone has done a conjuring trick. This department has been deceived and swindled. Who organized the deception is for you to find out—it may have been Ashton himself, for all we know. But I want to know who organized it, and why.'

'Why pick me? As Cregar made plain, I've not done too well up to now.'

Ogilvie raised his eyebrows. 'You think not? You've satisfied me, and I'm the only man who matters. There are several reasons why I've picked you. First, you're the totally unexpected choice. Secondly, you are still the inside man in the Ashton family. Thirdly, I have complete confidence in you.'

I stood up and went to the window. A couple of pigeons were engaged in amorous play on the window ledge but flew away as I approached. I turned and said, 'I'm grateful for your thirdly, but not too happy about your secondly. As you know, I dropped into the middle of the Ashton case sheerly by chance and ever since then my private life has been intolerably disturbed. I have just harried a man to his death and you expect me to be *persona grata* with his daughters?'

'Penelope Ashton doesn't know of your involvement. I made sure of that.'

'That's not the point, and you know it,' I said sharply. 'You're too intelligent a man not to know what I mean. You're asking me to live a lie with the woman I want to marry—if she still wants to marry me, that is.'

'I appreciate the difficulty,' said Ogilvie quietly. 'You mustn't think I don't. But ...'

'And don't ask me to do it for the good of the department,' I said. 'I hope I have higher loyalties than that.'

Ogilvie quirked his eyebrows. 'Your country, perhaps?'

'Even than that.'

'So you believe with E. M. Forster that if you had to choose between betraying your country and betraying your friend you would hope to have the guts to betray your country. Is that it?'

'I'm not aware that betraying my country comes into this,' I said stiffly.

'Oh, I don't know,' said Ogilvie musingly. 'Betrayal takes many forms. Inaction can be as much betrayal as action, especially for a man who has chosen your work of his own will. If you see a man walking on a bridge which you know to be unsafe, and you do not warn him so that he falls to his death, you are guilty in law of culpable homicide. So with betrayal.'

'Those are mere words,' I said coldly. 'You talk about betrayal of the country when all I see is an interdepartmental squabble in which your *amour-propre* has been dented. You loathe Cregar as much as he loathes you.'

Ogilvie looked up. 'How does Cregar come into this? Do you know something definite?'

'He's been trying to poke his nose in, hasn't he? Right from the very beginning.'

'Oh, is that all,' said Ogilvie tiredly. 'It's just the nature of the beast. He's a natural scorer of points; it feeds his enormous ego. I wouldn't jump to conclusions about Cregar.' He stood and faced me. 'But I really am sorry about your opinion of me. I thought I deserved better than that.'

'Oh, Christ!' I said. 'I'm sorry; I didn't really mean that. It's just that this thing with Penny has me all mixed up. The thought of talking to her—lying to her—makes me cringe inside.'

'Unfortunately it goes with the job. We're liars by profession, you and I. We say to the world we work for McCulloch and Ross, economic and industrial consultants, and that's a lie. Do you think my wife and daughters really know what I do? I lie to them every minute of every day merely by existing. At least Penny Ashton knows what you are.'

'Not all of it,' I said bitterly.

'You're not to blame for Ashton's death.'

I raised my voice. 'No? I drove him to it.'

'But you didn't kill him. Who did?'

'Benson did, damn it!'

Ogilvie raised his voice to a shout. 'Then find out why, for God's sake! Don't do it for me, or even for yourself. All her life that girl of yours has been living in the same house as the man who eventually murdered her father. Find out why he did it—you might even be doing it for her sake.'

We both stopped short suddenly and there was silence in the room. I said quietly, 'You might have made your point—at last.'

He sat down. 'You're a hard man to convince. You mean I've done it?'

'I suppose so.'

He sighed. 'Then sit down and listen to me.' I obliged him, and he said, 'You're going to be in disgrace for a while. Everybody will expect that, including the Minister. Some sort of downgrading is indicated, so I'm going to make you a courier. That gives you freedom of action to move around in this country, and even out of it.' He smiled. 'But I'd hesitate about going back to Sweden.'

So would I. Captain Morelius would become positively voluble, even to the extent of speaking three consecutive sentences. And I knew what he'd say.

'We've been making quite a noise in here,' said Ogilvie. 'Had a real shouting match. Well, that will add verisimilitude to an otherwise bald and unconvincing narrative. There's one thing about being in an organization of spies—news gets around fast. You may expect some comments from your colleagues; can you stand that?'

I shrugged. 'I've never worried much about what people think of me.'

'Yes,' he agreed. 'Cregar discovered that when he first met you. All right; you'll have complete autonomy on this job. You'll do it in the way you want to do it, but it will be a solo operation; you'll have all the assistance I can give you short of men. You'll report your results to me and to no one else. And I do expect results.'

He opened a drawer and took out a slim file. 'Now, as for Penny Ashton, I laid some groundwork which will possibly help you. As far as she knows you have been in America for the past few weeks. I hope you didn't write from Sweden.'

'I didn't.'

'Good. She has been tactfully informed that you have been away on some mysterious job that has debarred you from writing to her. Knowing what she thinks she knows about your work it should seem feasible to her. However, you were informed of her father's death through the department, and you sent this cable.'

He passed the slip of paper across the desk. It was a genuine Western Union carbon copy emanating from Los Angeles. The content was trite and conventional, but it would have to do.

Ogilvie said, 'You also arranged for wreaths at the funeral through a Los Angeles flower shop and Interflora. The receipt from the flower shop is in this file together with other bits and pieces which a man might expect to pick up on a visit and still retain. There are theatre ticket stubs for current shows in Los Angeles, some small denomination American bills, book matches from hotels, and so on. Empty your pockets.'

The request took me by surprise and I hesitated. 'Come now,' he said. 'Dump everything on the desk.'

184

I stripped my pockets. As I took out my wallet Ogilvie delved in the small change I had produced. 'You see,' he said in triumph, and held up a coin. 'A Swedish crown mixed with your English money. It could have been a dead give-away. I'll bet you have a couple of Swedish items in your wallet. Get rid of them.'

He was right. There was a duplicate bar bill from the Grand which had yet to be transferred to my expense account, and a list of pound-kroner exchange rates made when I was trying to keep up with the vagaries of the falling pound sterling. I exchanged them for the Americana, and said, 'You were sure of me, after all.'

'Pretty sure,' he said drily. 'You got back from the States yesterday. Here is your air ticket—you can leave it lying around conspicuously somewhere. Penny Ashton, to the best of my knowledge, is coming back from Scotland tomorrow. You didn't buy any Swedish clothing?'

'No.'

'There are a couple of shirts and some socks in that small case over there. Also some packets of cigarettes. All genuine American. Now, leave here, go back to your office and mope disconsolately. You've just been through the meat grinder and you can still feel the teeth. I expect Harrison will want to see you in about an hour. Don't try to score any points off him; let him have his little triumph. Remember you're a beaten man, Malcolm—and good luck.'

So I went back to the office and slumped behind my desk. Larry rustled his paper and avoided my eye, but presently he said, 'I hear you were with with the top brass all morning.'

'Yes,' I said shortly.

'Was Gregar there?'

'Yes.'

'Bad?'

'You'll know all about it soon,' I said gloomily. 'I don't think I'll be around here much longer.'

'Oh.' Larry fell silent for a while, then he turned a page and said, 'I'm sorry Malcolm. It wasn't your fault.'

'Somebody has to get the axe.'

'Mmm. No, what I meant is I'm sorry about you and Penny. It's going to be difficult.'

I smiled at him. 'Thanks, Larry. You're right, but I think I'll make out.'

Ogilvie was right in his prediction. Within the hour Harrison rang and told me to report to his office. I went in trying to appear subdued and for once did not address him as Joe, neither did I sit down.

He kept me standing. 'I understand from Mr Ogilvie that you are leaving this section.'

'I understand so, too.'

'You are to report to Mr Kerr tomorrow.' His eyes glinted with ill-suppressed joy. He had always thought me too big for my britches and now I was demoted to messenger-boy—thus are the mighty fallen. 'This is really very difficult, you know,' he said fretfully. 'I'm afraid I'll have to ask you to clean out your desk before you leave today. There'll be another man coming in, of course.'

'Of course,' I said colourlessly. 'I'll do that.'

'Right,' he said, and paused. I thought for a moment he was going to give me a homily on the subject of mending my ways, but all he said was, 'You may leave, Jaggard.'

I went and cleared out my desk.

TWENTY-SEVEN

I trotted in to see Kerr next morning. He was one of several Section heads, but his Section was the only one to make a financial profit because, among other things, it ran the legitimate side of McCulloch and Ross, the bit the public knew about. It made a good profit, too, and so it ought; if it made a loss with all the professional expertise of the other Sections behind it then Kerr ought to have been fired. Under Kerr also came several other miscellaneous bits and pieces including the couriers—the messenger-boys.

He seemed somewhat at a loss as to how to deal with me. 'Ah, yes—Jaggard. I think I have something here for you.' He handed me a large, thick envelope, heavily sealed. 'I'm told you know where to deliver that. It appears that ... er ... delivery may take some time, so you may be absent for a period.'

'That's so.'

'I see,' he said blankly. 'Will you be needing desk space—an office?'

'No, I don't think so.'

'I'm glad. We're tight for space.' He smiled. 'Glad to have you ... er ... with us,' he said uncertainly. I don't know what Ogilvie had told him but evidently he was baffled by my precise status.

In my car I opened the envelope and found £1000 in used fivers. That was thoughtful of Ogilvie but, after all, I could hardly claim expenses in the normal way on this operation. I put the money in the special locker built under the front passenger seat and drove to the police station in Marlow where I asked for Honnister. He came out front to meet me. 'You haven't been around for a while,' he said, almost accusingly. 'I've been trying to get you.'

'I've been in the States for a few weeks. What did you want me for?'

'Oh, just a chat,' he said vaguely. 'You must have been away when Ashton and Benson were killed in Sweden.'

'Yes, but I was told of it.'

'Funny thing, Ashton going away like that.' There was a glint in his eye. 'And then getting messily killed. Makes a man wonder.'

I took out a packet of cigarettes and offered it. 'Wonder what?'

'Well, a man like Ashton makes his pile by working hard and then, when he's still not too old to enjoy it, he suddenly gets dead.' He looked at the packet in my hand. 'No, I don't like American coffin nails. They take good Virginia tobacco, mix it with Turkish, then roast it and toast it and ultra-violet-ray it until it tastes like nothing on God's earth.'

I shrugged. 'Everybody dies. And you can't take it with you, although they tell me Howard Hughes tried.'

'Seen Penelope Ashton?'

'Not yet.' I lit a cigarette although I didn't like them, either. 'I'll be going to the house. I hear she's expected back today. If she's not there I'll see Gillian, anyway.'

'And she'll see you,' said Honnister. 'But only barely. I had a talk with Crammond. He tells me Mayberry hasn't been brought to trial, and it's not likely that he will. He's unfit to plead.'

'Yes, I know about that.'

Honnister eyed the desk sergeant and then pushed himself upright from the counter. 'Let's have a noggin,' he proposed. I agreed quickly because it meant he wanted to talk confidentially and I was short of information. On the way to the pub he said, 'You didn't come to chat for old times' sake. What are you after?'

I said, 'When we started investigating we concentrated on Ashton and didn't look too closely at Benson, although at one point it did cross my mind that he might have chucked the acid.'

'Not the act of an old family servant.'

Neither was drilling his master full of holes—but I didn't say that aloud. 'Did you check on him?'

We turned into the Coach and Horses. 'A bit; enough to put him in the clear.' Honnister addressed the landlord. 'Hi, Monte; a large scotch and a pint of Director's.'

'My shout,' I said.

'It's okay—I'm on an expense account.'

I smiled. 'So am I.' I paid for the drinks and we took them to a table. It happened to be the same table at which I'd proposed marriage to Penny; it seemed a lifetime ago. It was early, just before midday, and the pub was quiet. I said, 'I've developed an interest in Benson.'

Honnister sank his nose into his beer. When he came up for air he said, 'There's been something funny going on in the Ashton family. This will have to be tit-for-tat, you know.'

'I'll tell you as much as I'm allowed to.'

He grunted. 'A fat lot of good that'll do me.' He held up his hand. 'All right, I know your lips are sealed and all that bull, and that I'm just a bumbling country copper who doesn't know which end is up—but tell me one thing; was Ashton kidnapped?'

I smiled at Honnister's description of himself which was a downright lie. 'No, he went under his own steam. He specifically asked that the police not be involved.'

'So he thought we might be. That's interesting in itself. And Benson went with him. What do you want to know about him?'

'Anything you can tell me that I don't know already. I'm scraping the bottom of the barrel.'

'Bachelor—never married. Worked for Ashton since the dark ages—butler, valet, handyman, chauffeur—you name it. Age at death, sixty-four, if you can believe *The Times*.'

'Any family—brothers or sisters?'

'No family at all.' Honnister grinned at me. 'As soon as I saw that bit in *The Times* I got busy. The itch in my bump of curiosity was driving me mad. Benson had a bit of money, about fifteen thousand quid, which he left to Dr Barnado's Homes for Boys.'

'Anything else?' I asked, feeling depressed.

'Ever been in a war?' asked Honnister unexpectedly.

'No.'

'Seen any deaths by violence?'

'A few.'

'So have I, in my professional capacity. I've also seen the results of bombs and shellfire. It was a bit difficult to tell after a pathologist had been at them but I'd say Ashton had been shot in the back twice, and Benson shot through the head from the front. Caught in a shell blast, my arse!'

'*You've seen the bodies!*'

'I made it my business to—unofficially, of course. I went to the mortuary here. I told you my bump of curiosity was itching.'

'Charlie, you keep that under your bloody hat or you'll find yourself in dead trouble. I really mean that.'

'I told you before I can keep secrets,' he said equably. 'Anyway, Sweden isn't in my parish, so there's nothing I can do about it. If they were killed in Sweden,' he added as an afterthought.

'They were killed in Sweden,' I said. 'That's genuine. And they *were* killed in a Swedish battle practice area while manoeuvres were going on.' I paused. 'Probably *The Times* got the report wrong.'

'In a pig's eye,' said Honnister pointedly.

I shrugged. 'Anyone else here seen the bodies?'

'Not that I know of. The coffins arrived here sealed and complete with death certificates, probably signed by one of your department's tame doctors. Christ, talk about medical ethics! Anyway, they're underground now.'

'Any more about Benson?'

'Not much. He lived a quiet life. He had a woman in Slough but he gave that up about five years ago.'

'What's her name?'

'It won't do you any good,' he said. 'She died of cancer eighteen months ago. Benson paid for her treatment in a private ward—for old times' sake, I suppose. Other than that there's nothing I can tell you. There was nothing much to Benson; he was just a sort of old-maid bachelor with nothing remarkable about him. Except one thing.'

'What was that?'

'His face. He'd taken a hell of a beating at one time or other. Nature didn't make him like that—man did.'

'Yes,' I said. I was bloody tired of coming up against dead

ends. I thought about it and decided that my best bet would be to look into Benson's army career but I wasn't sanguine that anything would come of that.

'Another drink?'

'No, thanks, Charlie. I want to see the Ashtons.'

'Give them my regards,' he said.

I drove to the Ashton house and, to my surprise, bumped into Michaelis who was just leaving. Under his arm he carried a loose-leaf ledger about as big as two bibles. 'What the devil are you doing here?'

He grinned. 'Playing puff-puffs. You know I'm interested, and Miss Ashton gave me permission to mess about in the attic pretty nearly any time I like. It really is a fascinating set-up.'

I suppose it wasn't too weird that a counter-espionage agent should be nuts on model railways. I indicated the big book. 'What's that?'

'Now this really is interesting,' he said. 'Let me show you.' He rested the book on the bonnet of my car. The letters 'LMS' were inscribed on the leather-bound cover in gilt. 'This is a set of timetables for the old LMS—the London, Midland and Scottish railway that was before nationalization. Effectively speaking, the railways were nationalized in 1939 and all the trains were steam in those days.'

He opened the book and I saw column after column of figures. 'Ashton was duplicating the LMS timetable, but I haven't figured out which year he was using so I'm taking this home to check against some old Bradshaws I have. Ashton's system up there in the attic isn't what you'd call standard practice in the model world—most of us can't afford what he'd got. I told you about those microprocessors he can program. These figures give the settings needed to the control panel to duplicate parts of the LMS timetable. He'd also got similar books for other pre-war railway companies—the London and North-Eastern, the Great Western and so on. It's bloody remarkable.'

'Indeed it is,' I said. 'Which Miss Ashton gave you permission?'

'Gillian. I talked to her a lot in hospital, about her father at the beginning, but one thing led to another. She was lonely, you know, being all bandaged up like that. I used to read books and newspapers for her. Anyway, I talked about the model railway and she found I was interested so she said I could come and play.'

'I see.'

'Gillian's a very nice girl,' he said. 'We get on very well.' He paused. 'I don't spend all my time in the attic.'

I studied Michaelis in a new light. It occurred to me that he was unmarried like myself and, if all went well with both of us, I was probably talking to my future brother-in-law. 'Is Gillian home now?'

'Yes—and she's expecting Penny for lunch.' He slammed the ledger closed. 'I heard on the grapevine what's happened to you. I think it's a bloody disgrace. Who the hell was to know...'

I interrupted. 'The less said about it the better, even in private. Don't talk about it at all—ever. That way nothing will slip out accidentally.' I consulted my watch. 'If you're so chummy with Gillian I thought you might be staying for lunch.'

He shook his head. 'I don't feel like facing Penny so I made an excuse. You see, Penny hasn't told Gillian about us—the department, I mean. She doesn't know anything about it and that makes it easier. But I haven't seen Penny since we came back from Sweden and I haven't the guts to face her yet—not after what happened. I have a weird feeling she might read my mind.'

'Yes,' I agreed. 'It is bloody difficult.'

'You're more involved than I am,' he said. 'How do you feel about it?'

'Pretty much the same as you, but maybe a bit more so. Well, I'll go in and see Gillian. See you around.'

'Yes,' said Michaelis. 'I hope so.'

TWENTY-EIGHT

I had forgotten that Gillian was not very pretty to look at and she came as a renewed shock. Her face was puckered and drawn with scar tissue and her right eyelid was pulled almost closed. The first few moments were not at all easy; there was the double embarrassment of condoling on the death of her father and coping with her dreadful appearance, and I hoped my face did not reflect what I felt. But she put me at my ease, gave me a scotch and had a sherry herself.

Of her father she had little to say beyond expressing a puzzled sadness and a total lack of knowledge of his motives. 'What can I say? There *is* nothing to be said, except that I'm deeply sorry and totally bewildered.'

Of herself she had come to terms with her affliction and was prepared to talk about it. 'Of course, it will be better after the plastic surgery. I'm told the best man for that is in America, and Penny wants me to go over. But my face is not so nice now, and I don't go out much.' She smiled lopsidedly. 'I saw you talking to Peter Michaelis outside. Do you know him?'

I said carefully, 'I met him at the hospital.'

'Oh, yes; you would, of course.' She smiled again, and there was a happy sparkle in her good eye. 'One never thinks of policemen as ordinary human beings—just shadows dashing about on television arresting people. Peter is such a delightful man.'

I agreed that a policeman's lot, etc., 'Must cramp their social lives.'

'He just told me about Mayberry. It appears the man is quite insane. Penny told me about ... about the mistake.'

'So you know.'

'She waited until I'd been home a few days. I suppose she was right to withhold it until then. I wasn't in any condition to take more shocks. But how awful for her. It took a great deal of straight talking from me to make her carry on with Professor Lumsden.'

'I'm glad you did.'

Gillian looked at me closely. 'There's something wrong between you and Penny isn't there? I think she's unhappy about it. What is it, Malcolm?'

'I don't know if the trouble altogether concerns me,' I said. 'I rather think she's unhappy about what happened to you, and then to your father.'

'No,' she said pensively. 'She appears to involve you in it, and I don't know why. She won't talk about it, and that's unlike her.' She turned her head to the window as a car drew up. 'Here she is now. You'll stay for lunch, of course.'

'Glad to.'

I was pleased to find that Penny was pleased to see me. 'Oh, Malcolm!' she cried, and hurried to meet me. I met her half way across the room, took her in my arms, and kissed her.

'I was very sorry to hear about your father.'

She looked beyond me to where Gillian sat, and said quietly, 'I want to talk to you about that afterwards.'

I nodded. 'Very well.'

'A sherry,' she said. 'A sherry, to save my life. Lummy and I have talked our throats dry this morning.'

So we had lunch, at which we chatted amiably and kept away from controversial subjects. We discussed Gillian's forthcoming trip to the United States, and Penny asked about my experiences there. 'I was told where you were,' she said obliquely.

Later she said, 'Gillian and I have decided to sell the house. It's much too big for the two of us, so we've decided to set ourselves up in a decent flat in town. Gillian will be closer to the theatres and concert halls, and I won't have to commute to the lab.'

'That sounds sensible,' I said. 'When do you move?'

'I'll be going to America with Gillian,' she said. 'We're selecting some of the best pieces from here and the rest will be auctioned, the antiques at Sotheby's and the rest of the stuff from the house. But we'll be in America then. I couldn't bear to stay and see the place sold up. So I suppose the auction will be in about three weeks. I'm making the final arrangements this afternoon.'

And that would put paid to Michaelis's fun and games with the model railway. I wondered if he was preparing to put in a bid.

After lunch Gillian pleaded tiredness and went to rest in her room, but I rather think she wanted to leave us alone together. Penny and I sat before the blazing fire with a pot of coffee and I could tell she was getting set for a serious discussion. 'Malcolm,' she said, 'what's the truth about Daddy?'

I offered her one of my American cigarettes which she took. 'I don't think anyone will ever know.'

'Did he die the way they said? You must know, being who you are, even though you were in America at the time. You were investigating him, after all.'

'My information is that he was in a Swedish army proving ground where they were using live ammunition when he was killed.'

'And that's the truth?' she said steadily. 'You wouldn't lie to me?'

'That's the truth.' But not the whole truth, Jaggard, you bastard!

She was silent for a while, gazing into the flames. 'I don't understand,' she said at last. 'I don't understand any of it. What was he doing in Sweden?'

'Apparently nothing very much, from what I can gather. He was living quietly in Stockholm with Benson to look after him. He read a lot and went to the occasional concert. A quiet and placid life.'

'How do you know this?'

'The department checked, of course.'

'Of course,' she said colourlessly. 'I'm going to Sweden. I want to find out for myself. Will you come with me?'

That was a poser! I could imagine the expression on the face of the colonel of the Royal Södermanland Regiment if I poked my nose into Strängnäs again. I needed no imagination at all to picture the cold grey eyes of Captain Morelius of Swedish Army Intelligence.

'That may not be easy,' I said. 'I've just been transferred and my time isn't my own.'

'Transferred from your department?'

'No, just within the department, but I may be office-bound from now on. Still, I'll see what I can do.' Which would be precisely nothing. 'Look, Penny, how would it be if I arranged for you to talk with my chief? He can tell you all that's known about your father in Sweden.' And he can tell my damned lies for me, I thought savagely.

She thought about it, then said, 'Very well. But that doesn't mean I'm not going to Sweden.'

'I'll arrange it.' I rose to pour us some more coffee. 'Penny, what's happening to us? I still want to marry you, but every time I get near the subject you edge away. I'm very much in love with you and it's becoming damned frustrating. Have you turned off?'

She cried, 'Oh, Malcolm, I'm sorry; I really am. Everything turned topsy-turvy so suddenly. First there was Gillian, then Daddy—and then you. I've been going about looking at people I know and wondering if what I think I know is really so. Even Lummy has come under scrutiny—I'm beginning to worry him, I think. He imagines I'm going paranoid.'

'It's not been too easy for me, either,' I said. 'I didn't want to have anything to do with the Ashton case.'

'The Ashton case,' she repeated. 'Is that what they call it?' When I nodded, she said, 'That takes the humanity out of it, doesn't it? When it's a "case" it's easy to forget the flesh and blood because a case is mostly dockets and paperwork. How would you like to be referred to as the Jaggard case?'

'Not much,' I said sombrely.

Penny took my hand. 'Malcolm, you'll have to give me time. I think—no—I *know* I love you, but I'm still a bit mixed up; and I don't know that I'm too happy about what you do with your life. That's something else which needs thinking about.'

'My God!' I said. 'You make it sound as though I go about eating live babies. I'm just a dreary counter-espionage man specializing in industry and making sure too many secrets don't get pinched.'

'You mean weapons?'

I shook my head. 'Not necessarily. That's not our pigeon—and we're not interested in the latest toothpaste additive, either. But if an engineering firm has ploughed a couple of millions into research and come up with something revolutionary, then we don't want some foreign Johnny nicking it and going into competition with a head start. And, don't forget, the foreign Johnnies from the East are state supported.'

'But these things are patented, aren't they?'

'Patents are a dead giveaway. The really big stuff isn't patented, especially in electronics. If you produce a new electronic chip which does the work of eleventy thousand transistors the opposition can put the thing under a microscope and see what you've done, but how the hell you've done it is quite another thing, and our boys aren't telling. They're certainly not going to disclose the process in a published patent.'

'I see,' she said. 'But that means you're just another sort of policeman.'

'Most of the time,' I said. 'Our problem is that the theft of information, as such, is not illegal in this country. Suppose I stole a sheet of paper from your lab, say, and I was caught. I'd be found guilty of the theft of a piece of paper worth one penny, and I'd suffer the appropriate penalty. The fact that written on that paper was some formula worth a million quid wouldn't count.'

Her voice rose. 'But that's silly.'

'I agree,' I said. 'Do you want to hear something really silly? A few years ago a chap was caught tapping a post office line. The only charge they could get him on was the theft of a quantity of electricity, the property of the Postmaster-General. It was about a millionth of a watt.' Penny laughed, and I said, 'Anyway, that's my job, and it doesn't seem all that heinous to me.'

'Nor to me, now you've explained it. But where did Daddy come into this?'

I said, 'You may not realize how important a man your father was. The catalysts he was developing were revolutionizing the economics of the oil industry and helping the economics of the country. When a man like that goes missing we want to know if anyone has been putting pressure on him, and why. Of course, if he's just running away from a shrewish wife then it's his affair, and we drop it. That's happened before.'

'And what conclusions did you come to about Daddy?'

'At first we tied it in with the attack on Gillian,' I said. 'But that's a dead end; we know Mayberry was a loner. As it is, as far as the department could make out, your father was living quietly in Stockholm and apparently taking an extended holiday. There's nothing we could do about that.'

'No,' said Penny. 'We're not yet a police state. What's being done now?'

I shrugged. 'The committee of brains at the top has decided to drop the matter.'

'I see.' She stared into the fire for a long time, then shook her head. 'But you'll still have to give me time, Malcolm. Let me go to America. I'd like to get away from here and think. I'd like to . . .'

I held up my hand. 'Point taken—no further argument. Change of subject; what were you doing in Scotland?' I was damned glad to change the subject; I'd been shaving the truth a bit too finely.

'Oh, that. Acting as adviser in the reconstruction of a laboratory. It's been worrying me because they're only willing to go up to P3 and I'm recommending P4. I was arguing it out with Lumsden this morning and he thinks I'm a bit . . . well, paranoiac about it.'

'You've lost me,' I said. 'What's P3? To say nothing of P4.'

'Oh, I forgot.' She waved her hand at the room. 'I was so used to talking things out here with Daddy that I'd forgotten you're a layman.' She looked at me doubtfully. 'It's a bit technical,' she warned.

'That's all right. Mine is a technical job.'

'I suppose I'd better start with the big row,' she said. 'An American geneticist called Paul Berg . . .'

It seems that Berg blew the whistle. He thought the geneticists were diddling around with the gene in the same way the physicists had diddled around with the atom in the '20s and '30s, and the potential hazards were even more horrendous. He pointed out some of them.

It seems that the favourite laboratory animal of the geneticist is a bacterium called *Escherichia coli* and it is the most studied organism on earth—more is known about *E.coli* than about any other living thing. It was natural that this creature be used for genetic experimentation.

'There's only one snag about that,' said Penny. '*E.coli* is a natural inhabitant of the human gut, and I don't mean by ones and twos—I mean by the million. So if you start tinkering around with *E.coli* you're doing something potentially dangerous.'

'For example?' I asked.

'You remember Lummy's example of genetic transfer from *Rhizobium* to make an improved wheat. I said we'd have to be careful not to transfer another, more dangerous, gene. Now, consider this. Supposing you incorporated into *E.coli*, accidentally or on purpose, the gene specifying the male hormone, testosterone. And supposing that strain of *E.coli* escaped from the laboratory and entered the human population. It would inhabit the digestive tracts of women, too, you know. They might start growing beards and stop having babies.'

'Christ!' I said. 'It would be a catastrophe.'

'Berg and some of his concerned friends called an international conference at Asilomar in California in 1975. It was well attended by the world's geneticists but there was much controversy. Gradually a policy was hammered out involving the concept of biological containment. Certain dangerous experiments were to be banned pending the development of a strain of *E.coli* unable to survive outside the laboratory and unable to colonize the human gut. The specification laid down was that the survival rate of the new strain should not be more than one in a thousand million.'

I smiled. 'That sounds like certainty.'

'It's not,' said Penny soberly, 'considering the numbers of *E.coli* around, but it's close. I think that was the most important conference in the history of science. For the first time scientists had got together to police themselves without having restrictions thrust upon them. I think at the back of all our minds was the bad example set by the atomic physicists.'

Fifteen months later the development of the new strain was announced by the University of Alabama. Penny laughed. 'A writer in *New Scientist* put it very well. He called it "the world's first creature designed to choose death over liberty".'

I said slowly, 'The first creature *designed* ... That's a frightening concept.'

'In a way—but we've been designing creatures for a long

time. You don't suppose the modern dairy cow is as nature intended it to be?'

'Maybe, but this strikes me as being qualitatively different. It's one thing to guide evolution and quite another to by-pass it.'

'You're right,' she said. 'Sooner or later there'll be some hack or graduate student who will go ahead with a bright idea without taking the time to study the consequences of what he's doing. There'll be a bad mistake made one day—but not if I can help it. And that brings us to Scotland.'

'How?'

'What I've just described is biological containment. There's also physical containment to keep the bugs from escaping. Laboratories are classified from P1 to P4. P1 is the standard microbiological lab; P4 is the other extreme—the whole of the lab is under negative air pressure, there are air locks, showers inside and out, changes of clothing, special pressurized suits— all that kind of thing.'

'And you're running into trouble with your recommendations in Scotland?'

'They're upranking an existing P2 lab. In view of what they want to do I'm recommending P4, but they'll only go to P3. The trouble is that a P4 lab is dreadfully expensive, not only in the building, but in the running and maintenance.'

'Are there no statutory regulations?'

'Not in this field; it's too new. If they were working with recognized pathogens then, yes—there are regulations. But they'll be working with good old *E.coli*, a harmless bacterium. You have about a couple of hundred million of them in your digestive tract right now. They'll stay harmless, too, until some fool transfers the wrong gene.' She sighed. 'All we have are guidelines, not laws.'

'Sounds a bit like my job—not enough laws.'

She ruefully agreed, and our talk turned to other things. Just before I left she said, 'Malcolm; I want you to know that I think you're being very patient with me—patient and thoughtful. I'm not the vapouring sort of female, and I usually don't have much trouble in making up my mind; but events have been getting on top of me recently.'

'Not to worry,' I said lightly. 'I can wait.'

'And then there's Gillian,' she said. 'It may have been silly of me but I was worrying about her even before all this happened. She's never been too attractive to men and she looked like turning into an old maid; which would have been a pity because she'd make someone a marvellous wife. But now'— she shook her head—'I don't think there's a chance for her with that face.'

'I wouldn't worry about that, either,' I advised. 'Michaelis has a fond eye on her.' I laughed. 'With a bit of luck you'll not have one, but two, spies in the family.'

And with that startling thought I left her.

TWENTY-NINE

The British weekend being what it is I didn't get to the War Office until Monday. Anyone invading these islands would be advised to begin not earlier than four p.m. on a Friday; he'd have a walkover. I filled in the necessary form at the desk and was escorted by a porter to the wrong office. Two attempts later I found the man I needed, an elderly major called Gardner who was sitting on his bottom awaiting his pension. He heard what I had to say and looked at me with mournful eyes. 'Do you realize the war has been over for thirty years?'

I dislike people who ask self-evident questions. 'Yes, I'm aware of it; and I still want the information.'

He sighed, drew a sheet of paper towards him, and picked up a ball point pen. 'It's not going to be easy. Do you know how many millions of men were in the army? I suppose I'd better have the names.'

'I suppose you had.' I began to see why Gardner was still a grey-haired major. 'George Ashton, private in the Royal Electrical and Mechanical Engineers; demobilized 4 January, 1947.'

'In London?'

'Probably.'

'Could have been at Earl's Court; that was used as a demob centre. The other man?'

'Howard Greatorex Benson, sergeant in the Royal Army Service Corps. I don't know where he was demobilized.'

'Is that all you know of these men?'

'That's it.'

Gardner laid down his pen and looked at me glumly. 'Very well, I'll institute a search. You'd better give me your address or a phone number where I can find you.' He sniffed lugubriously. 'It'll take about a month, I should say.'

'That's not good enough. I need the information a damned sight faster than that.'

He waved a languid hand. 'So many records,' he said weakly. 'Millions of them.'

'Don't you have a system?'

'System? Oh, yes; we have a system—when it works.'

I set out to jolly him along and by a combination of sweet talk, name-dropping and unspoken threats got him out of his chair and into action, if one could dignify his speed by such a name. He stood up, regarding me owlishly, and said, 'You don't suppose we keep five million army records here, do you?'

I smiled. 'Shall we take your car or mine?'

I had what I wanted four hours later. At the time I thought I'd been lucky but later decided that luck had nothing to do with it because it had been planned that way thirty years earlier.

We started with the records of Earl's Court, now an exhibition hall devoted to such things as cars and boats, but then a vast emporium for the processing of soldiers into civilians. There they exchanged their uniforms for civilian clothing from the skin out—underwear, shirt, socks, shoes, suit, overcoat and the inevitable trilby or fedora hat of the 1940s. There was also the equivalent of a bank which took in no money but which lashed it out by the million; the serviceman's gratuity, a small—very small—donation from a grateful nation. At its peak the throughput of Earl's Court was 5000 men a day but by early 1947 it had dropped to a mere 2000.

The ledgers for 4 January were comparatively small; they had coped with only 1897 men—it had been a slack day. Infuriatingly, the ledgers were not listed in alphabetical order but by army number, which meant that every name and page had to be scanned. 'What was the name again?' said Gardner.

'Ashton.'

'Ashton,' he muttered, as he started on the first page of a ledger. 'Ashton ... Ashton ... Ashton.' I think he had to repeat the name to himself because he had the attention span of a retarded five-year-old.

I took another ledger and started to check it. It was like reading a war memorial with the difference that these were the survivors; a long list of Anglo-Saxon names with the odd quirky foreigner for spice, and even more boring than checking Heathrow passenger lists. Half an hour later Gardner said, 'What was that name again?'

I sighed. 'Ashton. George Ashton.'

'No—the other one.'

'Benson, Howard Greatorex.'

'He's here,' said Gardner placidly.

'*Benson!*' I went to the other side of the table and leaned over Gardner's shoulder. Sure enough, his finger rested under Benson's name, and the rest of the information fitted. Sergeant H. G. Benson, RASC, had been discharged on the same day, and from the same place, as Private G. Ashton, REME. I didn't think coincidence could stretch that far.

'That's a piece of luck,' said Gardner with smug satisfaction. 'Now we have his army number we shall find his file easily.'

'We haven't got Ashton yet,' I said, and we both applied ourselves to the ledgers. Ashton came up three-quarters of an hour later. Gardner scribbled on a piece of paper and drifted away in his somnambulistic manner to organize the search for the files, while I sat down and began to sort out what we'd found.

I tried to figure out the odds against two specific men in the British Army being demobilized on the same day and from the same place, but the mathematics were too much for me—I couldn't keep count of the zeroes, so I gave up.

It was stretching the long arm a bit too far to suggest that it had happened by chance to two men who subsequently lived together as master and servant for the next quarter of a century. So if it wasn't coincidence it must have been by arrangement.

So who arranged it?

I was still torturing my brain cells when Gardner came back an hour later with the files. There was a sticky moment when I said I wanted to take them away; he clung to them as though I was trying to kidnap his infant children. At last he agreed to accept my receipt and I left in triumph.

I studied the files at home, paying little attention to Ashton's file because it had nothing to do with the Ashton I knew, but I went over Benson's file in detail. His career was exactly as

Ogilvie had described. He joined the army in 1940 and after his primary training and square-bashing he was transferred to the RASC and his promotions came pretty quickly at first—to lance-corporal, to corporal, and then to sergeant where he stuck for the rest of the war. All his service was in England and he never went overseas. Most of his duties were concerned with store-keeping, and from the comments of his superiors written in the file, he was quite efficient, although there were a few complaints of lack of initiative and willingness to pass the buck. Not many, but enough to block his further promotion.

His pay-book showed that he was unmarried but was contributing to the upkeep of his mother. The payments ceased in 1943 when she died. From that time until his discharge his savings showed a marked increase. I thought that anyone who could save out of army pay back in those days must have lived a quiet life.

His medical record was similarly uneventful. Looked at *en masse* it appeared alarming, but closer inspection revealed just the normal ailments which might plague a man over a period of years. There were a couple of tooth extractions, two periods of hospitalization—one for a bout of influenza and the other when he dropped a six-inch shell on his left foot. Luckily the shell was defused.

My attention was caught by the last entry. Benson had complained of aches in his left arm which had been preliminarily diagnosed as twinges of rheumatism and he had been given the appropriate treatment. He was thirty-three then, and rheumatism seemed a bit odd to me, especially since Benson had a cushy billet for a soldier in wartime. Not for him route marches in the pouring rain or splashing about joyfully in the mud; he worked in a warm office and slept every night in a warm bed.

Evidently the medical officer had thought it odd, too, when the treatment didn't work. In a different coloured ink he had appended a question mark after the previous diagnosis of rheumatism, and had scribbled beneath, 'Suggest cardiogram.' The amendment was dated 18 December, 1946.

I went back to the general service file where I struck another oddity, because his immediate superior had written as the last entry, 'Suggested date of discharge—21 March, 1947.' Underneath another hand had written, 'Confirmed', and followed it with an indecipherable signature.

I sat back and wondered why, if it had been suggested and confirmed that Benson should be discharged in March, 1947, he should have been discharged three months earlier. I consulted the medical record again and then rang Tom Packer.

This account started with Tom Packer because it was at his place I first met Penny. I rang him now because he was a doctor and I wanted confirmation of the idea that was burgeoning. If he didn't know what I wanted he'd be certain to know who could tell me.

After a brief exchange of courtesies, I said, 'Tom, I want a bit of free medical advice.'

He chuckled. 'You and the rest of the population. What is it?'

'Supposing a man complains of a pain in his left arm. What would you diagnose?'

'Hell, it could be anything. Have you got such a pain?'

'This is hypothetical.'

'I see. Could be rheumatism. What's the hypothetical age of this hypothetical chap?'

'Thirty-three.'

'Then it's unlikely to be rheumatism if he's lived a normal civilized life. I say unlikely, but it could happen. Did he say pain or ache?'

I consulted the medical file. 'Actually, he said ache.'

'Um. Not much to go on. Doctors usually have real patients to examine, not wraiths of your imagination.'

I said, 'Supposing the man was treated for rheumatism and it didn't work, and then his doctor thought a cardiogram was indicated. What would you think then?'

'How long has the man been treated for rheumatism?'

'Hang on.' I checked the file. 'Three months.'

Tom's breath hissed in my ear. 'I'm inclined to think the doctor should be struck off. Do you mean to say it took him three months to recognize a classic symptom of ischæmia?'

'What's that?'

'Ischæmic heart disease—*angina pectoris*.'

I suddenly felt much happier. 'Would the man survive?'

'That's an imponderable question—very iffy. *If* he's had that ache in the arm for three months and *if* it is ischæmic and *if* he hasn't had treatment for his heart then he'll be in pretty bad shape. His future depends on the life he's been living, whether he smokes a lot, and whether he's been active or sedentary.'

I thought of Sergeant Benson in an army stores office. 'Let's say he's been sedentary and we'll assume he smokes.'

'Then I wouldn't be surprised to hear he's dropped dead of a coronary one morning. This *is* hypothetical, isn't it? Nobody I know?'

'No one you know,' I assured him. 'But not quite hypothetical. There was a man in that condition back in 1946. He died about a month ago. What do you think of that?'

'I think that I think I'm surprised, but then, medicine isn't a predictive sport and the damnedest things can happen. I wouldn't have thought it likely he'd make old bones.'

'Neither would I,' I said. 'Thanks for your trouble, Tom.'

'You'll get my bill,' he promised, and rang off.

I depressed the telephone rest, rang Penny, and asked her the name of Benson's doctor. She was faintly surprised but gave it to me when I said my boss wanted me to tidy up a few loose ends before I was transferred. 'It's just a matter of firm identification.'

The doctor's name was Hutchins and he was a shade reserved. 'Medical files are confidential, you know, Mr Jaggard.'

'I don't want you to break any confidences, Dr Hutchins,' I said. 'But the man is dead, after all. All I want to know is when Benson last had a heart attack.'

'Heart attack!' echoed Hutchins in surprise. 'I can certainly tell you all about that. It's no breach of confidentiality on a doctor's part if he says a man is perfectly well. There was absolutely nothing wrong with Benson's heart; it was in better condition than my own, and I'm a much younger man. He was as fit as a flea.'

'Thank you, Doctor,' I said warmly. 'That's all I wanted to know.' As I put down the telephone I thought I'd handled that rather well.

I sat back and checked off all the points.

ITEM: Sergeant Benson was suffering from heart disease at the end of 1946. His condition, according to Tom Packer, was grave enough so that no one would be surprised if he dropped dead.

HYPOTHESIS: Sergeant Benson had died of heart disease some time after 18 December, 1946 and before 4 January, 1947.

ITEM: Civilian Benson was discharged at Earl's Court on 4 January, 1947 and subsequently showed no trace of a bad heart condition.

HYPOTHESIS: Civilian Benson was a planted substitute for Sergeant Benson, exactly as Chelyuskin was a substitute for Private Ashton. The method was exactly the same and it happened on the same day and in the same place, so the likelihood of a connection was very high, particularly as Benson worked for Ashton for the rest of his life.

COROLLARY: Because the methods used were identical the likelihood was high that both substitutions were planned by the same mind. But Ogilvie had told me that the idea was Chelyuskin's own. Was Benson another Russian? Had two men been smuggled out?

It all hung together very prettily, but it still didn't tell me who Benson was and why he had shot Ashton.

THIRTY

Ogilvie was pleased about all that even though it got us no further into cracking the problem of why Benson should kill Ashton. At least we had seen the common linkage and he was confident that by probing hard enough and long enough we—or rather I—would come up with the truth. All the same he coppered his bet by having me do an intensive investigation into the life of Sergeant Benson before he joined the army. Ogilvie was a belt-and-braces man.

So I spent a long time in the West Country looking at school records in Exeter and work records in Plymouth. At Benson's school I found an old sepia class photograph with Benson in the third row; at least, I was assured it was Benson. The uniformed young face of that thirteen-year-old gazing solemnly at the camera told me nothing. Some time in the ensuing years Benson had had his features considerably rearranged.

There were no photographs of an older Benson to be found in Plymouth, but I did talk to a couple of people who knew him before the war. The opinion was that he wasn't a bad chap, reasonably good at his job, but not very ambitious. All according to the record. No, he hadn't been back since the war; he had no family and it was assumed there was nothing for him to go back for.

All this took time and I got back to London just as Penny and Gillian were about to leave for America. I drove them to Heathrow myself and we had a drink in the bar, toasting surgical success. 'How long will you be away?' I asked Gillian. She wore a broad-brimmed straw hat with a scarf tied wimple-fashion and large dark glasses; style coming to the aid of concealment.

'I don't know; it depends how the operations go, I suppose.' She sketched a mock shiver. 'I'm not looking forward to it. But Penny will be back next week.'

Penny said, 'I just want to see Gillian settled and to make sure everything is all right, then I'll be back. Lummy wants to go to Scotland with me.'

'So you undermined his certainty.'

'Perhaps,' she said noncommittally.

'Did you arrange for the auction?'

'It's on Wednesday—viewing day on Tuesday. We already have a flat in town.' She took a notebook and scribbled the address. 'That's where you'll find me when I come back, if I'm not in Scotland.'

Gillian excused herself and wandered in the direction of the ladies' room. I took the opportunity of asking, 'How did you get on with Ogilvie?' I had arranged the meeting with Ogilvie as promised. He hadn't liked it but I'd twisted his arm.

Penny's brow furrowed. 'Well enough, I suppose. He told me pretty much what you have. But there was something . . .'

'Something what?'

'I don't know. It was like speaking in a great empty hall. You expect an echo to come back and you're a bit surprised when there isn't one. There seemed to be something missing when Ogilvie talked. I can't explain it any better than that.'

Penny was right—there was a hell of a lot missing. Her psychic antennae were all a-quiver and she perceived a wrongness but had no way of identifying it. Below the level of consciousness her intelligence was telling her there was something wrong but she didn't have enough facts to prove it.

Ogilvie and I *knew* there was something wrong because we had more facts, but even we were blocked at that moment.

I saw them into the departure lounge, then went home and proceeded to draw up an elaborate chart containing everything I knew about the Ashton case. Lines (ruled) were drawn to connect the *dramatis personae* and representing factual knowledge; lines (dashed) were drawn representing hypotheses.

The whole silly exercise got me nowhere.

About this time I started to develop an itch in my mind. Perhaps it had been the drawing of the chart with its many connections which started it, but I had something buried within me which wanted to come to the surface. Someone had said something and someone else had said something else, apparently quite unrelated, and the little man Hunch who lived in the back of my skull was beginning to turn over in his sleep. I jabbed at him deliberately but he refused to wake up. He would do so in his own good time and with that I had to be content.

On the Tuesday I went to the Ashton house for the public viewing. It was crowded with hard-eyed dealers and hopeful innocents looking for bargains and not finding much because all the good stuff had gone to the London flat or to Sotheby's. Still, there was enough to keep them happy; the accumulated possessions of a happy family life of fifteen years. I could see why Penny didn't want to be there.

I wasn't there to buy anything, nor was I there out of mere curiosity. We had assumed Ashton had hidden something and, although we hadn't found it, that didn't mean it wasn't there. When I say 'we' I really mean Ogilvie, because I didn't wholly go along with him on that. But he could have been right, and I was on hand to see if any suspicious-looking characters were taking an undue interest. Of course, it was as futile an exercise as drawing the chart because the normal dealer looks furtive and suspicious to begin with.

During the morning I bumped into Mary Cope. 'Hello, Mary,' I said. 'Still here, then.'

'Yes, sir. I'm to live in the house until it's been sold. I still have my flat upstairs.' She surveyed the throng of inquisitive folk as they probed among the Ashton's possessions. 'It's a shame, sir, it really is. Everything was so beautiful before ... before...'

She was on the verge of tears. I said, 'A pity, Mary, but there it is. Any offers for the house yet?'

'Not that I know of, sir.'

'What will you do when it's sold?'

'I'm to go to London when Miss Penny and Miss Gillian come back from America. I don't know that I'll like London, though. Still, perhaps it will grow on me.'

'I'm sure it will.'

She looked up at me. 'I wish I knew what was in God's mind when he does a thing like this to a family like the Ashtons. You couldn't wish for better people, sir.'

God had nothing to do with it, I thought grimly; what happened to the Ashtons had been strictly man-made. But there was nothing I could say to answer such a question of simple faith.

'It's not only Mr Ashton, though,' said Mary wistfully. 'I miss Benson. He was such a funny man—always joking and light-hearted; and he never had a wrong word for anyone. He did make us laugh, sir; and to think that he and Mr Ashton should die like that, and in a foreign country.'

'Did Benson ever talk about himself, Mary?'

'About himself, sir? How do you mean?'

'Did he ever tell anecdotes—stories—about his early life, or when he was in the army?'

She thought about it, then shook her head. 'No, Benson was a man who lived in the present. He'd joke about politicians, and what he'd read in the papers or seen on telly. A real comedian, Benson was; had us in stitches a lot of the time. I used to tell him he should have been on the stage, but he always said he was too old.'

A real comedian! What an epitaph for a man whose last macabre joke was to shoot his master. I said, 'You'd better look sharp, Mary, or some of these people will be stealing the spoons.'

She laughed. 'Not much chance of that, sir. The auctioneer has Securicor men all over the place.' She hesitated. 'Would you like a cup of tea? I can make it in my flat.'

I smiled. 'No, thank you, Mary. I don't think I'll be staying long this morning.'

All the same, I was there next day for the actual auction, and why I was there I didn't really know. Perhaps it was the feeling that with the dispersal of the contents of the house the truth about the Ashton case was slipping away, perhaps to be lost forever. At any rate I was there, impotent with ignorance, but on the spot.

And there, to my surprise, was also Michaelis. I didn't see him until late morning and was only aware of him when he nudged me in the ribs. The auctioneer was nattering about a particularly fine specimen of something or other so we withdrew to Ashton's study, now stripped rather bare. 'What a bloody shame this is,' he said. 'I'm glad Gillian isn't here to see it. Have you heard anything yet?'

'No.'

'Neither have I,' he said broodily. 'I wrote to her but she hasn't replied.'

'She's only been gone four days,' I pointed out gently. 'The postal services weren't that good even in their palmy days.'

He grinned and seemed oddly shy. 'I suppose you think I'm making a damned fool of myself.'

'Not at all,' I said. 'No more than me. I wish you luck.'

'Think I have a chance?'

'I don't see why not. In fact, I think you have everything going for you, so cheer up. What are you doing here anyway?'

'That model railway still interests me. I thought that if it's broken up for sale I might put in a bid or two. Of course, in model railway terms to break up that system would be like cutting up the Mona Lisa and selling bits of it. But it won't be broken up and I won't have a chance. Lucas Hartman is here.'

'Who's he?'

'Oh, everybody in the model railway world knows Hartman. He's a real model railway buff, but he calls it railroad because he's an American. He's also quite rich.'

'And you think he'll buy it as it stands?'

'He's sure to. He's up in the attic gloating over it now.'

'How much do you think it will bring?' I asked curiously.

Michaelis shrugged. 'That's hard to say. It's not exactly standard stuff—there's so much extra built in that it's hard to put a price on it.'

'Have a try.'

'For the rail and rolling stock and normal control instrumentation, all of which is there, it would cost about £15,000 to build from scratch, so let's say it might bring between £7000 and £10,000 at auction. As for the other stuff built in, that's more difficult to assess. I'd say it'll double the price.'

'So you think it will bring somewhere between £15,000 and £20,000.'

'Something like that. Of course, the auctioneer will have a reserve price on it. Any way you look at it, Hartman will get it. He'll outbid the dealers.'

'Ah, well,' I said philosophically. 'It will fall into good hands—someone who appreciates it.'

'I suppose so,' said Michaelis gloomily. 'The bloody thing beat me in the end, you know.'

'What do you mean?'

'Well, you know those schedules I talked about—I showed you one of them.'

'The London, Midland and Scottish, I think it was.'

'That's right. I compared them against old Bradshaws and got nowhere. I even went right back to the mid-1800s and nothing made sense. The system doesn't seem to compare with any normal railway scheduling.'

'Not even when those schedules were clearly labelled "LMS" and so on,' I said slowly.

'They don't fit at any point,' said Michaelis. 'It beats me.'

There was a picture in my mind's eye of Ashton's clenched fist opening to reveal a railway timetable—Stockholm to Göteborg, and it was like a bomb going off in my skull. 'Jesus!'

Michaelis stared at me. 'What's wrong?'

'Come on. We're going to talk to that bloody auctioneer.'

I left the study at a fast stride and went into the crowded hall where the auction was taking place. The auctioneer had set up a portable rostrum at the foot of the stairs and, as I elbowed my way through the throng towards it, I took a business card from my wallet. Behind me Michaelis said, 'What's the rush?'

I flattened myself against the wall and scribbled on the card. 'Can't explain now.' I pushed the card at him. 'See the auctioneer gets this.'

Michaelis shrugged and fought his way through to the rostrum where he gave the card to one of the auctioneer's assistants. I walked up the stairs and stood where I could easily be seen. The auctioneer was in mid-spate, selling an eighteen-place Crown Derby dinner service; he took the card which was thrust under his nose, turned it over, looked up at me and nodded, and then continued with hardly a break in his chant.

Michaelis came back. 'What's the panic?'

'We must stop the sale of that railway.'

'I'm all for that,' he said. 'But what's your interest?'

The auctioneer's hammer came down with a sharp crack. 'Sold!'

'It's too complicated to tell you now.' The auctioneer had handed over to his assistant and was coming towards the stairs. 'It'll have to keep.'

The auctioneer came up the stairs. 'What can I do for you—er'—he glanced at the card—'Mr Jaggard.'

'I represent Penelope and Gillian Ashton. The model railway in the attic mustn't be sold.'

He frowned. 'Well, I don't know about that.'

I said, 'Can't we go somewhere a bit more quiet while I explain?'

He nodded and pointed up the stairs, so we went into one of the bedrooms. He said, 'You say you represent the Ashton sisters?'

'That's right.'

'Can you prove that?'

'Not with anything I carry with me. But I can give you written authority if you need it.'

'On your signature?'

'Yes.'

He shook his head. 'Sorry, Mr Jaggard, but that's not good enough. I was engaged by Penelope Ashton to sell the contents of this house. I can't vary that agreement without her authority. If you can give me a letter from her, that's different.'

'She's not easy to get hold of at short notice. She's in the United States.'

'I see. Then there's nothing to be done.' Something in my expression caused him to add quickly, 'Mr Jaggard, I don't know you. Now, I'm a professional man, engaged to conduct this sale. I can't possibly take instructions from any Tom, Dick or Harry who comes here telling me what to do or what not to do. I really don't conduct my business that way. Besides, the railway is one of the plums of the sale. The press is very interested; it makes a nice filler for a columnist.'

'Then what do you suggest? Would you take instruction from Miss Ashton's legal adviser?'

'Her solicitor? Yes, I might do that.' He frowned perplexedly. 'This all appears very odd to me. It seems, from what you say, that Miss Ashton knows nothing about this and it is something you are taking upon yourself. But if I have written instructions from her solicitor, then I'll withdraw the railway.'

'Thank you,' I said. 'I'll get in touch with him. Oh, by the way, what's the reserve price?'

He was affronted. 'I really can't tell you that,' he said coldly. 'And now you must excuse me. There are some important pieces coming up which I must handle myself.'

He turned to walk away, and I said desperately, 'Can you tell me when the railway will come up for sale?'

'Things are going briskly.' He looked at his watch. 'I'd say about three this afternoon.' He walked out.

'A telephone,' I said. 'My kingdom for a telephone.'

'There's one next door in Ashton's bedroom.' Michaelis looked at me a little oddly. 'This sudden interest in model railways doesn't seem kosher to me.'

I had a sudden thought. 'Where are those schedules?'

'In the attic; on a shelf under the control console. There are a dozen.'

'I want you in the attic on the double. Keep an eye on that railway and especially on those schedules. I don't want anything removed and I want note taken of anyone who takes a special interest. Now move.'

I went into Ashton's room and attacked the telephone. For the first time Ogilvie let me down; he wasn't in the office and no one knew where he was or when he'd be back. Neither was he at home. I left messages to say he should ring me at the Ashton house as soon as possible.

There were more frustrations. Mr Veasey of Michelmore, Veasey and Templeton, was away in the fastnesses of Wales talking to a valued but bedridden client. His clerk would not make a decision in the matter, and neither would any of the partners. They did say they would try to get hold of Veasey by telephone and I had to be satisfied with that. I had no great hopes of success—Veasey didn't know me and I had no standing.

I went up to the attic and found Michaelis brooding over the railway. Several small boys were larking about and being chased off by a Securicor guard. 'Any suspects?'

'Only Hartman. He's been checking through those schedules

all morning.' He nodded in the direction of the control console. 'There he is.'

Hartman was a broad-shouldered man of less than average height with a shock of white hair and a nut-brown lined face. He looked rather like Einstein might have looked if Einstein had been an American businessman. At that moment he was poring over one of the schedules and frowning.

I said, 'You're sure that *is* Hartman?'

'Oh, yes. I met him three years ago at a Model Railway Exhibition. What the hell are you really up to, Malcolm?'

I looked at the railway. 'You're the expert. Are there any other peculiarities about this other than the schedules?'

Michaelis stared at the spider web of rails. 'It did occur to me that there's an excessive number of sidings and marshalling yards.'

'Yes,' I said thoughtfully. 'There would be.'

'Why would there be?' Michaelis was baffled.

'Ashton was a clever bastard,' I said. 'He wanted to hide something so he stuck it right under our noses. Do you know how a computer works?'

'In a vague sort of way.'

I said, 'Supposing you instruct a computer that $A = 5$. That tells the computer to take the number five and put it in a location marked A. Suppose you gave the instruction $C = A + B$. That tells the computer to take whatever number is in A, add it to whatever number is in B, and put the result in C.' I jerked my head towards the railway. 'I think that's what this contraption is doing.'

Michaelis gaped. 'A *mechanical* computer!'

'Yes. And those schedules are the programs which run it—but God knows what they're about. Tell me, how many different kinds of rolling stock are there in the system? I'd say ten.'

'You'd be wrong. I counted sixty-three.'

'Hell!' I thought about it a little more. 'No, by God, I'm right! Ten for the numbers o to 9; twenty-six for the letters of the alphabet, and the rest for mathematical signs and punctuation. This bloody thing can probably talk English.'

'I think you're nuts,' said Michaelis.

I said, 'When Ashton was shot he couldn't talk but he was

trying to tell me something. He pulled something from his pocket and tried to give it to me. It was a railway timetable.'

'That's pretty thin,' said Michaelis. 'Larry had one, too.'

'But why should a man in his last extremity try to give me, of all things, a railway timetable? I think he was trying to tell me something.'

'I can see why you want the sale stopped,' admitted Michaelis. 'It's a nutty idea, but you may be right.'

'I haven't got very far,' I said gloomily. 'Ashton's law firm won't play and Ogilvie's gone missing. I'd better try him again.'

So I did, but with no joy. I tried every place I thought he might be—his clubs, the restaurant he had once taken me to, then back to the office and his home again. No Ogilvie.

At half past two Michaelis sought me out. 'They're about to start the bidding on the railway. What are you going to do?'

'Make another call.'

I rang my bank manager, who said, 'And what can I do for you this afternoon, Mr Jaggard?'

'Later today I'm going to write a largish cheque. There won't be enough funds to cover it, either in my current account or in the deposit account. I don't want it to bounce.'

'I see. How much will the cheque be for?'

'Perhaps £20,000.' I thought of Hartman. 'Maybe as much as £25,000. I don't quite know.'

'That's a lot of money, Mr Jaggard.'

I said, 'You know the state of my financial health, and you know I can cover it, not immediately but in a few weeks.'

'In effect, what you're asking for is a bridging loan for, say, a month.'

'That's it.'

'I don't see any difficulty there. We'll accept your cheque, but try to keep it down; and come in tomorrow—we'll need your signature.'

'Thanks.' I put down the telephone knowing that if I was wrong about the railway I was about to lose a lot of money. I couldn't see Ogilvie dipping into the department's funds to buy an elaborate toy, and the only person who might be happy about it would be Michaelis.

I went into the hall to see a small crowd gathered by the

rostrum listening to a man talking. Michaelis whispered, 'They've got old Hempson from *Model Railway News* to give a pep-talk. I suppose they think that'll drive up the price.'

Hempson was saying, '... core of the system is the most remarkable console I have ever seen, using the ultimate in modern technology. It is this which makes this example of the art unique and it is to be hoped that the system will be sold as a complete unit. It would be a disaster if such a fine example should be broken up. Thank you.'

He stepped down to a low murmur of agreement, and I saw Hartman nodding in approval. The auctioneer stepped up and lifted his gavel. 'Ladies and gentlemen: you have just heard Mr Hempson who is an acknowledged expert, and his opinion counts. So I am about to ask for bids for the complete system. It would be normal to do this on site, as it were, but even in so large a house the attic is not big enough to hold both the exhibit and the crowd gathered here. However, you have all had the opportunity of examining this fine example of the model-maker's art, and on the table over there is a representative collection of the rolling stock.'

He raised his gavel. 'Now what am I bid for the complete system? Who will start the bidding at £20,000?'

There was a sigh—a collective exhalation of breath. 'Come,' said the auctioneer cajoling. 'You just heard Mr Hempson. Who will bid £20,000? No one? Who will bid £18,000?'

He had no takers at that, and gradually his starting price came down until he had a bid of £8000. '£8000 I am bid—who will say nine? Eight-five I am bid—thank you, sir—who will say nine? Nine I am bid—who will say ten?'

Michaelis said, 'The dealers are coming in, but they won't stand a chance. Hartman will freeze them out.'

I had been watching Hartman who hadn't moved a muscle. The bidding crept up by 500s, hesitated at the £13,500 mark, and then went up by 250s to £15,000 where it stuck. 'Fifteen I am bid, fifteen I am bid,' chanted the auctioneer. 'Any advance on fifteen?'

Hartman flicked a finger. 'Sixteen I am bid,' said the auctioneer. '£16,000. Any advance on sixteen?' The dealers were frozen out.

I held up a finger. 'Seventeen I am bid. Any advance on

seventeen? Eighteen I am bid—and nineteen—and twenty. I have a bid of £20,000. Any advance on twenty?'

There was a growing rustle of interest as Hartman and I battled it out. At £25,000 he hesitated for the first time and raised his bid by £500. Then I knew I had him. I raised a single finger and the auctioneer said, 'Twenty-six and a half—any advance ... twenty-seven, thank you, sir—twenty-eight I am bid.'

And so it went. Hartman lost his nerve at thirty and gave up. The auctioneer said, 'Any advance on thirty-one? Any advance on thirty-one? Going once.' *Crack!* 'Going twice.' *Crack!* 'Sold to Mr Jaggard for £31,000.'

Crack!

I was now the proud owner of a railway. Maybe it wasn't British Rail but perhaps it might show more profit. I said to Michaelis, 'I wonder if Ogilvie has that much in the petty cash box?'

Hartman came over. 'I guess you wanted that very much, sir.'

'I did.'

'Perhaps you would be so kind as to let me study the layout some time. I am particularly interested in those schedules.'

I said, 'I'm sorry. I acted as agent in this matter. However, if you give me your address I'll pass it to the owner for his decision.'

He nodded. 'I suppose that will have to do.'

Then I was surrounded by pressmen wanting to know who, in his right mind, would pay that much money for a toy. I was rescued by Mary Cope. 'You're wanted on the telephone, Mr Jaggard.'

I made my escape into Ashton's study. It was Ogilvie. 'I understand you wanted me.'

'Yes,' I said, wishing he had rung half an hour earlier. 'The department owes me £31,000 plus bank charges.'

'What's that?'

'You now own a model railway.'

His language was unprintable.

THIRTY-ONE

I saw Ogilvie at his home that night. His welcome was somewhat cool and unenthusiastic and he looked curiously at the big ledger I carried as he ushered me into the study. I dumped it on his desk and sat down. Ogilvie warmed his coat tails at the fire, and said, 'Did you really spend £31,000 on a toy train set?'

I smiled. 'Yes, I did.'

'You're a damned lunatic,' he said. 'And if you think the department will reimburse you, then I'll get the quacks in and have you certified. No bloody model railway can be worth that much.'

'An American called Hartman thought it worth £30,000,' I observed. 'Because that's how much he bid. You haven't seen it. This is no toy you buy your kid for Christmas and assemble on the floor before the living-room fire to watch the chuff-chuff go round in circles. This is big and complex.'

'I don't care how big and complex it is. Where the hell do you think I'm going to put it in the department budget? The accountants would have *me* certified. And what makes you think the department wants it?'

'Because it holds what we've been looking for all the time. It's a computer.' I tapped the ledger. 'And this is the programing for it. One of the programs. There are eleven more which I put in the office vaults.'

I told him how Michaelis had unavailingly tried to sort out the schedules and how I'd made an intuitive jump based on the timetable in Ashton's hand. I said, 'It would be natural these days for a theoretician to use a computer, but Ashton knew we'd look into all his computer files and programs. So he built his own and disguised it.'

'It's the most improbable idea I've ever heard,' said Ogilvie. 'Michaelis is the train expert. What does he think?'

'He thinks I'm crazy.'

'He's not far wrong.' Ogilvie began to pace the room. 'I tell you what I think. If you're right then the thing is cheap at the price and the department will pay. If you're wrong then it's cost *you* £31,000.'

'Plus bank charges.' I shrugged. 'I stuck my neck out, so I'll take the chance.'

'I'll get the computer experts on it tomorrow.' He wagged his head sadly. 'But where are we to put it? If I have it installed in the department offices it'll only accelerate my retirement. Should the Minister hear of it he'll think I've gone senile—well into second childhood.'

'It will need a big room,' I said. 'Best to rent a warehouse.'

'I'll authorize that. You can get on with it. Where is it now?'

'Still in the Ashtons' attic. Michaelis is locked in with it for the night.'

'Enthusiastically playing trains, I suppose.' Ogilvie shook his head in sheer wonderment at the things his staff got up to. He joined me at the desk and tapped the schedule. 'Now tell me what you think this is all about.'

It took four days to dismantle the railway and reassemble it in a warehouse in South London. The computer boys thought my idea hilarious and to them the whole thing was a big giggle, but they went about the job competently enough. Ogilvie gave me Michaelis to assist. The department had never found the need for a model railway technician and Michaelis found himself suddenly elevated into the rank of expert, first class. He quite liked it.

The chief computer man was a systems analyst called Harrington. He took the job more seriously than most of the others but even that was only half-seriously. He installed a computer terminal in the warehouse and had it connected to a computer by post office land lines; not the big chap Nellie was hooked up to, but an ordinary commercial time-sharing computer in the City. Then we were ready to go.

About this time I got a letter from Penny. She wrote that Gillian was well and had just had the operation for the first of the skin grafts. She herself was not coming back immediately; Lumsden had suggested that she attend a seminar at Berkeley in California, so she wouldn't be back for a further week or ten days.

I showed the letter to Michaelis and he said he'd had one from Gillian, written just before the operation. 'She seemed a bit blue.'

'Not to worry; probably just pre-operation nerves.'

The itch at the back of my mind was still there, and so the buried connection was nothing to do with the railway. Little man Hunch was sitting up and rubbing his eyes but was still not yet awake. I badly needed to talk to Penny because I thought it was something she had said that had caused the itch. I was sorry she wasn't coming home for that reason among many.

One morning at ten o'clock Harrington opened the LNER schedule. 'The first few pages are concerned with the placement of the engines and the rolling stock,' he said. 'Now, let's get this right if we can. This is silly enough as it is without us putting our own bugs into the system.'

It took over an hour to get everything in the right place—checked and double checked. Harrington said, 'Page eleven to page twenty-three are concerned with the console settings.' He turned to me. 'If there's anything to your idea at all these Roms will have to be analysed to a fare-thee-well.'

'What's a Rom?'

'A read-only module—this row of boxes plugged in here. Your man, Michaelis, calls them microprocessors. They are pre-programed electronic chips—we'll have to analyse what they're programed to do. All right; let's get on with the setting.'

He began to call out numbers and an acolyte pressed buttons and turned knobs. When he had finished he started again from the beginning and another acolyte checked what the first had done. He caught three errors. 'See what I mean,' said Harrington. 'One bug is enough to make a program unworkable.'

'Are you ready to go now?'

'I think so—for the first stage.' He put his hand on the ledger. 'There are over two hundred pages here, so *if* this thing really is a computer and *if* this represents one program, then after a while everything should come to a stop and the console will have to be readjusted for the next part of the program. It's going to take a long time.'

'It will take even longer if we don't start,' I said tartly.

Harrington grinned and leaned over to snap a single switch. Things began to happen. Trains whizzed about the system, twenty or thirty on the move at once. Some travelled faster than others, and once I thought there was going to be a collision as two trains headed simultaneously for a junction; but one slowed just enough to let the other through and then picked up speed again.

Sidings and marshalling yards that had been empty began to fill up as engines pushed in rolling stock and then uncoupled to shoot off somewhere else. I watched one marshalling yard fill up and then begin to empty, the trains being broken up and reassembled into other patterns.

Harrington grunted. 'This is no good; it's too damned busy. Too much happening at once. If this is a computer it isn't working sequentially like an ordinary digital job; it's working in parallel. It's going to be hell to analyse.'

The system worked busily for nearly two hours. Trains shot back and forth, trucks were pushed here and there, abandoned temporarily and then picked up again in what seemed an arbitrary manner. To me it was bloody monotonous but Michaelis was enthralled and even Harrington appeared to be mildly interested. Then everything came to a dead stop.

Harrington said, 'I'll want a video-camera up there.' He pointed to the ceiling. 'I want to be able to focus on any marshalling yard and record it on tape. And I want it in colour because I have a feeling colour comes into this. And we can slow down a tape for study. Can you fix that?'

'You'll have it tomorrow morning,' I promised. 'But what do you think now?'

'It's an ingenious toy, but there may be something more to it,' he said, noncommittally. 'We have a long way to go yet.'

I didn't spend all my time in the warehouse but went back three days later because Harrington wanted to see me. I found him at a desk flanked by a video-recorder and a TV set. 'We may have something,' he said, and pointed to a collection of miniature rolling stock on the desk. 'There *is* a number characterization.'

I didn't know what he meant by that, and said so. He

smiled. 'I'm saying you were right. This railway is a computer. I think that any of this rolling stock which has red trim on it represents a digit.' He picked up a tank car which had ESSO lettered on the side in red. 'This one, for instance, I think represents a zero.'

He put down the tank car and I counted the trucks; there were nine, but one had no red on it. 'Shouldn't there be ten?'

'Eight,' he said. 'This gadget is working in octal instead of decimal. That's no problem—many computers work in octal internally.' He picked up a small black truck. 'And I think this little chap is an octal point—the equivalent of a decimal point.'

'Well, I'm damned! Can I tell Ogilvie?'

Harrington sighed. 'I'd rather you didn't—not yet. We haven't worked out to our satisfaction which number goes with which truck. Apart from that there is a total of sixty-three types of rolling stock; I rather think some of those represent letters of the alphabet to give the system alpha-numeric capability. Identification may be difficult. It should be reasonably easy to work out the numbers; all that takes is logic. But letters are different. I'll show you what I mean.'

He switched on the video-recorder and the TV set, then punched a button. An empty marshalling yard appeared on the screen, viewed from above. A train came into view and the engine stopped and uncoupled, then trundled off. Another train came in and the same thing happened; and yet again until the marshalling yard was nearly full. Harrington pressed a button and froze the picture.

'This marshalling yard is typical of a dozen in the system, all built to the same specification—to hold a maximum of eighty trucks. You'll notice there are no numbers in there—no red trucks.' With his pen he pointed out something else. 'And scattered at pretty regular intervals are these blue trucks.'

'Which are?'

Harrington leaned back. 'If I were to talk in normal computer terms—which may be jargon to you—I'd say I was looking at an alphameric character string with a maximum capacity of eighty characters, and the blue trucks represent the spaces between words.' He jabbed his finger at the screen. 'That is saying something to us, but we don't know what.'

I bent down and counted the blue trucks; there were thirteen. 'Thirteen words,' I said.

'Fourteen,' said Harrington. 'There's no blue truck at the end. Now, there are twelve marshalling yards like this, so the system has a capacity of holding at any one time about a hundred and sixty words in plain, straightforward English—about half a typed quarto sheet. I know it's not much, but it keeps changing all the time as the system runs; that's the equivalent of putting a new page in the typewriter and doing some more.' He smiled. 'I don't know who designed this contraption, but maybe it's a new way of writing a novel.'

'So all you have to do is to find out which truck equals which letter.'

'All!' said Harrington hollowly. He picked up a thick sheaf of colour photographs. 'We've been recording the strings as they form and I have a chap on the computer doing a statistical analysis. So far he's making heavy weather of it. But we'll get it, it's just another problem in cryptanalysis. Anyway, I just thought I'd let you know your hare-brained idea turned out to be right, after all.'

'Thanks,' I said, glad not to be £31,000 out of pocket. Plus bank charges.

Two days later Harrington rang me again. 'We've licked the numbers,' he said. 'And we're coming up with mathematical formulae now. But the alphabet is a dead loss. The statistical distribution of the letters is impossible for English, French, German, Spanish and Italian. That's as far as we've gone. It's a bit rum—there are too many letters.'

I thought about that. 'Try Russian; there are thirty-two letters in the Russian alphabet.' And the man who had designed the railway was a Russian, although I didn't say that to Harrington.

'That's a thought. I'll ring you back.'

Four hours later he rang again. 'It's Russian,' he said. 'But we'll need a linguist; we don't know enough about it here.'

'Now is the time to tell Ogilvie. We'll be down there in an hour.'

So I told Ogilvie. He said incredulously, 'You mean that bloody model railway speaks Russian?'

I grinned. 'Why not? It was built by a Russian.'

'You come up with the weirdest things,' he complained.

'I didn't,' I said soberly. 'Ashton did. Now you can make my bank manager happy by paying £35,000 into my account.'

Ogilvie narrowed his eyes. 'It cost you only £31,000.'

'"Thou shalt not muzzle the ox that treadeth the corn",' I quoted. 'It was a risky investment—I reckon I deserve a profit.'

He nodded. 'Very well. But it's going to look damned funny in the books—for one model railway, paid to M. Jaggard, £35,000.'

'Why don't you call it by its real name? A computing system.'

His brow cleared. 'That's it. Now let's take a look at this incredible thing.' We collected Larry Godwin as interpreter and went to the warehouse.

The first thing I noticed was that the system wasn't running and I asked Harrington why. 'No need,' he said cheerfully. 'Now we've got the character list sorted out we've duplicated the system in a computer—put it where it really belongs. We weren't running the entire program, you know; just small bits of it. To run through it all would have been impossible.'

I stared at him. 'Why?'

'Well, not really impossible. But look.' He opened the LNER schedule and flipped through. 'Take these five pages here. They contain reiterative loops. I estimate that to run these five pages on the system would take six days, at twenty-four hours a day. To run through the whole program would take about a month and a half—and this is one of the smaller programs. To put all twelve of them through would take about two years.'

He closed the schedule. 'I think the original programs were written on, and for, a real computer, and then transferred on to this system. But don't ask me why. Anyway, now we've put the system back into a computer we're geared to work at the speed of electrons and not on how fast a model railway engine can turn its wheels.'

Ogilvie said, 'Which computer?'

'One in the City; a time-sharing system.'

Ogilvie looked at me. 'Oh, we can't have that. I want everything you've put into that computer cleared out. We'll put it in our own computer.'

I said quickly, 'I wouldn't do that. I don't trust it. It lost Benson.'

Although Harrington could not know what we were talking about he caught the general drift. 'That's no problem.' He pointed to the railway. 'As a model railway that thing is very elaborate and complex, but as a computer it's relatively simple. There's nothing there that can't be duplicated in the Hewlett-Packard desk-top job I have in my own office. But I'll need a printer to handle Russian characters and, perhaps, a modified keyboard.'

Ogilvie said, 'That's a most satisfactory solution.' He walked over to the railway and looked at it. 'You're right; it is complex. Now show me how it works.'

Harrington smiled. 'I thought you'd ask that. Can you read Russian?'

Ogilvie indicated Larry. 'We've brought an interpreter.'

'I'm going to run through the program from the beginning; it's set up ready. I want you to keep an eye on that marshalling yard there. When it's full you can read it off, because I've labelled each truck with the character it represents. I'll stop the system at the right time.'

He switched on and the trains began to scurry about, and the marshalling yard, which was empty, began to fill up. Harrington stopped the system. 'There you are.'

Ogilvie leaned forward and looked. 'All right, Godwin. What does it say?'

Harrington handed Larry a small pair of opera glasses. 'You'll find these useful.'

Larry took them and focused on the trains. His lips moved silently but he said nothing, and Ogilvie demanded impatiently, 'Well?'

'As near as I can make out it says something like this: "First approximation using toroidal Legendre function of the first kind." '

'Well, I'll be damned!' said Ogilvie.

Later, back at the office, I said, 'So they're not going to use the railway.'

'And better not,' said Ogilvie. 'We can't wait two years to find out what this is all about.'

'What will you do with it? According to Harrington it's a pretty simple-minded computer. Without the schedules—the programs—it's just an elaborate rich man's toy.'

'I don't know what to do with it,' said Ogilvie. 'I'll have to think about that.'

'Do me a favour,' I said. 'Give it to Michaelis. It was he who figured those schedules were fakes. It'll make his day.'

THIRTY-TWO

So Harrington put the programs on tape acceptable to his own computer and the Russian character printer began to spew out yards of Russian text and international figures. When Larry translated the Russian it proved to be oddly uninformative— brief notes on what the computer was doing at the time, but not why it was doing it. I mean, if you read a knitting pattern and find 'knit 2, purl 1', that doesn't tell you if you're knitting a body-belt for a midget or a sweater for your hulking Rugby-playing boy-friend. And that's not really such a good analogy because if you're knitting you know you're knitting, while a computer program could be doing damned nearly anything from analysing the use of the subjunctive in Shakespeare's *Titus Andronicus* to designing a trajectory for a space shot to Pluto. The field was wide open so a selection of assorted boffins was brought in.

All this was beyond me so I left them to it. I had other things on my mind, the principal one being that Penny had cabled me, saying that she was returning and giving her flight number and time of arrival at Heathrow. I felt a lot better immediately because it meant she expected me to meet her, and she wouldn't have done it if her decision had not been in my favour.

When I met her she was tired. She had flown from Los Angeles to New York, stopped for a few hours only to see Gillian, and then flown the Atlantic. She was suffering from jet lag and her stomach and glands were about nine hours out of kilter. I took her to the hotel where I had booked her a room; she appreciated that, not wanting to move into an empty flat with nothing in the refrigerator.

I joined her in a coffee before she retired to her room, and she told me that the operation on Gillian was going well and would I pass that message to Michaelis. She smiled. 'Gillian particularly wants him to know.'

I grinned. 'We mustn't hinder the marriage of true minds.'

She talked briefly about what she had been doing in California and of a visit to the Harvard School of Medical Studies. 'They're doing good work there with PV40,' she said.

'What's that?'

'A virus—harmless to human beings.' She laughed. 'I keep forgetting you're not acquainted with the field.'

I said nothing to her about the model railway, although she would have to be told eventually. We couldn't just expropriate the knowledge to be found there—whatever it was—although the legal position would seem to be confused. The department had bought it, but whether the information it held came under the Copyright Act or not was something to keep the lawyers happy for years. In any case it was for Ogilvie to make the decision.

But she had just said something that had jerked little man Hunch out of bed and he was yelling his head off. I said, 'Did you talk over your work much with your father?'

'All the time,' she said.

'It doesn't seem a subject that would interest a man primarily versed in catalysts,' I said casually. 'Did he know much about it?'

'Quite a lot,' she said. 'Daddy was a man with a wide range of interests. He made one or two suggestions which really surprised Lummy when they worked in the laboratory.' She finished her coffee. 'I'm for bed. I feel I could sleep the clock around.'

I saw her to the lift, kissed her before she went up, then went back to the office at speed. Ogilvie wasn't in, so I went to see Harrington and found him short-tempered and tending to be querulous. 'The man who put these programs together was either quite mad or a genius. Either way we can't make sense out of them.'

Harrington knew nothing about Ashton and I didn't enlighten him beyond saying, 'I think you can discount insanity. What can you tell me about the programs—as a whole?'

'As a whole!' He frowned. 'Well, they seem to fall into two groups—a group of five and a group of seven. The group of seven is the later group.'

'Later! How do you know?'

'When we put them through the computer the last thing that comes out is a date. The first five seem to be totally unrelated to each other, but the group of seven appear to be linked in some way. They all use the same weird system of mathematics.'

I thought hard for some minutes and made a few calculations. 'Let me guess. The first of the group of seven begins about 1971, and the whole lot covers a period finishing, say, about six months ago.'

'Not bad,' said Harrington. 'You must know something I don't.'

'Yes,' I said. 'I rather think I do.'

I sought Ogilvie again and found he had returned. He took one look at my face, and said, 'You look like the cat that swallowed the canary. Why so smug?'

I grinned and sat down. 'Do you remember the time we had a late night session trying to figure what Ashton would have been working on? We agreed he would keep on theorizing, but we couldn't see what he could theorize about.'

'I remember,' said Ogilvie. 'And I still can't. What's more, neither can Harrington and he's actually working on the material itself.'

'You said he wouldn't be working in atomics because he hadn't kept up with the field.'

'He didn't keep up in any field with the exception of catalytic chemistry, and there he was mainly reworking his old ideas—nothing new.'

'You're wrong,' I said flatly.

'I don't see what he could have kept up in. We know the books he bought and read, and there was nothing.'

I said softly, 'What about the books Penny bought?'

Ogilvie went quite still. 'What are you getting at?'

'Penny said something just before she went to the States which slipped right past me. We were talking about some of the complications of her work and most of it was over my head. We were in her home at the time, and she said she was so used to talking with her father in that room she'd forgotten I was a layman.'

'The implication being that Ashton wasn't?'

'That's it. It came up again just now and this time it clicked. I've just been talking to Harrington, and he tells me there's a group of seven linked programs. I made an educated guess at the period they covered and got it right first time. They started when Penny first began her graduate work in genetics. I think Ashton educated himself in genetics alongside his daughter. This morning Penny said he'd made suggestions which surprised Lumsden when they worked in the laboratory. Now, Penny works with Lumsden, one of the top men in the field. Everything he knew and learned she could pass on to Ashton.

She read the relevant journals—and so did Ashton; she attended seminars and visited other laboratories—and passed everything back to Ashton. She could have been doing it quite unconsciously, glad to have someone near to her with whom she could discuss her work. He was right in the middle of some of the most exciting developments in science this century, and I'm not discounting atomic physics. What's more likely than that a man like Ashton should think and theorize about genetics?'

'You've made your point,' said Ogilvie. 'But what to do about it?'

'Penny must be brought in, of course.'

He shook his head. 'Not immediately. I can't make that decision off the cuff. The problem lies in the very fact that she *is* Ashton's daughter. She's intelligent enough to ask why her father should have considered it necessary to hide what he's doing; and that, as the Americans say, opens up a can of worms, including his early history and how and why he died. I doubt if the Minister would relish an angry young woman laying siege to his office or, much worse, talking to newspaper reporters. I'll have to ask him for a decision on this one.'

I said, 'You can't possibly suppress a thing like this.'

'Who is talking about suppressing it?' he said irritably. 'I'm merely saying we'll have to use tact in handling it. You'd better leave it with me. You haven't said anything to her about it, have you?'

'No.'

'Good. You've done well on this Malcolm. You'll get the credit for it when the time comes.'

I wasn't looking for credit, and I had an uneasy feeling that

233

Ogilvie wasn't being quite straight with me. It was the first time I had ever felt that about him, and I didn't like it.

I saw Penny the following afternoon, by arrangement, at University College. As I walked down the corridor towards her office the door of Lumsden's office opened and Cregar came out so that I had to sidestep smartly to avoid barging into him. He looked at me in astonishment and demanded, 'What are you doing here?'

Apart from the fact that it wasn't any of his business, I still felt sore enough at the roasting he had given me at the committee meeting to be inclined to give him a sharp answer. Instead I said, mildly enough, 'Just visiting.'

'That's no answer.'

'Perhaps that's because I neither liked the question nor the way it was put.'

He boggled a bit then said, 'You're aware the Ashton case is closed?'

'Yes.'

'Then I'll have to ask you again—what are you doing here?'

I said deliberately, 'The moon will turn into green cheese the day I have to ask your permission to visit my fiancée.'

'Oh!' he said inadequately. 'I'd forgotten.' I really think it had slipped his memory. Something in his eyes changed; belligerence gave way to speculation. 'Sorry about that. Yes, you're going to marry Dr Ashton, aren't you?'

At that moment I didn't know whether I was or not, but I wouldn't give Cregar that satisfaction. 'Yes, I am.'

'When is the wedding to be?'

'Soon, I hope.'

'Ah, yes.' He lowered his voice. 'A word to the wise. You are aware, of course, that it would be most undesirable if Miss Ashton should ever know what happened in Sweden.'

'Under the circumstances I'm the last person likely to tell her,' I said bitterly.

'Yes. A sad and strange business—very strange. I hope you'll accept my apology for my rather abrupt manner just now. And I hope you'll accept my good wishes for your future married life.'

'Of course—and thank you.'

'And now you must excuse me.' He turned and went back into Lumsden's office.

As I walked up the corridor I speculated on Cregar's immediate assumption that my presence in University College was linked to the Ashton case. Granted that he had genuinely forgotten I was to marry Penny, then what possible link could there be?

I escorted Penny to Fortnum's where she restocked her depleted larder. Most of the order was to be sent, but we took enough so that she could prepare a simple dinner for two. That evening, in the flat, as we started on the soup she said, 'I'm going to Scotland tomorrow.'

'With Lumsden?'

'He's busy and can't come. The extra time I spent in America has thrown our schedule out a bit.'

'When will you be back?'

'I don't think I'll be away as much as a week. Why?'

'There's a new play starting at the Haymarket next Tuesday which I thought you might like to see. Alec Guinness. Shall I book seats?'

She thought for a moment. 'I'll be back by then. Yes, I'd like that. I haven't been in a theatre for God knows how long.'

'Still having trouble in Scotland?'

'It's not really trouble. Just a difference of opinion.'

After dinner she made coffee, and said, 'I know you don't like brandy. There's a bottle of scotch in the cabinet.'

I smiled. 'That's thoughtful of you.'

'But I'll have a brandy.'

I poured the drinks and took them over to the coffee table. She brought in the coffee, and then we sat together on the settee. She poured two black coffees, and said quietly, 'When would you like us to get married, Malcolm?'

That was the night the new carpet became badly coffee-stained, and it was the night we went to bed together for the first time.

It had been quite long enough.

235

The rest of the week went slowly. Penny went to Scotland and I booked a couple of seats at the Haymarket Theatre. I also made enquiries into exactly how one gets married; it hadn't come up before. I felt pretty good.

Ogilvie was uncommunicative. He wasn't around the office much during the next few days and, even when he was, he didn't want to see me. He asked how I was getting on with the investigation of Benson and made no comment when I said I was stuck. Twice thereafter he refused to see me when I requested an audience. That worried me a little.

I checked with Harrington to find how he was doing and to see if any genetics experts had been brought in—not by asking outright but by tactful skating around the edges. No new boffins were on the job and certainly no biologists of any kind. That worried me, too, and I wondered why Ogilvie was dragging his heels.

Harrington's temper was becoming worse. 'Do you know what I've found?' he asked rhetorically. 'This joker is using Hamiltonian quaternions!' He made it sound like a heinous offence of the worst kind.

'Is that bad?'

He stared at me and echoed, 'Bad! No one, I repeat—*no one*—has used Hamiltonian quaternions since 1915 when tensor analysis was invented. It's like using a pick and shovel when you have a bulldozer available.'

I shrugged. 'If he used these Hamilton's whatsits he'd have a sound reason.'

Harrington stared at a print-out of the computer program with an angry and baffled expression. 'Then I wish I knew what the hell it is.' He went back to work.

And so did I, but my trouble was that I didn't know what to do. Benson was a dead issue—there seemed to be no possible way of getting a line on him. Ogilvie seemed to have lost interest, and since I didn't want to twiddle my thumbs in Kerr's section, I spent a lot of time in my flat catching up on my reading and waiting for Tuesday.

At the weekend I rang Penny hoping she'd be back but got no answer. I spent a stale weekend and on the Monday morning I rang Lumsden and asked if he'd heard from her. 'I spoke to her on Thursday,' he said. 'She hoped to be back in London for the weekend.'

'She wasn't.'

'Well, perhaps she'll be back today. If she comes in is there a message for her?'

'Not really. Just tell her I'll meet her at home at seven tomorrow evening.'

'I'll tell her,' said Lumsden, and rang off.

I went to the office feeling faintly dissatisfied and was lucky to catch Ogilvie at the lift. As we went up I asked bluntly, 'Why haven't you given Harrington a geneticist to work with him?'

'The situation is still under review' he said blandly.

'I don't think that's good enough.'

He gave me a sideways glance. 'I shouldn't have to remind you that you don't make policy here,' he said sharply. He added in a more placatory tone, 'The truth is that a lot of pressure is being brought to bear on us.'

I was tired of framing my words in a diplomatic mode. 'Who from—and why?' I asked shortly.

'I'm being asked to give up the computer programs to another department.'

'Before being interpreted?'

He nodded. 'The pressure is quite strong. The Minister may accede to the request.'

'Who the devil would want ...?' I stopped and remembered something Ogilvie had let drop. 'Don't tell me it's Cregar again?'

'Why should you think ...' He paused and reconsidered. 'Yes, it's Cregar. A persistent devil, isn't he?'

'Jesus!' I said. 'You know how he'll use it. You said he was into bacteriological warfare techniques. If there's anything important in there he'll use it himself and hush it up.'

The lift stopped and someone got in. Ogilvie said, 'I don't think we should discuss this further.' On arrival at our floor he strode away smartly.

Tuesday came and at seven in the evening I was at Penny's flat ringing the bell. There was no answer. I sat in my car outside the building for over an hour but she didn't arrive. She had stood me up without so much as a word. I didn't use the tickets for the show but went home feeling unhappy and depressed. I think even then I had an inkling that there was something terribly wrong. Little bits of a complicated jigsaw were fitting themselves together at the back of my mind but still out of reach of conscious reasoning power. The mental itch was intolerable.

The next morning, as early as was decent, I rang Lumsden again. He answered my questions good-humouredly enough at first, but I think he thought I was being rather a pest. No, Penny had not yet returned. No, he had not spoken to her since Thursday. No, it wasn't at all unusual; her work could be more difficult than she had expected.

I said, 'Can you give me her telephone number in Scotland?'

There was a silence at my ear, then Lumsden said, 'Er ... no—I don't think I can do that.'

'Why? Haven't you got it?'

'I have it, but I'm afraid it isn't available to you.'

I blinked at that curious statement, and filed it away for future reference. 'Then can you ring her and give her a message?'

Lumsden paused again, then said reluctantly, 'I suppose I can do that. What's the message?'

'It'll need an answer. Ask her where she put the letters from her father. I need to know.' As far as I knew that would be perfectly meaningless.

'All right,' he said. 'I'll pass it on.'

'Immediately,' I persisted. 'I'll wait here until you ring me back.' I gave him my number.

When I sorted the morning's post I found a slip from British Road Services; they had tried to deliver a package but to no avail because I was out—would I collect said package from the depot at Paddington? I put the slip in my wallet.

Lumsden rang nearly an hour later. 'She says she doesn't know which particular letters you mean.'

'Does she? That's curious. How did she sound?'

'I didn't speak to her myself; she wasn't available on an outside line. But the message was passed to her.'

I said, 'Professor Lumsden, I'd like you to ring again and speak to her personally this time. I . . .'

He interrupted. 'I'll do no such thing. I haven't the time to waste acting as messenger-boy.' There was a clatter and he was cut off.

I sat for a quarter of an hour wondering if I was making something out of nothing, chasing after insubstantial wisps as a puppy might chase an imaginary rabbit. Then I drove to Paddington to collect the package and was rather shattered to find that it was my own suitcase. Captain Morelius had taken his time in sending my possessions from Sweden.

I put it in the boot of my car and opened it. There seemed to be nothing missing although after such a length of time I couldn't be sure. What was certain was that Swedish Intelligence would have gone over everything with a microscope. But it gave me an idea. I went into Paddington Station and rang the Ashton house.

Mary Cope answered, and I said, 'This is Malcolm Jaggard. How are you, Mary?'

'I'm very well, sir.'

'Mary, has anything arrived at the house from Sweden? Suitcases or anything like that?'

'Why, yes, sir. Two suitcases came on Monday. I've been trying to ring Miss Penny to ask her what to do with them, but she hasn't been at home—I mean in the flat in London.'

'What did you do with them?'

'I put them in a box-room.'

'I'll be right out, Mary. In the meantime don't let anyone get near them.'

There were traffic jams on the way to Marlow. The congestion on the Hammersmith By-Pass drove me to a distraction of impatience, but after that the road was open and I had my foot on the floor as I drove down the M4. The gates of the house stood open. Who would think Mary Cope might need protection?

She answered the door at my ring, and I said immediately, 'Has anyone else asked about those cases?'

'Why, no, sir.'

'Where are they?'

'I'll show you.' She led me upstairs by the main staircase and up another flight and along a corridor. The house was bare and empty and our footsteps echoed. She opened a door. 'I put them in here out of the way.'

I regarded the two suitcases standing in the middle of the empty room, then turned to her and smiled. 'You may congratulate me, Mary. Penny and I are getting married.'

'Oh, I wish you all the best in the world,' she said.

'So I don't think you'll have to stay in London, after all. We'll probably have a house in the country somewhere. Not as big as this one, though.'

'Would you want me to stay?'

'Of course,' I said. 'Now, I'd like to look at this stuff alone. Do you mind?'

She looked at me a shade doubtfully, then made up her mind. So many strange things had happened in that house that one more wouldn't make any difference. She nodded and went out, closing the door behind her.

Both cases were locked. I didn't trouble with lock-picking but sprung open the catches with a knife. The first case was Ashton's and contained the little he had taken with him on the run from Stockholm. It also contained the clothes he had been wearing; the overcoat, jacket and shirt were torn-bullet holes —but there was no trace of blood. Everything had been cleaned.

It was Benson's case I was really interested in. In this two-cubic-foot space was all we had left of Howard Greatorex Benson, and if I couldn't find anything here then it was probable that the Ashton case would never be truly solved.

I emptied the case and spread everything on the floor. Overcoat, suit, fur hat, underwear, shirt, socks, shoes—everything he had died with. The fur hat had a hole in the back big enough to put my fist through. I gave everything a thorough going-over, aware that Captain Morelius would have done the same, and found nothing—no microfilm, beloved of the thriller writers, no hidden pockets in the clothing, nothing at all out of the usual.

There was a handful of Swedish coins and a slim sheaf of currency in a wallet. Also in the wallet were some stamps, British and Swedish; two newspaper cuttings, both of book reviews in English, and a scribbled shopping-list. Nothing there for me unless smoked salmon, water biscuits and Mocha coffee held a hidden meaning, which I doubted.

I was about to drop the wallet when I saw the silk lining was torn. Closer inspection showed it was not a tear but a cut, probably made by a razor blade. Captain Morelius left nothing to chance at all. I inserted my finger between the lining and the outer case and encountered a piece of paper. Gently I teased it out, then took my find to the window.

It was a letter:

TO WHOM IT MAY CONCERN

Howard Greatorex Benson is the bearer of this letter. Should his *bona fides* be doubted in any way the undersigned should be consulted immediately before further action is taken with regard to the bearer.

Stapled to the letter was a passport-type photograph of Benson, a much younger man than the Benson I remembered but still with the damaged features and the scar on the cheek. He looked to be in his early thirties. Confirmation of this came from the date of the letter—4 January 1947. At the bottom of the letter was an address and a telephone number; the address was in Mayfair and the number was in the old style with both letters and digits, long since defunct. The letter was signed by James Pallson.

The itch at the back of my mind was now assuaged, the jigsaw puzzle was almost complete. Although a few minor pieces were missing, enough pieces were assembled to show the picture, and I didn't like what I saw. I scanned the letter again and wondered what Morelius had made of it, then I put it into my wallet and went downstairs.

I telephoned Ogilvie but he was out, so after making my farewell to Mary Cope I drove back to London, going immediately to University College. Aware that Lumsden might refuse to see me, I avoided the receptionist and went straight to his office and went in without knocking.

241

He looked up and frowned in annoyance as he saw me. 'What the devil ... I won't be badgered like this.'

'Just a few words, Professor.'

'Now look here,' he snapped, 'I have work to do, and I haven't time to play post office between two love-birds.'

I strode to his desk and pushed the telephone towards him. 'Ring Penny.'

'I will not.' He picked up the card I flicked on to the desk, then said, 'I see. Not just a simple policeman, after all. But I can't see this makes any difference.'

I said, 'Where's this laboratory?'

'In Scotland.'

'Where in Scotland?'

'I'm sorry. I'm not at liberty to say.'

'Who runs it?'

He shrugged. 'Some government department, I believe.'

'What's being done there?'

'I really don't know. Something to do with agriculture, so I as told.'

'Who told you?'

'I can't say.'

'Can't or won't?' I held his eye for a moment and he twitched irritably. 'You don't really believe that guff about agriculture, do you? That wouldn't account for the secretive way you're behaving. What's so bloody secret about agricultural research? Cregar told you it was agriculture and you accepted it as a sop to your conscience, but you never really believed it. You're not as naïve as that.'

'We'll leave my conscience to me,' he snapped.

'And you're welcome to it. What's Penny doing there?'

'Giving general technical assistance.'

'Laboratory design for the handling of pathogens,' I suggested.

'That kind of thing.'

'Does she know Cregar is behind it?'

'You're the one who brought up Cregar,' said Lumsden. 'I didn't.'

'What did Cregar do to twist your arm? Did he threaten to cut off your research funds? Or was there a subtly-worded letter from a Cabinet Minister suggesting much the same thing? Co-operate with Cregar or else.' I studied him in silence for a moment. 'That doesn't really matter—but did Penny know of Cregar's involvement?'

'No,' he said sullenly.

'And she didn't know what the laboratory was for, but she was beginning to have suspicions. She had a row with you.'

'You seem to know it all,' said Lumsden tiredly, and shrugged. 'You're right in most of what you say.'

I said, 'Where is she?'

He looked surprised. 'At the laboratory. I thought we'd established that.'

'She was very worried about safety up there, wasn't she?'

'She was being emotional about it. And Cregar was pushing Carter hard. He wanted results.'

'Who is Carter?'

'The Chief Scientific Officer.'

I pointed to the telephone. 'I'll lay you a hundred pounds to a bent farthing that you won't be able to talk to her.'

He hesitated for a long time before he picked up the telephone and began to dial. Although he was being niggly on secrecy, on security he was lousy. As he dialled I watched his finger and memorized the number. 'Professor Lumsden here. I'd like to speak to Dr Ashton Yes, I'll hang on.'

He put his hand over the mouthpiece. 'They've gone to call her. They think she's in her room.'

'Don't bet on it.'

Lumsden hung on to the telephone for a long time, then suddenly said, 'Yes? ... I see ... the mainland. Well, ask her to ring me as soon as she comes back. I'll be in my office.' He put down the telephone and said dully, 'They say she's gone to the mainland.'

'So it's on an island.'

'Yes.' He looked up and his eyes were haunted. 'They could be right, you know.'

'Not a chance,' I said. 'Something has happened up there. You referred to your conscience; I'll leave you with it. Good day, Professor Lumsden.'

I strode into Ogilvie's outer office, said to his secretary, 'Is the boss in?' and breezed on through without waiting for an answer. There were going to be no more closed doors as far as I was concerned.

Ogilvie was just as annoyed as Lumsden at having his office invaded. 'I didn't send for you,' he said coldly.

'I've cracked Benson,' I said. 'He was Cregar's man.'

Ogilvie's eyes opened wide. 'I don't believe it.'

I tossed the letter before him. 'Signed, sealed and delivered. That was written on the fourth of January 1947, the day Benson was discharged from the army, and signed by the Honourable James Pallson who is now Lord Cregar. Christ, the man has no honour in him. Do you realize, that when Ashton and Benson skipped to Sweden and Cregar was doing his holier-than-thou bit, he knew where they were all the time. The bastard has been laughing at us.'

Ogilvie shook his head. 'No, it's too incredible.'

'What's so incredible about it? That letter says Benson has been Cregar's man for the past thirty years. I'd say Cregar made a deal with Ashton. Ashton was free to do as he wanted —to sink or swim in the capitalist sea—but only on condition he had a watchdog attached: Benson. And when the reorganization came and Cregar lost responsibility for Ashton he conveniently forgot to tell you about Benson. It also explains why Benson was lost from the computer files.'

Ogilvie drew in his breath. 'It fits,' he admitted. 'But it leaves a lot still to be explained.'

'You'll get your explanation from Cregar,' I said savagely. 'Just before I skin him and nail his hide to the barn door.'

'You'll stay away from Cregar,' he said curtly. 'I'll handle him.'

'That be damned for a tale. You don't understand. Penny Ashton has gone missing and Cregar has something to do with it. It will take more than you to keep me off Cregar's back.'

'What's all this?' He was bewildered.

I told him, then said, 'Do you know where this laboratory is?'

'No.'

I took a card from my wallet and dropped it on the desk. 'A telephone number. The post office won't tell me anything about it because it's unlisted. Do something.'

He glanced at the card but didn't pick it up. He said slowly, 'I don't know ...'

I cut in. 'I know something. That letter is enough to ruin Cregar, but I can't wait. Don't stop me. Just give me what I need and I'll give you more than that letter—I'll give you Cregar's head on a platter. But I'm not going to wait too long.'

He looked at me thoughtfully, then picked up the card and the telephone simultaneously. Five minutes later he said two words. 'Cladach Duillich.'

THIRTY-FOUR

Cladach Duillich was a hard place to get to. It was one of the Summer Isles, a scattering of rocks in an indentation of the North Minch into Ross and Cromarty. The area is a popular haunt of the biological dicers with death. Six miles to the south of Cladach Duillich lies Gruinard Island, uninhabited and uninhabitable. In 1942 the biological warfare boys made a trifling mistake and Gruinard was soaked with anthrax—a hundred years' danger. No wonder the Scots want devolution with that sort of foolishness emanating from the south.

I flew to Dalcross, the airport for Inverness, and there hired a car in which I drove the width of Scotland to Ullapool at the head of Loch Broom. It was a fine day; the sun was shining; the birds singing and the scenery magnificent—all of which left me cold because I was trying to make good speed on a road which is called in Scotland, 'Narrow, Class 1 (with passing places)'. I felt with a depressing certainty that time was a commodity which was running out fast.

It was latish in the day when I arrived in Ullapool. Cladach Duillich lay twelve miles further, out in the bay; say a four hour round trip for a local fishing boat. I dickered with a couple of fishermen but none was willing to take me out at that time. The sun was an hour from setting, clouds were building up in the west, and a raw wind blew down the narrow loch, ruffling water which had turned iron grey. I made a tentative deal with a man called Robbie Ferguson to take me out to the island at eight the next morning, weather permitting.

It was not yet the tourist season so I found a room in a pub quite easily. That evening I sat in the bar listening to the local gossip and putting in a word or two myself, not often but often enough to stake a conversational claim when I decided to do a small quiz on Cladach Duillich.

It was evident that the rising tide of Scottish nationalism

was in full rip in the West Highlands. There was talk of English absentee landlords and of 'Scottish' oil and of the ambivalent attitude of the Scottish Labour Party, all uttered in tones of amused and rather tired cynicism as though these people had lost faith in the promises of politicians. There was not much of it, just enough to spice the talk of fishing and the weather, but if I had been a bland habitué of the Westminster corridors of power it would have been enough to scare the hell out of me. Ullapool, it seemed, was further removed from London than Kalgoorlie, Australia.

I finished my half-pint of beer and switched to scotch, asking the barman which he recommended. The man next to me turned. 'The Talisker's not so bad,' he offered. He was a tall, lean man in his mid-fifties with a craggy face and the soft-set mouth found in Highlanders. He spoke in that soft West Highland accent which is about as far from Harry Lauder as you can get.

'Then that's what I'll have. Will you join me?'

He gave me a speculative look, then smiled. 'I don't see why not. You'll be from the south, I take it. It's early for folk like you.'

I ordered two large Taliskers. 'What sort am I, then?'

'A tourist, maybe?'

'Not a tourist— a journalist.'

'Is it so? Which paper?'

'Any that'll publish me. I'm a freelance. Can you tell me anything about Gruinard Island?'

He chuckled, and shook his head. 'Och, not again? Every year we get someone asking about Gruinard; the Island of Death they usually call it. It's all been written, man; written into the ground. There's nothing new in that.'

I shrugged. 'A good story is still a good story to anyone who hasn't heard it. There's a rising generation which thinks of 1942 as being in the Dark Ages. I've met kids who think Hitler was a British general. But perhaps you're right. Anything else of interest around here?'

'What would interest an English newspaper in Ullapool? There's no oil here; that's on the east coast.' He looked into his whisky glass thoughtfully. 'There's the helicopter which comes and goes and no one knowing why. Would that interest you?'

'It might,' I said. 'An oil company chopper?'

'Could be, could be. But it lands on one of the islands. I've seen it myself.'

'Which island?'

'Out in the bay—Cladach Duillich. It's just a wee rock with nothing much on it. I doubt if the oil is there. They put up a few buildings but no drilling rig.'

'Who put up the buildings?'

'They say the government rented the island from an English lord. Wattie Stevenson went over in his boat once, just to pass the time of day, you know, and to say that when the trouble came there'd always be someone in Ullapool to help. But they wouldn't as much as let him set foot on the rock. Not friendly neighbours at all.'

'What sort of trouble was your friend expecting?'

'The weather, you understand. The winter storms are very bad. It's said the waves pass right over Cladach Duillich. That's how it got its name.'

I frowned. 'I don't understand that.'

'Ah, you haven't the Gaelic. Well, long ago there was a fisherman out of Coigach and his boat sank in a storm on the other side of the islands out there. So he swam and he swam and he finally got ashore and thought he was safe. But he was drowned all the same, poor man, because the shore was Cladach Duillich. The water came right over. Cladach Duillich in the English would be the Sad Shore.'

If what I thought was correct it was well named. 'Do the people on Cladach Duillich ever come ashore here?'

'Not at all. I haven't seen a one of them. They fly south in the helicopter and no one knows where it goes or where it comes from. Not a penny piece do they spend in Ullapool. Very secret folk they are. There's just the one landing place on Cladach Duillich and they've put up a big notice about trespassers and what will be done to them.'

I noticed that his glass was empty and wondered when he'd sunk the whisky. He must have done it when I blinked. I said, 'Have another, Mr ... er ...'

'You'll have one with me.' He signalled to the barman, then said, 'My name is Archie Ferguson and it's my brother who'll be taking you out to Cladach Duillich tomorrow morn.' He

248

smiled sardonically at my evident discomfiture, and added, 'But I doubt if you'll set foot there.'

'I'm Malcolm Jaggard,' I said. 'And I think I will.'

'Malcolm's a good Scots name,' said Ferguson. 'I'll drink to your success, anyway; whatever it may be.'

'There's certainly something odd about the place,' I said. 'Do you think it's another Gruinard?'

Ferguson's face altered and for a moment he looked like the wrath of Almighty God. 'It had better not be so,' he said sternly. 'If we thought it was we would take the fire to it.'

I chewed that over together with my dinner, then made a telephone call—to Cladach Duillich. A voice said, 'How can I help you?'

'I'd like to speak to Dr Ashton. My name is Malcolm Jaggard.'

'Just a moment. I'll see if she's available.'

There was a four minute silence, then another voice said, 'I'm sorry, Mr Jaggard, but I'm told Dr Ashton went to the mainland and is not yet back.'

'Where on the mainland?'

There was a pause. 'Where are you speaking from, Mr Jaggard?'

'From London. Why?'

He didn't answer the question. 'She went to Ullapool—that's our local metropolis. She said she'd like to stretch her legs; there's not much scope for walking where we are. And she wanted to shop for a few things. May I ask how you got our number?'

'Dr Ashton gave it to me. When do you expect her back?'

'Oh, I don't know. The weather has closed in, so I don't think she'll be back until tomorrow morning. You could speak to her then.'

'Where would she stay in Ullapool? I don't know the place.'

'I really couldn't say, Mr Jaggard. But she'll be back tomorrow with the boat.'

'I see. May I ask who I'm speaking to?'

'I'm Dr Carter.'

'Thank you Dr Carter. I'll ring tomorrow.'

As I put down the telephone I reflected that someone was

lying—other than myself—and I didn't think it was Archie Ferguson. But to make sure I went into the bar and found him talking to Robbie, his brother. I joined them. 'Excuse me for butting in.'

'That's all right,' said Ferguson. 'I was just talking over with Robbie your chances of getting out to Cladach Duillich the morrow's morn.'

I looked at Robbie. 'Is there any doubt of it?'

'I think there'll be a wee blow,' he said. 'The glass is dropping as the weather forecast said. Have you a strong stomach, Mr Jaggard?'

'Strong enough.'

Archie Ferguson laughed. 'You'll need one of cast iron.'

I said, 'The people on Cladach Duillich also said the weather is closing in.'

Archie raised his eyebrows. 'You've been talking to them! How?'

'By telephone—how else?'

'Aye,' said Robbie. 'They had the cable laid.' He shook his head. 'Awful expensive.'

'A man there told me a woman came ashore today from Cladach Duillich—here in Ullapool. She's about five feet eight inches, dark hair, age twent...'

Robbie interrupted. 'How did she come?'

'By boat.'

'Then she didn't come,' he said positively. 'All the comings and goings are by that bluidy helicopter. There's no boat on Cladach Duillich.'

'Are you sure. I?'

'O' course I'm sure. I pass the place twice a day, most days. You can take my word—there's no boat.'

I had to make sure of it. 'Well, supposing she came anyway. Where would she stay in Ullapool?'

'Ullapool's not all that big,' said Archie. 'If she's here at all we can put our hands on her—in a manner o' speaking, that is. What would be the lassie's name?'

'Ashton—Penelope Ashton.'

'Rest easy, Mr Jaggard. You'll know within the hour.' He smiled genially at his brother. 'Do you not smell something awful romantic, Robbie?'

THIRTY-FIVE

The wind whistled about my ears as I stood on the pier at eight next morning. The sky was slate-grey and so was the loch, stippled with whitecaps whipped up by the wind. Below me Robbie Ferguson's boat pitched violently, the rubber tyre fenders squealing as they were compressed and rubbed on the stone wall. It looked much too fragile to be taken out on such a day, but Robbie seemed unconcerned. He had taken the cover off the engine and was swinging on a crank.

Beside me, Archie Ferguson said, 'So you think the young lady is still on Cladach Duillich?'

'I do.'

He pulled his coat closer about him 'Maybe we're wrong about the government,' he said. 'Could this be one of those queer religious groups we're importing from America these days? Moonies or some such? I've heard some remarkably funny things about them.'

'No, it's not that.' I looked at my watch. 'Mr Ferguson, could you do me a favour?'

'If I can.'

I estimated times. 'If I'm not back in eight hours—that's by four this afternoon—I want you to get the police and come looking for me.'

He thought about it for a moment. 'No harm in that. What if Robbie comes back and you don't?'

'Same thing applies. They might spin Robbie a yarn, tell him I've decided to stay. They'll be lying, but he's to accept the lie, come back here, and raise the alarm.'

Below, the diesel engine spluttered into life and settled down into a slow and steady thumping. Archie said, 'You know, Malcolm Jaggard, I don't believe you're a journalist at all.'

I took a card from my wallet and gave it to him. 'If I don't come back ring that number. Get hold of a man called Ogilvie and tell him about it.'

He studied the card. 'McCulloch and Ross—and Ogilvie. It seems we Scots have taken over the City of London.' He looked up. 'But you look less like a financier than you do a journalist. What's really going on out there on Cladach Duillich?'

'We spoke about it last night,' I said. 'And you talked of fire.'

A bleakness came over him. 'The government would do that again?'

'Governments are made of men. Some men would do that.'

'Aye, and some men can pay for it.' He looked at me closely. 'Malcolm Jaggard, when you come back you and I are going to have a bit of a talk. And you can tell yon laddies on Cladach Duillich that if you don't come back we'll be bringing the fire to them. A great cleanser is fire.'

'Stay out of it,' I said. 'It's a job for the police.'

'Don't be daft, man. Would the police go against the government? You leave this to me.' He looked down into the boat. 'Away with you; Robbie is waiting. And I'll away and have a talk with a few of my friends.'

I didn't argue with him. I climbed down the iron ladder which was slippery with water and seaweed and tried to time my drop into the boat to coincide with its erratic pitching. I fumbled it but was saved from sprawling full length by Robbie's strong arm.

He looked me up and down, then shook his head. 'You'll freeze, Mr Jaggard.' He turned and rummaged in a locker and brought out a seaman's guernsey. 'This'll keep you warm, and this'—he gave me a pair of trousers and an anorak, both waterproof—'this'll keep you dry.'

When I had put them on he said, 'Now sit you down and be easy.' He went forward, walking as easily in that tossing boat as another man would walk a city pavement. He cast off the forward line, then walked back, seemingly unconcerned that the bow was swinging in a great arc. As he passed the engine he pushed over a lever with his boot, then dexterously cast off the stern line. The throbbing note of the engine deepened and we began to move away from the quay wall. Robbie was standing with the tiller between his knees, looking forward and steering by swaying motions of his body while he coiled the stern line into a neat skein.

The wind strengthened as we got out into the loch and the waves were bigger. The wind was from the north-west and we plunged into the teeth of it. As the bow dipped downwards sheets of spray were blown aft and I appreciated the waterproofing. As it was, I knew I'd be thoroughly drenched by the time we got to Cladach Duillich.

Presently Robbie sat down, controlling the tiller with one booted foot. He pointed, and said, 'The Coigach shore.'

I ducked a lump of spray. 'What sort of man is your brother?'

'Archie?' Robbie thought a bit and then shrugged. 'He's my brother.'

'Would you call him a hot-headed man?'

'Archie hot-headed!' Robbie laughed. 'Why, the man's as cold as an iceberg. I'm the laddie in the family to take the chances. Archie weighs everything in a balance before he does anything. Why do you ask?'

'He was talking about what he'd do if I didn't come back from Cladach Duillich.'

'There's one thing certain about my brother—he does what he says he'll do. He's as reliable as death and taxes.'

That was comforting to know. I didn't know what lay ahead on Cladach Duillich, but I knew I wasn't going to get an easy answer. The knowledge that I had a reliable backstop gave me a warm feeling.

I said, 'If I go missing on that bloody bit of rock you'll take no for an answer. You'll swallow what they tell you, then go back and see your brother.'

He looked at me curiously. 'Are you expecting to disappear?'

'I wouldn't be surprised.'

He wiped spray from his face. 'I don't ken what this is about, but Archie seems to like you, and that's enough for me. He's the thinker.'

It was a long haul across Annat Bay towards the Summer Isles. The waves were short and steep, and the pitching was combined with rolling, giving a corkscrew motion which was nauseating. Robbie looked at me and grinned. 'We'd better talk; it'll take your mind off your belly. Look, there's Carn nan

Sgeir, with Eilean Dubh beyond. That's Black Island in the English.'

'Where's Cladach Duillich?'

'Away the other side of Eilean Dubh. We've a way to go yet.'

'Why don't they keep a boat there? If I lived on an island it's the first thing I'd think of.'

Robbie chuckled. 'You'll see when we get there—but I'll tell you anyway, just for the talking. There's but one place to land and a chancy place it is. There's no protection for boat or man. You can't just tie up as you can at Ullapool Pier. There'd be no boat when you got back if there was anything of a blow. It would be crushed on the rocks. I won't be waiting there for you, you know.'

'Oh? Where will you be?'

'Lying off somewhere within easy reach. There are more boats wrecked on land than at sea. It's the land that kills boats. I'll be doing a wee bit of fishing.'

I looked at the jumbled sea. 'In this!'

'Och, I'm used to it. You give me a time and I'll be there.'

'I'll tell you now. I want exactly two hours ashore.'

'Two hours you'll get,' he said. 'About the boat they haven't got on Cladach Duillich. When those folk first came they had a boat but it got smashed, so they got another and that was smashed. After they lost the third they began to get the idea. Then they thought that if they could take the boat ashore it would be all right, but it's an awful weary job pulling a boat ashore on Cladach Duillich because there's no beach. So they rigged davits just like on a ship and they could take the boat straight up a cliff and out of the water. Then a wave came one night and took the boat and the davits and they were never seen again. After that they gave up.'

'It sounds a grim place.'

'It is in bad weather. It won't be too bad today.' I looked at the reeling seas and wondered what Robbie called bad weather. He pointed. 'There it is—Cladach Duillich.'

It was just as Archie Ferguson had described it—a wee bit of rock. There were cliffs all around, not high but precipitous, and the sea boiled white underneath them. Off the island was a scattering of rocks like black fangs and I thought the people on

Cladach Duillich had been right when they decided this was no place for a boat.

As we drew nearer Robbie said, 'See that ravine? The landing place is at the bottom.'

There was a narrow crack in the cliff face at the bottom of which the sea seemed to be calmer—relatively speaking. Robbie swung the tiller over sharply to avoid a rock which slid astern three feet off the port quarter, then he swung hard the other way to avoid another. He grinned. 'This is when you hope the engine doesn't pack in. You'd better get right forrard—you'll have to jump for it, and I won't be able to hold her there long.'

I scrambled forward and stood right in the bows as he brought the boat in. Now I saw that the crack in the rock was wider than at first glance and there was a concrete platform built at the bottom. The engine note changed as Robbie throttled back for the final approach. It was an amazing feat, but in that swirling sea with its cross-currents he brought her in so the bow kissed the concrete with a touch as light as a feather. At his shout I jumped and went sprawling as my feet skidded from under me on the weed-covered surface. When I picked myself up the boat was thirty yards off-shore and moving away fast. Robbie waved and I waved back, and then he applied himself to the task of avoiding rocks.

I looked at my surroundings. The first thing I saw was the notice board Archie Ferguson had mentioned. It was weather-beaten and the paint was peeling and faded but it was still readable.

GOVERNMENT ESTABLISHMENT
Landing is Absolutely Prohibited
By Order

It did not say who had issued the order.

A path led from the concrete platform up the ravine, so I followed it. It climbed steeply and led to a plateau, sparsely grassed, in the centre of which was a group of buildings. They were low concrete structures which had the appearance of military blockhouses, probably because they were windowless. From what had been said about Cladach Duillich they were the only type of building which could survive there.

I had no more time to study the place because a man was

approaching at a run. He slowed as he came closer, and said abruptly, 'Can't you read?'

'I can read.'

'Then clear off.'

'The age of miracles is past, friend. Walking on the water has gone out of fashion. The boat's gone.'

'Well, you can't stay here. What do you want?'

'I want to talk to Dr Carter.'

He seemed slightly taken aback, and I studied him as he thought about it. He was big and he had hard eyes and a stubborn jaw. He said, 'What do you want to talk to Dr Carter about?'

'If Dr Carter wants you to know he'll tell you,' I said pleasantly.

He didn't like that but there wasn't much he could do about it. 'Who are you?'

'Same thing applies. You're out of your depth, friend. Let's go and see Carter.'

'No,' he said curtly. 'You stay here.'

I looked at him coldly. 'Not a chance. I'm wet through and I want to dry out.' I nodded to the buildings. 'Those look as bloody inhospitable as you behave, but I'm willing to bet they're warm and dry inside. Take me to Carter.'

His problem was that he didn't know me or my authority, but I was behaving as though I had a right to be there and making demands. He did as I thought he would and passed the buck. 'All right, follow me. You see Carter and you go nowhere else.'

THIRTY-SIX

As we walked towards the buildings I looked around at Cladach Duillich. It was not very big—about a third of a mile long
and a quarter-mile across. Life had a poor existence on this
rock. What grass had managed to gain a roothold was salt-
resistant marram, growing in crannies where a poor soil had
gathered, and even the dandelions were wizened and sickly
growths. The seabirds appeared to like it, though; the rocks
were white with their droppings and they wheeled overhead
screaming at our movements below.

There were three buildings, all identical, and I noted they
were connected by enclosed passages. To one side, on a level
bit of ground, was a helicopter pad, empty. I was conducted
around the corner of one of the buildings and ushered through a
doorway, bidden to wait, and then taken through another doorway. I looked back and realized I had gone through an air lock.

We turned sharply left and into a room where a man in a
white coat was sitting at a desk and writing on a pad. He was
slightly bald, had a thin face and wore bifocals. He looked up
and frowned as he saw me, then said to my escort, 'What's this,
Max?'

'I found him wandering about loose. He says he wants to see
you.'

Carter's attention switched to me. 'Who are you?'

I glanced sideways at Max, and said smoothly, 'Who I am is
for your ears only, Dr Carter.'

Carter sniffed. 'More cloak and dagger stuff. All right, Max.
I'll take care of this.'

Max nodded and left, and I stripped off the anorak. 'I hope
you don't mind me getting out of this stuff,' I said, as I began
to take off the waterproof trousers. 'Too warm for indoors.'

Carter tapped on the desk with his pen. 'All right. Who are
you, and what do you want?'

I tossed the trousers aside and sat down. 'I'm Malcolm Jaggard. I've come to see Dr Ashton.'

'Didn't you ring me last night? I told you she wasn't here—she's on the mainland.'

'I know what you told me,' I said evenly. 'You said she'd be back this morning, so I came to see her.'

He gestured. 'You've seen the weather. She wouldn't come over in this.'

'Why not? I did.'

'Well, she hasn't. She's still in Ullapool.'

I shook my head. 'She's not in Ullapool and she wasn't there last night, either.'

He frowned. 'Look here, when I asked last night you said you were ringing from London.'

'Did I? Must have been force of habit,' I said blandly. 'Does it make a difference where I rang from?'

'Er ... no.' Carter straightened and squared his shoulders. 'Now, you're not supposed to be here. This establishment is, shall we say, rather hush-hush. If it became known you were here you could be in trouble. Come to that, so could I, so I'll have to ask you to leave.'

'Not without seeing Penny Ashton. She's supposed to be here. Now isn't that a funny thing. I'm where I'm supposed not to be, and she's not where she's supposed to be. How do you account for it?'

'I don't have to account for anything to you.'

'You'll have to account for a lot, Dr Carter, if Penny Ashton doesn't turn up pretty damn quick. How did she get to Ullapool?'

'By boat, of course.'

'But this establishment doesn't have a boat. All journeys are by helicopter.'

He moistened his lips. 'You appear to be taking an unhealthy interest in this place, Mr Jaggard. I warn you that could be dangerous.'

'Are you threatening me, Dr Carter?'

'For any purpose prejudicial to the safety of the State, to approach, inspect or enter any prohibited place, or to—'

'Don't quote the Official Secrets Act at me,' I snapped. 'I probably know it better than you do.'

'I could have you arrested,' he said. 'No warrant is needed.'

'For a simple scientist you appear to know the Act very well,' I observed. 'So you'll know that to arrest me automatically brings in the Director of Public Prosecutions.' I leaned back. 'I doubt if your masters would relish that, seeing that Penny Ashton is missing from here. I told you, you'll have to account for a lot, Dr Carter.'

'But not to you,' he said, and put his hand on the telephone.

'I hope that's to give instructions to have Dr Ashton brought in here.'

A cool and amused voice behind me said, 'But Dr Carter really can't have her brought in here.' I turned my head and saw Cregar standing at the door with Max. Cregar said, 'Doctor, I'll trouble you for the use of your office for a moment. Max, see to Mr Jaggard.'

Carter was palpably relieved and scurried out. Max came over to me and searched me with quick, practised movements. 'No gun.'

'No?' said Cregar. 'Well, that can be rectified if necessary. What could happen to an armed man who breaks into a government establishment, Max?'

'He could get shot,' said Max unemotionally.

'So he could, but that would lead to an official enquiry which might be undesirable. Any other suggestions?'

'There are plenty of cliffs around here,' said Max. 'And the sea's big.'

It was a conversation I could do without. I said, 'Where's Penny Ashton?'

'Oh, she's here—you were quite right about that. You'll see her presently.' Cregar waved his hands as though dismissing a minor problem. 'You're a persistent devil. I almost find it in me to admire you. I could do with a few men of your calibre in my organization. As it is, I'm wondering what to do with you.'

'You'd better compound your offences,' I said. 'Whatever you do about me, you've already done for yourself. We've linked you with Benson. I wouldn't be surprised if the Minister hasn't already been informed of it.'

The corners of his mouth turned down. 'How could I be linked with Benson? What possible evidence could there be?'

'A letter dated the fourth of January, 1947, carried by Benson and signed by you.'

'A letter,' said Cregar blankly, and looked through me into the past. Comprehension came into his eyes. 'Are you telling me that Benson still carried that damned letter after thirty years?'

'He'd probably forgotten about it—just as you had,' I said. 'It was hidden in the lining of his wallet.'

'A brown calf wallet with a red silk lining?' I nodded and Cregar groaned. 'I gave Benson that wallet thirty years ago. It would seem I tripped myself.'

He bent his head, apparently studying the liver spots on the backs of his hands. 'Where is the letter?' he asked colourlessly.

'The original? Or the twenty photocopies Ogilvie will have already made?'

'I see,' he said softly and raised his head. 'What were your first thoughts on seeing the letter?'

'I knew you were linked with Ashton because you brought him out of Russia. Now you were linked with Benson, too. I thought of all the odd things that had happened, such as why a gentleman's gentleman should carry a gun, and why you tried to discount the fact he had shot Ashton when we had the meeting on my return from Sweden. It seemed hard to believe he was still your man after thirty years, but I was forced into it.'

Cregar lounged back in his chair and crossed his legs. 'Benson was a good man once, before the Germans got him.' He paused. 'Of course he wasn't Benson then, he was Jimmy Carlisle and my comrade in British Intelligence during the war. But he lived and died as Benson, so let him remain so. He was captured in a Gestapo round-up in '44 and they sent him to Sachsenhausen, where he stayed until the end of the war. That's where he got his broken nose and his other brutalized features. They beat him with clubs. I'd say they beat his brains out because he was never the same man afterwards.'

He leaned forward, elbows on the desk. 'He was in a mess after the war. He had no family—his father, mother and sister were killed in an air raid—and he had no money apart from a disability pension. His brains were addled and his earning capacity limited. He'd never be any good in our line of work after that, but he deserved well of us, and by 1947 I pulled enough weight to help him. I was coping with Chelyuskin's tantrums at the time, so I offered him the job of shepherd to Chelyuskin—Ashton as he became. It was a sinecure, of course, but he was pathetically grateful. You see, he thought it meant he wasn't finished in his job.'

Cregar took out a packet of cigarettes. 'Are you finding this ancient history interesting?' He held out the packet.

I took a cigarette. 'Very intcresting,' I assured him.

'Very well. We switched him into the person of Benson at the same time we switched Chelyusin to Ashton, then he hung around for a while. When Ashton got going Benson had a job in Ashton's office, and then later he became Ashton's factotum.'

'And Ashton knew what he was?'

'Oh, yes. Benson was the price Ashton had to pay for freedom. I knew that a man with that calibre of mind would not long be content to fiddle around in industry and I wanted to keep tabs on what he was doing.' He smiled. 'Benson was on to quite a good thing. We paid him a retainer and Ashton paid him too.'

He leaned forward and snapped a gold lighter into flame under my nose. 'When the reorganization came and I lost Ashton to Ogilvie I kept quiet about Benson. In fact, I paid his retainer out of my own pocket. He didn't cost much; the retainer wasn't raised and the erosion in the value of money made Benson dirt cheap. It was an investment for the future which would have paid off but for you.'

I said, 'Did you know Ashton was into genetics?'

'Of course. Benson caught on to that as soon as it started happening. His job was to *know* what Ashton was doing at all times and, being permanently in the house, he could hardly miss. It was an incredible stroke of luck—Ashton becoming interested in genetics, I mean—because after the reorganization I had moved into the biological field myself.' He waved his hand. 'As you have discovered.'

'Ogilvie told me.'

'Ogilvie appears to have told you too much. From what you have let fall he appears to have given you the run of Code Black. Very naughty of him, and something he may regret. I was fortunate enough to be able to put a block on the computer to cover Benson, but evidently it wasn't enough.' He stopped suddenly, and stared at me. 'Even I appear to be telling you too much. You have an ingratiating way with you.'

'I'm a good listener.'

'And I become garrulous as I grow old, a grave failing in a man of our profession.' He looked at his half-smoked cigarette distastefully, stubbed it out, and put his hands flat on the desk. 'I'm at a loss to know how to dispose of you, young Jaggard. Your revelation that Ogilvie has that letter makes my situation most difficult.'

'Yes, he's in a position to blast hell out of you,' I agreed. 'I don't think the Minister will be pleased. I rather think you've put yourself on the retirement list.'

'Very succinctly put. Nevertheless, I will find a way out of the difficulty. I have surmounted difficulties before and I see no reason why I should fail this time. All it takes is applied thought to the study of men's weaknesses.' He slapped his hands together. 'And that is what I must do immediately. Put him somewhere safe, Max.'

I ignored the hand on my shoulder. 'What about Penny Ashton?'

'You will see her in my good time,' said Cregar coldly. 'And only if I think it advisable.'

In my rage I wanted to lash out at him but I couldn't ignore that tightening hand. Max leaned over me. 'No tricks,' he advised. 'I have a gun. You won't see it but it's there.'

So I rose from the chair and went with him. He took me from the office and along a corridor. Because the place was windowless it was almost like being in a submarine; everything was quiet except that the air shivered with the distant rumble of a generator. At the other end of the corridor I saw movement on the other side of a glass partition as a man walked across. He was wearing totally enveloping overalls and his head was hooded.

I had no time to see more because Max stopped and opened a heavy door. 'In there,' he said curtly, so I walked through and he slammed the door, leaving me in total darkness because he had not seen fit to turn on a light. The first thing I did was to explore my prison and arrived at the conclusion that it was an unused refrigerated room. The walls were thick and solid, as was the door, and I soon came to the conclusion that the only way out was to be let out. I sat on the floor in a corner and contemplated possibilities.

It appeared to have been wise to tell Cregar of the letter. Up to then he had primarily been interested in discussing ways and means of transforming me into a corpse safely, but my disclosure that Ogilvie had the letter had put a stopper on that line of thought. But what a ruthless bastard he had turned out to be.

I don't know what makes men like Cregar tick, but there seem to be enough of the bastards around just as there are many Carters eager to help them. Somewhere in the world, I suppose, is the chemist who lovingly mixed a petroleum derivative with a palm oil derivative to produce napthenic acid palmetate, better know as napalm. To do that required a deliberate intellectual effort and a high degree of technical training, and why a man should put his brain to such a use is beyond me. Supervising that chemist would be an American Cregar whose motives are equally baffling, and at the top are the politicians ultimately responsible. Their motive is quite clear, of course: the ruthless grasp of sheer power. But why so many others should be willing to help them is beyond me.

It's hard to know who to blame. Is it the Lumsdens of the world who know what is going on but turn a blind eye, or is it the rest of us who don't know and don't take the trouble to find out? Sometimes I think the world is like a huge ant heap full of insects all busily manufacturing insecticide.

I was in the black room for a long time. The only light came from the luminous dial of my watch which told me of the hours ticking away. I was oppressed by the darkness and became claustrophobic and suffered strange fears. I got up and began to walk around the room, keeping to the walls; it was one way of taking exercise. The silence was solid except for the sound of my own movements and a new fear came upon me. What if Cladach Duillich had been abandoned—evacuated? I could stay in that room until the flesh rotted from my bones.

I stopped walking and sat in the corner again. I may have fallen asleep for a while, I don't remember. The hours I spent there are pretty much blanked out in my memory. But I was awake when the door opened to let in a flood of light as glaring as from arc lamps. I put my hands to my eyes and saw

Cregar at the door. He tut-tutted, and said, 'You didn't leave him a light, Max.'

'Must have forgotten,' said Max indifferently.

The light was quite ordinary light shed from fluorescent tubes in the ceiling of the corridor. I got up and went to the door. 'God damn you!' I said to Max.

He stood back a pace and lifted the pistol he held. Cregar said, 'Calm down. It wasn't intentional.' He saw me looking at the pistol. 'That's to warn you not to do anything silly, as well you might. You wanted to see the girl, didn't you? Well, you can see her now. Come with me.'

We walked along the corridor side by side with Max bringing up the rear. Cregar said conversationally, 'You won't see any of the staff because I've had them cleared out of this block. They're scientific types and a bit lily-livered. The sight of guns makes them nervous.'

I said nothing.

We walked a few more paces. 'I think I've found a way of confounding Ogilvie—there'll be no problem there—but that still leaves you. After we've seen Dr Ashton we'll have a talk.' He stopped at a door. 'In here,' he said, and let me precede him.

It was a strange room because one wall was almost entirely glass but the window looked, not upon the outside, but into another room. At first I didn't know what I was looking at, but Cregar said, 'There's Dr Ashton.' He pointed to a bed in the next room.

Penny was in the bed, seemingly asleep. Her face was pale and ravaged, she could have been a woman twice her age. Around the bed were various bits of hospital equipment among which I recognized two drip feeds, one of which appeared to contain blood. I said, 'In God's name, what happened?'

Cregar said, almost apologetically, 'We had ... er ... an accident here last week in which Dr Ashton was involved. I'm afraid she's rather ill. She's been in a coma for the last two days.' He picked up a microphone and snapped a switch. 'Dr Ashton, can you hear me?'

His voice came amplified and distorted from a loudspeaker in the next room. Penny made no movement.

I said tightly, 'What's she got?'

'That's rather hard to say. It's something nobody has ever had before. Something new. Carter has been trying to run it down but without much success.'

I was frightened and angry simultaneously. Frightened for Penny and angry at Cregar. 'It's something you brewed up here, isn't it? Something that got loose because you were too tight-fisted to have a P_4 laboratory as she wanted.'

'I see that Dr Ashton has been chattering about my business.' Cregar gestured. 'That's not a proper hospital ward of course; it's one of our laboratories. She had to be put somewhere safe.'

'Not safe for her,' I said bitterly. 'Safe for you.'

'Of course,' said Cregar. 'Whatever she's got we can't have spread about. Carter thinks it's most infectious.'

'Is Carter a medical doctor?'

'His degree is in biology not medicine, but he's a very capable man. She's getting the best of attention. We're transfusing whole blood and glucose, as you see.'

I turned to him. 'She should be in a hospital. This amateur lash-up is no good, and you know it. If she dies you'll be a murderer, and so will Carter and everybody else here.'

'You're probably right,' he said indifferently. 'About the hospital, I mean. But it's difficult to see how we could put her in a hospital and still maintain security.' His voice was remote and objective. 'I pride myself on my ability to solve problems but I haven't been able to solve that one.'

'Damn your security!'

'Coming from a man in your profession that smacks of heresy.' Cregar stepped back as he saw my expression, and gestured to Max who lifted the pistol warningly. 'She's having the best attention we can give her. Dr Carter is assiduous in his duties.'

'Carter is using her as a guinea pig and you damned well know it. She must be taken to a hospital—better still, to Porton. They understand high-risk pathogens there.'

'You're in no position to make demands,' he said. 'Come with me.' He turned his back and walked out.

I took a last look at Penny, then followed him with Max close behind. He walked up the corridor and opened a door on the other side. We entered a small vestibule and Cregar waited until Max had closed the outer door before proceeding. 'We do take precautions, in spite of anything you've been told,' he said. 'This is an air lock. The laboratory through there is under low air pressure. Do you know why?'

'If there's a leak air goes in and not out.'

He nodded in satisfaction as though I'd passed a test, and opened the inner door. My ears popped as the pressure changed. 'This is Carter's own laboratory. I'd like to show it to you.'

'Why?'

'You'll see.' He began a tour, behaving for all the world like a guide in one of those model factories where they show you what they're proud of and hide the bad bits. 'This is a centrifuge. You'll notice it's in an air-tight cabinet; that's to prevent anything escaping while it's in operation. No aerosols—microbes floating in the air.'

We passed on, and he indicated an array of glass-fronted cabinets covering one wall. 'The incubating cabinets, each containing its own petri dish and each petri dish isolated. Nothing can escape from there.'

'Something escaped from somewhere.'

He ignored that. 'Each cabinet can be removed in its entirety and the contents transferred elsewhere without coming into contact even with the air in the laboratory.'

I looked into a cabinet at the circular growth of a culture on a petri dish. 'What's the organism?'

'*Escherichia coli*, I believe. It's Carter's favourite.'

'The genetically weakened strain.'

Cregar raised his eyebrows. 'You seem well informed for a layman. I don't know; that's Carter's affair. I'm not the expert.'

I turned to face him. 'What's this all about?'

'I'm trying to show you that we do take all possible precautions. What happened to Dr Ashton was purely accidental—a million to one chance. It's very important to me that you believe that.'

'If you'd listened to her it wouldn't have happened, but I believe you,' I said. 'I don't think you did it on purpose. What's so important about it?'

'I can come to an accommodation with Ogilvie,' he said. 'I'll lose some advantage but not all. That leaves you.'

'Have you spoken with Ogilvie?'

'Yes.'

I felt sick. If Cregar could corrupt Ogilvie I wouldn't want to work with him again. I said steadily, 'What about me?'

'This. I can do a deal with Ogilvie all right, but I don't think I could make it stick if anything happened to you. He always was squeamish. That means you have to be around and able to talk for some time to come which, as you will appreciate, presents me with a problem.'

'How to keep my mouth shut without killing me.'

'Precisely. You are a man like myself—we cut to the heart of a problem. When you appeared in the Ashton case I had you investigated most thoroughly. To my surprise you had no handle I could get hold of, no peccadilloes to be exploited. You seem to be that rarity, the honest man.'

'I won't take compliments from you, damn it!'

'No compliment, I assure you. Just a damnable nuisance. I wanted something to hold over you, something with which to blackmail you. There was nothing. So I have to find something else to close your mouth. I think I've found it.'

'Well?'

'It will mean my giving up more of the advantage I have achieved over the years, but I'll retain the most of it. I'll trade the young lady in the next laboratory for your silence.'

I looked at him with disgust. He had said the solution to his problem would lie in the study of men's weaknesses and he had found mine. He said, 'As soon as you agree, the girl can be taken to hospital, in carefully controlled conditions, of course. Perhaps your suggestion that she be taken to Porton is best. I could arrange that.'

I said, 'What guarantee would you have that I won't talk when she's well? I can't think of anything but no doubt you can.'

'Indeed I can—and I have. In Carter's office there's a document I want you to sign. I should say it's a carefully constructed document which took all my ingenuity to concoct. Quite a literary gem.'

'About what?'

'You'll see. Well, do you agree?'

'I'll need to read it first.'

Cregar smiled. 'Of course you may read it, but I think you'll sign anyway. It's not much to ask—your signature for the life of your future wife.'

'You sicken me,' I said.

A telephone rang, startlingly loud. Cregar frowned, and said to Max, 'Answer it.' He held out his hand. 'I'll have the pistol. I don't trust him yet.'

Max gave him the gun and walked to the other end of the laboratory. Cregar said, 'Sticks and stones, etcetera. I don't care what you think of me as long as I get my way.'

'Show me what you want me to sign.'

'We'll wait for Max.'

Max talked in monosyllables in a low voice, then hung up and came back. 'Carter's got his knickers in a twist. He says a lot of men are landing. He reckons there are twenty boats out there.'

Cregar frowned. 'Who the hell are they?'

'He reckons they're local fishermen.'

'Damned Scotch peasants! Go and shoo them away, Max. Put the fear of God into them with the Official Secrets Act. Get rid of them any way you can. Threaten them with the police if you have to.'

'Just threaten or actually send for them?'

'You can send for them if you think the situation warrants it.'

Max nodded towards me. 'That may not be entirely safe.'

'Don't worry about Jaggard,' said Cregar. 'We've reached an agreement.' As Max left he turned to me. 'Is this your doing?'

'How could I start a popular uprising?' I asked. 'They've probably got wind of what you're doing here, and remembering Gruinard, are determined not to let it happen again.'

'Ignorant bastards,' he muttered. 'Max will put them in their place.'

I said, 'I want Penny in hospital fast. How do we get off here?'

'A phone call will bring the helicopter in two hours.'

'You'd better make the call, then.'

He looked down at the floor, rubbing the side of his jaw while he thought about it. It was then I hit him in the belly, knocking the wind out of him. The gun went off and a bullet

268

ricocheted from the wall and there was a smash of glass. I grabbed his wrist as he tried to bring up the gun and chopped him across the neck with the edge of my hand. He sagged to the floor.

When he painfully picked himself up I had the pistol. He glanced at it, then raised his eyes to mine. 'Where do you think this will get you?'

'I don't know about me, but it'll put you in prison.'

'You're a stupid romantic fool,' he said.

'What's the number to ring for the helicopter?'

He shook his head. 'You don't know how government works, damn it. I'll never go to prison, but you'll be in water so hot you'll wish you'd never heard of Ashton or me.'

I said, 'I don't like hitting old men but I'll hammer hell out of you if I don't get that number.'

He turned his head and froze, then a weird bubbling cry came from him. 'Oh, Christ! Look what you've done!' His hand quivered as he pointed to the wall.

I looked, being careful to step behind him. At first I didn't see it. 'No tricks. What am I supposed to see?'

'The cabinets. Two are broken.' He whirled on me. 'I'm getting out of here.'

Blindly he tried to push past me, ignoring the gun. He was in a frenzy of terror, his face working convulsively. I stiff-armed him but his panic gave him added strength and he got past me and headed for the door. I went after him, reversed the pistol and clubbed him over the head. He went down like a falling tree.

I dragged him away from the door and went back to see the damage. Two of the panes in the incubating cabinets were broken and fragments of the petri dishes were scattered on the floor as were slimy particles of the cultures they had contained.

I whirled around as the door of the laboratory burst open. There stood Archie Ferguson. 'You're right, Mr Jaggard,' he said. 'It's another damned Gruinard.'

'Get out!' I yelled. 'For your life, get out!' He looked at me with startled eyes, and I pointed to the glass wall at the end of the room. 'Go next door—I'll talk to you there. Move, man!'

The door slammed shut.

THIRTY-SEVEN

When I picked up the microphone my hand was shaking almost uncontrollably. I pushed the transmit button and heard a click. 'Can you hear me, Archie?' Ferguson, on the other side of the glass, nodded and spoke but I heard nothing. 'There's a microphone in front of you.'

He looked about him, then picked it up. 'What happened here, Malcolm?'

'This place is bloody dangerous. Tell your men not to enter any of the laboratories—especially this one and the one across the corridor. Do that now.'

'I'll have guards on the doors.' He dropped the microphone and left on the run.

I went across to Cregar who was breathing stertorously. His head was twisted in an awkward position so I straightened him out and he breathed easier but showed no signs of coming awake.

'Mr Jaggard—are you there?'

I went back to the window to find Archie and Robbie Ferguson and a third man, one of the biggest I've seen, who was introduced as Wattie Stevenson. Archie said, 'It would seem you have problems. Is the lassie across the corridor the one you looked for?'

'Yes. You haven't been in there, have you?'

'No. I saw her by this arrangement we have here.'

'Good. Keep out of there. What size of an army did you bring? I heard of twenty boats.'

'Who told you that? There's only the six.'

'Have any trouble?'

'Not much. A man has a broken jaw.'

I said, 'How many people are there in this place?'

'Not as many as I would have thought. Maybe a dozen.'

Ogilvie had been right. It didn't take much to run a microbiological laboratory; perhaps half a dozen technical staff and the same number of domestics and bottlewashers. 'Put the lot under arrest. You have my authority for it.'

Archie looked at me speculatively. 'And what authority would that be?' I took out my departmental card and held it against the glass. He said, 'It doesn't mean much to me, but it looks official.'

'It takes you off the hook for invading government property. You did it on my instruction and you're covered. Oh, if you find a character called Max I don't care how roughly he's handled.'

Robbie Ferguson laughed. 'He's the one with the broken jaw. Wattie, here, hit him.'

'Och, it wasna' more than a wee tap,' said Wattie. 'The man has a glass jaw.'

'Wattie won the hammer throwing at the last Highland Games,' said Archie, with a grim smile. 'Besides, it was the man, Max, who sent Wattie away with a flea in his ear when he offered to help. What's to do now?'

'Did you ring Ogilvie as I asked?'

'Aye. He said he already knew about it.'

I nodded. He would have talked with Cregar. 'I want you to ring him again and the call put through to this telephone in here. You'll find a switchboard somewhere.'

'You can't come out?'

'No. You have my permission to listen in when I talk.' There was a groan behind me and I turned to see Cregar stirring. I said, 'Tell your men guarding the laboratories it's just as important that no one comes out. In fact, it's more important. This place being what it is there's probably some guns somewhere. In emergency use them.'

Archie looked grave. 'Is it so fearsome a thing?'

'I don't know,' I said wearily. 'I'm just taking prophylactic measures. Get busy, will you?'

I went back to Cregar, helped him to get up, and sat him in a chair where he slumped flaccidly. He was dazed and in shock; to old to cope with the rough stuff any more. I said, 'Cregar, can you hear me?' He muttered something indistinguishable, and I slapped his cheek. 'Can you hear me?'

'Yes,' he whispered.

'Don't try to leave. There's a man outside with orders to shoot. Do you understand?'

He looked at me with glazed eyes, and nodded. 'Doesn't matter,' he muttered. 'I'm dead, anyway. So are you.'

'We'll all be dead in a hundred years,' I said, and went to look again at the cultures in the broken petri dishes. The stuff looked harmless enough but I was careful not to touch it. Penny had described the elaborate precautions which were taken to prevent the escape of dangerous organisms from laboratories and, according to her, the lab I was now in wasn't up to snuff for what Carter had been doing.

The cultures could have been ordinary *E.coli* and, as such, perfectly harmless. But if they were cultures of *E.coli* which Carter had diddled around with then they could be dangerous in totally unpredictable ways. Cregar wasn't a scientist but he knew what Carter was up to, and the broken dishes had been enough to scare him half to death. From now on no chances could be taken and I hoped there had not been an escape already when Archie had opened the door. I didn't think so— the laboratory had low air pressure and I'd got him out fast.

Twenty minutes later I had Ogilvie on the phone. I wasted no time on politeness and answered none of the questions he shot at me. I said, 'This is a matter for urgency so get it right the first time. Have you something to write with?'

'I'll record.' I heard a click.

'Cregar's laboratory on Cladach Duillich has run wild. There's one serious case of infection and two suspected. The organism causing it is new to medicine and probably man-made; it's also highly infectious. I don't know if it's a killer but it's highly likely. You'll have to set the alarm ringing and probably Lumsden, Penny's boss, is the best man to do it. Tell him hospitalization for three is needed in P4—repeat—P4 conditions. He'll know what that means. Tell him I suggest Porton Down, but he might have a better idea.'

'I'll get on to it immediately,' said Ogilvie. 'Who are the three?'

'The serious case is Penny Ashton.'

There was a sharp withdrawal of breath. 'Oh, Christ! I'm sorry, Malcolm.'

I went on, 'The suspected cases are Cregar and myself.'

'For the love of God!' said Ogilvie. 'What's been going on up there?'

I ignored him. 'There's a helicopter pad on Cladach Duillich so Lumsden had better use a chopper. Tell him the man to see here is a Dr Carter. He's the chap who cooked up whatever hellbrew has got loose.'

'I've got that.'

'Then make it quick. I think Penny is dying,' I said bleakly.

THIRTY-EIGHT

Cregar and I were in an odd position. Loathing each other beyond all belief, we were condemned to each other's company for an unspecified period. The next few hours were to be extremely uncomfortable, but I tried to make them as comfortable as possible.

Archie Ferguson came back as soon as I had spoken to Ogilvie and the expression on his face was terrifying. He looked like one of the Old Testament prophets might look after inditing one of the more dire chapters of the Bible. 'May their souls rot forever in hell!' he burst out.

'Take it easy,' I said. 'There are practical things to do.' I thought of Ogilvie recording my telephone conversation and it gave me an idea. 'See if you can find a tape-recorder. I'll need it.'

Archie simmered down. 'Aye, I'll see what I can do.'

'And we'll need food in here, but you can give us food once and once only. What you do is this. You open the outer door of the laboratory and put the food on the floor just inside. Tell me when you've closed the door and I'll come out and get it. It can be done once only because I can't risk contamination through the air lock, so you'd better give us enough for three meals. If you can find vacuum flasks for coffee that would be a help.'

Ferguson looked past me. 'Is yon man the Cregar you spoke of?'

'Yes.'

'Then he gets nothing from me.'

'You'll do as I say,' I said sharply. 'We both eat or neither of us eats.'

He took a deep breath, nodded curtly, then laid down the microphone and went away. Half an hour later he came back.

'Your food's there. I did better than flasks; there's a coffee percolator to make your own.'

'Thanks.' I had another idea. 'Archie, this laboratory is maintained at a lower air pressure than the outside. That means pumps, and pumps mean electricity. Put someone to watch the generator; I don't want it stopping, either by breakdown or lack of fuel. Will you see to that?'

'Aye. It won't stop.'

I went into the air lock and got the food—a pile of sandwiches—and also found a small battery-powered cassette tape-recorder. I put everything on the table next to the telephone. Cregar was apathetic and looked at the sandwiches without interest. I filled the percolator from a tap on one of the benches and got the coffee going. Cregar accepted coffee but he wouldn't eat.

Unobtrusively I switched on the recorder; I wanted Cregar condemned out of his own mouth. I said, 'We've a lot to talk about.'

'Have we?' he said without interest. 'Nothing matters any more.'

'You're not dead yet, and you may not be if Ogilvie does his stuff. When did Benson learn of Ashton's interests in genetics?'

He was silent for a moment, then said, 'Must have been 1971. He saw that Ashton was keeping up with the girl's studies, and then starting to do a lot of work on his own, usually at the weekend—a lot of calculating. He tried to get a look at it, but Ashton kept it locked away.' Cregar brooded. 'Ashton never did like me. I've often wondered if he knew what I was doing.' He waved his hand at the laboratory. 'This, I mean. It's supposed to be secret, but a man with money can usually find out what he wants to know.' He shrugged. 'Anyway, he made damned certain that Benson didn't lay an eye on his work.'

'That empty vault must have come as a shock.'

He nodded. 'Benson knew about the vault but never managed to get inside. And when Ogilvie told me it was empty I didn't believe him. It was only when he offered to let one of my forensic chaps look at the vault that I accepted the fact.' He looked up. 'You're a clever man. I never thought of the railway. I ought to have done. Ashton wasn't the man to fool about with toy trains.'

Now Cregar had started to talk he positively flowed. I suppose he thought there was no reason to keep his silence. It was a sort of deathbed confession.

I said, 'What I can't understand was how you engineered Mayberry's acid attack—and why. That's the bit that seems senseless.'

'It was senseless,' said Cregar. 'I had nothing to do with it. I didn't even know Mayberry existed until the police tracked him down. Do you remember when you appeared before the inter-departmental committee, Ogilvie said something about you "exploding Ashton out of Stockholm"? Well, I exploded him out of England.'

'How?'

He shrugged. 'Opportunism combined with planning. I'd been wanting to have a dig at Ashton for a long time. I wanted to get him out of that house so I could get into that vault. I thought whatever he had would be ripe. I'd already made preparations—rented the flat and opened the bank account in Stockholm, got the Israeli passport, and so on. All I needed was a trigger. Then along came that maniac, Mayberry—most opportunely. I got Benson to panic Ashton, talking of threats to the other girl, and so on. Benson told him my department couldn't cope with that sort of thing unless Ashton got out, that we were prepared to help and that we had a safe hideaway for him, which of course we had. And after all that the damned vault was empty.'

'But why did Benson kill Ashton?'

'Standing orders from thirty years ago,' said Cregar simply. 'Ashton wasn't to be allowed to go back to the Russians. If there was a chance of him falling into Russian hands Benson was to kill him. Benson had every reason to think you were Russians.'

'Jesus!' I said. 'What sort of man was Benson to kill Ashton after being with him thirty years?'

Cregar gave me a lopsided smile. 'He had gratitude, I suppose; and personal loyalty—to me.'

I remember my musings in the dark room and, out of curiosity, said, 'Cregar, why did you do all this?'

276

He looked at me in surprise. 'A man must leave his mark on the world.'

I felt chilled.

There wasn't much I wanted to know after that, but, the dam now broken, Cregar rambled on interminably, and I was glad when the telephone rang. It was Ogilvie. 'There'll be an RAF helicopter on its way with a medical team. Lumsden thinks you're right about Porton and he's made the arrangements.' He paused. 'He also wants me to pass on his apologies—I don't know why.'

'I do. Thank him for me. When will the chopper get here?'

'They're assembling the team now. I'd say six hours. How's Miss Ashton?'

'I don't know,' I said bitterly. 'I can't get to her. She's in a coma. You can tell that to Lumsden, too.'

Ogilvie was inclined to talk but I cut him off. I wasn't in the mood for that. Half an hour later the phone rang again and I found Archie Ferguson on the line. 'There's someone called Starkie wants to talk to the man Carter. Shall I let him?'

'Let me talk to Starkie.' The earphone crackled and a deep voice said, 'Richard Starkie here—is that Dr Carter?'

'Malcolm Jaggard here. Who are you?'

'I'm a doctor speaking from Porton Down. Are you one of the infected men?'

'Yes.'

'Any symptoms starting to show?'

'Not yet.'

'If Carter manufactured this bug he'll know more about it than anyone. I need the information.'

'Right,' I said. 'If you don't get satisfaction from him let me know. Are you on the line, Archie?'

'Aye.'

'Let them talk. If Carter wants persuading I'm sure you know what to do.'

They came for us seven hours later, dressed like spacemen in plastic clothing with self-contained breathing apparatus. They put us in plastic envelopes whole and entire, plugged in an air supply and sealed us up. We stopped in the air lock and the envelopes and themselves were drenched with a liquid, then we were carried out to the helicopter where I found Penny already installed in her own envelope. She was still unconscious.

THIRTY-NINE

A month later I was feeling pretty chipper because Starkie had given me a clean bill of health. 'For three weeks now we've inspected every damned *E.coli* bug that's come out of you and they're all normal. I don't know why you're still lying around here. What do you think this is, a doss house?'

He hadn't always been as cheerful as that. At the beginning I was placed in a sterile room and untouched by human hand for the next two weeks. Everything that was done to me was done by remote control. Later they told me that a team of thirty doctors and nurses was working on me alone.

Penny did better. For her they apparently mobilized the entire medical resources of the United Kingdom, plus sizeable chunks from the United States and the Continent, with a little bit from Australia. The bug she had was different from the one I'd caught, and it was a real frightener. It got the medical world into a dizzy tizzy and, although they were able to cure her, they wanted to make sure that the bug, whatever it was, was completely eradicated. So I came out of Porton Down a month before her.

Starkie once said soberly, 'If she'd have been left another day with the minimal attention she was getting I don't think we could have done it.' That made me think of Carter and I wondered what was being done about him. I never found out.

When I came out of purdah but before I was discharged I went to see her. I couldn't kiss her, or even touch her, but we could speak separated by a pane of glass, and she seemed cheerful enough. I told her something of what had happened, but not everything. Time enough for that when she was better. Then I said, 'I want you out of here pretty damned quick. I want to get married.'

She smiled brilliantly. 'Oh, yes, Malcolm.'

'I can't fix a day because of that bloody man Starkie,' I complained. 'He's likely to keep you in here forever, investigating the contents of your beautiful bowels.'

She said, 'How would you like a double wedding? I had a letter from Gillian in New York. Peter Michaelis flew over and proposed to her. She was lying in bed with her left arm strapped to her right cheek and swaddled in bandages when he asked her. She thought it was very funny.'

'I'll be damned!'

'It will be a little time yet. We all have to get out of our hospitals. Is four months too long to wait?'

'Yes,' I said promptly. 'But I'll wait.'

I didn't ask anyone how Cregar was doing because I didn't care.

On the day I came out of the sterile room Ogilvie came to see me, bearing the obligatory pound of grapes. I received him with some reserve. He asked after my health and I referred him to Starkie, then he said, 'We got the tape cassette after it had been decontaminated. Cregar won't be able to wriggle out of this one.'

I said, 'Had any success with Ashton's computer programs?'

'Oh, my God, they're fantastic. Everyone has claimed the man was a genius and he's proved it.'

'How?'

Ogilvie scratched his head. 'I don't know if I can explain—I'm no scientist—but it seems that Ashton has done for genetics what Einstein did for physics. He analysed the DNA molecule in a theoretical way and came up with a series of rather complicated equations. By applying these you can predict exactly which genes go where and why, and which genetic configurations are possible or not possible. It's a startling breakthrough; it's put genetics on a firm and mathematical grounding.'

'That should make Lumsden happy,' I said.

Ogilvie ate a grape. 'He doesn't know. It's still confidential. It hasn't been released publicly yet.'

'Why not?'

'The Minister seems to feel ... well, there are reasons why it shouldn't be released yet. Or so he says.'

That saddened me. The bloody politicians with their bloody reasons made me sick to the stomach. The Minister was another Cregar. He had found a power lever and wanted to stick to it.

Ogilvie took another grape. 'I asked Starkie when you'd be coming out but he isn't prepared to say. However, when you do I've a new job for you. As you may know, Kerr is retiring in two years. I want to groom you for his job.' Kerr was Ogilvie's second-in-command. He smiled. 'In seven years, when I go, you could be running the department.'

I said bluntly, 'Get lost.'

He was not a man who showed astonishment easily, but he did then. '*What did you say?*'

'You heard me. Get lost. You can take Kerr's job and your job and stuff them wherever you like. The Minister's backside might be a good place.'

'What the devil's got into you?' he demanded.

'I'll tell you,' I said. 'You were going to do a deal with Cregar.'

'Who said that?'

'Cregar did.'

'And you believed him? The man lies as naturally as he breathes.'

'Yes, I believed him because at that point he had no reason to lie. He did proposition you didn't he?'

'Well, we talked—yes.'

I nodded. 'That's why you won't get me back in the department. I'm tired of lies and evasions; I'm tired of self-interest masquerading as patriotism. It came to me when Cregar called me an honest man, not as a compliment but as someone to corrupt. I realized then that he was wrong. How could an honest man do what I did to Ashton?'

'I think you're being over-emotional about this,' Ogilvie said stiffly

'I'm emotional because I'm a man with feelings and not a bloody robot,' I retorted. 'And now you can take your bloody grapes and get the hell out of here.'

He went away moderately unhappy.

FORTY

And they all lived happily ever after. The hero married the principal girl, the second hero got the second girl, and they moved out of the poor woodcutter's cottage into the east wing of the king's palace.

But this is not a fairy tale.

On the day Penny came out of hospital she, Peter Michaelis and I went on a wing-ding in the West-End and the three of us became moderately alcoholic and distinctly merry. On the day Gillian arrived back from New York the four of us went on another wing-ding with similar effects. That American plastic surgeon must have been a genius because Gillian's new face was an improvement on the one she had before the acid was thrown. I was very glad for Peter.

The clanging of wedding bells could be heard in the near future. Penny and Gillian were dashing about London denuding the better stores of dresses and frillies for their trousseaux, while I scouted around for a house, introduced it to Penny, and then secured it with a cash deposit against the time the lawyers had finished their expensive wrangling over the deeds. It was all very exhilarating.

Ten days before the wedding I felt it incumbent on me to go back to see Starkie. He heard what I had to say and frowned, then took me into a laboratory where I was subjected to a battery of tests. He told me to go away and return in a week.

On the day I went back I read of Cregar's death in *The Times*. The obituary was sickening. Described as a faithful public servant who had served the country with no thought of self for many years, he was lauded as an example for coming generations to follow. I threw the paper out of the train window and was immediately sorry; that sort of stuff could pollute the countryside very seriously.

Starkie was serious, too, when I saw him, and I said, 'It's bad news.'

'Yes, it is,' he said directly. 'It's cancer.'

It was a blow, but I had half-expected it. 'How long do I have?'

He shrugged. 'Six months to a year, I'd say. Could be longer, but not much.'

I walked to his office window and looked out. I can't remember what I saw there. 'Cregar's dead,' I said. 'Same thing?'

'Yes.'

'How?'

Starkie sighed. 'That damned fool, Carter, was doing shotgun experiments. That means he was chopping up DNA molecules into short lengths, putting them into *E.coli*, and standing back to see what happened. It's not a bad technique if you know what you're doing and take the proper precautions.'

'He was taking precautions,' I said. 'The stuff got loose because of my own damned foolishness.'

'He wasn't,' snapped Starkie. 'Cregar was putting pressure on him—wanting fast results. He couldn't wait for a consignment of genetically weakened *E.coli* from the States so he used the normal bug. There was no biological containment at all. The stuff went straight into your gut and started to breed happily.'

'To cause cancer?' It didn't seem likely.

'I'll try to explain this as simply as possible,' said Starkie. 'We believe that in the genetic material of all normal cells there are genes which can produce tumour-forming chemicals, but they are normally repressed by other genes. Now, if you do a shotgun experiment and introduce a short length of DNA into *E.coli* you're in danger of introducing a tumour gene without the one that represses it. That's what's happened to you. The *E.coli* in your gut was producing tumour-forming chemicals.'

'But you said the *E.coli* coming out of me was normal,' I objected.

'I know I did, and so it was. One of the most difficult things to do in these experiments is to get a new strain to breed true. They're very unstable. What happened was that this strain began to breed back to normal *E.coli* almost immediately. But it was in your gut long enough to do the damage.'

'I see.' I felt a sudden chill. 'What about Penny?'

'She's all right. That was a different bug entirely. We made sure of that.'

I said, 'Thank you, Dr Starkie. You've been very direct and I appreciate it. What's the next step?'

He rubbed his jaw. 'If you hadn't come to see me I'd have sent for you—on the basis of what happened to Lord Cregar. This is a type of cancer we haven't come across before; at least it hasn't been reported in the literature in this particular form. Cregar went very fast, but that may have been because of his age. Older cellular structures are more susceptible to cancers. I think you have a better chance.'

But not much better, I thought. Starkie spoke in the flat, even tone used by doctors when they want to break the bad news slowly. He scribbled on a sheet of paper. 'Go to this man. He's very good and knows about your case. He'll probably put you on tumour-reducing drugs and, possibly, radiation therapy.' He paused. 'And put your affairs in order as any sensible man should.'

I thanked him again, took the address, and went back to London where I heard another instalment of bad news. Then I told Penny. I had no need to give her Starkie's explanation because she grasped that immediately. It was her job, after all. I said, 'Of course, the marriage is off.'

'Oh, no; Malcolm!'

And so we had another row—which I won. I said, 'I have no objection to living in sin. Come live with me and be my love. I know a place in the south of Ireland where the mountains are green and the sea is blue when the sun shines, which it does quite often, and green when it's cloudy and the rollers come in from the Atlantic. I could do with six months of that if you're with me.'

We went to Ireland immediately after Peter and Gillian were married. It was not the happy occasion one would have wished; the men were sombre and the women weepy, but it had to be gone through.

At one time I thought of suicide; taking the Hemingway out, to perpetrate a bad pun. But then I thought I had a job to do, which was to write an account of the Ashton case, leaving nothing out and making it as truthful as possible, and certainly not putting any cosmetics on my own blemishes. God knows I'm not proud of my own part in it. Penny has read the manuscript; parts of it have amused her, other parts have shattered her. She has typed it all herself.

We live here very simply if you discount the resident medical staff of a doctor and three nurses which Penny insisted upon. The doctor is a mild young American who plays bad chess and the nurses are pretty which Penny doesn't mind. It helps to have a wealthy woman for a mistress. For the first few months I used to go to Dublin once a fortnight where they'd prod and probe and shoot atoms into me. But I stopped that because it wasn't doing any good.

Now time is becoming short. This account and myself are coming to an end. I have written it for publication, partly because I think people ought to know what is done in their name, and partly because the work of Ashton on genetics has not yet been released. It would be a pity if his work, which could do so much good in the right hands, should be withheld and perhaps diverted to malignant uses in the hands of another Cregar. There are many Cregars about in high office.

Whether publication will be possible at all I don't know. The wrath of the Establishment can be mighty and its instruments of suppression strong and subtle. Nevertheless Penny and I have been plotting our campaign to ensure that these words are not lost.

A wise one-legged American, in adapting the words of a naval hero, once said, 'We have met the enemy, and he is us.'

God help you all if he is right.